Silent Whispers of Hope

A novel by
Kimberly Morton Cuthrell

SERENITY LEGACY PUBLISHING

Published 2022
Paperback ISBN: 978-1-7367665-4-5
eBook ISBN: 978-1-7367665-5-2
Library of Congress Control Number (LCCN): 2022912647

The following is a work of fiction. Any names, nicknames, characters, sceneries, places, locales, events, descriptions, incidents, and issues are the product of the author's imagination. All character developments in this work are fictitious. Any resemblance to persons, living or dead, is entirely coincidental. The development of activity corners and worksheets are the product of the author's imagination and creativity.

Serenity Legacy Publishing
P.O. Box 2825
Greensboro, N.C. 27402

www.serenitylegacypublishing.com

Printed in the United States of America.

Dedicated to:

Those who aspire to be heard, but live in silence.

Table of Contents

Prologue...1
Chapter 1 3
Chapter 2 10
Chapter 3 14
Chapter 4 20
Chapter 5 26
Chapter 6 32
Chapter 7 36
Chapter 8 40
Chapter 9 44
Chapter 10 49
Chapter 11 54
Chapter 12 58
Chapter 13 62
Chapter 14 66
Chapter 15 71
Chapter 16 75
Chapter 17 79
Chapter 18 83
Chapter 19 86
Chapter 20 91
Chapter 21 95
Chapter 22 100
Chapter 23 107
Chapter 24 112
Chapter 25 117
Chapter 26 120
Chapter 27 124
Chapter 28 130
Chapter 29 137
Chapter 30 140

Chapter 31..144
Chapter 32..148
Chapter 33..154
Chapter 34..160
Chapter 35..164
Chapter 36..168
Chapter 37..172
Chapter 38..177
Chapter 39..182
Chapter 40..186
Chapter 41..191
Chapter 42..197
Chapter 43..201
Chapter 44..206
Chapter 45..211
Chapter 46..216
Chapter 47..221
Chapter 48..226
Chapter 49..233
Chapter 50..238
Chapter 51..243
Chapter 52..246
Chapter 53..252
Chapter 54..258
Chapter 55..263
Chapter 56..265
Chapter 57..269
Chapter 58..273
Chapter 59..278
Chapter 60..284
Chapter 61..288
Chapter 62..292
Chapter 63..298
Chapter 64..303

Chapter 65 306
Chapter 66 312
Chapter 67 318
Chapter 68 321
Chapter 69 326
Chapter 70 330
Author's Quotes..333
About Dr. & Atty. Kimberly Morton Cuthrell 334

Prologue

Hope Rankin-Glover exhaled as she drove along Highway I-85 South, bypassing the outskirts of North Carolina Correctional Institution for Women. A single tear slid down her oval shaped face, not for the women confined behind the prison walls but for the stroke of fate that nearly constricted her heart, mind, and body to a life sentence of human trafficking.

The sun beamed inside her white Range Rover, casting a streak of heat against her face. Firmly gripping the steering wheel, moisture formed between Hope's slender fingers as she reflected on the damnation of being shuffled as a child through drug-infested abandoned buildings. Fleeing from her mother's unstable nest after graduating from high school didn't erase the dreadful memories of Hope's childhood. Fleeing surely didn't prevent Hope from weaving a web of resentment toward her *later* rehabilitated drug-free mother or instill any degree of sympathy in Hope's heart for her *now* ill-stricken, dying mother, Gloria Rankin.

A stream of cool air flowed out of the vents inside the Range Rover, brushing against Hope's pink shirt. Listening to soft jazz pressing against her eardrums, Hope embraced the invaluable gift of being able to hear. Sadly, this gift did not transcend to her children, fraternal twins at birth, causing Hope's fragile heart to splinter into a million pieces.

Wiping a tear from her cheekbone, Hope reminisced about the daily struggles of learning American Sign Language ("ASL") to communicate with her twins, Jayla and Jayden. With every thought of her twins being deaf, bitterness settled at the core of Hope's heart which forced her to question the true essence of motherhood.

Hope winced, wondering whether her experience with her twins was an act of Karma. She had lived several years of voluntarily refusing to communicate with her mother, and especially with her sister, Ivey, who was the apple of their mother's eye. After several years of rediscovering the art of forgiveness, her twins' involuntary silence intersected with a stream of fate.

Loud screeching sounds penetrated through the tinted glass windows.

Glancing in the rearview mirror, Hope stared at the wide, asphalt highway with puddles of tears in her eyes. She was determined to leave the past behind and reestablish a life absent from mental bondage, emotional turmoil, and manmade secret dungeons.

A sharp pain knifed through her heart as she thought about the diabolic, heartless secrets of her so-called husband, Sloan. Swallowing hard, Hope flinched recalling how his treacherous, masterminded deeds had defied the crux of humanity.

Pastures of red, yellow, violet, and white perennial flowers aligned Highway I-85 South creating a peaceful scenery. Struggling to smile as she passed by the flowers, Hope appreciated how the court had granted her a voided marriage which allowed her to return to using her birth name—Hope Michele Rankin. She no longer had to suffer the wrath of Sloan's obsessive demands. She no longer had to unknowingly help him paint a picture-perfect family image to mask his worldwide servitude scheme.

It all began a year ago. A year that had redefined the depths of survival for her. A year that had forged a new level of hatred and deceit. A year that unveiled a cyclone of secrets, fears, and regrets. A year that preyed upon countless innocent lives. A year that bordered on the cuffs of life and death. Through a twist of fate, it was a year that had promised wishful hopes for Hope, her twins, and her mother. Unfortunately, it was also a year that challenged the validity of Hope's sanity and freedom outside of prison walls.

Chapter 1

One year earlier, the bright Friday morning sun beamed beyond the endless horizon. Yellowish-brown oak trees, upscale venues, affluent communities, and cutting-edge universities sprouted throughout Raleigh, North Carolina. Sleep was on the verge of interruption but not before the last seconds of a nightmare stormed through Hope Glover.

Hope drifted into a deep sleep as her past trauma sprung forward while she dreamed, reminding her of the pain she had endured as a little girl. "No . . . no . . . *please* don't hurt me again," cried Hope as tears trickled down her five-year-old innocent face. "I want to go back into the building with my mama," she cried as a wide alabaster white hand firmly thrust her slender body down forcing her back to nestle against the black leather police patrol car's backseat.

"You can cry all you want . . . nobody's going to rescue you . . . nobody can see us in this *cut* in the woods," said the officer in a harsh tone. "Not even your *own cracked out* mama," he chuckled.

A loud sound pierced the room from an alarm clock causing Hope's body to jerk to an upright position on her bed then launched her feet to level to the floor before she left her bedroom heading to her husband's office in the basement.

Her alarm clock rang just in time to break the cycle of her recurring nightmares. She dreaded falling asleep. She had lost pleasure in daydreaming because her childhood painful memories had a way of catching up with her. She wished she could sleep without having traumatic flashbacks . . . without having nightmares . . . without remembering that she was ever a child growing up in abandoned buildings near Cloverdale. Her childhood memories seemed to never cease, causing her to relive every day the traumatic memories of being a poor, black child living in Cloverdale under the vicious and corrupted reign of the now deceased Sergeant Paul Smith. His murder was a day of celebration instead of mourning for people living in Cloverdale. They had suffered heavily at the wrath and mercy of his treacherous hands.

Hope tiptoed beside her husband, Sloan Glover, as her chiffon-pink dress shifted across her melon shaped breasts like a windshield wiper. She wrapped her golden brown slender arms around Sloan as she planted a kiss on his cheek. Sloan had shown her *real* love and had helped her to *mentally* escape the wrath of danger and fear—at least that's what she thought.

"Nice dress," grinned Sloan as his gaze surveyed Hope's physique.

"Yes, it is," giggled Hope as she seductively slid her hands along the ridges of her hips. "You have good taste," she said while glancing at her dress.

"Well, you know my wife must have the finest clothing."

"I know," sighed Hope as uncertainty trailed in her voice. She often wondered why Sloan insisted that she dressed up every day—even in the house. She was not allowed to wear jogging pants, T-shirts, or anything unappealing— not even to the mailbox or to empty the trash can. Her closet was organized by the colors of garments with a specific section for her lingerie, upscale dresses, designer business suits, and fashionable hats. Before her feet hit her bedroom's plush carpet in the mornings, Sloan made sure she had a specific attire selected for the day as if she was preparing to become a model . . . or something else, she often thought.

A crisp scent of Cucumber-Melon candle drifted inside Sloan's office creating a pleasant smell for the first day of summer in June. Hope winced for a split second. She noticed that the Cucumber-Melon scent slightly mingled with the strong aroma of a flowery perfume as if a woman had suddenly vanished from Sloan's office.

"Why do I smell a woman's perfume in here," squinted Hope while glancing around the office and noticing that only she and Sloan were in the office. She was certain another woman had been in here. *But where was she now?* she thought. She had no doubt that the strange perfume scent did not belong to her. Sloan was meticulous with ordering only one type of perfume for her which was imported. She was only allowed to wear E'Zanti perfume which had a unique, noticeable scent.

Sloan glared at her for a few seconds before allowing his luscious lips to drift apart. "Hope, what are you talking about?" he sneered. "I've been in *this* house with you and our twins for the past two days . . . working. Maybe you are smelling my new cologne."

Hope glanced around the spacious office. Five-tiered mahogany bookshelves lined the sandalwood painted walls creating a mini-library. Sovereigns positioned on the bookshelves from Portugal, Greece, Turkey, Italy, Spain, and other exciting places that Sloan had taken Hope. A lifestyle Hope had dreamed of, but she did not realize that Sloan had planned for the trips to be more than just a romantic vacation. Somehow, he managed to secretly mix business with pleasure right under her nose. She often questioned why he had to leave her in luxury hotels for hours during their trips. But he always had the perfect excuse which came with upscale massages, facials, and pampering to keep her occupied while he was gone.

The office *appeared* to have one door, granting an entrance and exit. At least Hope thought. As the flowery perfume scent slowly faded, Hope was certain no one had exited the office door when she entered.

"You are right," she smiled realizing that Sloan was *possibly* correct.

He had been in the house with her and their five-year-old fraternal twins for the past two days.

"Do I detect some jealousy?" smiled Sloan while gently grabbing Hope's hands.

"Whatever, Sloan," chuckled Hope as she glanced at his black laptop before he slightly tilted the screen preventing a view. "Whatcha working on, baby?" she asked while massaging his large butterscotch brown hand.

She perched her buttocks on the edge of the black desk. Her eyes darted around the almond painted office—a cozy spot in their oversized basement.

"Why don't you get an office, Sloan?" she asked knowing their household income was more than enough for him to get an executive-style office downtown.

"It is best if I work from home. This basement is large enough," he smiled. "Plus, I need a lot of privacy and quietness for the technology work that I do."

"Whatcha working on, baby?" she asked again.

A warm charming smile stretched across Sloan's smooth face. He pressed his back firmly into the black padded chair and inched it closer to Hope. His neatly trimmed mustache, light brown eyes, and tamed eyebrows accentuated his chiseled attractive appearance. He stroked his hands up and down Hope's hips like a sculptor molding a masterpiece.

"Do you mean, 'What are you working on,' darling?" gritted Sloan in a harsh tone while moving strands of hair that dangled near her lavish eyelashes.

For some reason, Sloan always felt the need to correct Hope's grammar and to tease her about her southern accent—further weakening her self-esteem. He was aware that she had grown up in Cloverdale Assisted Housing Community—a project in Charlotte, North Carolina. In particular, he knew people in the Cloverdale project shared a unique English dialect that was recognized among community members but criticized by outsiders who spoke the King's English.

Sloan was forty years old which made Hope's twenty-five-year-old mind appear to be less tactful than his. Even though she was from North Carolina, her level of *street knowledge* matched his New York level. Cloverdale had provided her with a *crash course* in street knowledge. Yet, she played the *naïve game* with Sloan.

"What are you working on?" she asked as frustration flowed through her.

In a deep baritone voice, Sloan replied, "Doing some last minute touches to Mr. Gavino's website." He paused as if he was searching for his next words. "I've developed an easier way for him to track sales at the pizza pubs.

Plus, he is opening another spot."

"Where?" she asked, recalling that Mr. Gavino had several *Worldwide Express Pizza, Inc.,* delivery pizza pubs along Highway I-85 and Highway I-95 from Richmond, Virginia to Miami, Florida. The pizza pubs were unique. Routine customers often requested different types of cheeses and *specific* sizes of pizzas—something that was normal. But Hope thought it was odd based on her gut feeling because the pizza descriptions matched the physical features (size and skin tone) of the women on the brochures. Yet, the pizza was delicious. There was also an amusement section in the pizza pubs where children could play games. The only drawback was that cash was not accepted. All transactions were processed through credit cards—as if Mr. Gavino wanted to keep track of his customers' names.

"He is opening a pub in Charlotte," said Sloan as he closed the browser on his computer, preventing Hope from seeing what he was doing. His computer was *off limits*.

"Charlotte, North Carolina?" she asked as unpleasant memories of living with her mother in Charlotte flashed before her.

"Yes. I have to meet him at ten this morning in Charlotte," said Sloan while glancing at his high-tech watch that was *also* off limits to Hope. The face on the watch was larger than a fifty-cent coin as if Sloan wanted to track time for the universe.

An uneasy feeling nestled inside Hope's stomach. Her gut feeling forced her to realize that Sloan's watch did more than just track time.

"You've been down here for hours working on this project for him already," said Hope in a puzzled tone as if Sloan was not forthcoming about something with her.

Hope's honey-blonde bob hairstyle shifted in the air as she moved, creating an elegant classy look around her diamond shaped face. She was fortunate to have a full head of hair. Her hair had undergone much damage before sprouting healthy roots. As a child, she had a history of pulling her hair to cope with the nerve-wracking abuse she endured from her mother. She had more patches on her scalp than a quilt. Her mother camouflaged Hope's patches by keeping her hair in a ponytail. Needless to say, Hope developed trichotillomania and posttraumatic stress disorder as a child but never received behavioral health therapy or treatment. She tried to cope with her conditions the best way she could and struggled to do so even now. She had considered therapy but did not pursue it because she learned from people in Cloverdale that therapy was taboo. Little did she know that her perception of therapy would change.

Hope gazed at Sloan for a few seconds. Sloan had been diagnosed with obsessive compulsive disorder. He would labor from dusk to dawn on a task until it was impeccable. Hope recalled on their first date how Sloan tied his shoestrings several times within an hour until they were perfect. Something she found quite strange. But Sloan's charming ways had won her over. He could tie a warehouse of tennis shoes and she'll still love him—especially after Sloan introduced Hope to his *iron rod.*

Truth be told, Hope didn't know much about men. She was eighteen when she met Sloan. She had never understood true love—not even the bonding process with her *own* mother. She had spent a large part of her life searching for love to fill the void in her heart that her mother had caused. Sloan was God's gift to Hope—at least it felt that way.

Sloan was the closest thing to what she thought love should be. But Hope did not like how Sloan was obsessed with her *grammar,* sheltered her from other men—especially drug dealers—and kept her on a routine schedule to *issue* him sexual treatment at least twice a week as if he wanted to make sure Hope depleted his royal oaks to prevent him from *creeping* out on her. Yet, Hope pondered why Sloan's sex drive was peaked every time he returned from flying to different states with Mr. Gavino. Deep down, Hope knew something wasn't right but her love for Sloan often overshadowed her doubts.

Hope rubbed Sloan's arms, giving them long smooth strokes.

"It seems like my hubby has skills," said Hope, hoping her grammar was correct.

Hope's small hands grazed Sloan's chest as if she was spreading a deck of cards. His powdered blue polo shirt snuggled nicely against his muscular chest.

Sloan stood, pressing his chest against Hope's melon shaped breasts. "I was born with skills," smiled Sloan before launching a kiss on Hope's neck. Hope closed her eyes, sighing softly. Sloan's voice echoed inside her eardrums, vibrating in her heart. His large hands palmed Hope's buttocks.

A growing object bulged through his khaki pants, pressing against Hope's thigh.

"I'm glad you came in here. I needed to find a stopping point," grinned Sloan as he hugged Hope. The smell of peppermint candy flowed out of his mouth, leaving no evidence of their tasteful breakfast.

A slight giggle escaped Hope's mouth. She skimmed the office, looking at the computer on the black desk, the file cabinets, and the bookshelves. Sloan's bachelor's and master's degrees in electrical and computer engineering with a specialization in information technology adorned the wall. Accolades from the study abroad program he attended in Spain, during college, showcased his superb intelligence and fluency in Spanish. His credentials certainly overshadowed Hope's associate degrees in culinary arts and concentration in business administration. But Hope was satisfied with her own accomplishments. Her heart was set on becoming a master chef and opening a restaurant and culinary school.

Hope glanced at the clock. It was ten o'clock in the morning. The thought of stroking Sloan's *iron rod* crossed Hope's mind. But she knew Sloan always ordered two *scoops of sex*—every time. One scoop was never enough.

"Do you want to take a quick shower together?" she invited, hoping to caress Sloan's *royal oats* before he left the house.

Sloan glanced at his watch. "A quick *shower* sounds good, but I don't want to be late for my meeting."

Sloan's six-foot-seven muscular body towered over Hope's five-foot-six full-figured frame. The crisp smell of his freshly-scented cologne swept across Hope's nose. What a pleasant aroma to inhale—especially a scent wafting off the body of a man who looked like he had jumped out of a fashion magazine. His sexy, muscular physique sent waves of passion through Hope's body. Their mattress could testify to that claim.

"Hey, darling, don't forget we are going to the museum on Sunday afternoon."

"I haven't forgotten," grinned Hope at the thought of going on a *family date*. It made a warm feeling flow through her. But she was certain that the date came with *rules*.

Sloan seldom took Hope on dates and when they did go, he preferred to travel to another city or state. Since his high-tech digital business surged, Sloan had little to no time for family activities—except at home.

"I'm pretty sure the twins haven't forgotten either," Hope said while glancing at their family picture in the small gold picture frame on Sloan's desk.

Jayla's picture-perfect smile brightened the image and Jayden's light brown eyes sparkled with joy. Hope often wondered why Sloan was adamant that he didn't want to name their son, Sloan Junior. But he agreed that his son should at least have his middle name—*Lamar*. Their twins were definitely a blessing from God—a gift. Hope never thought she could conceive after being molested as a child.

Hope stretched her long arms. "I don't know why I stay tired," she said while sipping on some lemon tea that Sloan had prepared for her.

Sloan cleared his throat before speaking. "Your mother called this morning," he said as if he was trying to change the subject.

Chill bumps rippled up and down Hope's slender arms like a cluster of hives. She had tried desperately to block the images of that woman's face out of her mind.

"When?" Hope asked in a low tone as her gaze landed on the oatmeal tan carpet.

Sloan caressed Hope's hands before saying, "While you were feeding the twins," muffled Sloan.

Hope was not interested in speaking with her mother. She slowly parted her lips to ask, "How did she get my number?"

Hope had moved from Charlotte, North Carolina to Raleigh, North Carolina the day after she graduated from high school, seven years ago, just to get away from her mother. Hope had saved every penny she earned while working at summer camps in high school to pay for a one-way Greyhound bus ticket to Raleigh—a place she had seen only once on television that was known for having several culinary arts schools.

Hope didn't have a pot to piss in when she arrived in Raleigh. She didn't care if she had to live in a shelter until she got on her feet as long as she was miles away from her mother. Luckily, Hope received a job at Green Leaf Tavern—an elegant vegan tavern. Between learning fine dining etiquette tips at the tavern and watching Mrs. Lena Brown bake and sell cakes in Cloverdale projects, she mustered the nerve to open her own catering business. Although Hope did not have a location yet, she conducted all transactions through her company's website—Serenity Catering Services. Plus, she established a contract with the local temporary agency to employ individuals to assist with catering jobs.

Sloan caressed Hope's shoulders, pulling her closer. Hope sensed more was yet to come. Butterflies swarmed in Hope's stomach as she waited for Sloan's mouth to open. She planted her head on his chest. The slow steady beat of his heart fluttered in her ears.

While Hope had thought she had already experienced her worst nightmares as a child growing up in Cloverdale, she wasn't prepared for what was yet to come as an adult living under the seductive wrath of Sloan.

Chapter 2

A soft crisp smell lingered on Sloan's six-foot-seven body as he nestled against Hope.

His luscious lips slowly opened before saying, "Ivey called," in his deep New York accent.

"Why is she is calling me? First Gloria called and now Ivey. What did she say?" Hope asked while feeling a tug of drama en route.

"She wants you to call her," asserted Sloan.

Hope paused before speaking. "I figured Ivey would be too busy fleeing from the police with her drug-dealing boyfriend. I wonder if she is still dating him. I've never dated a drug dealer."

"I hope not!" blurted Sloan as he looked at Hope with a questionable frown—a look that plastered on his face every time Hope mentioned the word 'drug dealers' as if Sloan despised them. Hope assumed Sloan reacted this way because he knew a drug dealer had molested her as a child . . . or perhaps it was for an unknown reason that Sloan had never disclosed to her.

"First of all, she was shocked that you were married. She said you never told her," uttered Sloan as he walked toward a family portrait on the wall. He slid the picture to the side, revealing a hidden safe behind the picture. Hope was forbidden to touch it.

Hope stared at Sloan as he took off his brown watch and placed it inside the small fireproof wall safe. Her mind floated like a balloon in the air as she observed him retrieving a black watch from the safe. He had positioned his body in such a way that Hope couldn't see inside the safe, something he always did if she was in his office when he opened the safe.

Hope slightly leaned to the side to peek inside the safe. She could see a small box inside. But she didn't know what was inside it. She didn't know what else was inside the safe. She didn't even know the code. Her gut told her that Sloan was hiding something. Hope was determined to get inside the safe one day.

Sloan walked toward his bookshelf. The large spotless bookshelf created an elegant appearance in the office. He adjusted a small family picture, making sure it was centered on the shelf. He was obsessed with things being centered and neat.

"That is a nice family picture," said Hope as she reached for the picture.

"Hope, please don't touch anything on my bookshelf," he chided her as if she had violated a house rule. "You know how I like to keep things neat. So, please, *don't* touch my bookshelf. And please *don't ever* come into my office when I'm not home."

Hope exhaled, releasing tension in the air. Sloan didn't have to worry about her entering his office when he was not at home. He kept his office locked at all times as if he was an undercover secret service agent for the president.

He paused as if he wanted to reiterate to Hope that his bookshelf was off limits.

"Now, back to what we were talking about. Why you did not tell your sister you were married?" he asked while tightening his watch on his wrist.

Sloan was correct. Hope had vanished without a trace seven years ago from her family and friends. They probably thought she was dead by now.

"I didn't have to tell her," she muffled as she glanced out of the window, looking at a bluebird prancing on a tree limb. "I haven't spoken to her in years . . . and I don't plan on starting."

A faint machinery sounded through the office from outside. Apparently, a distant neighbor was mowing the fresh summer grass.

"Why did you talk to her?" asked Hope in a distressed tone.

"Hope, she called our home," blurted Sloan without pausing.

"You typically don't answer the telephone when other people call. What else did she say?" asked Hope in an uninterested manner.

"Ivey told me to tell you that your mother was sick."

"*So!*" huffed Hope. "What else did she say?"

"She also told me to tell you that your mother needs you."

"*Need* me for what!" shrieked Hope in a hasty tone. "I thought Gloria would be dead by now," She recalled her mother's painful words that ripped through her heart daily as a child when she was called—*A Bad Seed*.

Chirping sounds came into the office as a blue jay landed on the windowsill.

"I don't know why *Gloria* is calling me. I haven't spoken to her in years," mumbled Hope as she recalled how her mother used to demand that she massage her scalp to help ease her troubled mind. Instead of massaging her mother's scalp, Hope wished she would've strangled her mother for all of her wrongdoings.

"Why do you call your mother by her first name?" asked Sloan in a calm tone as if Hope had never told him about her dreadful childhood. "I wish I knew who my mother and father were," he said as Hope suddenly remembered he had never met his parents. He had bounced around foster homes.

"Gloria does not *deserve* to be called my mother," said Hope as she fumbled with her manicured fingernails. "She robbed me of my childhood. I loved going to school just to get away from her. I hated the weekends. I hated the holidays. I hated summer breaks."

11

A sense of happiness flowed through Hope's veins as she thought about the friends she had met in school. She had never forgotten Tiffany Brown and her other friends from high school. Hope's mother refused to allow her 'projected' friends to visit her—not to mention the fact her mother didn't want Hope or her sister Ivey to ride on the same school bus with the kids from Cloverdale Assisting Housing Community. Hope's mother didn't have to worry about Ivey befriending the *projected* kids because she was not allowed to do so.

As fate would have it, the high horse that Hope's mother was riding on came to a sudden halt. They had to move into Cloverdale. It was a sad day for her mother because her husband had died. But it was a happy day for Hope. She was able to see her friends. Hope learned to avoid Sergeant Smith—the community officer—who reigned over the projects with crooked rules, deadly deals, and unwarranted sexual favors. Hope had a brush of bad luck with him—an event she would never forget.

"The twins need to meet their grandmother one day, Hope," uttered Sloan.

"That will *never* happen," she insisted as memories of her bruised arm flashed before her eyes. Hope's mother routinely pinched her as punishment, to the point that bruises clustered along Hope's shoulders. Hope had to permanently wear buttoned-up shirts to cover her shoulders even during the summers. She paused before speaking again. "I'm not calling *Gloria*," she said while rubbing her temples with her knuckles as if she could erase away the painful memories of her mother.

"Relax," sighed Sloan as he planted a kiss on Hope's forehead while palming her buttocks before walking out the front door. "I'll be back. I have to meet Mr. Gavino in Charlotte." He glanced up at one of the many cameras he had installed throughout their house as if they lived inside a maximum security prison. Hope never questioned it. She figured Sloan wanted a high-tech alarm system in their home.

Hope exhaled slowly as if she was blowing up a balloon.

"Go and check on the twins," ordered Sloan as he strolled out of the office while Hope trailed behind to the front doors.

Hope detected he had a hidden mean streak. Somehow, he managed to control it.

Thirty minutes later, a sharp sound pierced the air as the telephone rang. Hope glanced at the high-tech caller ID system that Sloan had designed for their house. He had built a state-of-the-art system that permitted Hope to see a caller's name, address, and a picture of the caller. Sloan had applied his computer engineering skills to interlink with the internet to quickly search for the identity of individuals who called their home. He had developed the same system for Mr. Gavino's pizza pubs. He told Hope that Mr. Gavino needed a high-tech caller ID system to ensure the safety of his pizza delivery drivers.

Hope's heart pulsated rapidly. It was a North Carolina telephone number. It was not Mrs. Lena Brown's number. Mrs. Brown had kept the same number since the extinction of dinosaurs. Hope's heart pulsated rapidly as the picture of the caller flashed on the high-tech caller ID system.

Today had suddenly turned into a nightmare for Hope.

Chapter 3

Mrs. Lena Brown sat at the oval shaped maple wood table in her small kitchen. Her apartment nestled in the heart of Cloverdale Assisted Housing Community. She leaned back, reading the *Charlotte Observer* while eating her breakfast. Her black wire rimmed glasses rested on the bridge of her nose.

A shaft of the Friday morning sunlight beamed inside the kitchen, granting additional light for Mrs. Brown to read the newspaper. Her unblemished dark brown skin sparkled as the rays touched her heart shaped face. A lovely smile plastered on her bow shaped lips.

A sharp sound echoed from the front screen door into the kitchen, drowning out the gospel music that flowed out of a small radio.

"Who is it?" yelled Mrs. Brown as she stood, pushing her chair under the table.

Mrs. Brown wobbled from side to side as she walked toward the front door while her lavender ankle-length dress shifted with every step. The savory smell of a lemon pound cake permeated the air. Mrs. Brown had baked the pound cake for the postman who often placed orders for several coworkers at the post office. When it came to baking homemade cakes, pies, and cookies, everyone loved Mrs. Brown's special touch. Her cakes were so good that people in Cloverdale paid her to bake for birthdays, graduations, weddings, and other special events—decreasing the nearby bakery's profit which caused the bakery to report Mrs. Brown to the office manager. The office manager, Floyd, tried to increase Mrs. Brown's rent by implying that the income she earned from baking cakes was a steady source of income. Floyd's tactics didn't last long after Mrs. Brown baked Floyd a homemade red velvet cake, erasing all thoughts of increasing her rent.

"It's me, Mrs. Brown," said Ruth in a rapid tone. "Hurry up. I need your help."

"My help?" Mrs. Brown asked, placing her dark brown weathered hand on her chest. She was known in Cloverdale as the neighborhood counselor, chef, and minister.

Mrs. Brown wasn't in a rush to answer the door. Nothing surprised her in Cloverdale—it was the projects. Anything was possible. She had seen and heard it all. The steady flow of negativity in the community was enough to declare Cloverdale as a hazardous zone because of the *Hill*. The Hill was a drug-infested area in Cloverdale that was engulfed with a heavy traffic flow of hustlers and prostitutes. It was a large open space with no grass that led to several alleys, abandoned buildings, woods and a creek. The grass on the Hill had been trampled on so much that the grass refused to grow there.

"Ruth, you're yelling like you need God," blurted Mrs. Brown as she inched closer to the screen door, passing a chocolate cake that was on a clear tray on the table.

Mrs. Brown had two more cakes to bake for customers before the sun swept behind the moon—not to mention the lemon pound cake that was still cooling down.

"Can I please come in?" asked Ruth as her light brown eyes peered inside the apartment.

"Ruth, why are you peeking in my apartment?" asked Mrs. Brown.

"I'm . . . I'm not peeking," babbled Ruth.

"Whatcha call it then, Ruth?" said Mrs. Brown as she glanced at a family portrait that was mounted on the almond painted wall. Her heart melted with joy every time she looked at the picture of her children. Her daughter, Tiffany, was a gynecologist and her son, Tony, was a dentist. Her children had achieved more than Mrs. Brown had ever dreamed.

A warm breeze drifted through the window, bouncing against the gold curtains.

"Mrs. Brown, please let me in," mumbled Ruth. "I need to talk with you."

A sharp pain gripped Mrs. Brown's ankles as she wobbled to the door. Her ankles were rooted in arthritis. They had carried her body for sixty-nine years.

She unlocked the screen door, pushing it open so Ruth could enter.

"Come on in, Ruth," said Mrs. Brown as she peeked down the sidewalk toward Ruth's apartment, trying to make sure Ruth wasn't running from the law.

Mrs. Brown's gaze landed on her neighbor, Gloria Rankin, who lived across the street. Her heart clenched as she watched Gloria struggle to walk from her mailbox to her apartment. She recalled Gloria crying about her failing health.

"Thank you, Mrs. Brown, for opening the door," said Ruth while trudging through the door like a bat out of hell, nearly knocking over a lamp on the maple wood end table.

Gunshots fired in the air, sending crackling noises into the apartment. Mrs. Brown didn't flinch. She was used to gunshots in Cloverdale, especially when Sergeant Smith used to allow drug dealers to fire guns in the air to scare tenants. Tenants were glad that someone had finally killed Sergeant Smith. Some of them still had nightmares about him.

"Slow down!" Mrs. Brown said, grabbing the lamp while gawking at Ruth. She wondered whether Ruth was still mad because her rent had increased by two dollars.

"Where's the fire, Ruth?" she asked as she stared out of the front door.

Her gaze swept across the scenery, landing on the piled-up trash near the dumpsters, the potholes in the street and the broken glass on the sidewalk. Regardless of the poor maintenance of the neighborhood and the low quality of life the community offered its tenants, Cloverdale was home to Mrs. Brown. A place she'd grown to love. A place where she felt safe. A place where she was highly respected.

Ruth's hip-hugger jeans were so tight, appearing to be cutting off circulation from her hips to her toes. Her wide curvaceous hips bulged against the seams of the jeans. Her well-built physique had captured the eye of nearly every man in Cloverdale. She was known as the *Queen of Cougars*. She dated men between the ages of twenty-one to thirty-five. Ruth was brushing on the hills on sixty. But she didn't look a day past forty.

Ruth slouched down on the navy-blue sectional chair.

"Child, don't flop down on my sofa," blurted Mrs. Brown as she stood near the front door, hoping that Ruth's visit would be short so she could finish baking her cakes. "My children worked hard to get me this. I'm going to take good care of it."

Ruth's glittery red painted lips curled into a frown. "The *social worker* is on her way," she huffed as her face sagged as though the world had caved in on her.

"What social worker?" asked Mrs. Brown.

"The one who's bringing my grandkids that I've never met," mumbled Ruth as her penciled eyebrows connected creating wrinkles on her mahogany brown forehead. "She did a home study last week to make sure my apartment was okay for my grandkids. She even did all types of background checks on me," huffed Ruth. "But I didn't think she was bringing my grandkids this fast."

Mrs. Brown waved her hand back and forth trying to create a cool breeze.

"Mrs. Hall told me that my daughter, Julia, died two weeks ago, and now I'm stuck with taking care of her children," blurted Ruth as bitterness crept into her voice. "I don't know what happened to Julia." A single tear trickled down her round shaped face. "I wonder why the kids' father can't get custody of them. I've never met him. I didn't even know Julia had children. All I know is Julia called me on my birthday . . . fourteen years ago to tell me that she was moving to Miami with a man named Rock. She was only eighteen. To this day, I still don't know why Julia left. She never called me after that."

A sharp sound pierced the air as police sirens echoed in the apartment.

"Mrs. Hall said prostitutes helped Julia with the kids when she escaped from *somewhere*. Drug dealers fed them," sighed Ruth. "And pit bulls protected them while they slept in abandoned buildings. I don't know what condition these kids are in."

A delicious aroma wafted from the kitchen into the living room.

"You must be baking a cake," said Ruth as a sense of calmness overtook her.

"Yes," said Mrs. Brown as she glanced at her small hands. "I'm not sure how much longer these hands are going to keep up. My arthritis is acting up again. I've got to start turning down customers. I'll be seventy soon and won't bake anymore." She slowly exhaled while reminiscing how she had previously taught many people in Cloverdale how to cook, even Hope who was destined to become a famous chef. "I'll have to stop baking soon."

Ruth's face crumpled to a frown. "Who's gonna bake our cakes?"

"I'm sure there's someone else who can. I've taught a lot of folks."

Ruth's lips curled into a sneer. "Nobody can *bake* like you, Mrs. Brown. Besides, people in Cloverdale ain't gonna eat nobody's cakes or pies but yours."

"What time is the worker coming?" asked Mrs. Brown while looking at the clock.

"In four hours," hissed Ruth as she folded her slender arms across her cantaloupe shaped breasts. "But I'm not ready for all of this. 'Sides I was thinking 'bout getting a top-level job."

"A top-level job," blurted Mrs. Brown while rubbing her hands together as if she could remove arthritis. "The only job that starts on the top is a graveyard digger."

Mrs. Brown had never held a top-level position herself. In fact, she didn't have much education. Yet, she could work wonders with an oven to make ends meet. She recalled pulling a red metal wagon, the type that children played with, on a long narrow road to the furniture plant to serve meals where her husband, Anthony Sr., worked. Like clockwork, she would haul two canisters, one with coffee and the other with homemade lemonade to the furniture plant.

Homemade buttermilk biscuits, gravy, cheesy eggs, and fried chicken spread around the canisters, tucked away on trays, to sell to her husband's coworkers. Her husband would stand in the back of the line as if he were embarrassed that his wife had to take on such a job—just to make ends meet. But Mrs. Brown never allowed her husband's pride to stand in her way. It wasn't long before her husband's coworkers quickly realized Mrs. Brown had golden hands. His co-workers flocked in lines, especially white folks, to order breakfast and lunch.

Growling noises resonated in the apartment, capturing Ruth's attention. A herd of men trotted past the apartment with pit bulls, heading toward the Hill. The musty smell of marijuana drifted into the apartment. Ruth looked out the window. A wide smile inched across her face as if she was indeed a Cougar overseeing her flock of *cubs*.

"Don't turn your back on your grandkids," said Mrs. Brown in a hasty tone.

Ruth sucked in air through her pearly white teeth, the ones that she claimed were not false teeth. "I don't want to raise my grandkids. They'll slow me down," she snapped while rubbing her arms as if ants were crawling on them.

"It seems like there is something else that is bothering you," said Mrs. Brown as she stood and walked into the kitchen to check on her cake while Ruth trailed behind.

"I'm going to tell the social worker that I can't keep my grandkids."

"Why would you do that to those kids, Ruth?"

Ruth dropped her head as if a tidal wave of disappointment had set within her.

"I can't read," mumbled Ruth. "And I don't want my grandkids finding out."

"Ruth, don't let that stop you from helping those kids."

A frown formed on Ruth's face before she said, "It's more than just that, Mrs. Brown. My granddaughters are better off living in a foster home than living here in Cloverdale. I don't want them getting on drugs. I don't want them getting raped. I don't want them falling at the mercy of these crooked police officers in Cloverdale. I don't want a stray bullet hitting them. I don't want them becoming *secret* girlfriends or mistresses or baby mamas of the businessmen, doctors, lawyers and preachers who creep through here. Mrs. Brown, you know those rich white men and black men are not coming to Cloverdale for nothing. They sit in their fancy offices and *bad mouth* poor black people but they are quick to secretly crawl into our beds and pay *big dollars* for services. I use condoms all the time. But, some of them have bizarre sexual interests like . . ."

"I don't want to know," interjected Mrs. Brown.

"Well, I don't want my granddaughter to experience that life. But don't get me wrong, I don't want for anything. My customers take good care of me. But I don't want my granddaughters being like me."

"What do you mean?" asked Mrs. Brown as she pulled the cake out of the oven.

Ruth closed her eyes before solely saying, "I crave sex, Mrs. Brown. I like it . . . I love it."

"You what?" asked Mrs. Brown as she closed the oven.

"I'm addicted to sex. Older men can't please me. So, I date young men," sighed Ruth. "But I don't want to risk having my male friends being around my granddaughters. She scratched her head creating a part in her cinnamon red wig that draped close to her belt. Ruth closed her eyes. "I need you to pray for me."

Ruth needed more than prayer. She needed a permanent chastity belt.

Chapter 4

The bright Friday morning sun continued to glisten across the blue sky, sending a beam of light into Hope's cozy living room.

Hope inhaled, reeling in the delicate scent of a cucumber melon candle that wafted in the air.

A sharp sound pierced the air throughout the house as the telephone rang.

"Hello, Hope," said a soft voice as Hope leaned back on the black sofa.

"Why are you calling me!" shrieked Hope, nearly echoing from the living room into the playroom where the twins were playing. "How did you get my number?"

"Hope, how are you doing?" asked Ivey, Hope's sister, in an uneasy soprano voice.

Silence streamed through the phone as the nerves in Hope's body tensed up.

"I'm fine," said Hope in a hasty tone. "What do you want, Ivey?"

"I need to talk to you. I'm still your little sister," said Ivey as if Hope didn't know that she was five years older than Ivey.

"Whatever, Ivey. Look, I'm getting ready to hang up. What do you want?"

"Hope, please don't hang up. Mama has been trying to get in touch with you."

"For what!" Hope said in a lifeless flat tone. "What does Gloria want? It's been seven years since I spoke with that woman!"

"Come on, Hope. Things have changed," said Ivey as her voice came to a halt. "Mama *needs* you."

"*Needs* me," laughed Hope. "I needed her when I was a child!"

"Hope, please don't do this."

"*Girl*, please. Whatever, I'm hanging up now," said Hope as a busload of irritation knifed through her heart. "I can't believe *Gloria needs* me. Girl, bye!"

"Hope, please, don't hang up."

"How did you get my number, Ivey?" gasped Hope in an annoying tone.

"The internet. I've called you several times over the years," said Ivey as she cleared her throat. "But every time I got your number, you changed it."

Ivey's words were indeed true. Hope changed her telephone number more than a mechanic changed tires. But she had never changed her catering business' number. Hope doubted if Ivey knew she had a small catering business.

"Why are you calling me?" she demanded as she walked toward her twins' playroom. "Please do not call me anymore."

Jayden and Jayla were sound asleep. Their five-year-old bodies had been napping for at least an hour. Rosemary pink sheets draped around Jayla's twin-sized bed while powdered blue sheets adorned Jayden's bed.

"Don't do this, Hope. I know you're going to change your number."

Hope gazed at the soft lilac painted walls in the living room, hoping Ivey would hang up. Hope hadn't seen nor spoken with Ivey in several years—all because of the bitterness rooted in Hope from the harsh treatment she had endured from her mother.

"Hope, mama is sick," said Ivey in a caring tone.

Not a twinge of remorse seeped through Hope's veins.

"*Karma* is something. Why can't you *nurse* her back to health since you're a nurse? I'm sure Gloria would prefer that you help her instead of me! You were always her favorite . . . did you forget, Ivey?"

Hope flopped down on the black sofa as she dazed out of the bay window.

She recalled when she was twelve years old that her mother had beaten her with an Ajax can, crushing the can on her head and causing the white substance to splatter all over her face. Hope had forgotten to clean the tub before Ivey took a bath. Hope's heart clenched as she recalled how seven-year-old Ivey had laughed—not realizing the emotional turmoil Hope felt. Her mind never allowed her to forget how Gloria had made her scrub the front porch with Ajax nearly every day as a permanent chore thereafter.

Chirping noise resonated in the living room, breaking Hope's daze.

"Are you still dating that lowlife drug dealer?" asked Hope, trying to stray from the subject.

"*Hope*! Mama is going to die if she can't get a donor," said Ivey in a soft tone.

"So!" screeched Hope in an insensible tone. "What do you expect me to do? I'm not a nurse. I'm not a doctor. I'm not a miracle worker and I sure ain't *God*!"

"The doctor said mama has leukemia. It's like having cancer in her blood," said Ivey in a sympathetic tone. "Mama will die if she doesn't get a bone marrow transplant."

"A what?" asked Hope as a pinch of bitterness settled in her heart.

"A bone marrow transplant," said Ivey in a heartfelt tone. "And she needs someone who is a match to donate bone marrow to her."

"Why are you telling me this? I don't care! Whatever Gloria needs, give it to her."

"I can't, Hope. I'm not a match for her," mumbled Ivey in a kindhearted tone.

"Me, neither," said Hope in a short and snappy tone as she sighed heavily.

"You are . . . Hope," said Ivey. "Mama's blood showed that you *may be* a match."

"Girl, *please*, whatever!" shrieked Hope as she flopped on her black leather sofa. "You think Gloria is good as gold! Please spare me! You don't know the Gloria I knew as a child! The Gloria I knew was a crack addict who shuffled me with her to alleys, shelters, and slums. You don't know the things that happened to me. I saw her perform many tricks for crack. She told me crack was candy for adults. Gloria doesn't even know who my father is."

"Hope, please stop speaking negatively about mama."

"Whatever, Ivey! Gloria used to call me a 'Bad Seed' as if it was my fault that she got pregnant with me while she was out tricking," uttered Hope. "Nobody helped me . . . not even social services because Gloria did a good job covering up stuff."

"Hope, mama has changed. So, please, stop it," begged Ivey.

"No, Ivey. You had it made! Gloria had gotten clean before she had you. That's only because Gloria met your father and he helped get Gloria's nasty tail cleaned up. She stopped smoking crack, but it was hard. Your father made sure Gloria attended her drug treatment program. But before then, Gloria sure didn't stop smoking crack even after I told her that her nasty dope man molested me," screamed Hope as tears rolled down her face. "Gloria didn't even believe me. She was too busy getting high. Her dope dealer had messed me up inside. I was in pain for weeks."

"Hope, mama has changed," muffled Ivey. "She needs you. You're a match."

Hope paused for a second. "Wait! How do you know Gloria's blood shows that I'm a match for her?" asked Hope completely confused.

"There is a process called fetal microchimeric."

"Ivey, what are you talking about? What is that?"

Ivey cleared her throat before speaking. "The easiest way to explain this is . . . it is called *mother-child cell sharing*. But some people call it *fetal stem cell sharing*."

"Huh," snapped Hope in a puzzled tone. "Fetal . . . what? I hope you didn't call me to give me a crash course in biology because I'm not in the mood for it!"

"Hope, just listen so I can explain everything to you," said Ivey in a low tone. "When a woman is pregnant, she can pass cells to a fetus. Research also shows that a fetus passes stem cells to its mother. The stem cells can remain in a mother for decades."

"Ivey, stop playing," interrupted Hope. "Don't be using medical words with me just because you're a nurse," said Hope as she noticed that Ivey spoke 'proper English' as Sloan often requested Hope to do. Apparently, Ivey had improved her grammar when she went to college to become a nurse even though she was raised in Cloverdale.

"Hope, please let me finish telling you," said Ivey as she cleared her throat. "Doctors are able to test a mother's blood to detect fetal microchimeric. Research shows that there is a link between cancer and fetal microchimeric. Some mothers have been able to eliminate their risk of cancer or force their cancer into remission."

"Okay. So, what does that mean?" asked Hope as she scratched her hair. "If you are trying to say my stuff is in mama's body then your stuff is, too."

"Yes, our fetal stem cells are still in mama. But I can't donate bone marrow."

"Why not?" sneered Hope as she closed her eyes. "This isn't making any sense."

"Hope, mama only has two children. She's only been pregnant twice."

"I doubt that . . . especially with all of the tricks she used to perform," smirked Hope.

"Hope, please stop it and listen to me. The doctors confirmed that mama only had fetal microchimeric from two different babies. This had to be from you and me."

"Please get to the point Ivey 'cause this medical stuff is over my head."

"The doctors examined the fetal microchimeric *or* in simple terms the fetal stem cells in mama that we left inside her," sighed Ivey. "Somehow, the cells stayed in her."

"Something else should've remained inside her," said Hope in a pathetic tone.

A roaring siren sound pierced the air from an ambulance driving down the street.

"Hope, mama can't get a bone marrow transplant from me," muffled Ivey. "This means mama can't get a stem cell transfusion from me because I have fibromyalgia."

"You have what?" asked Hope.

Ivey sighed, "Fibromyalgia is an autoimmune disorder. It makes the nerves in my body hurt . . . and it messed up my cells. Since I have it, I cannot be a bone marrow donor."

The sun drifted behind the clouds, blocking light from entering the living room.

"Well, Gloria has a serious problem if you can't donate whatever she needs."

"Hope, please listen. There is a chance that mama can use your cells and bone marrow to treat her leukemia," said Ivey in an empathetic tone. "She hasn't been able to find someone who is a match. But based on the fetal stem cells in mama, you might be able to give her more cells and bone marrow to help treat her leukemia. But, of course, there are other tests that the doctor has to run to make sure you can donate bone marrow."

"Do you hear yourself, Ivey? You sound crazy!" said Hope in a heartless manner.

"Hope, if you would just . . . ."

"No!" shrieked Hope, interrupting Ivey. "I don't even understand all of this."

A tingling sensation pressed against Hope's right leg. The twins tugged at her leg.

Hope reached toward Jayla and Jayden, hugging them tight to prevent them from seeing the tears flow down her face. Jayla's jet black ponytails dangled along her shoulders. Jayden's warm small hand pressed against Hope's back.

"Let me call you back, Ivey," said Hope while smiling at Jayla and Jayden.

Hope's fingers fluidly moved in the air as her twins watched her fingers and lips move. Hope's heart clenched, knowing that her twins were deaf. She had learned ASL to communicate with them. Sloan's skills were still rusty. The twins were scheduled to get a cochlear implant surgery in a few months—a medical procedure that Hope and Sloan prayed would help the twins to be able to hear.

"Let me call you back, Ivey. My twins are up now," spouted Hope.

"Your twins!" blurted Ivey in a shocking tone. "I didn't know you had children."

"There's a lot you don't know about me."

"Hope, I would love to see my nieces or nephews one day. Hope, what about mama?" asked Ivey in a calm tone. "Please help her."

A shaft of bitterness pumped through Hope's heart. She pressed her lips firmly into the telephone's receiver, making sure that Jayla and Jayden could not see her lips moving. They were getting better at reading lips and Hope was too.

"I'm not giving Gloria anything," bellowed Hope in a frenzied manner. "Tell Gloria to take out an ad in the *Charlotte Observer.*"

"Hope," sobbed Ivey. "Mama is going to die *if* she can't find a donor soon."

"Well, I guess you better start planning funeral arrangements."

Chapter 5

Mrs. Lena Brown inched toward the gray sofa inside Ruth's apartment while peeking at a white chubby woman with disheveled kids pinned to her side as they walked toward the front door. The children resembled mannequins in a second-hand clothing store. They stood speechless with bleach-stained jeans and hand-me-down shoes.

The sweet smell of chocolate chip cookies lingered in the air. Mrs. Brown had prepared the cookies for Ruth's grandkids.

Mrs. Brown chuckled, staring at Ruth's shoulder-length charcoal black wig. The cinnamon red wig Ruth had on earlier wasn't suitable for the occasion. She had more wigs than a hair supply store chain.

"I'm over here. You can walk through the grass," yelled Ruth as she walked toward her front door with her face faintly twisted into a frown while looking toward the parking lot.

She turned slightly toward Mrs. Brown with a puzzled looked plastered on her face. "I thought Mrs. Hall was bringing two girls."

"Hush," said Mrs. Brown, tapping Mrs. Ruth on the knee while noticing one of the kid's hair. The child had more patches on her scalp than a cow grazing on pasture.

Music traveled into the apartment as a blue BMW X5 cruised down the street. A smile flashed across Ruth's lips as she looked out the window. "That's Chauncey, Donovan, Stone, and Chance," whispered Mrs. Ruth to Mrs. Brown as if she was doing a roll call. "They are from Florida. They host great parties . . . lingerie parties, wig shows, and swingers' events."

Mrs. Brown slowly exhaled while shaking her head side to side. "You need to cut that out, Ruth."

"Oh, no, Mrs. Brown. They are not my cup of tea. But they are cool."

Mrs. Brown slowly exhaled.

"Come in," said Ruth as she peered out the front door with a fake smile.

The short, hefty lady gripped the door handle, then escorted the children inside the sable white painted living room, carrying a briefcase. The children held on to their brown suitcases like the luggage was surgically connected to their hands. There was no doubt that Mrs. Hall intended to leave the children with Mrs. Ruth.

"Good morning, Mrs. Ruth Turner," Mrs. Hall said, ushering the children inside Ruth's apartment. A black briefcase dangled from her alabaster white hand. Mrs. Hall marshaled the children to a gray loveseat that was positioned in the corner near a five-foot artificial silk palm tree. The children's wrinkled jeans draped the floor as they moved. Their pants were clearly too big.

A fresh smell of Dove soap trailed behind the children as they walked past Mrs. Brown. Their feet shuffled as if they were walking through quicksand.

"Good morning to you, Mrs. Hall," said Ruth in a shaky tone. "This is my neighbor, Mrs. Brown. She wants to meet my grandkids."

The children's gazes fixated on the tile floor as if they were embarrassed.

"That's good," said Mrs. Hall while sitting down as she pulled out a form from her black briefcase. Her platinum-blonde, curly hair bounced on her shoulders. "I'm glad we were able to track you down." Her hands moved at a rapid pace, filling out the information on the form as if she was in a rush to drop off the kids.

"Oh, really," Mrs. Ruth said with a smirk on her round shaped face.

Mrs. Hall's big blue eyes averted from Mrs. Ruth to her watch. The children gripped each other's hands as though they were preparing for rejection.

Mrs. Brown nudged Ruth as Mrs. Hall reached down in her briefcase for another form, her eyes widened as her gaze landed on the expensive décor in Ruth's apartment. A 5 x 8 plush rustic tan carpet positioned in the middle of the white ceramic tile floor between the gray sofa and loveseat, underneath a leaf shaped ceiling fan, creating a dazzling appearance. A 60-inch flat screen television snuggled against the sable white wall. A Bose stereo system positioned in a corner. Ruth's upscale apartment was too fashionable to be nestled in the midst of Cloverdale projects. Mrs. Brown was certain Ruth's *cubs* paid for the furniture.

"How did you find me?" asked Ruth as her light brown eyes narrowed to mere slits as if she was a character in a mini-documentary movie.

Mrs. Hall cleared her throat while adjusting her glasses on her pointy nose. "Um . . . this is Jasmine Turner. She is thirteen," said Mrs. Hall as she pointed at the light brown eyed teenager whose shaggy sandy brown hair dangled over her narrow shoulders.

A screeching sound reaped through the air as a car slammed on breaks, nearly hitting a kid who dashed across the street.

Mrs. Ruth's neck nearly popped off, trying to look out of the window. "I've told Quest to stop speeding in his Volvo through here. I will talk to him about it again. I'll see him later tonight."

"It seems like you know a lot of people in Cloverdale," said Mrs. Hall as she adjusted her glasses again.

Mrs. Ruth dismissed Mrs. Hall's comment. "So, how did you find me?" she inquired again.

"Jasmine told the police in Atlanta, Georgia that her grandmother,

Ruth Turner, lived in Charlotte, North Carolina," uttered Mrs. Hall as she paused for a few seconds while tapping her ink pen on a form.

Mrs. Ruth penciled eyebrows drew in. "How did you know that, Jasmine?" asked Ruth, leering at Jasmine before shifting her gaze toward Mrs. Hall.

Jasmine slowly lifted her head. "My mother told me before she was killed," said Jasmine as her eyes filled with sorrow. There was definitely too much pain for a thirteen-year-old teenager to bear—the same heartfelt pain Mrs. Brown saw in her children's eyes when her husband rested on his deathbed with cancer. "Somebody had her cremated."

An eerie silence filtered into the room.

Mrs. Hall pressed her pink lips together. "The kids wanted to keep Julia's ashes in this urn," said Mrs. Hall as she tapped on a black bag that obviously stored the urn.

Mrs. Brown sighed slowly. She clutched her fingers together, saying a silent prayer without moving her lips.

"How did you know my name?" asked Ruth as she looked at Jasmine.

"I—I told the police," said a weak and shaky voice. "My mother carved your name on a wall in the abandoned building we slept in."

Mrs. Brown cleared her throat as she leaned back in the chair, staring at the other child who was sitting on the chair. "What's your name?" asked Mrs. Brown while handing the tray of cookies to the kids.

Fear built up in the kids' eyes. They rejected the cookies as if they had been taught never to accept cookies from anyone.

"Oh, that is Taylor," Mrs. Hall said, pointing at the other kid as if she suddenly remembered another child was in the room. "She is twelve years old."

Mrs. Ruth slid to the edge of the chair, frowning as she looked at Mrs. Hall. "She?" inquired Ruth as her gaze shifted from Mrs. Hall to the slender kid whose hazel brown eyes widened like walnuts. "I thought this was a boy."

Confusion flooded Mrs. Brown's mind as she looked at that kid whose appearance resembled a male image.

"She isn't a boy," said Jasmine in a low tone as she gripped Taylor's hand tightly.

"Well, please don't tell me she's gay," blurted Ruth as a smirk wrapped her red painted lips. "There's a lot of that going on," she said while crossing her thick legs. "There's a new breed of kids growing up these days. But I'm cool with it if that is how she is."

Taylor pressed her palms against her golden brown face as sobbing noises escaped her cupid shaped mouth. Her auburn brown patchy hair scattered on her scalp.

"Ruth, behave yourself," shrieked Mrs. Brown as she glared at Ruth.

Jasmine wrapped her slender arms around Taylor, providing a sense of comfort and protection as if she wanted to demonstrate their strong sibling bond. It was a bond that Mrs. Brown recalled that her children, Tiffany and Tony, shared.

"No ma'am, she's not gay," said Jasmine as she paused to wipe Taylor's face with her small pecan brown hand. "I cut her hair with some scissors."

Mrs. Ruth's eyes widened in shock. Her red painted lips clamped together as though she was lost for words.

"Why?" Mrs. Brown asked, staring at Jasmine.

Silence drifted into the room for a few seconds.

Jasmine rubbed Taylor's hands. "That was the only way I could keep her safe."

"Safe?" asked Ruth as curiosity trailed in her voice.

Jasmine hugged Taylor. A tear trickled down her diamond shaped face. "If the businessmen and drug dealers," mumbled Jasmine as she dropped her head before continuing, "If businessmen and drug dealers thought Taylor was a boy . . . then she had a better chance of not getting raped. They didn't mess with the boys."

Mrs. Brown's heart felt as though a knife had stabbed through it. Painful memories of when her daughter was raped by Sergeant Smith stormed through her mind.

"*Rape?*" shrieked Mrs. Ruth as if her grandmotherly instincts had kicked in. She stood and walked over to the chair to sit with Jasmine and Taylor.

Jasmine tilted her head toward the popcorn ceiling. "I had to protect Taylor," said Jasmine as she rubbed her arms as if she could erase the memories. "I used to hide Taylor from the *men,* so she didn't have to go through what I went through."

Ruth wrapped her arms around Jasmine and Taylor as tears formed in the crease of her eyelids. There was no doubt that Jasmine had been raped.

Taylor tied up her sneakers before speaking. "A lot of men came in the abandoned buildings where we lived. I was scared. Jasmine told me she was my *Guardian Angel.* She didn't let the men hurt me."

Jasmine reached into her pocket and pulled out an envelope. She handed it to Ruth. "This is for you. My mother told me to give it to you."

Mrs. Ruth stared at the envelope for a few seconds before opening it. Ruth pulled a letter and a picture of her daughter out of the envelope. Ruth propped her hand under her chin, staring at the picture. A tear rolled down her face.

Tires screeched, causing Mrs. Hall to drop her ink pen.

Taylor tugged on her pocket, capturing Mrs. Ruth's attention.

"What's in your pocket?" asked Mrs. Ruth, wondering if Taylor had something to give her as well.

"It's my mom's perfume bottle," said Taylor as she pulled the small bottle out of her pocket.

"She never parts away from that bottle," commented Mrs. Hall. "It was the perfume her mother wore."

Mrs. Ruth pressed her lips together. "Can I see it?"

"Yes," responded Taylor as she handed it to Mrs. Ruth. "Please do not spray it. I want to keep it as long as I can before it evaporates."

"I think it will take a long time to evaporate," smiled Mrs. Brown, embracing the love that Taylor had for her mother.

"Oh, this has a unique, pleasant smell," said Mrs. Ruth as she sniffed the perfume bottle while closing her eyes as if she could visualize Julia. "What type of perfume is it?"

"Mama said it was expensive and imported. It was the only perfume that daddy allowed her to wear. She couldn't wear any other type," said Jasmine.

"Why not?" inquired Mrs. Brown as she smelt the perfume realizing it was a unique scent, one that she doubted she would ever forget.

"Daddy said it was his way in knowing if mama had been in a certain area," mumbled Jasmine.

Mrs. Ruth gasped for air. "Tell me about the kids," she said while glancing at the picture of her daughter again before tucking it inside the Bible on the glass coffee table.

Mrs. Hall scribbled something on a form before looking up at Ruth. "These kids have been exposed to a lot. They've lived on the streets most of their lives," she said while glancing around. "They were in different cities and states."

"Different cities and states? I thought she was in Miami."

"Yes, she was. But from what we know, your grandchildren's father forced your daughter, Julia, into a lifestyle of human trafficking at an early age. She was forced to travel around the country with him and other women and children," uttered Mrs. Hall. "The kids said she hitched a ride with a truck driver to escape from Rock. But somehow the truck driver took her back as if he was also a part of the human trafficking ring," babbled Mrs. Hall. "The kids told us that Julia called the police to get away. But even the police officer took her back there. So, Julia was basically trapped there."

"Human trafficking!" blurted Ruth as if she finally realized why Julia had vanished without a trace with Rock. "Where is their father?" asked Ruth.

Growling sounds traveled into the apartment. Thugs trotted past the apartment, showcasing their vicious pit bulls as if they were in a dog contest.

"We don't know," said Mrs. Hall. "But we know his nickname is Rock."

"Do you know Rock's real name?" asked Mrs. Brown in a soft pleasant tone.

"No, but mama used to call him Rock. He didn't come around as much."

"Do you remember what he looked like?" curiously asked Ruth.

"Yes," mumbled Jasmine as her head lowered. "The police showed us pictures of men who had been in trouble for human trafficking but none of them were him."

Ruth exhaled slowly before her lips parted. "It seems like you and Taylor have been through a lot," she said in a sincere tone.

A loud sob escaped Jasmine's mouth. "Yes, ma'am. A lot of bad things happened to me. But I tried my best to protect Taylor. Mama couldn't do it. We were always separated from mama in the houses or warehouses."

Ruth tilted her head toward the ceiling as if she was contemplating whether or not to take Jasmine and Taylor.

Today was destined to reveal the heartfelt experience of human trafficking through the eyes of children.

Chapter 6

A cool breeze flowed through the twin's playroom, mingling with the scent of ginger cookies that Hope had prepared for them. She chuckled, recalling a boy from Cloverdale named Blake who used to love ginger cookies. Blake had a crush on Hope in high school. But Hope dismissed all of his advances toward her. But she never forgot that day when Blake told her that she would be his wife one day. Hope figured Blake was heartbroken by now because that dream never came true.

Hope sat at the small colorful square shaped table, painting with her twins. Pictures of cartoon characters adorned the sunflower painted walls. A large canvas board positioned in a corner creating enough space for the twins to craft and express their creativity.

A silent peal of laughter brightened their faces as they played and laughed. Hope took pride in spending family time with her twins, to ingrain in their hearts, bodies, and souls the value of the love that she had for them. Yet, Hope's heart tugged at the fact that her twins were deaf.

Hope reached for her cell phone. Her slender fingers pressed firmly on the numbers to dial Mrs. Brown's telephone number. It had been a few weeks since Hope spoke with her. Hope always enjoyed talking to her as if she had wished that Mrs. Brown were her mother. She recalled crying many nights as a child because she wished the doctors had switched her at birth and given her to Mrs. Brown. A pinch of disappointment seized Hope as she waited for Mrs. Brown to answer the telephone. To Hope's surprise, she was not at home which was rare unless she was visiting a neighbor or with her children. She never checked her answering machine. She thought answering machines were a waste of money, but Tiffany had purchased one for her.

A pleasant feeling surrounded Hope as she reminisced upon fond memories of Mrs. Brown teaching her how to cook, bake and sew. Hope glanced at her twins, vowing to herself to be the best mother that she possibly could be. She was determined not to be like her mother.

A warm feeling simmered in her heart as she reflected upon how she met their father, Sloan, on a rainy day . . .

Large, gloomy clouds spread across the gray morning sky as a rumbling sound echoed overhead. Rain beat down on Hope's straggly black umbrella, soaking up her black chef uniform and shoes. She lived in a hotel four miles from her job. She walked to work six days a week working eight to ten hours every day. The distance didn't bother her—not even the rain. As long as she had peace of mind away from her mother.

A pearl white Mercedes-Maybach S650 pulled up to the shoulder of the curve.

"Excuse me, do you want a ride?" said Sloan as he lowered the car window.

The rain brushed against Hope's wet face, preventing a clear vision of the driver. "No, thank you," Hope said as she picked up the pace, gripping her pink purse. "My job isn't far. I can walk there."

"Are you sure?" asked Sloan as his car inched down the street slowly beside Hope with the hazardous lights flashing. "It's thundering and lightning. I can give you a ride."

"I said no," insisted Hope as her feet moved swiftly on the muddy sidewalk.

A streak of lightning flashed across the sky, causing Hope to flinch.

"Listen, lady, I'm not going to hurt you," shouted Sloan over the rumbling noise that echoed from the sky. "I just want to give you a ride."

"I'll be fine. I'm just going up the street."

Gray, puffy clouds stretched across the gloomy sky, preventing the sun from shining through the rain.

Sloan scrambled around in his glove compartment and pulled something out.

Adrenal pumped through Hope's veins. Her feet moved at a rapid pace. She detoured off the sidewalk, nearly sprinting toward a curb market. She dashed past a homeless man standing outside as if the rain was his only means of a shower.

"Hey, where are you going?" yelled Sloan from his car window. "I'm not going to hurt you," he bellowed while pulling into the curb market's parking lot. "I only want to give you a ride," he said in a sincere tone as he exited his car and handed Hope his umbrella. His pristine navy blue business suit shifted as he walked toward Hope.

Water piled up to her ankles. The rain came down harder and faster. Her umbrella had taken a beating from the rain and was falling apart.

Hope stared into the man's eyes as if she was trying to read his mind. She inched toward the car, scanning the inside of it. "Here, take this," he said as he handed Hope his driver's license. "This is what I was reaching for in my glove compartment. Call your job and tell your boss that you're riding with me."

Hope winced. His charming personality rattled her mind, clouding her judgment. She stared at the license, making sure his face matched the picture on it. She glanced at his date of birth, noting that he was older than her. Hope slowly pulled out her cell phone and called her job. She gave her boss the information on the license.

As Hope drew closer to the car, Sloan dashed to the passenger's door to open it for Hope. "Get in before you drown out here."

Rain beat down on Sloan, making his navy blue suit look black. Somehow his mannerism chiseled away Hope's fear.

Hope glanced around inside the car before Sloan hopped in. The interior of the car was spotless as if Sloan had a daily cleaning service. The brown leather upholstery presented an elegant backdrop for the wood trim. Sloan's six-foot-seven muscular body slid inside the car. He opened the glove compartment and handed Hope a napkin. Hope rubbed the napkin across her face wiping the rain off.

"What is your name?"

"Hope."

"That is a beautiful name."

"I'm going up the street to *my job*. It's straight up the street on the left," Hope said as she kept her hands glued to the door handle the entire time as Sloan drove. Hope glanced at Sloan's business suit. "Are you going to work too?" she asked bashfully admiring the interior view of the car.

"Fasten your seatbelt, please," ordered Sloan as he gripped the steering wheel. "I'm coming from the courthouse."

"Court!" said Hope as her body flinched. "What did you do?"

"Nothing. My . . . ," he slowly said as if the next words were too embarrassing for him to say. "I had to file a restraining order against my ex-girlfriend."

"What happened?" Hope asked as she leaned back in the chair.

An ocean mist scent wafted in the car.

"She was a jealous woman. I didn't feel safe around her anymore, especially after she hit me with a bat."

"Are you serious?" asked Hope as an unquenchable curiosity quickly replaced the fear she had. She looked out of the window, hoping Sloan's ex-girlfriend was not following them. "Did you hit her back?"

Wrinkles flashed across Sloan's butterscotch-brown forehead. "*Never,*" he said in a sheepish tone. "I'm not that type of guy."

A Dodge Durango whizzed, causing water to splash on the windshield.

"Was there a reason for her to hit you with the bat?" inquired Hope.

"No." He changed lanes, avoiding a puddle of water. "This made my second time going to court to file a restraining order against her."

"Second time!" Hope cringed, sneering. "What happened the first time?"

Sloan paused before speaking. "The timeframe for the first restraining order was ending. I wanted to make sure I filed another one," he said while scratching his black well-tamed hair. "I doubt that she knows where I live now because I've moved." Hope was lost for words. She had never heard of a woman abusing a man. Perhaps, this was the reason why she later fell in love with him because he was a victim of abuse like her.

"What about you?" asked Sloan as he adjusted the rearview mirror.

"What do you mean?" inquired Hope.

"What is the story about your boyfriend?" grinned Sloan as he plucked a lint ball from Hope's shoulder, causing her to flinch.

"I don't have a boyfriend."

"I'm sure you're dating somebody," said Sloan while glancing at her thighs.

Hope felt puzzled. Her mind fluttered as she wondered why this stranger was asking her if she was dating. She placed her hand on the door handle just in case she had to jump out of the car.

Chapter 7

The Friday midday sun shined inside Ruth's eggshell painted apartment. Mrs. Hall glanced at her watch as if she was on a timer. She had been sitting in Mrs. Ruth's apartment for nearly an hour. Without a doubt, she was ready to leave.

"Mama told me that my daddy, Rock, stole her from you," sobbed Jasmine.

Ruth's light brown eyes filled up with tears. "Why would Rock do that to Julia?" snapped Ruth as if she wanted to round up her cubs to go and look for Rock.

Silence filled the air as if sound had been sucked up in a vacuum.

"He left mama," uttered Jasmine as she hugged Taylor. "Mama told me . . . she was a virgin when daddy took her from you. Mama said he kept her for himself for a few years . . . and . . . and . . . locked her in a house somewhere. She could never go out. She got pregnant with us."

"Tell the other part, Jasmine," winced Taylor.

Jasmine slowly exhaled as if she was blowing out candles on a cake. "Mama told us that she tried to kill herself a lot of times," said Jasmine as her gaze plummeted to the floor. "One time she drank some Clorox. Another time, she cut her wrist and took a lot of pills."

A tear trickled down Ruth's face.

"Mama told us that she was tired of being trapped in the house with daddy."

"Did she get help at the hospital?" asked Mrs. Brown in a sympathetic tone.

"No, ma'am," mumbled Taylor. "Mama said daddy got a doctor to come to the house to check on her. Mama said the doctor was part of the trafficking group too."

A whirlwind of conversations flowed through the window as three teenage girls walked past Ruth's apartment. Their colorful tight jeans clung to their curvy hips.

Jasmine stared out the window, looking at the teenage girls. She shook her small head as if she wanted to forewarn the girls that their skin-tight jeans could make them an easy target for human trafficking.

"Why was she trying to kill herself?" asked Ruth as her voice trembled.

"Mama said she got tired of feeling trapped. Plus, daddy used to take me and Taylor with him for days and leave mama by herself. He would handcuff her hands and feet to pipes on the heater that was connected to the wall," muffled

Jasmine.

Mrs. Hall rubbed her blushed pink cheek.

"Why did he leave her tied up for days?" asked Mrs. Hall in a soft tone.

"Taylor and I were about six and seven. Daddy used to do that to *punish* mama for trying to kill herself . . . or for asking him to let her go."

Silence surged through the apartment.

Taylor slowly opened her mouth. "He didn't leave mama any food . . . or anything. Mama had to use the bathroom on herself because she couldn't get loose from the pipe on the heater," said Taylor in a humiliating tone.

A loud sound echoed through the living room as a midnight black Mercedes-Benz crept down the street with music pumping out the car, causing Taylor to shake worse than a washer machine spinning.

"Mama told me daddy got tired of her trying to kill herself. So, daddy found another virgin younger than her," winced Jasmine as she lowered her head. "I heard him tell mama that he couldn't keep her longer than seven years."

"What are you talking about, Jasmine?" asked Ruth while pressing her lips together.

"I really don't know," responded Jasmine. "But I heard daddy tell mama that his brother *had a seven-year rule.*"

"What is a seven-year rule?" asked Mrs. Brown.

Taylor rubbed her eyes. "I overheard daddy tell mama that his brother would only allow him to keep mama for seven years," she sniffled.

"Why was there a limit of seven years?" asked Ruth in a baffled tone.

"I really don't know," responded Mrs. Hall. "But we *speculate* that the leaders may have had an insurance scheme going on too."

"What do you mean?" asked Mrs. Brown in a disoriented tone.

"I don't know all of the details, but I was told if a person is missing for seven years, then the beneficiary can be awarded money from that person's life insurance policy."

Screeching noise ricocheted through the apartment.

Ruth cracked her knuckles. "Did someone have a life insurance policy on Julia?"

"It is hard for us to quickly determine that since there are a lot of life insurance companies," responded Mrs. Hall. "But we are checking into it."

"So, what did Rock do to Julia?" asked Mrs. Brown.

Jasmine's gaze lowered toward the floor. "After seven years, daddy had to sell mama or kill her. So, one day daddy sold mama."

"Sold her," cringed Ruth as if life had been sucked out of her.

"Yes, ma'am," mumbled Jasmine. "Daddy let mama take us with her to one of the human trafficking houses. We were at that house for several years.

Mama kept trying to find a way for us to escape," sobbed Jasmine. "We were scared. The leaders kept bringing new women, girls and boys to the house all the time."

"Where were they coming from?" asked Mrs. Brown in a nervous tone.

"We don't know," answered Jasmine. "But some of them spoke different languages. They were scared."

"I saw them bring in women with their children," said Taylor. "Mama said some of the women had to be traded in like her."

Sirens roared in the air as a police cruiser sped down the street.

"Sometimes, kids were brought to the house without their mothers or fathers," muffled Taylor. "They used to cry for a long time. They were terrified."

Mrs. Hall leaned forward. "From what I know, some of the human trafficking leaders prey on young girls and boys who live in the projects," she said while looking around inside Ruth's spotless apartment. "Or young girls and boys who are caught walking alone or whose families don't really care about them. But there are other situations where people have gotten involved in human trafficking."

"So, I guess Cloverdale projects or other projects must be a harvesting center for people doing human trafficking stuff. That is wrong!" yelled Ruth.

"To be honest, I was told that other girls from this project and, of course, from other projects have been forced into human trafficking," said Mrs. Hall. "Whether it was drug traffic, sex traffic, labor traffic, baby traffic, or other stuff."

"Baby traffic?" inquired Ruth as her eyebrow elevated.

"Yes," said Mrs. Hall. "Some women are forced to get pregnant. After they have the babies, the leaders sell the babies on *Black Market* to couples who can't have babies."

Ruth slumped in the chair as if the information was too much for her to bear.

The sound of stray cats scrambling for food in the piled-up trash echoed in the apartment. The cats caused wine bottles to plunge to the ground.

"Did the kids go to school?" Mrs. Brown asked as if she wanted to *soften* the conversation, noticing Mrs. Hall was anxiously keeping up with the time.

Mrs. Hall glanced at her watch. This made it her fifth time staring at her watch within an hour as if being in Cloverdale projects made her feel uncomfortable.

"When we used to live in a large house with other women and children, the leaders had kidnapped a lady that they found out was a school teacher. They made her teach all of us at the large house."

"What large house?" asked Ruth as a bizarre look overshadowed her face.

"The leaders of the human trafficking group kept the women and children in large secluded houses," said Mrs. Hall. "The police couldn't locate any of them."

"We can't trust the police," cringed Taylor.

"Why not?" asked Mrs. Brown curiously.

"The leaders paid some police to do stuff for them," gasped Jasmine in a disheartened tone. "The leaders even had doctors come in to give checkups and stuff."

Mrs. Brown clasped her hands together as she bowed her head.

Seconds had passed before anyone said a word.

"It seems like you remembered a lot," said Mrs. Brown as she looked at Jasmine.

"Yes, ma'am. My mama taught us. She repeated stuff because she didn't want us to forget . . . just in case we escaped and got help," said Jasmine as her voice rattled.

Taylor slowly opened her mouth. "Mama was always trying to find ways to escape with me and Jasmine. The last time she tried . . ." sobbed Taylor.

"One of the leaders ordered for mama to be killed," interjected Jasmine as she rubbed Taylor's eyes.

A tear trickled down Taylor's face. "I think it was my dad's brother who ordered mama to be killed."

"His brother?" shrieked Mrs. Ruth in a heartfelt tone.

Silence gripped the living room as Taylor hid her face in Jasmine's chest.

Chapter 8

Time moved slower than a snail on Friday afternoon. Hope glanced at the clock, hoping that Sloan would return soon from his business trip.

A river of love flowed through Hope as she looked at her twins playing together. Hope slowly exhaled as she allowed her mind to venture to the day that she met Sloan . . .

"So, you mean to tell me that you have *never* had a boyfriend," inquired Sloan as he licked his lips.

Hope swallowed before responding. A sudden river of fear stormed through her body. "Can you please pull over and let me out of the car?" asked Hope as her voice slightly trembled.

Sloan paused for a split second.

"I cannot do that."

"Why not?" asked Hope as she gripped the handle on the door.

"First of all, I want you to calm down," he ordered. "I am not going to hurt you. All I want to do is to give you a ride to work." Sloan's entire demeanor changed to a calm and supportive approach.

A cool breeze swept through the car.

"I just find it amazing that a beautiful woman like yourself has never had a boyfriend."

Hope closed her eyes as she slowly exhaled, praying that Sloan would arrive at her job soon.

"I don't have a boyfriend," she uttered hoping that Sloan wouldn't ask her any further questions.

"What about before? I am sure you have had a boyfriend before?"

"Why are you asking me if I have a boyfriend?" blurted Hope in a low tone as she glanced out the window wishing Sloan would change the subject.

"No reason," smirked Sloan, pausing before speaking. "Well, do you have a girlfriend?"

A peal of laughter trailed off Hope's tongue removing a layer of fear.

"That is funny," smirked Hope. "I don't have a girlfriend. I don't have a boyfriend. I have never had a girlfriend and I have never had a boyfriend. So, please stop asking me."

A bewildered look inched across Sloan's face as if he suddenly had a change of plan about something. Hope pressed her wet back against the passenger seat wondering what was going through his mind. But a sense of ease swept through her body as she noticed that he did not lock her door. Hope wanted to make sure she was able to make a fast break—if deemed necessary.

Soft jazz flowed through the speakers in the car.

"So, what type of work do you do?" she asked, hoping to change the subject.

"I'm an engineer. I work with computers and devices."

"So, this is where you work?" asked Sloan as he pulled up in front of Classic Touch Tavern.

Hope flinched wondering how Sloan knew exactly where she worked without her telling him. It was as if he had been following her previously.

"Yes," Hope slowly said as Sloan parked the car. "How did you know exactly where I worked?"

"I figured out of all of the restaurants, you look like you would work at the most upscale spot on this street," chuckled Sloan. "I can see that you are wearing a restaurant uniform."

"But the name of the restaurant isn't on my shirt," sighed Hope.

"It wasn't hard for me to figure it out, Hope," he said, revealing a dimple on his right cheek.

Hope paused for a few seconds. She figured Sloan had given her an okay explanation. Plus, she was delighted that a decent man had finally approached her. Though her guard was still up, she was tired of lifeless men trying to take her on dates—all of which she had turned down.

"I'm a cook. I'm in culinary school. I will have my own catering business one day," smiled Hope as she opened the car door.

"Wait, let me get the door and umbrella for you," said Sloan as he quickly hopped out of the car. He walked Hope to the front door, barricading her from the rain. "I'll be back for lunch," said Sloan as a smile unfolded on his lips.

Sloan ate at Classic Touch Tavern every day until Hope agreed to go on a date with him, resulting in them being married a year later. She didn't even really know Sloan's family. She didn't even know much about his past life. At that time, she didn't even know anyone other than her co-workers. She had never been on a date. She had no one to talk to other than Mrs. Brown. She didn't even know what to expect from a man. She didn't even try to figure it out. She thought she was in love. She thought Sloan was the man for her. Plus, she was tired of being *alone*. But little did Hope know, there was much more to Sloan beyond his well-groomed charismatic appearance.

A sharp noise pierced the air, snapping Hope out of her daydream. Jayden had knocked over a bucket of colorful blocks on the oatmeal colored carpet. Hope smiled as Jayla rushed over to help Jayden pick up the blocks.

Suddenly, ringing sounds echoed throughout the house.

A busload of anxiety stormed through Hope's body. She didn't want to talk to Ivey again. She certainly didn't want to talk to her mother. A sense of calm overtook her when she realized it was her business telephone ringing. She didn't bother to look at the high-tech caller ID since her business telephone had rung instead of the house telephone. She figured her customers had legitimate reasons to call her.

"Thank you for calling Serenity Catering Services. How may I help you?" asked Hope in a pleasant voice while opening her stationary pad. She took the pad with her everywhere because she was always ready to take orders.

"Hello, my mother is having her seventieth birthday next month," said a lady in an upbeat tone that Hope thought she recognized but she was uncertain about. "My brother and I would like to have a small gathering catered to her. We want this to be very special. My mother likes to do a lot of cooking and baking."

Hope paused for a second, realizing that the caller's voice sounded familiar.

"Me too," said Hope in an excited tone as she handed Jayden a blue block.

"My mother typically cooks meals and bakes cakes for other people. But my brother and I want to surprise her by having food catered for her birthday."

"Well, that will be a wonderful surprise," said Hope in a cheerful tone. "I definitely know how to personalize my catering services to fit any occasion. I can cater particularly any gourmet meal, dessert, pastry, or fruit salad," said Hope in a confident tone. "I can e-mail you some pictures of the events that I have catered. I can also prepare a small dish for you to sample. Plus, I can provide you with some references."

"Of course, I would like to sample the dishes. I'm sure my brother would want to do the same. He might eat up all of the samples," laughed the lady.

"It wouldn't be the first time that has happened," said Hope as she joined the lady in laughter. "What is your name and where will the event take place?" asked Hope as she watched Jayla color a picture.

"My name is Tiffany Brown-Carson and the event will take place in Charlotte, North Carolina. I see that you are located in Raleigh," she paused. "I had to find a catering company in a different city other than Charlotte because my mother knows particularly everyone in the catering business nearby."

Hope exhaled. At this point, there was no doubt that she recognized the caller's voice. But she hoped that the caller didn't recognize her.

Hope's lips slightly trembled as she asked, "What is your mother's name?"

"Mrs. Lena Brown," said Tiffany in a heartfelt tone.

Hope slumped in the chair as her blood came to a sudden halt.

Chapter 9

Hope leaned back in the chair, reminiscing about her telephone call with Tiffany. Without a doubt, Hope was delighted to have the opportunity to cater Mrs. Lena Brown's event. Sadly, Hope realized that Tiffany hadn't recognized her voice. It had been over seven years since Hope had spoken with Tiffany. The thought of returning to Charlotte made Hope's heart clench. More compelling, Mrs. Lena Brown lived across the street from Hope's mother in Cloverdale projects. Hope definitely didn't want to risk seeing her mother. In fact, Hope didn't want to be anywhere near her mother.

Two hours later, a cool breeze flowed through the sunflower painted playroom, mingling with the smell of peanut butter and jelly sandwiches that Hope had prepared for the twins. Small slices of red apples clustered on a gold saucer in front of Jayla and Jayden, presenting a delicious treat for them.

After the twins finished eating, Hope walked toward the forty-inch television mounted in the corner on the wall. She scanned the DVDs, searching for the twins' favorite cartoon. Hope specially ordered their cartoons to make sure the characters communicated by using ASL. Also, the cartoons were specially crafted to permit the twins to practice their lip-reading skills.

Hope sighed, glancing at the television. She took pride in her children having a television, something she never had as a child. As an adult, she had no interest in watching television, unless it was an educational program for her children. She didn't even watch the news. She had lost interest in the news, especially when all of the events seemed to be about crime in the Cloverdale community.

Hope glanced at the rainbow colored clock on the wall, noticing that Sloan had been gone nearly two hours. She recalled Sloan stating that he would be with Mr. Gavino for a couple of hours working on a project. On one end, Hope was delighted that Sloan was not at home. She didn't have to worry about correcting her grammar in his absence nor subdue to the pressure she typically endured as a result of Sloan's obsessive compulsive disorder.

Soft chirping sounds came in through the double pan window.

Hope's heart tightened as she thought about how Sloan had a unique way in which the canned foods had to be positioned in the cabinets, how the towels had to be folded, how the shoes and clothes in the closet had to be organized and how his clothes needed to be ironed. Hope could never iron Sloan's clothing to his likeness. He finally resorted to taking his clothes to the cleaners. Of course, Hope was relieved.

A burst of sunlight inched through the olive green curtains, casting sun rays on the oatmeal tan carpet.

Hope sat on the burgundy sofa in the playroom with the twins watching cartoons. A smile stretched across Jayden's pecan-tan face as he looked at the cartoon. Jayla's pearly white teeth glistened as she laughed while watching cartoons. Hope enjoyed watching cartoons with her twins. She was fond of their ability to read the cartoon character's lips.

Hope's fingers gracefully moved as she communicated in ASL with her twins. She paused the cartoon to practice lip reading with her twins. Hope slowly opened her mouth to say words and her twins responded in unison in ASL to spell out the words that Hope had said to them. Hope wrapped her slender arms around her twins as a warm lovely feeling engulfed her. She was delighted that they had improved their ASL and lip-reading skills.

Hope turned back on the television to allow her twins to finish watching their favorite cartoon.

A sharp sound pierced the air as the telephone rang, causing Hope's heart to flutter like butterflies. She glanced down at her cell phone. She felt a sense of relief as she noticed the telephone number was associated with a telemarketer.

A sharp sound pierced the air again. Hope's gaze scanned the telephone number.

"Hello," said Hope in a soft tone.

"I was calling to check on you and the twins," said Sloan in a deep tone.

"The twins are watching cartoons," said Hope as she tapped on the twins' shoulders to signal to them that she was speaking to their father on the telephone.

"Hey, when is that event at the twins' summer camp?" asked Sloan.

"The father-son and mother-daughter activities day is in a few weeks," said Hope in an excited tone. She liked doing activities with the twins.

"Okay. So, what are you doing?" asked Sloan as if he was questioning Hope.

"I was sitting here . . . thinking about my lovely husband."

"Yeah, right. You probably are enjoying the break from me," chuckled Sloan.

Hope paused for a few seconds, trying to detect any sound in Sloan's background. Hope noticed that every time Sloan called her, he always managed to make sure his background was silent.

"Hey, don't forget we are still going to the museum on Sunday afternoon."

"I haven't forgotten, Sloan," said Hope in a submissive tone.

"Make sure you wear something semi-sexy."

She felt proud as she reflected upon how Sloan took pride in her appearance. He had a fetish for high heels. Hope was required to wear them around the house—even when they went to the grocery store. Her closet aligned with name-brand clothing and shoes—a wardrobe she could never afford on her own. Sloan made sure Hope and the twins were always presentable as if his family were in a fashion show.

A beeping sound penetrated Hope's ear as another call seeped through the phone. Hope looked at the high-tech caller ID. It was Mrs. Brown. Although Hope wanted to speak with her, she wanted to talk to Sloan for a few more minutes.

"Sloan," said Hope in an upbeat tone. "I've got a potential new customer today." A sense of excitement ran through her. "This makes my tenth customer in the first month of operating my catering business."

"Hope, it is not *got* . . . it is *received*," blurted Sloan without even acknowledging Hope's excitement about her steadily increasing customers within one month.

Sloan paused before uttering another word. He typically would not speak until Hope corrected her grammar.

Hope exhaled as if she was a dragon blowing out a fire. Sloan had struck a nerve inside Hope's heart. She felt like a child in a preparatory grammar class. She cleared her thoughts before repeating herself.

"Sloan, I've received a potential new customer today," mumbled Hope as a touch of agony knifed through her heart.

"That is great, Hope. I am proud of you. How many customers do you have now?" he asked as if he didn't already know.

Hope was certain Sloan kept track of her list of customers. Hell, he had created a state-of-the-art website for her. In fact, he had recommended that Hope processed all catering transactions through the website. This made life much easier for her. Yet, she was certain Sloan used the website to track her catering sales and her actions.

On the other hand, Hope understood why Sloan had launched a niche in the business arena for his computer engineering expertise. He had established his own company and executed multiple contracts with specific types of businesses only to develop their websites. He was highly demanded. But for some strange reason, he preferred to contract with *delivery* companies only—especially pizza pubs. In particular, Sloan vested a lot of time in overseeing Mr. Gavino's website to track the pizza pub's deliveries and sales. Hope often wondered why Mr. Gavino had insisted that Sloan incorporate a system on the website to screen every customer's telephone number. When Hope asked Sloan about this bizarre practice, Sloan politely reminded Hope that Mr. Gavino wanted to ensure the safety of his staff when they made deliveries. Yet, Hope was still clueless about why Mr. Gavino offered a variety of cheeses—other than the typical customary types. Perhaps this was the trademark for Mr. Gavino's *Worldwide Express, Inc.'s* pizza delivery pub.

"I have ten regular customers and one new potential customer."

"Your catering business is making steady progress in just one month."

"I've always envisioned having my own catering company ever since I was a teenager. I used to watch Mrs. Brown cook meals and bake desserts," said Hope in a soft tone. "She could make a meal from scraps."

"*Scraps*," laughed Sloan. "Mrs. Brown must be a food magician."

"She is," said Hope, suddenly recalling that she had not seen Mrs. Brown in several years. Yet, she spoke with Mrs. Brown at least once or twice a month.

"I can't wait until I meet this infamous Mrs. Brown one day," blurted Sloan.

"Speaking of that," said Hope in a slow tone. "My potential new customer is Mrs. Brown's daughter, Tiffany. She called today to place an order for Mrs. Brown's seventieth birthday event that is scheduled within two months."

"Are you serious?" laughed Sloan. "I know you are excited about this, Hope."

"I am," said Hope as her voice weakened.

"What's wrong?" asked Sloan in a concerned tone.

Silence engulfed the telephone for a few seconds.

"Tiffany didn't recognize my voice," mumbled Hope. "Even though it has been more than seven years since I spoke with her, I assumed she would remember my voice."

"Did you remember her voice?" asked Sloan.

"Not at first," Hope sighed. "But after she told me her name . . . I did."

"Well, it seems as though you didn't recall her voice either," said Sloan. "But how do you speak with Mrs. Brown all the time and never speak with Tiffany?"

"Mrs. Brown and Tiffany don't live together, Sloan," responded Hope. "When I call Mrs. Brown, Tiffany is never at her mother's house."

"Oh, by the way . . . why did you say '*potential new customer*' earlier?"

Hope gasped for air, hoping Sloan would change the subject. She was not in the mood to explain to Sloan that she might decline catering Mrs. Brown's seventieth birthday event because Mrs. Brown lived near her mother.

A soft hand tugged at Hope's arm. Jayla alerted Hope that the cartoon had ended, saving Hope from having to provide Sloan a response to his question.

"Hold on for a second," said Hope. "The cartoon has ended."

"Go ahead and take care of the twins. I will be home in a few hours."

An unfamiliar voice traveled through Sloan's cell phone to Hope's eardrums.

"Sloan, the accountant needs you," said a man with a Saint Vincent Island accent.

Even though Hope had never seen Mr. Gavino, she was certain it was not his voice because he had an Italian accent. She recalled Sloan telling her that Mr. Gavino spoke English, Italian, French and Spanish and that he had pizza pubs in various countries.

Silence filtered through the telephone as if Sloan had muzzled the sound to prevent Hope from hearing his conversation with the man.

"Tell Mr. Gavino I'll be there in a minute," said Sloan in a stern tone as if the man had interrupted his conversation with Hope. "Hold on, Hope," he snapped before muting the call. A few seconds later, the sound slowly resurfaced on the phone. "Hope, I have to fly out of town with Mr. Gavino this evening. I will return on Sunday morning."

"Really, Sloan! Today is Friday and you're telling me you will be back on Sunday? Where are you going this time?" she asked.

Sloan exhaled heavily on the phone without answering Hope's questions.

"I will be back on Sunday, Hope. I will call you later."

Hope slowly hung up the phone, trying to detect any degree of lingering sounds on the other end. She often worried about how Sloan managed to be surrounded by silence every time he called. Even though she trusted him, an uneasy feeling floated in her gut slowly convincing her otherwise. Sloan was too perfect. He was too smart. He was too handsome and he never left any clues behind. He was bound to slip up and that day was coming.

Chapter 10

Ruth's apartment felt eerie. The Friday afternoon seemed to have presented more heartfelt conversations than Ruth was prepared to hear.

Jasmine protectively rubbed Taylor's arm.

Jasmine's mouth slowly opened. "One of the leaders ordered that mama be killed. The next day, mama was gone. They killed her in front of other women to teach them a lesson," said Jasmine before pausing. "One of the women who was my mama's friend begged the leaders to bury mama. The leaders were going to let the wild dogs eat her like they did another woman," mumbled Jasmine as her body shivered like leaves on a windy day. "But somebody told them to burn up mama's body."

"Burn!" bellowed Ruth.

"Yes, so that Taylor and I could keep her ashes. I was so scared. I thought they were going to kill me and Taylor too. But the next day the leaders moved us from Miami, Florida to Atlanta, Georgia. I guess, to sell us to somebody," sobbed Jasmine.

"*Sell*!" shrieked Ruth, causing her wig to wobble.

Tears flowed down Taylor's face. "I heard them say they would lose money if they killed Jasmine and me," she paused. "I saw the leader kill my mama."

Jasmine leaned toward Taylor, causing her red shirt to wrinkle. "They decided to take me and Taylor to a restaurant in Atlanta. But I don't think we were going there to eat. I think they wanted to sell us to people at the restaurant. I remember the leaders used to make mama do nasty stuff with people who ordered her."

"What do you mean? *Ordered* her! You mean to tell me that human trafficking is a business for some people. This is absolutely crazy!" shrieked Ruth.

"Yes, it is a serious issue in several countries," muffled Mrs. Hall. "It is a good thing that Jasmine and Taylor were not trafficked to another country."

"Where were Jasmine and Taylor born?" asked Ruth.

"Mama said we were born in a house. But I don't remember what city or state she told me about. The leaders got doctors to come to the house to deliver us," uttered Jasmine.

Loud music drifted from a white Cadillac Escalade into the apartment as the driver pulled over to the curb, causing Jasmine and Taylor to shiver like falling leaves. A nervous look spread across their faces at the onset of the sudden loud noise. Mrs. Brown recalled the same traumatized look that her brother,

Lamont Brown, also known as June Bug, had after he returned from serving in the military as a sergeant. Mrs. Brown was certain that the kids had posttraumatic stress disorder like her brother. Unfortunately, her brother resorted to using crack and then elevated to heroin to self-medicate his disorder. With the massive opioid epidemic, he had no problem finding a nearby fix. But he was fortunate to survive an overdose that redefined his life.

Ruth peered out of the window at the well-groomed driver as a wide smile flashed on her face. "That's Forest playing that loud music. He's probably looking for me. I forgot that I was scheduled to . . . meet with him today. We have a weekly appointment."

"An appointment?" inquired Mrs. Hall.

Mrs. Ruth glanced at Mrs. Hall before rolling her eyes.

"How did Jasmine and Taylor get from Miami to Atlanta?" asked Mrs. Brown, trying to interrupt Mrs. Hall and redirecting Mrs. Ruth's attention.

"A Spanish lady and a French man were talking to a tall black lady about us," said Jasmine.

"How do you know they were Spanish and French?" asked Mrs. Ruth in a puzzled way.

"The leaders made mama learn a lot of languages and she taught us. The leaders got mama tutors. She learned Spanish, French, Italian, and Russian. They wanted mama to be part of the human trafficking business because she had learned the languages fast. But she refused to do it," responded Jasmine.

"Really? Julia could speak, read and write all of those languages?" inquired Ruth. She was delighted to know that her daughter was multi-lingual but she was not happy with the circumstance in which her daughter had learned the languages.

"Yes," mumbled Taylor. "Jasmine and I can too."

Silence flowed in the air.

"How did you all get from Miami to Atlanta?" repeated Mrs. Brown as she tried to break the silence.

"The tall black lady made us get in an 18-wheeler truck with a short fat white truck driver. He had a lot of chickens in the back of the truck," said Jasmine.

"Chickens," bawled Ruth.

"Yes, that's how they hid us," muffled Jasmine as she held Taylor's hand.

"What do you mean?" asked Mrs. Brown in a shocking tone.

Jasmine exhaled slowly.

"It's okay. You don't have to talk about it anymore," uttered Mrs. Brown.

Taylor wrapped her small narrow arms around Jasmine.

"The lady hid us between the chicken cages in the back of the truck.

"What! A woman was in on this too?" blurted Ruth.

"Yes, they are called Madams. They help the leaders control the other women and children," mumbled Jasmine as tears formed in her eyelids.

A cluster of laughter soared into the apartment as children played outside.

"The lady put some of the cages in front of us so nobody could see us if someone opened the back door of the truck. There were seven other girls like Taylor and I in the back of the truck with the chickens. The girls said they were taken from different states. One girl didn't speak English. She spoke Chinese. She got sick 'cause the chickens didn't smell right," sighed Jasmine.

"There was one girl who spoke Russian and another girl who spoke Arabic," said Taylor.

"How long were you on the truck?" asked Ruth in a cautious manner.

"A long time. The lady gave us some bread to eat and a bottle of water. She said it would be a long trip from Miami to Atlanta," mumbled Jasmine. "She told the truck driver where to take us in Atlanta. The lady didn't ride with us."

A loud noise traveled in the apartment as a cluster of motorcycles rolled past the apartment.

"Oh, they are called biker boys. A lot of them came down here from Baltimore, Maryland," smiled Mrs. Ruth as if her attention span was designed as a radar that only allowed her to focus on men. "I've been on a few of their motorcycles. Onyx has the best motorcycle."

"How did the kids escape to get from Atlanta, Georgia to Charlotte, North Carolina?" asked Mrs. Brown as curiosity leaped through her while trying to divert Mrs. Hall's focus from Mrs. Ruth.

"It's a complex story," said Mrs. Hall as if she didn't want to answer Ruth.

Jasmine tilted her head toward the popcorn ceiling. "I'll tell her."

Words ceased through the apartment like wildflowers.

"When the truck driver took us to Atlanta, he didn't go straight to the restaurant to drop us off. He parked the truck in the middle of some woods," babbled Jasmine as her bottom lip trembled. "The truck driver pulled a Spanish talking girl off the truck to do some nasty stuff to her." Her head lowered.

Jasmine paused, placing her small golden brown hands on her head as if the memories of her human trafficking experience were too painful to rehash.

"The truck driver left the door unlocked while he was messing with that girl in the woods. I was scared. But I wanted to get me and Taylor out of that truck," said Jasmine as her body shivered slightly like Jell-O. "I tried to get the other girls to run with us, but they were too scared. So, I grabbed Taylor's hand and we ran and ran and ran until we couldn't run anymore."

"Oh, my God," blurted Mrs. Brown while noticing darkness inch across the sky.

"Me and Taylor hid in the woods for a few days," mumbled Jasmine. "We still had the bread and water that the lady gave us. Plus, the other girls on the truck gave us some of their bread to take with us. They didn't want to leave with us. They probably thought Taylor and I were going to get killed."

"How did you find help?" asked Ruth as she hugged Jasmine and Taylor.

"I found an abandoned building for Taylor and me to hide in and sleep. I remembered that is what mama used to do when she escaped with us."

Mrs. Brown planted her dark brown hand over her heart as she mumbled a prayer.

"We were too scared to go to the police because we had learned that we couldn't trust them.

The police had taken mama back to the leaders twice. One time when we were in Richmond and another time when we were in Miami."

"Richmond," said Ruth as if she was shocked that Julia had been trafficked to several states with Jasmine and Taylor.

"So how did you find help for you and Taylor?" asked Mrs. Brown in a calm tone.

"I learned from my mama that the leaders had a lot of women lure kids for them."

A frown stretched across Ruth's face, causing her penciled eyebrows to cave in.

"I knew I couldn't trust some teachers, cab drivers, truck drivers, doctors . . . social workers, airport workers, dentists, lawyers, or preachers," mumbled Jasmine. "I learned from mama that some of them help the leaders too. The doctors used to come to check some of the girls to make sure they were not pregnant or had a disease, even though I used to hear the leaders tell the men that they had to use condoms. A few dentists used to come as well because the leaders liked for our teeth to be pretty to attract customers," she exhaled, while rubbing her hands together. "About two beauticians used to do our hair and they got paid a lot of money."

"Really?" spouted Ruth. "This is terrible. Human trafficking is scary. It seems like it is an underground empire business."

"It seems like," mumbled Mrs. Brown.

"That is why Taylor and I want to become lawyers one day to help stop human trafficking leaders from doing bad things. There are a lot of people who secretly work for the leaders. Nobody can be trusted." Jasmine slowly closed her eyes before, saying. "Taylor and I knew that we couldn't trust some homeless people either because they are watchers."

"*Watchers*?" asked Ruth in a puzzling tone.

"Yes, they are people who keep the leaders informed about what's happening in the streets," said Jasmine as she exhaled. "Especially, if they see certain girls or boys wandering by themselves on the streets or walking home from school or in other places."

"Are you serious," said Mrs. Brown as a touch of agony flowed through her.

"I learned quickly how to spot who was a watcher for the traffic leaders," said Jasmine as she lowered her head. "My mama taught me."

"Mama told us not to trust some restaurant owners," mumbled Taylor.

"Why not?" asked Mrs. Brown.

"Mama told us that some young girls and women were taken to private fancy restaurants to work," said Taylor.

"Work?" inquired Mrs. Brown

"Men could order the type of young girl or woman that they wanted to eat breakfast, lunch or dinner with and then they went to secret rooms in the restaurants to have sex," replied Jasmine as if she had to respond for Taylor.

"Why didn't the young girls and women try to escape from the restaurants?" inquired Ruth.

"They couldn't because the leaders had *runners* who watched them. Plus, mama said some of the young girls and women got tired of trying to leave and they started liking that lifestyle because the leaders bought them nice clothe," said Jasmine. "Mama used to beg the leaders not to take us to the restaurants. Mama prayed that someone would help us."

"So, who helped you?" asked Ruth in a painstaking tone. "Or . . .what did you have to do to get some help for you and Taylor?" she inquired at a slow pace.

"I have to leave. I'll be back in the morning," said Mrs. Hall in a nervous tone as if she was anxious to depart from Cloverdale before darkness settled in. Plus, it was obvious Mrs. Hall couldn't withstand hearing Jasmine speak about human trafficking.

Mrs. Brown exhaled slowly, knowing that the next words that came out of Jasmine's mouth would cause a ripple of chills to pierce through her heart.

Chapter 11

A soft scent of cucumber-melon drifted into the den creating a crisp pleasant aroma for the Saturday morning. Hope exhaled, wondering why Sloan had to quickly fly out of town with Mr. Gavino yesterday evening. "What is going on," said Hope to herself.

She leaned back in the Italian designed cream love seat gazing at the lemon flower-painted walls. The den was definitely off limits for the twins.

Hope was fond of the 5,000 square feet house that Sloan was adamant had to be built from the ground. The four bedroom house provided enough space for Sloan and Hope to expand their family. But for the moment, Hope was satisfied with only having two children. The house was nestled on ten acres that were enclosed by tall skyscraping pine trees, preventing any view of the house from neighbors and the street.

Hope placed her 15-inch laptop on her leg, browsing through her catering company's website. Colorful entrees adorned upscale dishes creating a unique image of home-cooked meals, inexpensive party trays, gourmet cuisine meals, and homemade cakes and pastries. A warm feeling flowed through her as she read customers' surveys about her services. She took pride in providing quality catering services. The feeling that once warmed her came to a sudden halt. Tiffany had requested to meet with Hope to taste some samples.

Hope slowly exhaled as she contemplated whether she wanted to decline Tiffany's request. An ounce of misery crept through Hope as she battled with risking the chance of seeing her mother if she catered Tiffany's mother's seventieth birthday party. Her heart tugged at the fact that she wanted to see Mrs. Brown. But she didn't want to be anywhere near her mother.

A sharp noise pierced the air, causing Hope to flinch. A car's horn blew as it passed by her house—apparently blowing at another driver.

Hope surfed the internet, narrowing her focus to Mr. Gavino's Worldwide Express, Inc.'s pizza pub. She browsed through the pizza pub's website. Her gaze focused on the different types of cheese. Two lists outlined the types of cheeses that the pizza pub offered. On the left-hand side of the webpage, a list of traditional cheeses assembled down the page. On the right-hand side of the webpage, a list of unique cheeses neatly aligned down the page. The advertisement created an appealing image.

She felt a knot in her gut as she viewed the advertisement of the *unique* cheeses. The website showcased female employees holding different types of pizzas. Even though it was an advertisement, she felt as though something wasn't right.

Hope squinted as she looked at the advertisement for a white cheddar cheese pizza that was displayed on the webpage. A slender attractive woman who was visibly white stood near the pizza as her employee uniform snuggled around the crescent of her watermelon shaped breasts. Hope's gaze shifted to an advertisement for a Mexican cheese pizza. Ironically, a full-figured eye-catching woman who was visibly Mexican stood near the pizza as her employee uniform pressed firmly against her well-defined curves.

Hope scrolled down the computer's screen, noting an advertisement for brunost cheese pizza—a brown colored cheese. Hope's curiosity peaked as she noticed an astounding golden-brown woman positioned close to the brunost cheese pizza. The women's pizza uniform cradled her perky breasts. The woman was too beautiful. *Why is she working at this pizza pub?* wondered Hope.

"What is Sloan doing for Mr. Gavino," mumbled Hope. She recalled Sloan had set up the website for Mr. Gavino. Sloan had created the entire web-based system and high-tech caller ID system for all of Mr. Gavino's Worldwide Express Pizza pubs. "Why does Sloan wear those high-tech watches?" she pondered.

Hope leaned back on the love seat, thinking about the astounding appearances of the women on Worldwide Express Pizza's website. The women's astonishing features resembled more like patent beauty queens than typically pizza restaurant staff. Yet, Hope considered herself as being highly attractive. She recalled the days she labored in restaurants to make ends meet. So, she could relate to why the women were working at Mr. Gavino's pizza pub. Plus, Hope recalled Sloan saying Mr. Gavino paid his staff well. This may be the primary reason his employee retention rate remained high, revealing that his employees worked with him for several years.

A roaring sound echoed inside the den as an ambulance drove past.

Hope exhaled slowly, reflecting on her conversation with her sister Ivey. An ounce of bitterness reaped through Hope as memories of her dreadful childhood soared through her head. Hope pressed her back firmly into the love seat, slowly allowing her mind to drift down memory lane . . .

A surge of winter cold air brushed against Hope's boney five-year-old body as her teeth rattled. Her thin brown flimsy jacket barely prevented the air from seeping through. The poorly lit abandoned building welcomed lifeless bodies throughout the night. There was enough light for Hope to see filthy activities as if she was watching a triple X movie.

Hope's innocent eyes scanned every corner of the building, taking in the sinful scenes before her eyes. Shattered windows lined the three-story building. Broken glass bottles, crack pipes and rusted needles scattered on the scraped cemented floors. Debris piled up in a corner on the other side of the building as if it was the designated garbage disposal center. Stray cats rumbled through the trash like a scavenger hunt. A whiff of urine drifted inside the building. Male and female prostitutes assembled in dark corners, performing countless tricks in exchange for drugs.

"Give me my *dope*," yelled a short cocoa brown woman as she pulled up her dingy hot pink pants while following a man in a navy blue business suit. Suddenly, several drug addicts glared in the man's direction as if they were prepared to come to the woman's rescue. The man stopped in his tracks as he plunged his alabaster white hand into his pocket. Hope watched as the man tossed a small object toward the woman. The woman dove toward the object as if she was a baseball player.

Hope sat in a corner with three other children, near a small fire that burnt inside a trash can. They were forbidden to talk or move as if they were hostages taking in an ounce of warmth. Two skinny pale white little girls clustered together, trying to stay warm as their mother injected heroin. An almond tan little boy whispered something in Spanish as he looked at his father disappearing into a corner with another man. Hope couldn't understand the little boy because she didn't speak Spanish. Broken toys dispersed around the kids as the kids were in a miniature playroom.

Hope's muscles tightened in her stomach as hunger took over. She only had a candy bar to eat all day. She licked her teeth, hoping the residue from the candy bar still remained. Her school was out for the Christmas break, preventing Hope from eating breakfast and lunch daily.

A tear welled up in the corner of her eyes as she glanced at her mother. Gloria's bow shaped lips wrapped around a clear crack pipe as if she could care less about Hope at the moment. Gloria preferred to come to the abandoned building to smoke crack rather than in her small two-bedroom house. She didn't want to risk being evicted for having crack in her house. Surely, she didn't want to lose her Section 8 voucher. Instead, she compromised Hope's safety by hauling her to different abandoned buildings and houses—several times a week—especially on the weekends.

Gloria and the other crackheads and heroin addicts had organized a shady homeowners' association at abandoned buildings and houses throughout Charlotte, North Carolina. They often met at lifeless buildings to perform tricks and do drugs—in a so-called safe environment. Gloria always mingled with the same crackheads and heroin addicts as if they were safety patrol monitors.

The herd of crackheads and heroin addicts formed an amateur gang-like group to protect one another. As a child, Hope quickly learned that crackheads and heroin addicts could run faster than a speeding bullet. They had perfected the art of stealing. They had more con-artist skills than a crooked salesman. They could detect danger faster than a rat running through a sewer. Despite their flaws, they made sure their customers never harmed the kids in the abandoned buildings and houses. But there was only so much crackheads and heroin addicts could monitor when they were high, resulting in Hope being sexually molested while no one watched or helped—a painful memory Hope had tried endlessly to erase from her mind.

Scuffling sounds surfaced in a corner as Hope noticed two crackheads tussled over the last hit on a crack pipe. Hope had learned that crackheads didn't like sharing their crack.

Hope pulled her small body to an upright position to stand. She slowly walked toward Gloria, dreading that she would be beaten or pinched but she was hungry. Every step she took toward her mother scared her more and more.

"Mama, I'm hungry," said Hope in a low tone as her voice trembled.

Gloria stared at Hope as her eyes widened like quarters. Her shaggy unkempt sandy brown hair was scattered on her head. "Go sit down," shrieked Gloria as if Hope had weakened her high, causing Hope to urinate on herself. "You'll eat when I'm finished!"

A pinch of hatred sparked in Hope's little heart toward her mother as she retreated to the area where she congregated with the other kids. She laid on the cold cemented floor, planting her head on her folded arms as she forced herself to go to sleep to subdue the hunger pains.

A soft touch tugged at Hope's smooth hand interrupting her painstaking venture down memory lane. Hope was delighted that her twins had ended her daydream just in time before she had reflected upon the most heart-wrenching memory that forced her to hate her mother. Plus, Hope preferred to focus on preparing breakfast for her twins instead of reminiscing about the agonizing memories of her childhood.

It was the day that five-year-old Hope lost all respect and love for her mother.

Chapter 12

A cool breeze circulated through Ruth's apartment from the gold ceiling fan. Mrs. Hall returned to Ruth's house before the sun had peaked over the morning clouds. She glanced at her watch before peering at a form that she had retrieved from her black briefcase.

"Good morning, Mrs. Hall. I'm surprised you returned since it is Saturday," said Ruth as she adjusted a button on her candy apple red shirt. "I thought social workers only worked Monday through Friday."

"Good morning, Mrs. Turner. I'm on-call this weekend," said Mrs. Hall as she glanced at her watch. "And good morning to you, Mrs. Brown."

"Good morning," said Mrs. Brown in a peaceful manner as she rubbed her wrist.

"I have a few questions about Jasmine and Taylor's experience," said Ruth in an uneasy tone. "I want to make sure I understand what they went through so I can try to help them."

"I'm sure Jasmine or Taylor can answer your questions," blurted Mrs. Hall as if speaking about their human trafficking experience made her feel uncomfortable.

Ruth inched toward Jasmine. "So, how did you find help for you and Taylor?" inquired Ruth as her gaze shifted between Jasmine and Taylor.

Jasmine scratched her sandy brown hair as if she wanted to erase the memories of her painful experience.

"I remembered mama told me if I ever escaped, I needed to find a daycare center. She told me that daycares were responsible for watching children," sighed Jasmine. "She said daycares took care of children. Mama told me that they had to return children every day back to their parents without harming them. She said there was no way children in daycare could go missing without the police having to really do something about it. I was scared to go there. But Taylor and I were hungry. We had run out of bread."

Chirping noise flowed through the apartment as a mockingbird flew by.

"Mama was right. The daycare helped Taylor and me," said Jasmine as she looked at Ruth. The daycare center director, Mrs. Bailey, stayed with us until we got some help. She fed and protected us. She was really nice and we will never forget her. But Taylor was nervous at first to trust Mrs. Bailey because was had an accent. She told us that she was from Saint Vincent Island."

"Why was Taylor afraid because of Mrs. Bailey's accent?" asked Ruth.

"The majority of the people whom the leaders spoke with had accents.

So, Taylor was scared. Mrs. Bailey assured Taylor that she would be safe. I trusted Mrs. Bailey because she did do certain things like most people involved in human trafficking," commented Jasmine.

"Like what?" asked Mrs. Brown.

"Like being too nice or whispering on the cell phone or speaking with secret codes or making certain hand signals or doing other things. But Mrs. Bailey did not do those things. So, Taylor eventually trusted her," responded Jasmine.

"I arranged for Jasmine and Taylor to speak to Mrs. Bailey when we found you, Mrs. Ruth. She was glad that the girls had reunited with a family member," said Mrs. Hall.

"Reunite?" mumbled Mrs. Ruth as she slightly tilted her head to the side while a blank look unfolded on her face as if she wanted to tell Mrs. Hall that she had not agreed to reunite with Taylor and Jasmine, yet.

"How did Mrs. Bailey help you and Taylor?" asked Mrs. Brown as if she wanted to erase the tension that was slowly forming from Mrs. Ruth.

Jasmine cleared her throat before saying, "Mrs. Bailey and the daycare center's corporate office in Atlanta got in touch with a company that didn't like human trafficking stuff. The company helped Taylor and me to get in touch with a safe haven in Charlotte," uttered Jasmine as she pressed her lips together.

"Why did they bring you and Taylor to Charlotte?" asked Mrs. Brown.

"Mama told us that she was from Charlotte. So, I told the people at the company that we will like to go there," exhaled Taylor.

Jasmine coughed before speaking. "The company in Atlanta made sure we arrived safely in Charlotte. Somehow, they got in touch with Mrs. Hall."

"The anti-human trafficking company got in touch with the social services agency where I work," interjected Mrs. Hall. "The company sent several advocates with Jasmine and Taylor to make sure that services were coordinated properly."

Taylor lifted her head. "The advocates recommended that our names be changed. My name wasn't Taylor before," she said looking at Mrs. Hall.

"That is correct. We had to change their names to ensure their safety," said Mrs. Hall while wiping a beam of sweat from her forehead.

"What about my safety?" blurted Ruth. "What if Rock tells the leaders where I live? What if somebody comes here looking for Jasmine and Taylor since they escaped from that truck driver?"

Soaring noise stormed through the air as an ambulance dashed down the street.

"Mama told us that daddy didn't know where you lived. He only knew that mama was from Charlotte," muffled Taylor in a soft shaky voice.

Jasmine cleared her throat. "Mama said daddy snatched her when she was coming from the store on your birthday," said Jasmine as she glanced at Ruth. "She said daddy made her call you and say that she was moving to Miami with her boyfriend, Rock. She said she never told him where you lived or your full name."

Mrs. Brown's gaze swept the floor landing near Ruth's black stiletto shoes.

Tears streamed down Ruth's face. "That was the last time I heard from Julia."

Mrs. Brown scanned the tidy living room. Her gaze shifted to a picture of Julia on the eggshell painted wall. A gold frame outlined the oval shaped portrait of Julia, permitting her almond brown skin to showcase her hazel eyes and high cheekbones. Her full-figured body created a stunning image of her curvaceous shape. Her dark brown straight hair brushed against her thin neck creating a dazzling appearance around her heart shaped face.

Mrs. Hall handed Ruth a form. "I need to you sign, here, here and here."

Ruth looked at the forms as if she had to sign her life away. She stood and walked over to the chair where Mrs. Brown was sitting. Mrs. Brown knew why Ruth strolled over to her with the form. She recalled that Ruth couldn't read.

"Ruth, let me see the form while you continue to talk with Mrs. Hall and your grandchildren," said Mrs. Brown, trying to conceal the fact that Ruth could not read.

"I'm glad Jasmine and Taylor are finally with a family member," said Mrs. Hall as she smiled at Ruth.

Ruth's black eyelashes flickered as she looked at Mrs. Hall as if Mrs. Hall had plucked her nerves.

"Ruth, please sign here, here, and here," ordered Mrs. Brown. "You will have temporary custody of the kids until social services process a few more papers."

Mrs. Hall stood and grabbed her briefcase. There was no doubt that Mrs. Hall was ready to leave. "Jasmine and Taylor, you're going to be happy with your grandmother."

"Grandmother?" blurted Ruth, causing Jasmine and Taylor to flinch.

Mrs. Hall's eyes and mouth stopped moving as if her face had frozen in time.

"I don't want anybody calling me Grandmother," said Ruth while fingering through her charcoal black wig as if she was a young jiggle bug.

"Ruth, stop that nonsense," said Mrs. Brown as she squinted.

Mrs. Ruth rolled her eyes. "They can call me . . . um . . . I'll think of something."

Mrs. Hall swallowed hard. She appeared to be lost for words. "I'll make sure their insurance cards and other aid come here," she said as she stood. "Also, I scheduled them to see a therapist. Their first appointment is on Monday," declared Mrs. Hall as she walked closer to Ruth to hand her an ink pen to sign the forms. "Oh, by the way, they shouldn't be around any men anytime soon."

Ruth's eyebrows connected as a frown formed on her face. "Wait, I haven't agreed to nothing yet. I haven't signed any papers. So, slow your horses," blurted Ruth as if she was contemplating whether or not she was prepared to care for Jasmine and Taylor . . . or willing to suddenly change her lifestyle.

Mrs. Ruth leered at Mrs. Hall as she exhaled slowly. She looked at Jasmine and Taylor before casting her gaze toward Mrs. Brown.

Jasmine sat on the gray sofa, hugging Taylor as if they were glued together.

Loud music floated inside the apartment, capturing Ruth's attention. Ruth stared out of the window for a few seconds.

"Goodness, that music is loud," said Mrs. Brown.

Mrs. Ruth glanced out the window. "Oh, that's Onyx," she smiled. "He's one of my friends." Her right eyebrow arched toward the ceiling while she slightly swayed from side to side as if she was reminiscing on an enchanting counter she had with Onyx.

Mrs. Brown cleared her throat, interrupting Ruth's train of thought.

Ruth looked at Mrs. Brown as a puzzled look stretched across her face.

Mrs. Brown clamped her dark brown hands together in a praying position. She nodded as if she were reassuring Ruth that she could care for Jasmine and Taylor.

Ruth stared at the black ink pen as if it was a torch.

Time seemed to have come to a standstill as Ruth signed the forms.

Today definitely marked the end of Ruth's reign as being the Queen of Cougars.

Chapter 13

The bright Sunday morning sun flowed into Hope's master suite bathroom. Metallic gold heated tile floors adorned the bathroom floor. Artichoke vintage green painted walls marched around the bathroom. A rectangular glass walk-in shower positioned elegantly in a corner. A cascade of natural stones paraded inside the shower against the wall creating an astounding appearance.

Hope stepped out of the shower, hoping to prepare breakfast before her twins woke up. She typically woke up an hour before the twins every morning. She draped the towel over her face wiping away the water. She exhaled, realizing that Sloan hadn't called her last night or this morning. She closed her eyes as she wrapped the towel around her flawless body.

"Take the towel off," said Sloan as he snuck up behind Hope in the bathroom, causing her body to flinch.

Sloan pressed a small button on the wall, permitting soft melodies to flow out the flushed speakers in the bathroom.

"Well, good morning to you, Sloan. I'm glad you remembered *where* you lived," said Hope in a sarcastic tone. "I was getting ready to fix breakfast and get the twins ready for church."

"Take the towel off and get back in the shower," ordered Sloan as he scanned Hope's body while unfastening his black slacks.

Hope paused for a few seconds, detecting a mean streak flowing within Sloan. She watched as Sloan took items out of his pocket, placing them on the vanity in the bathroom. Her gaze locked in on the airplane ticket, noticing that Sloan had flown to Miami, Florida. She quickly realized that Mr. Gavino had a pizza pub in Miami.

"Is there a problem, Hope?" frowned Sloan as he picked Hope's panties off the floor, pressing them against his unblemished nose as if he was trying to detect whether Hope had sex with someone while he was out of town.

Hope stared at Sloan as a touch of disbelief rippled through her body as she watched him smell her panties. She swallowed slowly, recalling that Sloan always had a high-peaked sex drive every time he returned home from traveling out of town on business trips with Mr. Gavino.

"Are you okay, Sloan?" asked Hope in an uneasy tone.

Sloan's well-groomed eyebrows connected, forming a stern look on his butterscotch-brown face. "The question is, are you okay? It should *never* be a problem if I want to spend some quality time with my wife."

Hope exhaled slowly. "Sloan, it's not a problem. But I don't like your tone," blurted Hope as she allowed the towel to fall to the floor, permitting every curve of her body to showcase in front of him.

"That's more like it," said Sloan as he licked his luscious lips while staring at Hope's naked body. "Turn around so I can see every inch of your body."

Hope pressed her lips together as a glimpse of uneasiness flowed through her.

"Sloan, you are acting different," whispered Hope as she lovingly reached for Sloan's hand.

Sloan locked eyes with Hope as if he wanted to assert his dominance over her. "Listen, Hope! Just do *what* I ask you to do . . . *when* I ask you to do it . . . and *how* I ask you to do it," snapped Sloan as he pulled his hand from Hope while removing his cream shirt and tie.

A pinch of discomfort drifted through Hope's body as she noticed a significant change in Sloan's demeanor. Hope closed her eyes, recalling that Sloan always reacted differently toward her every time he returned home from attending business trips with Mr. Gavino. Hope exhaled wondering if the business trips were causing Sloan to act as if he had to portray an image of a misogynist that devalued and dominated women. Hope's heart clenched wondering why Sloan struggled to be a loving and respectful husband to her— for a few days—every time he returned from the business trips.

What is going on, pondered Hope to herself. She was convinced that something wasn't right.

"Get back in the shower, Hope," ordered Sloan in a firm tone.

Hope strolled over to the walk-in shower as Sloan trailed behind her.

"Did you check on the twins?" asked Hope as the shower water bounced against her melon shaped breasts.

"Hope, it is 6:15 a.m. They are still sleeping," said Sloan as he licked his lips again. "So, I should be able to get two rounds out of you before they wake up," whispered Sloan in Hope's ear in a seductive tone. He paused. "When we are finished, I want you to walk around in our bedroom naked for me with the new yellow stilettos I bought you when I was out of town."

Hope was silent for a few seconds. She often wondered why Sloan wanted her to prance around naked wearing stilettos and sometimes lingerie. *Did he have a fetish?* she wondered. Hope glanced at Sloan's hand. He held her favorite colored flowers. White roses always made her feel elegant. She watched as Sloan sprinkled a few rose petals—something that always made her heart melt.

Sloan pulled Hope close to his chiseled body as his iron rod protruded in front of him like a compass. He caressed the soft skin that nestled between

Hope's breasts. His long fingers strolled along the ridges of Hope's thighs as if he was playing a piano.

Sloan knelt in front of Hope's jewel box as droplets of water bounced from his jet black hair. He inched his wide hands around the smoothness of Hope's hips, thrusting her jewel box toward his face. Sloan dangled his long tongue through the neatly trimmed hairs that bordered Hope's jewel box.

Hope's body clamored with a mixture of pleasurable sensations and an ounce of uneasiness. Her body clinched as Sloan launched his tongue against the silkiness of her walls, causing a warm moist feeling to form inside her. She planted her small golden brown hands on top of Sloan's head as if she were palming a basketball. She thrust her hips side to side like a pendulum, trying to enjoy every second of the sexual gratification that Sloan sprung upon her. She arched her right leg over Sloan's broad shoulder, forcing his tongue to plunge deeper inside her.

"Oh, yes, Sloan," she moaned as her body shivered like a leaf on a windy day.

"You like this, baby?" teased Sloan as if he was slowly returning back to the loving and respectful husband that Hope knew. "I want to please you first, baby, before I get my *two scoops.*"

Hope closed her eyes, trying to enjoy every inch of Sloan's tongue that slid gently against her moist walls. Hope could feel Sloan nibbling around the outer part of her jewel box, causing her body to quiver like Jell-O.

"Yes, Sloan . . . oh, yes," moaned Hope as she gripped Sloan's head firmly.

"That's what I want to hear *every time*, baby," mumbled Sloan as he launched his tongue back inside Hope.

Sloan gripped Hope's hips firmly, forcing her body to move at the speed of his tongue. He pressed his head firmly between her thighs, causing his shoulder to elevate her leg as his tongue traveled inside her jewel box as if he was looking for a hidden treasure.

A warm sensation boiled inside her like hot lava, causing the muscles inside her walls to clamp around Sloan's long tongue. An intense level of passion rushed through Hope. She pressed her back firmly against the glass shower, using it to brace her body.

"Oh, Sloan," moaned Hope as a warm sensation flowed through her body, nearly causing her body to become numb.

"I know it was good to you, baby," teased Sloan as he stood, pressing his well-built body against Hope's voluptuous physique.

Sloan gripped Hope's right thigh, elevating it so he could launch his iron rod inside her. He thrust back and forth like a pendulum, causing Hope's breasts to jiggle.

"Oh, Hope," moaned Sloan as he plunged deeper and deeper inside Hope like a construction worker drilling concrete.

Sloan licked on Hope's neck as if he was eating ice cream. He cradled Hope's leg while penetrating through the finest creases of her moist walls.

"Um, Sloan," moaned Hope as Sloan lunged toward her cervix, causing a mixture of pain and pleasure to vibrate through Hope's body.

Sloan caressed Hope's inner thighs. He thrust faster and faster inside her, causing her head to brush against the shower's glass. He scooped Hope up, straddling her legs around his waist.

"Oh, this is good," mumbled Sloan as his heart pounded rapidly against Hope's breasts.

Hope could feel a throbbing sensation pound against her walls as Sloan's hips moved faster and faster and faster.

"Oh, yes," moaned Sloan as his body jerked with ecstasy. Hope could feel a burst of warm liquid splatter against her walls as Sloan's body went limp for a few seconds.

Soreness overpowered the ridges of Hope's jewel box. She glanced at Sloan as he gasped for air, hoping that one scoop of sex had quenched Sloan's needs. Yet, Hope knew Sloan had a hefty sexual appetite.

"Go get on the bed," whispered Sloan as he continued to gasp for air. "And get on your knees."

Like clockwork, Sloan needed two scoops of sex to smooth the savage beast that lurked within him.

Chapter 14

The clear blue sky stretched across the warm Sunday afternoon sky creating an atmosphere of fun and excitement without any rain.

Hope felt excited as she strolled through Creative Marbles Museum with Sloan and the twins. But her jewel box was still recovering from Sloan's order of two scoops of sex this morning that rendered her a mixture of pain and pleasure.

Bright colorful small and large rocks decorated the elegant walls creating a dazzling appearance for children. Large play areas spread throughout the museum, offering an intriguing playful arena for them.

"I'm glad you brought the twins and me here," smiled Hope while wondering how Sloan knew about the museum since it was located close to the Virginia state line.

Sloan stretched his chiseled butterscotch brown arm toward Hope, as his white linen sleeveless suit glistened with the elegant marbles. "Nothing but the best for my queen and children," grinned Sloan as he caressed Hope's narrow chin. "But you know the rules," blurted Sloan in a serious tone.

"Yes, Sloan," said Hope. "I know I must watch them at all times. They are not allowed to go to the bathroom without me. They are not allowed to walk at a distance from me. They are not allowed to talk to any strangers. They are not allowed to be near grown men or women," said Hope as she paused to briefly capture her breath. "I am not permitted to hold conversations with anyone to the point that I am distracted from watching the twins. I must make sure that the children are dressed at all times. I must make sure that I look presentable every day. My make-up and hair must be flawless. My fingernail and toenail polish must be perfect," said Hope as if she had to recite the ground rules.

For some strange reason, Sloan was overly protective of the twins and her as if he feared someone would harm or kidnap them.

A soft touch tugged at Hope's golden-brown hand as Hope glanced down at her twins, interrupting her recital to Sloan.

Hope's fingers slowly moved in front of the twins as she communicated with pride with her children. Jayla's caramel brown fingers glided in the air to respond to Hope. A small smile stretched across Jayla's face as her eyes glistened with excitement, highlighting the blossom pink outfit.

"What did she say, Hope?" asked Sloan as he smiled at Jayla.

"Jayla said she loves this place," said Hope as she suddenly remembered Sloan still struggled to understand ASL.

Hope strolled through the museum as her icy teal colored French-designed summer dress glided with every step she took. Her voluptuous hips pressed firmly against the threads in the dress revealing a glimpse of her flawless shape. Her icy teal heels with toasted oatmeal colored straps complimented her high-class dress and her teal sun hat. Her pearl necklace displayed a graceful image, showcasing her unblemished gorgeous face. Her hat was perfect to shield the sun when she took the twins outside to see the colorful marbled water fountains and walking trails.

Hope's gaze darted around as she watched Jayden run from one area to another as if he was overly rejoiced to be in the museum. His navy blue pressed short set shifted as he ran. Hope walked at a fast pace behind Jayden. She had perfected the art of walking and running in heels.

"Thank you for coming to the Marbles Kids Museum," said a short golden tanned white woman in a charming voice. "Please let me know if you need any assistance."

"Thank you," said Hope in a soft pleasant tone.

Sloan strolled behind Hope as if he was getting a glimpse of his *trophy wife* from behind.

Hope watched as Jayla joined Jayden in a play area as her long jet-black ponytails dangled past her tiny shoulders. Hope's heart slightly prickled as she noticed other children in the play area made efforts to speak to Jayden and Jayla. The other children's innocent minds quickly realized that Jayden and Jayla couldn't hear or speak. Yet, this didn't stop the other children from playing with them.

"You look absolutely beautiful, Hope," said Sloan as his eyes lowered to Hope's melon shaped breasts before locking into her hazel-brown eyes. "You look like a fashion model."

"Well, thank you, Sloan. You look nice yourself," smiled Hope as Sloan moved a strand of hair that dangled on her eyelash. Everything had to be perfect for Sloan which chiseled away at Hope's heart.

"I feel like the luckiest man alive," uttered Sloan as he caressed Hope's hand.

A pleasant feeling surged through Hope as she blushed.

Hope knew she had to keep their conversations *only* about their family. Sloan didn't like mixing conversations about his business ventures or Hope's catering company with their family time.

"The twins have another appointment with Dr. Ericsson in a few weeks before they get their operation," said Hope, hoping her grammar was correct. She had improved her understanding of the *King's English.*

Sloan glanced at Hope for a few seconds as if he was making a mental note that Hope had communicated in a grammatically correct manner—as if he was a professor.

"I hope the operation works," mumbled Sloan as he glanced around the museum, obviously looking at the children who could speak.

Hope paused, reflecting that they had to travel to Charlotte, North Carolina for the twins' appointment with Dr. Ericsson. Her heart rattled at the thought of going to the city where her mother lived. Yet, Dr. Ericsson was a well-known surgeon who specialized in performing the procedure that the twins needed.

Hope knew Sloan disliked the fact that their twins were deaf. Yet, Sloan always displayed a great deal of love for the twins without a doubt.

"Dr. Ericsson has performed the cochlear operation on several children. She has helped a lot of children gain their ability to hear and talk."

"I know that Dr. Ericsson told us that. But I am hoping it works for *our* children," said Sloan while staring at a group of kids walking by.

A gentle crisp scent of Sloan's cologne wafted in the air past Hope's nose.

Hope and Sloan continued to wander through the museum, trailing behind their twins as they rotated from one play area to the next.

"Time to go, Hope," said Sloan while casting a quick glance at a tall model shaped almond brown woman whose beauty radiated as she walked beside a European well-groomed man who held a little cocoa brown girl's hand. Hope noticed how the little girl appeared to be disinterested in the activities in the museum—something Hope found to be quite strange since the museum had several activities to meet every child's interest.

Hope walked toward the twins. Her fingers elegantly moved into the air as she used ASL to communicate with the twins. A frown stretched across Jayden's chestnut brown face, displaying a reluctance to leave the fun activities. A small tear formed in the corner of Jayla's eye as if she didn't want to abandon the fun either.

"They can play for a few more minutes," whispered Sloan as he looked at his Rolex watch.

Within a split second, Jayden and Jayla dashed back to the area that had a cascade of colorful pebbled rocks.

"How did they know what I said before you communicated it in sign language to them?" asked Sloan in a slow inquisitive manner.

A soft chuckle escaped Hope's mouth. "They can read lips," smiled Hope.

Sloan's eyes widened bigger than walnuts as if he was in a state of shock.

Hope cleared her throat before whispering, "Remember, Sloan, it is not called sign language. The correct term is American Sign Language, but many people say ASL."

Sloan squinted.

Hope watched as the European well-groomed man walked toward an area where a group of unattended children were playing. Although the man's action was normal, Hope noticed that the man had left the little girl that he once held hands with near the model shaped woman which Hope found to be odd.

A few minutes later, Hope noticed that man flirting with a short mocha brown woman who was walking with her little girl. Hope thought this was definitely odd since the woman who had come with him sat quietly as the man continued to flirt with the woman.

Suddenly, the European man's gaze boldly locked in on Hope. The man didn't break his stare, even though Sloan was standing beside Hope.

Hope winced. She noticed the attractive woman who had entered the marble museum with the European man smiled at her as if she wanted Hope to join her at a nearby table.

"*Hope* . . . get the twins and let's go," ordered Sloan in a harsh tone, immediately capturing Hope's attention as if he knew something that she didn't.

"But you said the twins could play for a few more minutes," whispered Hope.

"Do what I tell you to do, right now!" gritted Sloan through his pearly white teeth while he kept his gaze firmly on the European man.

Hope dashed toward the twins, signaling to them that it was time to go right now.

Sloan ushered Hope and the twins out of Creative Marbles Museum as if they were doing a bomb evacuation drill. He wasted no time hauling them to his Mercedes-Maybach S680. The soft jazz he usually played in the car had been muted.

"What is wrong, Sloan?" asked Hope in a soft curious tone as Sloan drove off.

Sloan remained silent for a few seconds.

"You wouldn't understand, Hope," said Sloan in a stern voice. "But I'll never . . . never let anyone harm you or the twins!" blurted Sloan as he peered in his rearview mirror.

"Sloan, are you okay?" asked Hope as she stared at the right side of his face while he drove like a deranged person.

"We are not taking the twins back to Creative Marbles Museum *ever* again," shrieked Sloan, causing Hope's body to flinch. "And don't *ask* me any questions about it," ordered Sloan as he sped up the highway, heading toward their home.

There was definitely more to this story than what Sloan disclosed and Hope was destined to find out. She was no fool and did not doubt that Sloan's behavior and the things that were happening to their family were not normal.

Chapter 15

The grayish-black clouds hung in the sky, casting darkness over Cloverdale.

"Thank you for cooking breakfast for us, Mrs. Brown," said Ruth as she shelved a spoonful of grits into her bow shaped mouth.

"Thank you, Mrs. Brown," mumbled Jasmine as she nibbled on a homemade biscuit.

"These eggs are good," said Taylor as she glanced at Mrs. Brown.

"You are welcome," said Mrs. Brown as she unfastened the brown apron and placed it on a rack in the corner of the kitchen.

The tasty smell of buttery cheese grits, golden-brown eggs and buttered homemade biscuits continued to linger in the air.

"Mrs. Brown, we're going to miss these home-cooked meals when you stop cooking and baking for folks," sighed Ruth.

"Well, my arthritis keeps bothering me. So, I have to stop cooking and baking at some point." She paused. "I'm thinking about giving my customers to Hope. The last time I spoke with her, she was trying to open her own chef business."

"You spoke with Hope?" inquired Ruth with a puzzled look on her face.

Soft gospel music played on a tiny radio that was positioned on the kitchen countertop as Mrs. Brown pressed her lips firmly together.

"It's been years since the last time I spoke with Hope," said Ruth as if she noticed that Mrs. Brown had intentionally ignored her question about Hope. Ruth was aware that people in Cloverdale knew that Mrs. Brown had a soft spot in her heart for Hope. If anyone knew anything about Hope, Mrs. Brown was sure to be the person. But she certainly was not saying anything.

"How did you sleep last night?" asked Ruth as she looked at Jasmine while shifting her gaze from Mrs. Brown.

"I had a dream that I was playing a game with the leaders."

"Playing a game," inquired Mrs. Brown as she smeared molasses on a biscuit. She preferred molasses to jelly.

Jasmine's gaze landed on the wooden table. "When I was much younger, the leaders used to take me to playgrounds. A different pretty lady was always with us. They held my hand as we walked through the playground. I was so happy to go to there," she sighed in a heartfelt manner. "I thought they took me to the park to be nice. But after going with them a few times, I realized that it was a game."

"What do you mean a game?" asked Ruth as a puzzled look flashed in her eyes.

"Every time we left the park, there was always a new woman in the car with us."

"What!" shrieked Ruth.

"I realized that they took me to the playgrounds just to kidnap young women who were at the parks with their children."

"They are called madams," mumbled Jasmine. "They help the leaders."

Ruth slowly closed her eyes. "Did your mother ever help lure other women?" she asked in an embarrassed tone.

"She used to get beat really bad because she didn't want to do it," said Taylor as a tear trickled down her face. "I remember one of the leaders gave her a black eye for refusing to do it."

"But another leader got mad at him for blackening mama's eyes. He said it messed up their money for the week," muffled Jasmine.

A cloud of fear floated through the kitchen like miniature drones.

"They used to make different women in the houses help them lure other women," mumbled Taylor. "They used different children, too."

"But how did the leaders get the victims into their cars?"

"The women looked like they were dizzy when they were in the cars with us," muffled Jasmine. "But they didn't look like that when they were playing with their children on the playground."

"Where were the women's children?" asked Ruth while shoving more grits inside her mouth.

"They would bring the children with us," babbled Jasmine.

"Maybe they drugged the women," exhaled Mrs. Brown.

"I saw one leader put something against a woman's nose," whimpered Taylor. "She got dizzy and fell into his arms like they were hugging. The leader kept hugging her as they walked toward the car," mumbled Taylor. "I guess he wanted people to think that they were still hugging."

"Could the woman walk?" inquired Mrs. Brown in a remorseful tone.

"Yes, but she looked dizzy," responded Taylor in a low tone, barely above a whisper as her gaze lowered toward her jungle green colored shirt.

"They used to take me to different parks, malls, stores, skating rinks and other places," muffled Jasmine. "They stopped when I got older."

"Why?" asked Ruth as she gnawed on a buttered biscuit.

"I heard them say they didn't want to risk taking the older kids with them to play the game 'cause they didn't want the kids to try to run away," muffled Jasmine.

A shaft of sunlight finally inched through the dark clouds permitting a single ray of light in the kitchen.

"Where are those women and children now?" asked Mrs. Brown as she pressed her glasses on the ridges on her nose.

"The leaders took them to different houses," sighed Jasmine. "Sometimes we had to drive really far before we got there. But the women were still dizzy the entire time we drove to the drop off houses."

"Drop off houses?" inquired Mrs. Brown.

"That's what the leaders called it," said Taylor as she wiped her mouth. "The drop off houses were in different cities . . . maybe different states. I remember we were in the car for a long time."

"How did they know which house to take the women to?" asked Ruth as if Jasmine and Taylor were hosting an information session on human trafficking.

"I don't know," muffled Jasmine. "But they used to look at a small thing in their hands as they drove.

"Maybe it was an iPod or cell phone or something," said Ruth as if she was technologically savvy.

"I don't know," said Jasmine. "But somehow they knew which house to take the women every time."

"The leaders really operate as if they are conducting a real business," angrily uttered Ruth. "They are destroying people's lives."

Jasmine brushed a crumb off her peach orchid colored shirt.

"I hope you're going to sweep my floor," said Mrs. Brown as she looked at Jasmine.

"Yes, ma'am, I will," said Jasmine in a soft tone.

A soft chuckle flowed out of Taylor's mouth as she looked at Jasmine.

"Where did the leaders take the women?" asked Ruth while tucking the strands of her charcoal black wig behind her ears.

"It was always a house in a different city or state than where the leaders *stole* the women."

"Why?" asked Mrs. Brown curiously.

"The leaders said it was best if they were taken to a city they didn't know."

Sirens soared through the air as police cars dashed through Cloverdale projects.

"I don't even know why police come over here," blurted Ruth. "They don't care nothing about folks in Cloverdale. I bet they are coming over here to check on their dope dealers or to meet up with their secret lovers."

"What are you talking about now, Ruth? Who has a secret lover?"

"Mrs. Brown, please don't let these policemen fool you. Most of them have secret lovers in the projects. They love these young girls," said Ruth.

"Hush with that foolishness, Ruth," blurted Mrs. Brown.

"I'm telling the truth, Mrs. Brown. Trust me, I know from experience," Ruth sighed. "And most of them are married."

"That is a sin," muffled Mrs. Brown as she swallowed a mouthful of grits.

"Well, it's been going on for a long time," uttered Ruth. "The sad thing about it is some of the police and businessmen act like they don't like us in front of their friends. But behind the scenes they are creeping through these projects looking for young black girls to accept them as their sugar daddies," she sighed. "Some of them even have babies with these girls. They take care of the kids. But I'm sure their wives don't know."

Conversations in the kitchen evaporated like a bubble.

Chapter 16

A week later, Hope strolled through a colorful long hallway. There were computers on several desks in every room. Children gathered together, playing an array of activities. Their fingers shifted smoothly in the air as they communicated in ASL with one another. Hope was delighted to find a summer camp for the twins that specialized in providing services to children who were deaf.

"Good morning, Mrs. Glover," said a short white lady as Hope walked toward Jayla and Jayden's summer camp classroom.

"Good morning, Mrs. Jones. I came to participate in the hand painting activity with Jayla and Jayden today."

"Oh, yes, Mrs. Randy told me that you were coming today," uttered Mrs. Jones. "I'm glad that you did. It's time for the mother-daughter activity."

"Jayla made sure I didn't forget," smiled Hope.

"We had the father-son activity this morning. Your husband came."

"I know," said Hope. "We came together. But he had to leave," said Hope, recalling that Sloan had a business meeting. "It was nice to see Jayden put the paint on my husband's hands," laughed Hope. "Now, I guess it's time for Jayla to paint my hands."

A walnut-brown child walked toward Mrs. Jones. The child's fingers moved swiftly in the air as he communicated with Mrs. Jones.

Hope glanced at the child, observing as he communicated that he had permission to go to the bathroom.

"Are your parents coming to the event today?" asked Mrs. Jones.

Hope cleared her throat. "No, my parents are not coming to the event today," responded Hope in an unwavering tone.

"What about your husband's parents?"

"Our parents don't live here," replied Hope.

"That's right," said Mrs. Jones. "I forgot that you told me that before."

"No, problem," said Hope as she continued to stroll toward the twins' classroom.

Mrs. Jones walked beside Hope as if Hope needed an escort.

"I hope your mother gets better."

Hope came to a sudden halt.

"How do you know Gloria is ill?" inquired Hope as a touch of uneasiness reaped through her.

Mrs. Jones winced as if she noticed that Hope referred to her mother by her first name. "I saw Jayla *sign* it to one of her friends that her grandmother was sick. I typically look at the children's fingers as they communicate to one another," said Mrs. Jones.

Hope paused, wondering how Jayla knew that her mother was sick. Hope winced, recalling that Jayla had stared at her lips as she talked to Ivey on the telephone about her mother's failing health. Hope was curious as to what else Jayla knew.

A clean scent lingered in the air, mingling with the cool breeze that drifted from the air conditioner.

"Just so you know, Jayla's friend's mother and grandmother are here," uttered Mrs. Jones. "Her friend asked Jayla if her mother and grandmother were coming today, too."

Mrs. Jones is bold. I hope she's not trying to embarrass me, thought Hope. *This is a sensitive matter and I don't have to explain anything to her.*

Silence drifted between Hope and Mrs. Jones for a few seconds. Hope could count on her hands and feet how many times her twins were deprived of participating in activities that required the presence of their grandmother.

Mrs. Jones cleared her throat. "I heard you have a catering company," blurted Mrs. Jones as a smile stretched across her oval shaped wrinkled face.

Hope paused, wondering how Mrs. Jones knew about her catering company. Hope stood wondering if Jayla had told Mrs. Jones.

"Yes, I do," smiled Hope. "It is called Serenity Catering Service," said Hope as she continued to walk toward her twins' classroom. "How did you know?" asked Hope.

"I saw your brochure," said Mrs. Jones as her blue dress shifted as she walked.

"Okay," grinned Hope. "I've received several new customers after I started distributing the brochures."

"I heard your service is good," uttered Mrs. Jones. "You catered the mayor's niece's high school graduation event."

"Oh, yes, Hannah-Rose. I remember her."

"I figured if you could satisfy Hannah-Rose and her mother," sneered Mrs. Jones. "Then your service must be good." Mrs. Jones looked around before speaking. "I heard they are hard to please," she whispered.

Hope reflected upon the evening when she had catered Hannah-Rose's graduation event. Hope stood on the natural stone paved driveway that accentuated the Courtland Country Clubhouse waiting to greet Hannah-Rose with her friends and family. Hope recalled that Hannah-Rose pulled up in front of the clubhouse in a convertible white Bentley Continental Coupe GT—clearly an extraordinary high school graduation present. Hope winced, recalling how Hannah's mother sneered as she walked through the clubhouse looking at the catered food on the gold plates. Heather's sneer quickly faded when the food landed on her small pink tongue.

A cluster of footsteps approached Hope and Mrs. Jones as children walked up the hallway, heading outside to play.

"If you bring me some of your brochures, I will give them to the parents."

"I will put some in Jayla's bag. I will tell her to give them to you."

"Great," said Mrs. Jones. "Oh, by the way . . . if you cater food again for Hannah-Rose or Heather, please don't tell them what I said about them," whispered Mrs. Jones as her blue eyes gazed at Hope. "Definitely, please don't tell the mayor."

"I will not. Do not worry," whispered Hope.

"If you ask me, the mayor needs to do something about these missing young girls. It's been all over the news," whispered Mrs. Jones as her eyebrows connected. "Parents can't even go places without fearing that someone might take their child."

"That is sad," said Hope as she approached her twins' classroom door.

"It's bad when a child is taken from a museum."

Hope stood speechless for a few seconds before speaking. "A museum?"

"Yes," muffled Mrs. Jones. "A young woman and her daughter were abducted from Creative Marbles Museum a few weeks ago."

"Really? My family and I went there a few weeks ago," said Hope as she tried to recall the exact day that Sloan had taken the twins and her there.

"Well, it's been all over the news," whispered Mrs. Jones as she planted her hand over her mouth. "The camera at the museum only captured a side view of the man," she sighed. "He looked like a European man."

Hope didn't want to tell Mrs. Jones that she did not watch the news, not even television shows. She figured everything was always about crime lurking in Cloverdale. Plus, even when she did try watching the news, Sloan became furious and prohibited her from watching it. He told her that the news was a mixture of lies and corruption. Sadly, she believed him.

A nervous feeling captured Hope as she recalled that Sloan's demeanor crumbled when he saw a well-groomed European man looking at a few children playing inside a den of marbles. She also recalled the man talking to a short mocha-brown woman. She wondered if Sloan had detected something strange about that man. Hope figured this was why Sloan has always drilled her about watching the twins at all times. Between preparing catering meals, tending to the twins, and performing her wifely duties for Sloan, she didn't have time to watch the news. But Hope realized that she needed to start making time to watch it.

Hope strolled into the classroom, looking for Jayla and Jayden. Large canvasses scattered throughout the room with colorful designs plastered on them. Children clung to their mothers while painting animals, flowers, and shapes. The twins dashed over to Hope with smiles glued to their faces.

"Hello, Mrs. Glover," said an ebony brown lady.

"Hello, Mrs. Randy," replied Hope.

"I see that you are back," smiled Mrs. Randy who was the twins' camp teacher.

"Yes, I am," laughed Hope. "I have to do the activities with Jayla now."

Jayla grabbed Hope's hand, guiding her to their table. Jayden trailed behind. Hope drafted a cape over her pink summer dress. She grabbed a brown paintbrush as Jayla tapped on her hand. Hope looked as Jayla pointed to a dove white little girl. A warm feeling flowed through Hope as she read Jayla's fingers as she communicated that the little girl was her friend, Zoe.

Hope watched as Zoe slowly walked toward them. Her blonde ponytails shifted in the air. Hope observed as Zoe and Jayla talked. She glanced up as Jayden galloped to a table to get the green paint while stopping to play with friends.

Hope smiled as Jayla introduced Zoe. A bright smile spread across Jayla's face. Hope observed as Zoe signed to Jayla that her mother and grandmother were at her table painting. Hope trailed Zoe's fingers as she communicated with Jayla.

A rattling sound flowed through the room as a little boy knocked over some paint.

Hope applied the brush to the white paper, trying to ignore Zoe's questions. A soft touch landed on Hope's hand as Jayla signaled to Hope that Zoe was still signing to her. Hope shifted her gaze to Jayden as he sat beside her, applying different colors to the canvass. Hope exhaled as Jayla looked at her.

Hope watched as Zoe signed the same question again. Hope's felt as though her fingers were moving through quicksand as she slowly responded to Zoe.

"No, Jayla's grandmother is not coming," signed Hope, as an ounce of uneasiness overtook her.

Jayla's smile crumbled into a frown.

Chapter 17

A gust of wind bounced against Hope's office window in her home as the gloomy sky made room for a rainstorm. Large green leaves dangled from tree limbs as the wind swirled through the air, permitting a dimmed Friday mid-day shaft of sunlight to flow inside the house.

Hope pressed her back against the black leather chair in her office. Her office walls were painted a soft lemon color. A mahogany wood desk with a black trim positioned in the middle of the office created a professional appearance. A small credenza rested underneath the window, permitting a resting place for her small lucky bamboo plant. Hope was delighted that the house had four bedrooms so that she could convert one into her office.

She browsed through her catering company's website, trying to review her upcoming scheduled events. She had already taken the twins to summer camp, prepared dinner and completed her routine house chores. She double checked the kitchen cabinets to make sure that the canned foods were organized. Sloan was obsessed with how the canned foods were organized in the cabinets, how the towels were folded, and how their clothes and shoes were arranged in their closets. Sloan's obsessive compulsive disorder was pushing Hope nearly over the edge.

A pleasant feeling crept through Hope as she noticed the increase in potential new customers. Hope read every customer's inquiry. She sent e-mails to them with pictures of meals, events and arrangements that she had already catered.

She leaned back as she reflected upon how Sloan had treated her to some ice cream at the nearby creamery factory earlier today. He had taken his laptop to the creamery with him to do some work while Hope reviewed her orders for the month on her laptop. She figured Sloan wanted to spend time with her before he left on a two-day business trip to Richmond, Virginia.

Hope wondered why she felt as though she hadn't slept in days. Something was wrong. But Sloan had convinced her not to go to the doctor. He told Hope that she was fatigued from working and taking care of the twins. He always convinced her to drink a cup of lemon tea to help soothe her.

A ringing sound echoed through the house. She peered at the high-tech caller ID. It was Mrs. Brown.

"Hello, Mrs. Brown," she said in an upbeat tone.

"Hello, Hope," said Mrs. Brown in a charming tone. "I was calling to check on you."

"That is so nice of you. I'm doing fine. My twins are doing good and my husband is well."

"That's good to hear," said Mrs. Brown. "How's your catering business coming along?"

"Great! My orders have been increasing. I am so happy."

"Have you found a business location?"

"No. But I will start looking in a few weeks. I would like to find a location in downtown Raleigh. But the rental prices may be beyond my budget," chuckled Hope. "I hope to open my own culinary school one day. I've been researching it."

"What about equipment?"

"I have a lot of equipment and supplies already in my storage."

A loud rumbling echoed through the house as lightning flashed across the sky.

"How's your husband, Hope?"

"He's doing fine."

The conversation lowered and fizzled out on the telephone.

"Is he still traveling a lot?"

"Yes, ma'am."

"When are you coming to see me?"

Hope tilted her head toward the vintage white painted ceiling.

"I don't know, Mrs. Brown," mumbled Hope. "I don't mind coming to see you. But I . . . I don't want to see Gloria."

Mrs. Brown exhaled heavily on the telephone. "Hope, it's been over seven years since you've spoken with your mother," she said in a calm tone. "At some point in your life, you've got to forgive her."

"Well, I'm not at that point yet," mumbled Hope. "With all due respect, Mrs. Brown, you don't know the misery that Gloria put me through. You don't know the Gloria that I knew as a child."

"Hope, people do change."

"I know. But my heart just can't allow me to accept that Gloria is my mother. She put me in dangerous conditions as a child. I was molested while she got high on crack. I went days without eating sometimes, Mrs. Brown."

"I will pray for you and your mother," sighed Mrs. Brown. "I think you should give her a chance to explain a few things."

"I think it's too late for her to try to explain anything to me."

"It's never too late, Hope," said Mrs. Brown in a calm tone. "I pray that you and Gloria can make peace."

A pinch of hatred entered Hope's heart as she reflected upon her childhood, living with Gloria.

"I don't know if I would ever find peace in my heart for her," said Hope as a tear rolled down her face. "When I left seven years ago, I had no plans of ever talking to her again," sobbed Hope. "I wanted her to think that I was dead. I didn't want her to come looking for me. I wanted her to forget that I was her daughter."

Quietness traveled through the telephone for a few seconds.

"Hope, it seems like your heart is still filled with hatred," mumbled Mrs. Brown in a low tone. "Even though Gloria didn't treat you right . . . she's still your mother. It is so disheartening to know that you were molested," muffled Mrs. Brown. "I know it may be hard to do but one day you have to make peace with her," said Mrs. Brown. "I'm not sure if you know that your mother is really sick."

Tears rolled down Hope's golden-brown face. Her heart forced her to ignore Mrs. Brown's last statement.

"Mrs. Brown, how's your catering services?" asked Hope as if she wanted to avoid talking about her mother's health.

Mrs. Brown delayed in responding to Hope as if she knew Hope had intentionally changed the topic.

"I'm still baking cakes and cooking some meals for people. But my arthritis has been acting up a lot lately," sighed Mrs. Brown. "I don't know how much longer I will be able to go on. "

"Who's going to take your place?" asked Hope, knowing that Mrs. Brown was well-known in Cloverdale and nearby communities for her superb baking and cooking.

"I don't know. I was hoping . . . well I don't know," she paused before continuing in a slow tone. "Maybe if you were here . . . I could give you, my customers. I've tasted your baking and cooking in the past. I'm sure your skills have gotten better," she chuckled. "I've taught you well. So, I know your skills are excellent now."

Hope laughed as she said, "My skills are exceptional now, Mrs. Brown." Hope paused before speaking again. "But I can't take your customers."

"Why not?" inquired Mrs. Brown in a puzzled tone.

"I don't know if I want to move back to Charlotte. I don't want to be anywhere near Gloria."

A peeping noise soared inside Hope's office. She glanced at her laptop. It was powering down. Hope looked around for her laptop charger cord as she continued to talk to Mrs. Brown. She figured she had left her laptop charger in Sloan's car when they returned from the ice cream factory.

"Hold on, Mrs. Brown, I have to go to my husband's car to get my laptop charger. I will call you back."

"Don't hang up, Hope. I can hold on. I hardly get a chance to talk to you."

"Okay," smiled Hope. "I'll talk to you for a few more minutes."

Hope continued to talk to Mrs. Brown on the telephone as she strolled up the lilac painted hallway, heading toward the garage. She opened the garage door.

Toasted oatmeal painted walls surrounded Hope inside the three-car garage. Custom-made bookshelves aligned on one wall, presenting an upscale appearance. A thirty-two-inch television mounted in a corner creating an opportunity for Sloan to watch television as well as monitor the identity of callers on the high-tech caller ID. The garage floor had grayish-white concrete floors.

Hope strolled toward Sloan's car. The door was locked. She went back to the house to look for his car key.

"What's all of that noise?" asked Mrs. Brown.

"I'm looking for the key to my husband's car."

"Oh, it sounds like you are rattling through some chains," snickered Mrs. Brown.

Hope searched the key station where Sloan typically hung his keys but they weren't there. She paused, wondering why Sloan had taken all of his keys. Suddenly, she recalled seeing Sloan tuck a set of spare keys inside a toolbox in the garage. Sloan was unaware that Hope knew about the spare keys.

"Have you found the key?" asked Mrs. Brown in a soft tone.

"No, I'm still looking," responded Hope.

"You should have a spare key to his car," uttered Mrs. Brown.

Hope swallowed hard. "He never gave it to me."

"That doesn't make sense. You're his wife. You should have a key to his car."

Hope strolled toward the toolbox. She slowly opened it. The toolbox had two layers. She opened the second layer. As expected, a set of spare keys were tucked in the corner, underneath a few tools.

Hope winced as her gaze landed on an oddly shaped key. *What is this mysterious key for?* she thought. She was determined to find out.

A sudden river of curiosity flowed through Hope, leaving her speechless.

"Why are you so quiet?" asked Mrs. Brown.

The sight of the oddly shaped key forced a thorn through Hope's soul.

Chapter 18

Five minutes later, Hope glanced around the garage. She scratched her head, trying to figure out why Sloan was hiding an oddly shaped key in the toolbox.

"Hope, what's wrong?" asked Mrs. Brown. "Why are you so quiet?"

"I just found an oddly shaped key in my husband's toolbox."

"Oh," sighed Mrs. Brown.

"I've never seen this key before," said Hope as she gawked at the key.

"What type of key is it?" inquired Mrs. Brown.

"I don't know. But it looks like one of those old-fashioned keys from medieval times."

A soft chuckle flowed through the telephone as Mrs. Brown laughed.

"I'm serious," laughed Hope. "It looks like a key to a dungeon or something."

Hope glanced around the garage. Her mind raced while trying to determine whether the key opened something in the garage.

"Well, just ask your husband when he comes home," laughed Mrs. Brown.

"Oh, no," said Hope. "I don't want him to know that I was in his toolbox. He doesn't know that I saw him put these spare keys there."

"Oh," said Mrs. Brown as her voice trailed away.

Hope stared at the key. An unwavering feeling stormed through her body.

"Something isn't right about this key, Mrs. Brown," said Hope in a rattled tone.

"Why do you say that?" asked Mrs. Brown.

"I don't know," muffled Hope, twirling the odd shaped key in her soft hands.

"Well, you have to follow your gut feeling," uttered Mrs. Brown.

Silence filtered through the telephone.

"Got it," said Hope as she strolled back to the garage. "I've found the spare key."

"Good," said Mrs. Brown. "Now, put that other key back."

"I did," said Hope.

Hope galloped over to Sloan's midnight black Jaguar. She inserted the key into the car door. Hope's gaze landed on her black laptop charger. She had left it on the floor inside the car.

A soft chuckle escaped her mouth. "I'm sure Sloan didn't see this laptop charger on the floor. He would have had a fit."

"What do you mean?" asked Mrs. Brown.

"Sloan has obsessive compulsive disorder. He likes everything to be in a neat fashion," she said while tugging on the laptop charger.

Hope winced. The laptop charger seemed to have snagged onto something.

"Hold on, Mrs. Brown. I have to place the telephone down for a second."

"What's going on now, Hope?" asked Mrs. Brown.

"It seems like my laptop charger is stuck onto something under the seat," responded Hope.

"Under what seat?" asked Mrs. Brown.

"The passenger seat in Sloan's car," frowned Hope, trying to figure out what her laptop was stuck on.

"It seems like you've got a lot going on right now," said Mrs. Brown.

"Not really," said Hope before pressing her lips together.

Quietness drifted through the telephone for several seconds.

"Just call me back later, Hope."

"Okay, I will call you later," she said as she hung up the telephone.

She bent her small head to look under the passenger's seat. Her gaze landed on a black object.

A black folder protruded from under the passenger's seat. A professional bracket neatly marched around the folder, securing the content inside it.

Hope winced, wondering why a black folder was strapped underneath the seat.

Curiosity pumped through Hope's veins as her manicured fingers slowly opened the folder. A sense of calmness flowed through Hope as she noticed that the black folder consisted of Worldwide Express Pizza, Inc.'s business plan and several brochures as if Sloan had planned to market the pizza pub.

A puzzling feeling reaped through Hope as she peered at the brochure. She noticed that two-digit numbers, from 18 to 30, were printed underneath pictures of women who advertised different types of pizzas while wearing their employee uniforms. But Hope was certain that pizzas did not have that many slices.

What do these numbers represent? pondered Hope as she retrieved one of the brochures to keep for herself, hoping that Sloan would never find out.

"Why is Sloan hiding the brochures under the seat?" she uttered.

Hope tapped her fingers on the brochure as she stared at it.

A loud sound pierced the air.

Hope glanced at the high-tech caller ID that Sloan had positioned in nearly every room of the house—even the garage. The telephone number was blocked which was odd. Sloan had designed the caller ID to unblock nearly every telephone number. She couldn't even see a picture of the caller.

"Hello," said Hope in a puzzling tone.

"What are you doing in my car, Hope?" yelled Sloan.

Chapter 19

The Friday afternoon sun sunk into the sky, casting a massive shadow over the Cloverdale community. Hustlers competed for drug transactions on *The Hill*. Loud music flowed out of cars as if there were tailgate parties on every corner. Prostitutes attracted more customers than a supermarket. The clusters of zombie-like people who roamed through Cloverdale made the community look like a zoo with death lurking on every corner.

"*God*, please have mercy on their souls," mumbled Mrs. Brown as she stared out of the window, looking at the strung-out drug addicts.

A sense of uneasiness washed over her as she stared at the mindless addicts. She remembered the days when her brother, Lamont a.k.a June Bug, used to risk his life, soul and dignity for dope. Crack and heroin had nearly destroyed Lamont's life, forcing him to rob people to supply his high. He had the mentality that he was the Ginger Bread Man—he felt like the police couldn't catch him. Now that he was drug-free, Lamont no longer wanted people to refer to him as June Bug anymore.

Mrs. Brown exhaled slowly as she reflected upon what had pushed Lamont to nearly a point of no return. Lamont's wife had forced him over the edge. He caught her in the bed with another man and woman—something he found out she had been doing with several guys on his military base. Instead of killing his wife which was his first intention, Lamont left behind his twenty-year military career, his two-story luxury home and two children in exchange for a twenty-dollar crack piece and a vial of heroin.

A peaceful feeling filtered through Mrs. Brown as she recalled how Lamont had successfully completed his recovery process. Now, he was a Peer Recovery Specialist at a local mental health and substance use agency. Lamont took pride in discussing his past mental health and substance use experiences to help mentor individuals as they transitioned through their treatment and recovery processes.

Soft melodies of bells ringing flowed inside Mrs. Brown's apartment creating a cheerful sound. An ice cream truck cruised down the street, playing loud music to capture ice cream lovers' attention. Mrs. Brown laughed, nearly popping a button off her sunset orange color dress as she watched a boney tall man chase after the truck. She glanced at the clock on the eggshell painted wall. It was 5:00 p.m. Her children, Tiffany and Tony and her brother, Lamont were en route to enjoy their routine Friday evening dinner with her.

Arthritis hurt her body as she wobbled from side to side toward the oval shaped mirror on the wall, trying to make sure her hair was intact. Her unblemished dark brown skin sparkled with grace. Her grayish-black hair glowed with a radiance of wisdom. A warm, lovely smile was permanently painted on her heart shaped face.

Her small hands slightly shook as she pulled several items out of the refrigerator. Old age was surely settling in her body. Yet, she worked diligently to prepare her routine Friday meal for Tiffany, Tony, and Lamont: fried fish, homemade coleslaw and baked beans.

She glanced out of her small kitchen window, chuckling as she noticed how the skinny white mailman crept to the mailbox to toss mail in the mailboxes. His hairline recessed significantly from his wrinkled forehead as if he had been stressing all of his life. He nearly tripped over his shoe strings while dashing back to the truck as if he wanted to vanish without anyone noticing his presence in Cloverdale. After serving as the mailman in Cloverdale for the past fifteen years, Mrs. Brown figured he should be used to the daily crime scenes by now.

As she dipped the fish into her homemade seafood batter, her mind drifted down memory lane to when her children took her to an upscale seafood restaurant . . .

A musty, strong odor wafted from under the driver's flabby armpits in the taxi. Mrs. Brown cracked the back window, permitting a breath of fresh air to rush in. Her son, Tony, rubbed his eyes as if the musty odor was burning his eyes. Her daughter, Tiffany, coughed like cotton was in her throat. The driver stared at them as if he didn't know what was wrong.

Frustration settled in the lower region of her stomach because the driver had refused to pick them up in Cloverdale. They had to walk ten blocks to the library for a pick-up which was rough on Mrs. Brown's ankles. Hustlers and addicts messed it up for everyone. They had a reputation for robbing taxi cab drivers. After a few robberies, the taxi cab had bulletproof protective glass windows. Even with this protection, some taxi cab drivers didn't want to risk their lives by entering Cloverdale.

"You better have money to pay me," warned the driver, banging on the partition.

"We have money," snapped Tony as his soft brown eyes narrowed.

A sense of pride rolled over Mrs. Brown. Her son had worked all summer, cutting grass, cleaning windows, and washing cars just to save enough money to treat his mother and sister to a nice dinner at a restaurant. Tony was a hardworking young man just like his father had been before he passed away from cancer.

"Don't get too sassy with me, young blood," said the taxi cab driver as he pressed on the brakes as though he was ready to put them out on the curve.

Tony squinted, casting an icy glare at the driver. Mrs. Brown rubbed Tony's hand, knowing how overprotective he was of her and his sister. He would fight a lion to ensure his mother and sister's safety and respect. He was a skinny, sixteen-year-old young man but he was tall as a skyscraper and strong as an ox.

"Sir, we have money," said Mrs. Brown while watching the driver's pudgy nose curl up into a sneer as he stared at them through his rearview mirror.

"Mama, are we getting closer?" asked Tiffany as she tugged on her mother's navy blue dress while a glint of nervousness flashed in her light brown eyes.

Mrs. Brown wrapped her slender arm around Tiffany to provide a sense of comfort. "We're almost there."

The evening sun drifted beyond the horizon, allowing the moon to slowly take its place in the sky.

The taxi sped down the street, driving toward a more affluent side of town. An area Mrs. Brown surely couldn't afford to live in. Her children's eyes brightened like fireworks as they passed a house that resembled a mansion with a swimming pool.

Tires screeched in the air. The taxi came to a sudden halt, causing the driver's drink to splatter on the front seat. A possum ran across the street, cutting in front of the taxi. The driver balled up his fist, slamming it against the horn.

"I should've killed that possum!" blurted the deranged smelly driver. The words leaped between the large gaps in his teeth as he wiped the splattered drink from his white wrinkled face. His voice carried the magnitude of loud thunder.

Tiffany tugged on her mother's dress again.

Mrs. Brown winked as she pinched Tiffany's cheek. "It's okay," she whispered.

Five minutes later, they pulled up in front of a well-lit building—a place Mrs. Brown had never visited before. But Tony had visited the restaurant, a month ago, with his high school basketball team for a summer team-building event.

"Give me my money!" demanded the taxi driver.

"How much is it?" asked Tony as he stretched his narrow neck toward the front seat to look at the black device on the dashboard that displayed the price.

Mrs. Brown was grateful Tony had saved up the money he made over the summer, cutting grass. With her house cleaning job, she could barely make ends meet.

The driver pointed with his long index finger at the device.

Tony shoved his hand into his pocket and pulled out the money. He placed the money on the tray. "Keep the change. You'll need it to buy a better attitude," uttered Tony as he exited the taxi.

The taxi driver launched an alarming smile.

Mrs. Brown gripped Tony's arm as she planted her swollen feet on the paved parking lot, trying to maneuver out of the taxi. Her dress flared around her black tennis shoes. She couldn't wear heels. Her ankles popped every time she took a step. Arthritis had formed in her middle-aged body settling into areas she didn't know existed.

A pang of uneasiness hovered over Mrs. Brown as her gaze connected with staring eyes and gaped mouths. Parking attendants and customers stood motionless like they were shocked to see someone pull up to the upscale restaurant in a taxi.

Luxury cars, tailor-made suits and fancy dresses paraded through the large parking lot. A huge cascade water fountain, surrounded by yellow and purple tulips, mounted in the middle of the landscaped lush green grass. White diamond shaped pebbles lined the sidewalk, providing a pathway to the entrance door.

Muffled giggles and whispers seeped into the air as white and brown noses tilted toward the ceiling.

Mrs. Brown straightened her floral pink scarf around her neck, giving her a sense of comfort. The scarf accented her navy blue dress. Her neatly pinned-up hairstyle glistened as the sunlight pressed against it.

The French doors abruptly flung open as they approached the entrance.

"Sorry, this is Friday night. It's our busiest night of the week. You must have a reservation to enter," said the doorman, preventing them from entering the restaurant. His creased black pants and starched white shirt snuggled against his barrel shaped body.

Mrs. Brown paused for a second. She wondered why the doorman assumed that they didn't have a reservation. Mrs. Brown glanced at her children's attire. Tony had on a pair of black slacks, a white shirt and black shoes. Even though Tony didn't have the finest clothes, his attire was clean, neat and ironed. Tiffany's sunflower yellow dress draped around her knees, presenting a dazzling appearance for a seventeen-year-old girl.

"Yes, we know," said Tony, gripping his mother's elbow to provide support as he walked her closer to the door. "I have reservations for us. It's under Anthony Brown."

Soft classical music flowed out of the overhead speakers.

The doorman slowly glanced at the reservation list while sporadically looking up at the other customers who were gawking in their direction.

Mrs. Brown peered through the French glass doors as they waited for the doorman to confirm their reservations. Bright lights glistened from a Victorian chandelier that dangled from the toasted oak painted ceiling. A gold oval shaped mirror mounted on the satin-emerald painted wall. Elegant, honey-gold high-back chairs snuggled neatly under the round rustic cream color tables. Flower arrangements radiated a mixture of colors positioned in every corner— creating an astounding appearance.

"Welcome to Country Club Seafood Tavern," said the doorman with a fake smile spread across his thin pink lips as he opened the French doors . . .

A loud pounding noise echoed from Mrs. Brown's front door, interrupting her trip down memory lane as the smell of savory fried fish wafted through the apartment.

"Mama, open the door. The fish smells delicious," said Tiffany and Tony in unison as their voices traveled through the locked screen door.

"Come on, Lena, open the door. We're starving," chuckled her brother, Lamont, as he tugged on the screen door, peering inside.

A pleasant feeling warmed Mrs. Brown.

Today was going to be a great day.

Chapter 20

The bright, early morning sun arched above the blue clouds on the cozy Saturday morning.

Hope strolled along the beige caramel carpet toward her twins' bedrooms. She peaked her head inside Jayla's pink, princess décor room. Jayla was still asleep. Hope pivoted toward Jayden's blue adorned bedroom. Jayden was sound asleep. Since the twins were asleep, Hope figured she would take this time to review her catering orders that may have fluttered her website overnight.

Hope pressed her back against the black leather chair in her office. She reflected upon the interrogation that she had endured from Sloan on the telephone yesterday. Hope recalled feeling like a child as she explained to Sloan, repeatedly, why she had entered his car. She knew Sloan's cars were off limits— just like his office—whenever he was not present with her. She never understood why Sloan needed two cars. But as long as she had her own car, she was fine. Somehow, Hope had managed to reassure Sloan that she had entered his car to retrieve her laptop charger. He had no clue that she had seen the folder. But Hope could not stop thinking about a picture inside the folder with women on it. She recalled one of the women resembled the woman talking to the European man at the museum. She was determined to find out, even if that meant sneaking back into Sloan's car.

Hope glanced over at the small lucky bamboo tree that rested on top of the credenza. She lifted the small bamboo tree's wide vase. She had tucked the brochure inside a ziplock bag and placed it underneath the wide vase. She kept the brochure to read it because Sloan had never discussed the details about the pizza pub with her. She was certain that Sloan would never find her hiding spot.

Hope slowly opened the ziplock bag to retrieve Worldwide Express Pizza Inc.'s brochure, hoping to make sense of it. She gazed at the brochure, observing that the women who appeared to be Mexican were advertising Mexican cheese pizzas.

A cool breeze flowed through the office, mingling with a crisp scent from the lemon-lavender candle.

Hope scanned the brochure, hoping to figure out what the numbers underneath the women represented. She glanced at several women on the brochure. They were advertising Mexican cheese pizzas, white cheddar cheese pizzas, brunost cheese pizzas, asiago cheese pizza, Greek feta cheese and so forth. Instantly, Hope realized that the women's skin tone and facial features resembled the names of the different types of cheese pizzas on the brochure.

A beam of sweat trickled down Hope's golden-brown face, competing with the cool breeze that flowed inside the office. She glanced at the words at the bottom of the brochure that revealed 'Staff Roster List,' which created a sense of ease for her.

Hope exhaled slowly. Her conscience would not allow her to forget about the numbers that appeared underneath the pictures of the women. Hope figured that the two-digit numbers reflected something that related to the pizza. But she wondered why Sloan had the black folder strapped underneath the passenger's seat in his car. On the contrary, Hope knew Sloan was a *neat freak*. He preferred that all items were neatly stored away.

Hope continued to peer at the brochure. She noticed that the brochure advertised small, large, extra-large, and deluxe sized pizzas which was typical. An uneasy feeling crept through Hope as she continued to review the brochure. She swallowed hard as she noticed that small sized, beautiful women were advertising small pizzas, medium-sized women were advertising medium sized pizzas and so forth.

Hope stood, hoping that her mind was not playing any tricks on her. She paced the oatmeal tan carpet in her office as she continued to review the brochure. She closed her eyes, realizing that something wasn't right. Her gut feeling told her that there was some connection between the sizes of the women and pizzas.

Hope's mind started racing as she recalled that Worldwide Express Pizza's website had advertisements with several beautiful young women. She kept thinking about the numbers that appeared underneath the women on the brochures. She scanned the numbers again; they ranged from 18 to 30. For a quick second, Hope wondered whether the numbers underneath the women represented how many years the women had been working at the pizza pub.

But that wouldn't make sense. The women looked young, Hope thought. She even pondered whether the numbers underneath the women represented how many pizzas had been sold for a specific period of time.

Hope scratched her head, causing her hair to bounce on her face. She fingered through her hair to push it behind her perky ears as she flopped into her office chair. She tapped her slender fingers on the brochure as bizarre thoughts continued to storm through her mind. Hope pressed her back firmly in the chair. She wondered if the numbers underneath the women represented their employee id numbers. "Perhaps, this is what the numbers represent," sighed Hope.

She glanced out of the window for a few seconds as her mind continued to force her to speculate about the numbers underneath the pictures of the women. She rubbed her eyes. "What do these numbers represent," she huffed.

Hope's conscious continued to persuade her to think *intensely* about the numbers. Her gaze shifted from the pictures of the women to the numbers underneath them—multiple times. She shook her head, hoping that the numbers underneath the women on the brochure didn't represent the women's ages.

Hope exhaled, thinking that the brochure was forcing her to speculate on something *crazy*. A soft chuckle flowed out of her mouth as she figured that Sloan would have a *good* explanation about the brochure. She wasn't in the mood for another interrogation. But Hope's gut feeling convinced her that something was not right. *"Why do the brochures have numbers marked on them. Why did Sloan have a picture of a woman in the folder,"* she thought.

Chirping sounds flowed through the office's window.

Hope slowly flipped over the brochure to look at the back of it. She had been so occupied with looking at the women on the front side of the brochure that she never looked at the back. Hope's gaze landed on a few men wearing employee uniforms like the women on the front page. The appearance of the men brought a sense of ease to Hope. But for some reason, the men's pictures were smaller than the women's pictures. Hope noticed that the men wore badges that identified them as being managers and delivery drivers. Hope continued to review the brochure.

A sense of relief filled her as she noticed several women that were advertising pizzas on the back had on employee badges that identified them as managers, waiters and delivery drivers as well. But the badges didn't display the employees' names. "I was getting worked up for nothing," mumbled Hope. She was used to high-profile officials covering up dirt in Cloverdale. So, she thought Sloan was doing the same. She still wondered why the women on the front side of the brochure didn't have on badges. Yet, she still felt as though Worldwide Express Pizza was a legitimate business.

A sense of guilt seized her. She felt as though she did not have any business going through Sloan's things. She leaned toward the small black shredder positioned beside her desk. A rumbling sound pierced the air as Hope inserted the brochure into it. She definitely couldn't return the brochure to the folder inside Sloan's car. She glanced inside the shredder, hoping that the brochure was cut into tiny pieces. It had destroyed the brochure beyond recognition.

Hope slowly closed her eyes, trying to figure out why Sloan was hiding the business plan and brochures in a folder underneath the passenger's chair.

Footsteps quickly approached Hope, forcing her eyelids to separate.

"What were you shredding, Hope?" asked Sloan in a hasty tone.

A sudden river of nervousness burst through Hope. "I thought you were going to be gone for two days," responded Hope in a nervous tone.

Sloan squinted. "I figured since you were acting like a detective inside my car yesterday, I needed to cut my business trip short," he uttered in a firm tone. "So, answer my question, Hope. What were you shredding?" inquired Sloan as if he already knew that Hope had retrieved a brochure from the folder. He had obsessive compulsive disorder and he knew when Hope tampered with his items.

Hope swallowed hard, forcing her throat to nearly cave inward. She was on a mission to find out why Sloan was a mysterious puzzle. Hope felt that she was married to a stranger.

Chapter 21

A week later, the bright morning sun flowed through the bay window in the living room. Hope glanced out of the window as Sloan inched his midnight black Jaguar out of their three car garage. Hope paused, trying to speculate why Sloan was not driving his pearl white Mercedes-Maybach S650 to meet Mr. Gavino. For some reason, Sloan switched up cars whenever he traveled to different pizza pubs. He even rented cars sometimes—something Hope thought was odd. Sloan justified his actions by telling Hope that he didn't want to put several miles on his cars. Yet, he never drove Hope's white Range Rover.

Hope glanced at her itinerary on her website, reviewing her catering orders for the day. An ounce of discomfort flowed through Hope as she sent an e-mail to Tiffany to confirm a time to meet to provide a few samples of her catering dishes. The thought of hosting Mrs. Brown's seventieth birthday brought a sense of excitement for Hope. Hope hoped that the event wouldn't be held at Mrs. Brown's apartment so she could avoid seeing her mother who lived across the street from Mrs. Brown.

Hope had hauled the twins off to camp just as the sun was peeking through the morning clouds at 7:00 a.m. Now, she had the entire day to prepare her two scheduled catering orders, deliver them and set up for the events. A small chuckle flowed out of Hope's mouth as she noticed that the orders consisted of a ten-year-old little girl who shared the same birthday as a one-hundred-year-old woman. Regardless of their vast age difference, they both wanted accents of pink and yellow on their birthday cakes and cupcakes.

A sharp sound rang through the house as Hope walked toward the kitchen to prepare the catering orders. Hope glanced at the caller ID, hoping that it was not Ivey. She had been calling Hope and leaving messages at least twice a week for the past three weeks. A pinch of resentment flowed through Hope as Ivey's picture appeared on the high-tech caller ID.

"Hello, Ivey. Please stop calling my house!" said Hope in a hasty tone.

"How are you doing, Hope?" asked Ivey in a soft tone. "I've been calling you. But you haven't returned my call."

"I know," said Hope. "That should have been your clue that I didn't want to be bothered."

"Hope, I am still your sister."

"Ivey, please get to the point. What do you want?" snapped Hope. "I already told you that I'm not helping Gloria. So, I hope that is not what you are calling me about."

Silence filtered through the phone like pollen.

"How are your twins, Hope?

"Fine."

"What are their names?"

"Why?"

Ivey paused before speaking. "I want to know. They are my niece and nephew."

"Whatever, Ivey," said Hope as she mixed the batter for her cakes. "Their names are Jayla and Jayden."

"Those are beautiful names," uttered Ivey. "Hope, why are you so hateful toward me? I never did anything to you."

"Ivey, what do you want from me!" blurted Hope as she turned on the blender, hoping to drown out Ivey's voice.

"I need to talk to you," said Ivey as her voice leaped through the telephone.

A clattering sound echoed through the kitchen as Hope turned the blender to full speed to ensure that the batter did not have any lumps. Hope was known for making soft, moist, delicious homemade cakes.

"Ivey, I'll call you back. I am trying to make a few cakes."

"I will hold on 'because I need to talk to you," said Ivey as if she was desperate to talk to Hope. "What are you making?"

Hope exhaled slowly, hoping Ivey would end their telephone call. Hope turned off the blender, poured the batter into the cake pans and poured the remaining mixture into the non-stick baking trays for the cupcakes.

"I am making a few desserts," said Hope as if she didn't want Ivey to know she had a catering company. "Go ahead, Ivey. I am listening," said Hope as she continued to prepare her two catering orders.

"Hope, I know you don't want to talk about mama. But she is sick."

"So! You were the apple of Gloria's eyes. So, you need to help her."

"I didn't know any better, Hope. I was only a child, " mumbled Ivey as her sharp tone struck Hope's heart.

"I was, too. But I went through a lot of trauma in that house with mama."

"But daddy was good to you, Hope. He took care of you."

"Eugene wasn't my daddy! He was your daddy," snapped Hope. "And mama made sure I knew that. Besides, even though your daddy used to tell mama that it was wrong for her to show favoritism, she still did it."

"But daddy treated you good, Hope . . . like you were his child."

Words ceased as if the noise level had been sucked up in a vacuum.

A tear formed in Hope's eyes as she remembered how Ivey's father,

Eugene, had forced Gloria to enter a drug treatment center. Eugene had taken care of Hope while her mother underwent treatment. Those were the best three months of Hope's life. Hope exhaled as she recalled Gloria had relapsed a few more times and Eugene had paid for Gloria to enter into the drug rehab each time.

Eugene was a researcher at a nearby pharmaceutical company. Yet, he barely looked in any mirrors due to his blemished facial appearance. He had a large burn on his face that he received in a house fire as a child. Although he had a good spirit, money and a charming personality, his selection of women was slim to none due to his unappealing appearance. So, Hope often wondered if he purposely searched for a crackhead that he could restore. Hope felt that Eugene had forced himself to devote time and money toward Gloria's treatment to fulfill his passion. It finally worked and Gloria and Eugene got married and had Ivey. Somehow, Gloria convinced Eugene to undergo plastic surgery which improved his overall facial appearance.

"I didn't know the things that mama was doing to you were so wrong until I grew up."

A tear tumbled down Hope's high cheekbone. She didn't want Ivey to know she was crying. "Gloria wouldn't let me eat with you and her. I had to clean up the whole house like I was Cinderella. She used to call me—*A Bad Seed*."

Weeping sounds flowed through the telephone. "But daddy treated you nice. He *never* mistreated you, Hope. He treated you like you were his own flesh and blood."

Hope's heart uplifted, thinking about the happy times she had with Eugene. Hope recalled crying when Eugene had died of a heart attack. Hope was so distraught that she wanted to sleep in the grave with Eugene rather than live in the house with her mother. She was in high school and Ivey was in middle school. Gloria had spent up Eugene's life insurance money on a new boyfriend that she had suddenly met. The boyfriend wasted no time in spending the life insurance money, resulting in Gloria dragging Hope and Ivey to an apartment in the heart of Cloverdale projects. As soon as the money was gone, Gloria's so-called boyfriend left.

Whimpering sounds travelled through the telephone. "I love you, Hope."

Chirping sounds pressed against the kitchen window.

"Hope, have you thought about helping mama?" asked Ivey in a soft tone.

"No," blurted Hope without any remorse.

"But mama's doctor thinks you could be a donor for mama."

"So," bawled Hope as she felt a slight tug pull on her heart.

"D*addy* always told us that we had to show love even when we have been mistreated."

Hope's heart pumped a river of blood through her body. "So, why did you used to laugh when Gloria mistreated me?"

Painful images flashed in Hope's mind as she remembered how her mother used to hit her in the head with the *Holy Bible* as she called Hope a *Bad Seed*. The hits came so frequently that Hope thought they were part of the family's daily prayer.

"I didn't know any better, Hope," muffled Ivey as her voice flattened.

Hope gnawed on her bottom lip as a tear rolled down her face.

"Ivey, stop it. You know mama hated me . . . for something that wasn't my fault," said Hope while pulling out the cakes and cupcakes from the oven. She placed them on trays so they could cool down.

"I used to tell mama that it wasn't your fault that those drug dealers *raped* her . . . and . . . she got pregnant with you."

Hope's heart slammed against her chest. "Ivey, stop it! Please stop!" screamed Hope as if remembering that she was a product of rape diminished her self-worth.

Keys jiggled at the garage back door. Sloan had returned home sooner than Hope had expected. Apparently, he didn't go to his meeting with Mr. Gavino.

"I have to go, Ivey," said Hope while wiping the tears from her face.

"Hope, don't hang up. Please give mama another chance," begged Ivey.

"I can't, Ivey," sobbed Hope as she glanced at the cakes and cupcakes in the oven.

"Mama has changed, Hope. She has tried to find you for several years."

Hope walked inside the living room trying to avoid Sloan from seeing her when he entered the house. Hope balled up on the love seat with the cordless telephone glued to her ear. She glanced at her cellphone wondering if Sloan had called.

"But Gloria took everything out on me, Ivey," said Hope as tears trickled down her face. "Gloria said, every time she looked at me . . . she thought about the drug dealers who had raped her," muffled Hope as her voice slurred. "I still remember when I was five years old and Gloria told me that she could *never* love me."

"Hope, mama does love you. She was on drugs when she said those means words to you," wept Ivey. "I love you and I know daddy did, too."

The sound of footsteps slowly drew nearer to the living room.

"I have to go, Ivey," mumbled Hope as Sloan's footsteps were getting closer.

"Hope, please don't avoid my calls. I—I want us to be close," sobbed Ivey as she released a loud wailing sound on the telephone. "Hope, please help mama."

Sloan strolled into the living room with a dozen white roses in his hands. His charming smile melted into an alarming frown. "What's wrong, darling?" he whispered.

Hope pressed the telephone to her melon shaped breasts, trying to prevent Ivey from hearing her conversation with Sloan. "I'm talking to my sister."

Sloan caressed Hope's golden-brown hand. Hope lifted the telephone back to her perky ear as Sloan's eyes filled with confusion.

"Call me back later, Ivey."

"What about Mama, Hope?" inquired Ivey. "She has an appointment in two weeks at 8:30 in the morning. She wants you to go with her."

"Do you hear yourself, Ivey?" asked Hope as a tear rolled down her face.

Sloan rubbed the tear from Hope's high cheekbone. Sloan reached for the telephone to press the loudspeaker button so he could hear Hope and Ivey's conversation. Hope looked at Sloan as if she wanted to turn him into a pillar of salt.

"Mama said she has been calling you, Hope."

"I know, Ivey. I heard her pitiful messages asking me to call her," said Hope as the heartless words leaped out of her mouth. "I wish Gloria would stop calling me."

"Hope, please think about it. I will go to the doctor's appointment with you and mama," sniffled Ivey. "Mama is going to die, Hope, if she can't find a donor soon."

Hope slowly exhaled as she looked toward the clover white painted ceiling.

"Ivey, please listen to me carefully . . . I am not helping Gloria!"

Chapter 22

A cluster of bright colorful lights flashed across the evening sky, trailing behind crackling noises. The Fourth of July created an atmosphere of fun, food, and activities.

Hope walked through the brightly lit kitchen, reflecting upon Sloan's bizarre demeanor at Creative Marbles Museum and about the brochure that she had found underneath the passenger's seat in his car. An ounce of confusion pierced through Hope's heart, forcing her to question whether she really knew her husband.

Hope stood in the Spanish style kitchen, cutting up red plump tomatoes for the veggie burgers on a glass tray. Dove white cabinets hung on the dandelion yellow painted walls. Elegant Santa Cecilia granite countertop created an astounding appearance in the kitchen. Classy recessed lights assembled across the cottage white ceiling. Stainless steel appliances decorated the kitchen in an orderly fashion.

Soft jazz flowed through the house creating a cozy feeling to enjoy the holiday.

Hope peeked out of the kitchen window, noticing that Sloan was on the patio talking on his cell phone. A sharp pain knifed through Hope as she read Sloan's lips as he said, "Why do you need more customers? You have enough for now. The pizza is selling good," laughed Sloan. "I think it will be a huge risk if you expand to more states."

A few minutes later, Sloan tiptoed behind Hope tugging on her black apron. "The food smells good," he said while landing a soft kiss on Hope's neck.

"Sit down and eat, Sloan," laughed Hope while noticing Sloan's slightly uptight demeanor. "You've been downstairs in the basement working a long time."

"I had to take care of a few things," chuckled Sloan as reached over to give Hope a peck on the cheeks.

"You look *mighty tasty* in this black summer dress," said Sloan as he walked around Hope as if he was trying to get a full view of her body. "The apron is hiding most of your goodies," he chuckled as he pulled on the strings of the black apron.

A peach scent wafted underneath Hope's nose as Sloan leaned toward her, resembling a pleasant perfume smell. "Why do you smell like a woman's perfume?" inquired Hope.

"What are you talking about?" snickered Sloan. "I've been in this house all day and night for the past couple of days. Maybe it is the new lotion I am using that you are smelling," he said as he hugged Hope.

Hope paused. Sloan had a point. He had been in the house for several days.

Hope glanced at the twins who were already sitting at the oval shaped glass table, eating a veggie burger. Wide smiles stretched across their faces as they looked at their parents. Hope blew a kiss toward the twins as a warm feeling flowed to her heart. Jayden reached in the air as if he was a pitcher, trying to catch Hope's kiss.

Hope drifted through the kitchen, preparing plates for her family. The savory smell of veggie burgers, fruit salad, fried fish and potato chips wafted through the kitchen.

"Where are the hot dogs?" asked Sloan as he clamped down on a veggie burger.

"You know I don't feed my family hot dogs," said Hope in a short manner.

"Come on, Hope. The Fourth of July is not a holiday without hot dogs," he said, handing her a glass of his famous lemon tea. It was his famous recipe, he would say.

Hope stared at Sloan. "The holiday is not just about hot dogs, Sloan."

Clattering sounds rippled in the kitchen as Jayla shoved her small hand inside the barbeque potato chip bag. Hope's slender fingers motioned in the air, signaling for Jayla to put the chips back in the bag. A muffled chuckle leaped out of Jayden's mouth as he laughed while watching Jayla drop chips in the bag as if she was releasing pennies into a wishing well.

"Hope, let her have some chips. She already ate all of her food," chuckled Sloan

"See, there you go trying to spoil Jayla," laughed Hope. "I already told her that she could eat the chips when we go outside in a few minutes," said Hope, noticing that Sloan still hadn't developed a full understanding of ASL.

The moon slowly arched over the clouds as darkness stretched across the sky.

Hope escorted Jayla and Jayden outside onto the paradise designed patio capturing a glimpse of the fireworks that burst in the air from a distance. A cascade of granite rocks congregated around the outdoor fireplace and large grill, displaying elegant décors. The stainless steel outdoor kitchen created a dazzling appearance, complementing the Tuscany beige tile on the patio's floor. Ocean blue furniture assembled around the patio creating space for a few orange pillows. An encased aquarium stretched on one side of the patio, showcasing tropical fish to create a paradise illusion. Natural pebble stone walls accentuated the sparkling clear water in the swimming pool, showcasing an elegant reflection under the blue sky.

"Why did you leave me inside the house?" chuckled Sloan.

"I figured you wanted to keep pouting about nasty hot dogs," grimaced Hope.

"I see you have jokes," laughed Sloan while pinching Hope's soft cheek.

A warmth settled inside Hope as she looked at Sloan and her twins. Hope watched as Jayden's eyes widened like walnuts as colorful fireworks leaped across the sky. Jayla was busy eating potato chips as if she was in an eating contest.

"Maybe we can have a romantic evening after I put the twins to bed," whispered Hope, barely above a whisper.

"That sounds like a plan," smiled Sloan. "And I need you to put on those clear stilettos for me. I have a special outfit for you to wear tonight." He paused before whispering, "I think we should start video recording our hot sex scenes. It would give me something to watch when I travel on business."

Hope winced. "No, Sloan, I do not feel comfortable doing that."

"Why not? We are married. It is okay. Nobody will ever see it but me."

Hope exhaled slowly. "I've never done anything like that before."

"I know, but I want to spice up a few things," he said barely above a whisper.

"Are you trying to say I am not *spicy* enough?"

"You are more than spicy, Hope. I want to enhance our sex life to make it special for you."

Hope exhaled. "I will think about it, Sloan. I'll put the twins to bed soon."

Sloan glanced at his watch, reading something that had captured his attention. "Hope, I have to work on a project tonight in the basement."

"Really, Sloan?" asked Hope wondering what was more important than their romantic evening.

"We are still going to have our date tonight in the bedroom. I hope you are not asleep after I finish," he grinned. "But for now, I want to spend some quality time with my family," he said while smiling at Jayla and Jayden.

Thought of Hope having her own family made her feel at ease. For several years, she had spent every holiday alone with Sloan and her twins. Sloan never invited any of his family to their home for the holidays. In fact, Sloan despised the years of growing up in foster care. Hope, on the other hand, wished she could erase the memories of her family.

"Why didn't you invite any of your business friends over, Sloan?" asked Hope in a questioning manner while taking notice of Sloan's facial expression.

"You know I don't like mixing business with my family," blurted Sloan as if Hope had struck a nerve. "Besides, I don't want any of them around you or the twins."

"Why not?" asked Hope, recalling that she had never met any of Sloan's friends.

"I already told you that I *don't* have any friends," said Sloan in a serious tone.

A nighttime clattery song resonated in the air. Crickets had gathered in the freshly, cut grass.

"What about Mr. Gavino?" asked Hope. "It seems like Mr. Gavino is your friend."

Sloan paused before speaking. "First of all, Hope . . . are you trying to question me about something?" uttered Sloan as he sipped on a glass of iced tea while glaring at Hope.

"No, Sloan. I want to know why you have never introduced me to your friends."

Sloan leaned toward Hope while squinting as he asked, "Why are you so concerned about meeting my friends?"

"Sloan, what are you talking about? You know I'm not like that," mumbled Hope as she turned toward Sloan to prevent the twins from reading her lips.

A rattled noise traveled from Sloan's round shaped mouth as he gritted his teeth.

"So, why are you asking me about my friends?"

"I just wanted to meet your friends' wives or girlfriends."

"Why?" inquired Sloan as a frown formed on his butterscotch-brown face.

"So, we can do family activities together with our kids," sighed Hope. "You have always told me that I couldn't have anyone at our house. I feel like I'm in a prison. You don't even want me to have any friends," complained Hope as her voice slightly trembled.

"Hope, what friends do you even have?" shrieked Sloan. "I know you are not talking about the two girls at the tavern that you used to work with."

"Yes, I am talking about Harmony and Melody. They were my friends at work."

Sloan stared at Hope as a sneer formed on his face before glancing at his watch.

"Hope, you didn't know those girls!" said Sloan as if he knew something Hope didn't know. "You were young and naïve when you started working at that tavern."

A loud fluttering sound echoed across the sky as fireworks flashed across the sky.

"Those girls worked at the tavern during the day and at the strip club at night."

"Strip club!" gasped Hope as curiosity gripped her.

"Yes, Hope. They worked at the strip club. Go ahead and ask me, Hope," said Sloan as he pressed his back firmly against the crescent orange pillow.

"Ask you what, Sloan?" asked Hope as she noticed a shift in Sloan's demeanor.

"I know you are dying to ask me how I know that they worked at the strip club."

A streak of frustration flowed through Hope. "I have already figured that part out," said Hope while glancing at the twins as they walked toward the fish aquarium.

"So, now, you know why I never wanted Harmony or Melody in my house. They were whores. I definitely didn't want them converting you into a whore like them."

"That will not be a problem," uttered Hope. "I haven't seen them in years. During my last week at the tavern, Harmony and Melody didn't show up for work."

"Really," said Sloan as his gaze shifted from Hope to the sky as if he was trying to ignore Hope. "Maybe they started working at the strip club full-time."

"I wouldn't know about that," said Hope while taking notice of Sloan's nonchalant attitude. "But the police came to the tavern to question the manager because their families reported them missing."

"Really?" said Sloan as his eyebrows connected. "Missing? Are you serious?"

"Yes. The police said they were missing."

"You never told me that before," said Sloan as he looked at his watch again.

"I told you a few years ago," said Hope as she wondered why Sloan was trying to act as if she had never told him that Harmony and Melody were missing.

"That is right. You did tell me," said Sloan as if he suddenly recalled that Hope had told him. "There is no telling what happened to them. It seems like a lot of young girls are being abducted everywhere," muffled Sloan. "That is why I am so overprotective of you, Hope. I don't want anything to happen to you." He planted a kiss on Hope's hand. "Look, I don't mind if you have one or two friends but they can never come to our house. I mean *never*, Hope, I don't like being around gossiping women. So, don't ever bring them to our house," he said before glancing at his watch.

"Why do you look at your watch so much?" inquired Hope, totally discrediting his permission to allow her to have friends because she knew he would later disapprove of it.

Jayla leaped onto Sloan's lap while Jayden stared at the fireworks.

"I have to look at a few things on Mr. Gavino's website tonight."

"It's a holiday, Sloan. You shouldn't have to work," blurted Hope as she recalled that Sloan had designed his watch to monitor every activity on Mr. Gavino's website.

"Worldwide Express Pizza is open every day, Hope . . . even on holidays," said Sloan as he pointed at the fireworks that flashed across the sky to get the twins to look toward the colorful lights instead of at his lips. "I am sure somebody will order pizza today, Hope, even though it is the Fourth of July," said Sloan in a puzzling manner.

"I bet so. Especially when sexy women are advertising the pizza on the website," uttered Hope in a condescending tone.

Hope motioned for the twins to go play so she could talk with Sloan. She knew they could read lips well. She sensed that the conversation was about to turn up a few degrees with tension.

Jayla slowly inched off Sloan's lap as if she was disappointed.

Crackling sounds pierced the air as fireworks sparked. Hope exhaled, recalling the only fireworks she saw as a child on the Fourth of July were from Gloria's crack pipe.

"Listen, Hope, Mr. Gavino pays me big bucks to monitor his website, the calls and the sales every day . . . every night . . . every minute . . . every second . . . and every holiday!"

Hope cleared her throat. "Why do *you* have to do all of that monitoring for him?"

"Because it is my largest contract that pays for this *big house!*" snapped Sloan. "So, please don't ever ask me questions about what I do for Mr. Gavino. There are so many things that you do not know. Some things that I want to share with you, but I just cannot."

"Like what, Sloan?"

"What did I just say, Hope? Some things are better that you do not know about."

"But I am your wife. Why are you keeping secrets from me?"

"Secrets! Listen, one day I will tell you everything but that day is not today."

"Really, Sloan?"

"Hope, I love you . . . I really do." He cleared his throat. "I never knew what real love was until I met you," he said while firmly clamping his lips as if he was trying to trap his darkest secrets from seeping through his mouth. "I just cannot tell you certain things. It is best that I do not so that you are not involved."

"Involved in what, Sloan?"

"What did I say, Hope! You do not need to know," blurted Sloan while rubbing his temples. "I have already said enough. It is the end of that conversation. I do not ever want to talk about this topic with you ever . . . never again!"

A tear wedged in the corner of Hope's eye. There was no doubt that Sloan was hiding something. But what?

Sloan stood before trailing toward the patio door to enter the house. "There are so many things about me that you do not know. I wish I could tell you, but I cannot and I may never tell you. Just know that I will always . . . protect you and our twins. I will never . . . ," his words came to a sudden halt as if his next statement would release clues to his darkest secrets. "I have work to do." He bit his bottom lip before speaking as if he was trying to hold back words. "I'll fix you a cup of lemon tea so you can calm your nerves."

An eerie feeling overtook Hope. Sloan always made her a cup of tea before he went out of town or after they had an argument. She noticed that she always felt relaxed after drinking the tea. But the delicious taste along with the enchanting foot massages that Sloan gave convinced her that he was not spiking up the tea. But was he?

"By the way, I will not have time to give you a massage," snapped Sloan before dashing into the house.

Hope winced. The romantic evening that she had planned for them evaporated in her mind like a bubble.

A shaft of curiosity stormed through Hope as her gut feeling convinced her that something was not right. She was determined to piece together the clues to Sloan's past.

Chapter 23

The hot mid-July sizzling sun beamed inside Mrs. Brown's house, forcing her small fan to compete with the hot air. She leaned back on her burgundy sofa, looking at the air conditioner installed in her window. Even though her children had the air conditioner installed in her living room window, she barely used it because she was accustomed to using her small fan. She believed that the air conditioner had contributed to her unbearable arthritis, causing her to elect to suffer the wrath of the hot sun instead of enjoying a gentle cool breeze.

"Mama, it is *hot* in here. Do you have a custom-made wood stove?" laughed Tiffany as she stepped inside Mrs. Brown's apartment.

Tiffany closed the door and walked toward the air conditioner, turning it on full blast.

"Tiffany that thing has caused my arthritis to flare up," said Mrs. Brown as she wiped her wet forehead.

"Mama, the heat in here will cause you to have a stroke."

"Well, Tiffany, I don't know which one is worse . . . having arthritis or dying from a heat stroke."

A cool breeze wafted through the living room, overpowering the scorching heat inside Mrs. Brown's apartment.

"What made you stop by, Tiffany?" asked Mrs. Brown as she looked at the air conditioner as if she really wanted Tiffany to turn it off. "I thought you had to work today."

"I do. But I left my clinic to come by here to check on you," said Tiffany as she walked toward Mrs. Brown's answering machine to check the messages—something Mrs. Brown rarely did.

"Why?" asked Mrs. Brown, her cream dress shifting as she walked.

"I know my mother," smiled Tiffany. "I figured since it was hot outside . . . I needed to make a community caretaker stop at your apartment."

"A *what*?"

"I knew you didn't have the air conditioner on and it is too hot for you to be relying on that small fan," said Tiffany as she glanced at the small box shaped fan.

"Well, my arthritis has been acting up lately."

"Mama," said Tiffany as she looked at the answering machine. "You have a lot of messages."

"I know. But most of the messages are from new customers," sighed Mrs. Brown. "I can't accept any new customers because of my arthritis. I'm trying to find someone to take the customers that I have had over the years and the new customers that keep calling me."

"Well, that is going to be tough, mama. You know people in Cloverdale and nearby only like your cakes, cookies and meals."

"I know," exhaled Mrs. Brown. "I'm sure there is somebody that can cook and bake like me."

"Where?" laughed Tiffany while her apple green summer dress snuggled against her slender body.

Mrs. Brown looked at her withered hands.

"Oh, I see Hope called you, mama," said Tiffany. "I wonder what she has been up to lately."

"How do you know that Hope called me?" asked Mrs. Brown as if she didn't want Tiffany to know that she had been talking to Hope. Mrs. Brown had made a vow to Hope, several years ago, that she would keep their telephone calls a secret.

"She left you a voice message, mama," said Tiffany as a slight frown formed on her face as if she wanted to know why Mrs. Brown was keeping it a secret. "I think . . . I spoke with her a few weeks ago," said Tiffany as she paused as if she was trying to refresh her memory. "I spoke with a lady at a catering company. It sounded similar to this voice. Plus, we were friends for years as kids. But I know people's voices can change."

"Well, Tiffany, you haven't spoken with Hope in several years. So, people's voices do change."

"I know. But Hope's voice on this answering machine was very close to the lady's voice I spoke to a few weeks ago," said Tiffany as a puzzled look plastered on her face.

Mrs. Brown glanced out of her window, looking at a white dove that soared in the blue sky.

Tiffany cleared her throat. "I saw Mrs. Gloria. She looked really sick," said Tiffany as her voice flattened.

"She is really bad off," mumbled Mrs. Brown. "Sickness has settled into her blood and bones."

"This is sad," said Tiffany in an unpleasant tone. "I saw a nurse helping Mrs. Gloria walk to her mailbox."

"That is her daily exercise," said Mrs. Brown in a calm tone. "Gloria told me that she has leukemia."

"Oh, no," said Tiffany.

"Gloria said she needs someone to donate something to her. I can't remember the big word she told me."

"I pray that she can find a donor," muffled Tiffany.

"Gloria told me that she will die if she can't get a donor."

A gentle breeze swept through the apartment from the air conditioner.

"Are Hope and Ivey helping Mrs. Gloria?"

"Gloria said whatever she needs, Ivey can't help her."

"What about Hope?" inquired Tiffany. "Can she help Gloria?"

"I don't know," said Mrs. Brown. "But I know Hope hasn't spoken to Gloria in over seven years."

A gust of cool air flowed out of the air conditioner.

"I didn't know it had been that long, mama," muffled Tiffany. "But I do remember how Mrs. Gloria used to mistreat Hope. I felt bad for Hope. I used to cry when I saw Hope crying."

"I know you did, sugar. Hope was your friend," said Mrs. Brown as she slowly closed her eyes.

"I remember she used to come over here just to watch you cook and bake," smiled Tiffany. "Then again, maybe Hope came over here to escape from Mrs. Gloria. This was the only place where Mrs. Gloria would let Hope visit."

A hovering sound flowed out of the air conditioner, washing out their conversation for a few seconds.

"Tiffany, earlier you mentioned something about calling a caterer. What were you doing calling a catering company?" asked Mrs. Brown.

"Mama," Tiffany said as she looked around the apartment as if she was trying to ignore Mrs. Brown's question. "Please let Tony and me move you to another place."

"Tiffany, sugar, I have had this conversation with you and Tony a million times. I ain't moving out of Cloverdale. This is all I know," said Mrs. Brown in an unwavering tone. "I know you are a doctor and Tony is a dentist. I am proud of the careers that my children have. But that doesn't mean you and Tony have to get me a place. I am fine."

A sweet savory smell of lemon cookies wafted through the living room.

Mrs. Brown exhaled slowly before speaking. "Ruth and her grandchildren are coming over in a few minutes. I made some cookies for them," said Mrs. Brown as if she wanted to change the subject.

"Her grandchildren!" blurted Tiffany as her arched eyebrows connected. "Are you talking about Cougar Ruth who dates young men?"

Mrs. Brown's pressed her lips firmly together. "Tiffany, be nice," said Mrs. Brown. "Her granddaughters have made a big difference in Ruth's life."

"That is good to hear," said Tiffany as she pressed her back firmly against the burgundy sofa. "Are they Julia's children?" asked Tiffany in an uneasy tone.

"Yes, they are Julia's children," said Mrs. Brown at a slow pace as she recalled that Tiffany had grown up with Julia in Cloverdale projects.

"What's wrong, mama?" asked Tiffany.

Silence flowed through the apartment.

"Social services placed the children with Ruth last month," said Mrs. Brown, recalling that she hadn't told Tiffany that Ruth had custody of her granddaughters.

"Why?" asked Tiffany. "What happened?"

Mrs. Brown inhaled. A mixture of anger and sympathy seized her heart as she told Tiffany about Jasmine and Taylor's traumatic experience with human trafficking. Her heart sunk as she informed Tiffany that Jasmine and Taylor's mother, Julia, had been murdered. Mrs. Brown watched as tears formed in Tiffany's light brown eyes.

"Human trafficking," mumbled Tiffany. "There's been an increase in girls and boys being abducted lately."

"That is really sad," said Mrs. Brown as she rubbed her hands together.

"Vance is working on a huge case," said Tiffany as she glanced out of the window. "He hasn't told me much about it, but I know it involves human trafficking in several states."

"Goodness," said Mrs. Brown, recalling that Vance was the chief attorney with the FBI. "Please tell my son-in-law to be careful," said Mrs. Brown.

"My doctor friends and I have had an increase in patients lately who have been victims of human trafficking. I wonder what type of scheme the ringleaders have organized to keep transporting victims from state to state," said Tiffany in an inquisitive manner as she shook her head from side to side.

"What type of scheme do you think it is?" asked Mrs. Brown.

"I don't know. But I know Vance and his team of FBI agents may be steps away from uncovering it."

A soft clean scent of Lysol swirled through the air.

"I can't even imagine what those young girls and women have been through," sighed Mrs. Brown, remembering that Tiffany was a gynecologist who specialized in delivering babies and providing care to women who had been raped.

A gentle breeze wafted through the living room, mingling with Tiffany's perfume.

Mrs. Brown winced as she noticed Tiffany close her eyes.

"I try to sympathize with the women. I can relate to how they feel," paused Tiffany. "Women who have been raped never forget their experience," said Tiffany as her gaze drifted toward the floor.

Mrs. Brown reached over, tapping Tiffany's hand in a comforting manner. She dreaded the memory of the day that Sergeant Smith had raped Tiffany.

"I always commend the young girls and women for being strong enough to escape from human traffickers . . . and for having the courage to share their stories," said Tiffany.

A pounding noise vibrated from Mrs. Brown's front door.

"Who is it?" asked Mrs. Brown as Tiffany approached the door to open it.

"Hey, *Doctor* Tiffany," said Ruth in an upbeat voice. "Give me a hug. I'm so proud of you," she uttered while wrapping her mahogany brown arms around Tiffany.

"Hello, Mrs. Ruth," said Tiffany in a soft voice.

"I hear you are a big-time doctor with your own clinic," said Ruth.

"I wouldn't say all of that," smiled Tiffany.

Ruth strolled toward the sofa, wearing blue stiletto heels as her granddaughters trailed behind her. Her bluish-black curly wig bounced in the wind as she moved. Surely, Ruth was still holding on to a small glimpse of her Cougar memories.

"I'm glad to know that you made something out of your life, Tiffany. It's tough growing up in Cloverdale," said Ruth in an unpleasant tone. "A lot of bad things happen to people in Cloverdale, especially young girls."

"I know," confirmed Tiffany. "But it is possible for a young girl to heal from her past trauma in Cloverdale and have a successful life."

"You're right," smiled Ruth as she leaned forward to gently pinch Tiffany's cheek.

Though Mrs. Brown despised the day that Tiffany was raped, she felt at ease knowing that Tiffany viewed herself as a trauma survivor with powerful advocacy skills to help others.

Chapter 24

A peal of laughter pierced Hope's ears as she strolled through Silver Leaf Senior Recreation Center. After talking to Ivey on the telephone earlier today, she had managed to pull herself together to make it to her last customer's event just in time. The thought of knowing that her mother was terminally ill started to tug at Hope's heart. But not enough to convince Hope to visit her mother or to help her.

She felt uncomfortable as she briefly reflected upon her conversation with Sloan on the Fourth of July. She hoped that one day Sloan would share his secrets with her so that she would not feel like she was married to a stranger.

A sense of pride swept through Hope as she glanced down at her catering attire. Her white catering uniform pressed neatly against her body. Pristine, white buttons lined the front of her shirt. Hunter green embroidery thread etched her company's name on the upper left side of her shirt, showcasing Serenity Catering Services. A small gold spoon and fork positioned underneath her company's name, presenting a classy trademark.

Hope glanced down at her cell phone, hoping that Sloan had not called her. She preferred to devote all of her attention to her customers whenever she was hosting an event. However, she was certain that Sloan has installed a tracking device on her cell phone that alerted him to her whereabouts at all times.

Hope whispered a quick prayer, thanking God for blessing her with the gift of cooking. She stood quietly as her gaze darted from table to table. She took a few minutes, reading people's lips as they engaged in conversations with one another. She had prepared just enough food for Mrs. Parker's one-hundredth birthday event. She was delighted that she had secured a contract with the local temporary agency to hire individuals for this event. A sense of pride straightened her shoulders as she looked at the contracted employees wearing her catering company's uniform.

Soft instrumental music flowed through the speakers creating a cozy environment.

Elderly men and women, filled with years of wisdom, came in through the doors for a special event in their finest clothes. Elegant rose pink satin chair sashes assembled through a small dazzling ballroom, snuggling around white comfortable chairs. Sunflower yellow tablecloths draped over round shaped tables. White magnolia flowers floated inside crystal vases on each table creating an astounding appearance.

The small ballroom was an appropriate setting for the celebration of a one-hundredth birthday. Mrs. Parker's long silver-gray hair draped around the edges of her round ebony-brown face. She was Hope's oldest customer. Her seven children had coordinated the special event with Hope. A herd of grandchildren and great-grandchildren surrounded her reflecting the love shared by generations.

Hope glanced around the ballroom taking note of how people thrust food inside their mouths as if it were their last meal. A warm feeling engulfed Hope as she observed smiles plastered on faces throughout the ballroom.

The bubbly feeling suddenly evaporated, permitting a streak of bitterness to flow through her as she watched children talking with each other. She yearned for the day when her twins could talk.

The delicious savory smell of smothered baked chicken breasts, buttered asparagus and garlic scallop potatoes wafted through the ballroom, mingling with the homemade lemon pound cake. Chicken fingers swirled in the children's hands as they chattered with laughter at the tables.

"*Chef* Hope, this food is delicious," said Mrs. Parker's oldest daughter, Mary-Elizabeth, as she shoved a piece of salmon in her mouth. "You're too young to know how to cook *this* good. You sure you cooked this food?" teased Mary-Elizabeth.

"Yes, ma'am. I cooked it all by myself," grinned Hope in a confident manner.

Mary-Elizabeth paused for a few seconds as if she doubted that Hope had cooked the delicious meal. "Well, this is a beautiful way for us to celebrate our mother's birthday with her," she uttered while looking at her siblings at the table.

"Mary-Elizabeth, leave Chef Hope alone. You're just messing with her 'because you can't cook," mumbled Mrs. Parker's youngest daughter, Renee, who had a mouthful of potatoes in her round mouth.

"Maybe 'because I was too busy babysitting you for mama," grimaced Mary-Elizabeth. "Maybe if I wasn't using my hands to change your stinky diapers, I could've used my hand to learn how to cook."

A muffled laugh drifted around the table. "Thank you for making sure I didn't get a diaper rash, Mary-Elizabeth," chuckled Renee.

Hope glanced around the small ballroom, trying to detect whether someone needed any food or drinks. The group was small enough for Hope to oversee without any help.

"Chef Hope, you've done a great job. We'll definitely recommend your services to others," uttered Renee as her cocoa-brown hand gripped a glass of water.

A warm feeling spread through Hope as she noticed how Mrs. Parker's children shared a level of love that Hope wished she had with her own mother.

"I am glad you are pleased with my services," responded Hope in a positive manner while noticing how Mrs. Parker's children assembled in a line to plant kisses on her forehead.

"This is our mother's favorite meal," whispered Mrs. Parker's youngest son, Michael while clamping down on some asparagus. "So, my sisters and brothers are glad you were able to *spice up* this meal the right way," said Michael as he glanced down at Hope's wedding ring. "Oh, so you're married."

"I can only eat a little bit of food . . . but it was good," said Mrs. Parker, interrupting Michael from talking to Hope. "I've gotten older . . . and my stomach has gotten smaller," said Mrs. Parker as her voice rattled.

Hope walked closer to her, trying to inch slowly away from Michael.

"So, how long have you been cooking, Chef Hope?" asked Mrs. Parker.

"Since I was a teenager," smiled Hope as her heart bubbled with joy.

"Your mother did a good job, teaching you how to cook," said Mrs. Parker as she planted a spoonful of potato inside her bow shaped mouth.

Hope's heart cringed. "My mother didn't teach me, Mrs. Parker," smiled Hope. "A nice lady named Mrs. Lena Brown taught me how to cook and bake . . . and a lot of other things," grinned Hope with a great deal of pride. "Mrs. Brown is my Godmother."

Mrs. Parker looked at Hope with curiosity in her eyes. "Even if your mother didn't teach you how to cook and bake, I'm sure your mother taught you something, Chef Hope," sighed Mrs. Parker.

Hope forced a smile on her face, trying to conceal her true feelings. She dreaded the mention of her mother.

"Okay," mumbled Hope as bitterness stormed through every fiber of her heart.

A loud rattling, clamorous sound pierced the air as a plate fell on the floor, interrupting Hope's conversation with Mrs. Parker.

Hope glanced around as the staff at Silver Leaf Senior Recreation Center rushed to the area to clean up the broken plate.

Mrs. Parker clamped her small hands around a clear glass, sipping on water. She tapped her slender fingers on the table as she looked at Hope. "You only have *one* mother, Chef Hope," said Mrs. Parker as if she had detected a discord between Hope and her mother.

Why does everyone keep judging me and feeling sorry for Gloria without knowing all the details? Hope thought.

"I know, Mrs. Parker," said Hope as she pressed her lips firmly together. "It was nice talking with you. I hope you enjoy your event." She smiled trying to edge away from Mrs. Parke.

"Chef Hope, please have a seat," ordered Mrs. Parker in a soft gentle tone as she adjusted a button on her oatmeal beige dress. She cut a tiny piece of salmon and placed it in her mouth.

"You can take a break for a few seconds, Chef Hope," said one of Mrs. Parker's twin daughters, Ashlyn, who looked identical to the lady sitting beside her.

"Yes, please have a seat," said Ashley, Mrs. Parker's other twin daughter.

Hope inhaled slowly as she sat at the table that had space for eight people.

"Mama, Chef Hope has to finish serving the meals," whispered Mary-Elizabeth.

Mrs. Parker cleared her throat before speaking. "Mary-Elizabeth, this is more important right now," said Mrs. Parker as she tapped on Hope's golden-brown hand.

A bright smile flashed across Mary-Elizabeth's olive-brown face as if she knew her mother was about to give Hope a spiritual aura.

Mrs. Parker's lips slowly parted. "I didn't see the sparkle in your eyes when I asked you about your mother," she muttered, before sipping on her glass of water again. "I saw a dim . . . dim light in your eyes which isn't good, Chef Hope," muttered Mrs. Parker as if God was using her as a *vessel* to communicate to Hope.

Hope sat quietly, listening to Mrs. Parker as if she were confined to the chair.

"No matter what you and your mother have been through . . . God can fix it," muffled Mrs. Parker in a soft tone barely above a whisper.

Hope sighed as if she was blowing out a row of candles. She had vowed never to mix business with personal matters. But Mrs. Parker had Hope's undivided attention.

"Chef Hope, I have been on this earth one hundred years. These eyes have seen it all. These ears have heard it all," she said leaning back in her chair.

"She is telling the truth," chuckled Renee. "We couldn't get away with nothing."

Mrs. Parker cleared her throat as if talking placed a strain on her vocal cord. "After many years of tears . . . my children are happy now. But it was by the grace of God that all of them stuck with me over the years," she sighed.

"Amen to that," chuckled Mrs. Parker's daughter, Faye, who elbowed Renee.

Mrs. Parker squinted while gazing at Faye as if she was casting a motherly dominance.

"I'm just kidding, mama. You know I love you," said Faye in a respectful tone while rubbing her chestnut brown hands together.

"That's the one who gave our mother the most problems," chattered Mary-Elizabeth while pointing at her sister Faye. "She used to stuff her bras with socks."

A cloud of laughter formed at the table.

"Be nice, Mary-Elizabeth and Faye," ordered Mrs. Parker.

The soft, enchanting sounds from a violin streamed through the ballroom.

Mrs. Parker rubbed her skinny ebony brown arm. "My children and I had some good times . . . and we had a lot of bad times," said Mrs. Parker. "I've done things that I'm not proud of. But my children forgave me for all of the wrongs I did to them," she mumbled as she rubbed her eyes, pressing against her thin gray eyelashes.

"We sure did forgive her," said Mrs. Parker's oldest son, Christopher, as he sat at the table while his black clergy robe clung to his barrel shaped body.

"So, no matter what you've been through with your mother," uttered Mrs. Parker. "I'm sure God will help you to forgive her . . . like my children forgave me."

Hope slowly stood, pushing her chair under the white round shaped table. "Thank you, Mrs. Parker. I appreciate you talking to me. Please enjoy your meal," smiled Hope.

"Thank you for listening to my mother," chuckled Mary-Elizabeth.

A sharp sound flowed out of Mrs. Parker's mouth as she coughed. "Chef Hope," she uttered, causing Hope to come to a sudden halt. "If you don't remember anything I said to you today," said Mrs. Parker as her voice weakened. "I want you to remember that there is nothing under the sun that can't be forgiven. So, find a way in your heart to forgive your mother."

Mrs. Parker's words traveled through Hope's ears straight to her heart.

Hope stood as if she had been hypnotized.

Chapter 25

Ruth strutted toward Mrs. Brown's burgundy sofa as if she was on a runway. A pleasant, light scent of Sand and Sable perfume trailed behind her.

"Tiffany, these are my granddaughters Jasmine and Taylor," smiled Ruth as she looked at her granddaughters.

"Hey, I am Tiffany. I am Mrs. Brown's daughter."

"Hello," said Jasmine and Taylor in unison.

Tiffany paused before opening her mouth. "You two look just like your mother, Julia," said Tiffany in a heartfelt manner while staring them.

"You knew my mother?" muffled Taylor in a soft squeaky voice.

"Yes, she was my friend," replied Tiffany in a serene tone.

Ruth leaped into the conversation. "Tiffany, your mother told me you deliver babies."

"Yes, I deliver babies and give women check-ups," smiled Tiffany.

Mrs. Brown noticed that Taylor clinched Jasmine's pecan brown hand as if the thought of Tiffany giving women check-ups sparked fear inside of Taylor.

"What type of check-ups?" asked Jasmine as her voice trembled.

"I do different types of check-ups to help women," said Tiffany in a comforting tone as if she had noticed a change in Jasmine and Taylor's demeanors.

Loud screeching sounds drifted inside the apartment from outside as a car slammed on its brakes.

"Do you want a cookie, children?" interjected Mrs. Brown as if she wanted to change the subject. "Here are the delicious cookies that I made for you two."

Jasmine leaned forward to grab some cookies. Her candy apple red shirt gently shifted as the wind from the air condition pressed on it. Her sandy brown hair bounced with radiance as she moved creating a pretty youthful image of her face.

"Here you are, Taylor," said Tiffany as she handed Taylor some cookies. "It's okay." Her auburn-brown hair had started to grow, permitting the patches on her scalp to slowly disappear.

Taylor placed her golden-brown fingers around the cookies. "Thank you."

"I'll take two cookies myself," said Ruth as she stretched her long arm toward the tray, causing her breasts to protrude forward.

"So, you give women check-ups, Doctor Tiffany?" said Jasmine as she nibbled on a cookie.

"Yes, the same type of check-up that you and Taylor had to get done last month before your social worker brought you to me," said Ruth as her gaze shifted between Jasmine and Tiffany.

Jasmine's gaze tumbled toward the floor.

"It's okay, Mrs. Ruth. I can explain it to Jasmine," said Tiffany in a compassionate tone.

Tiffany could relate to Jasmine and Taylor's experiences of being raped. Tiffany had been raped as a teenager by Sergeant Smith who used to be the community patrol officer in Cloverdale—before he was mysteriously murdered. Now, Tiffany not only delivered babies and gave women their annual exams but also specialized in providing gynecological services to women and children who had been raped. However, she was never a victim of human trafficking.

A smile stretched across Mrs. Brown's face as she listened to Tiffany explain to Jasmine and Taylor about the types of medical services she provided to children and women. Tiffany communicated with them on a child-like level to ensure that they understood the information.

"Thank you, Doctor Tiffany," said Jasmine as she nibbled on another cookie.

"You are welcome," smiled Tiffany as she stood. "Are you ready for school to start? It starts in another month."

Their quietness made it evident that the thought of attending school for the first time in their lives scared them.

Ruth cleared her throat. "I'm not sure what type of school they will attend," said Ruth as she slowly exhaled. "They were victims of human trafficking. So, we have to be careful about a lot of stuff."

"Excuse me, grandma," said Jasmine in a soft respectful tone. "My therapist said we are not victims of human trafficking anymore . . . we are survivors now."

"I like the word survivors," said Tiffany in a calm voice as she smiled at them.

"Me too. I like the word survivor also," grinned Ruth. "It sounds better."

Mrs. Brown bowed her head to mumble a prayer.

"I have to go back to work, mama," said Tiffany.

"Please drive carefully," said Mrs. Brown as a sense of pride flowed through her.

"I will, mama."

"Give my grandchildren a kiss for me," smiled Mrs. Brown.

"Okay, mama. But you got to stop spoiling them," giggled Tiffany.

"You have children, Doctor Tiffany?" asked Taylor in a soft flat tone.

"Yes. I have twins. They are one," said Tiffany as she walked toward the door and opened it.

"It was nice meeting you, Jasmine and Taylor," smiled Tiffany as she looked at them. "I hope I will see you two again."

Hot air flew inside the apartment as Tiffany opened the door, mingling with the cool air.

"It was nice meeting you, Doctor Tiffany," muffled Taylor as she *freely* maintained eye contact with Tiffany which was a surprise to Mrs. Brown.

"I hope I will see you again, too," said Jasmine in a soft voice as if she had developed a comfort level to talk with Tiffany.

Tiffany slowly closed the door behind her. Mrs. Brown stood and wobbled toward the air conditioner. She pressed the knob to turn it off.

"Time to go," blurted Ruth as she leaped off the chair, looking at Jasmine and Taylor. "I don't have time for my wig to start sweating."

Instantly, Taylor's face crumbled into a slight frown. She rubbed her small golden brown hand along the ridges of her scalp as if she wished she could wear a wig.

Mrs. Brown's heart fluttered as she observed Jasmine hugging Taylor as if she could sense the feeling that bothered Taylor.

Chapter 26

Droplets of rain brushed against the large window, blocking the sun from peeking inside the doctor's office. Antique white walls adorned the room. Tan ceramic tile covered the floor like a blanket. Colorful posters assembled on the wall, providing resources to patients.

Hope exhaled, praying that the doctor's appointment would draw her twins one step closer to being able to hear and speak. Hope's heart slightly clinched as she remembered that her mother had a doctor's appointment today as well. Yet, Hope wasn't interested in accompanying her mother to the appointment. Her heart pulsated, knowing that she had to bring the twins from Raleigh to Charlotte. She hoped that her mother did not have an appointment at the same medical center.

"Good morning, Mr. and Mrs. Glover," said a petite olive cream woman with a middle-eastern accent.

"Good morning, Dr. Ericsson," said Hope.

Hope looked at Jayla and Jayden as they sat on the beige miniature medical bed playing with the disposable bed sheets.

"I have reviewed Jayden's medical records. If you still want Jayden to undergo the cochlear implant procedure, we can schedule it before school starts back," announced Dr. Ericsson as she looked at a form in Jayden's medical chart.

"What about Jayla?" interjected Sloan as he leaned forward in the chair.

Dr. Ericsson glanced up at Sloan. "I typically discuss one patient at a time, Mr. Glover."

Sloan pressed his back firmly in the chair while looking at Jayla with a sparkle of empathy in his eyes.

"As you know, Jayden and Jayla were born with sensorineural hearing loss in both of their ears," said Dr. Ericsson as if she wanted to make sure she discussed both children to ease Sloan's impulsive demeanor. "But I have conducted the procedure on several children who were born with the same medical condition as them."

"Did they develop the ability to hear and speak?" interrupted Sloan as if he was anxious for

Dr. Ericsson to get to the point.

Dr. Ericsson paused for a few seconds before speaking. "Yes, they did. But they developed skills at different levels. So, I can't predict the outcome that Jayden will have."

"But were they able to at least hear and speak some?" blurted Sloan.

Hope cleared her throat as she looked at Sloan for a few seconds. Her gaze darted around the room, noticing posters plastered on the walls of human trafficking, HIPAA compliance, opioid misuse, and domestic violence.

"Dr. Ericsson, this has been a difficult situation for my husband and me," said Hope as she noticed how Sloan's gaze fixated on the poster about human trafficking.

"I see," said Dr. Ericsson, as a slight smile flashed on her bow shaped lips. "Let me ask you a question. Why did you wait until your twins were six years old to request the cochlear implant procedure?"

Hope glanced at Sloan before responding. "My husband and I needed time to think about it," uttered Hope while noticing that Sloan was still reading the information on the poster. "We used to think that this was how God wanted our twins to be," said Hope in a puzzled manner as she noticed Sloan sneering as he continued to read the poster. "But we figured that God allowed this to happen to our twins for a reason."

Sloan pressed his lips together before contributing to the conversation. "This experience has changed me a lot," said Sloan as if he had a hidden secret that he had never shared with Hope. "For one, I was excited that my wife and I had *twins*. I think having twins is something really special. So, I figured having twins who are deaf is God's way of getting my attention. I mean our attention," said Sloan as if the twins had made a major impact on his life—an impact that was unknown to Hope. "So, my wife and I waited until we were certain that we wanted to take a chance in seeing if this procedure would help our twins."

A beeping sound echoed from inside Sloan's pocket. Sloan reached inside his navy blue slacks and pulled out his cell phone. He turned off his cell phone while looking at his watch.

Hope squinted as she looked at Sloan.

"We pray that the procedure will help our twins to hear and speak," sighed Sloan.

"I understand."

"I will do my very best," said Dr. Ericsson in a confident tone. "After the procedure, Jayden will have to undergo habilitation treatment."

"What is habilitation treatment?" asked Hope as she noticed that Jayla and Jayden were reading their lips.

"Habilitation is a process that is done after the cochlear implant procedure is completed. It is a treatment process for individuals who are born totally deaf," said Dr. Ericsson. "It is different from rehabilitation."

"What is the difference?" asked Sloan.

"Habilitation is done for individuals who are born totally deaf.

Rehabilitation treatment is done for individuals who are born partially deaf," declared Dr. Ericsson. "Both treatment processes require an individual to learn to hear and speak."

Tapping noises bounced against the window as rain thrust against the glass.

"What about Jayla," repeated Sloan. "You keep referring only to Jayden."

Dr. Ericsson stared at Sloan as if she were diagnosing him. She placed Jayden's chart on the white cabinet and picked up Jayla's.

"Jayla has a history of being diagnosed with pediatric anemia. Like with any procedure, there could be some risk factors when a person is anemic," declared Dr. Ericsson. "And there could . . ."

"Listen, Dr. Ericsson, with all due respect," interjected Sloan in a harsh manner. "If you are about to tell us that Jayden can have the surgery but Jayla cannot, then I would rather that the procedure is not done," said Sloan as he glanced out of the window.

Jayla slid off the bed and walked toward Sloan. She grabbed his hands and placed them over her ears as her lilac summer dress clung to her small framed body.

Silence tumbled through the room.

A tear formed in Sloan's right eye.

"Dr. Ericsson, can Jayla get the procedure done?" asked Hope in a remorseful tone as she watched Jayden slide off the bed and walk toward Jayla. His cream and brown outfit shifted as he walked.

"I want to run a few more tests on Jayla before we move forward with the cochlear implant for her."

"Can you run the tests today?" asked Sloan in a calm tone as he hugged Jayla and Jayden.

"Yes," said Dr. Ericsson. "And I would like to repeat the test in a week."

"Is there anything we can do to help her?" asked Hope in a sympathetic tone.

A gush of wind pressed against the window, mixing with rain.

"Yes, I will provide you with some information. If everything goes well, we can look at scheduling their procedures in a few weeks before school starts," said Dr. Ericsson.

A touch of compassion flowed through Hope as she observed Jayden holding Jayla's caramel brown hand. Jayden's love for Jayla reflected a strong sibling bond that must have been formed when they were inside Hope's womb together.

"We can schedule a date for Jayden to have the procedure done," uttered Dr. Ericsson. "I'll give both of them a check up today and run some lab work on Jayla. After I look at the results, we can discuss Jayla getting the procedure on the same day as Jayden."

Hope tilted her head toward the ceiling. She leaned back in the black padded chair, exhaling as if she was blowing a dandelion flower.

"Dr. Ericsson, please do whatever you have to do to make sure both of our twins can have the procedure done on the same day," said Hope as a tear rolled down her face. "The thought of having only one twin gain the ability to hear and speak . . . will crush our hearts," said Hope as Jayla walked toward her, rubbing a tear from Hope's eye.

For a split second, Hope embraced the love and affection that Jayla was displaying. She tried to recall if she had ever loved her mother this way when she was a child.

"I can't make any promises, Mr. and Mrs. Glover, whether Jayla will be able to have the procedure done. But I will definitely look at all of Jayla's medical results before giving you a final decision," the doctor said.

A sharp pain knifed through Hope's heart. The thought of having only one of her twins gain the gift of hearing and speaking shattered her heart.

Chapter 27

A shaft of light inched through the burgundy curtains pouring onto the oatmeal tile floor. A cool breeze drifted from the window fan creating a comfortable temperature in the living room. A cream sectional chair stretched along the eggshell painted walls.

"I came as fast as I could, Gloria," said Mrs. Brown in a raspy tone as her gaze landed on two other women sitting in the living room. "My arthritis has been acting up lately. So, it was painful for me to walk across the street to your apartment."

A soft scent of lemon mist wafted in the air.

"Thank you for coming, Mrs. Brown. I've been sick . . . real sick," Gloria said while coughing and wiping her mouth.

A red line had formed under Gloria's nose apparently from wiping it nearly every minute. Dark patches clustered underneath her eyelashes overshadowing her hazel brown eyes. Sickness had settled inside Gloria's body without shedding any mercy.

"I know," said Mrs. Brown as she pressed her lips together. "Have you eaten today?" she asked recalling that Gloria was forty-five, but her sickness made her look as if she was drawing near to seventy-five.

"I don't really have much of an appetite," said Gloria as her mahogany brown hands trembled.

"I see," said Mrs. Brown while taking notice of Gloria's skinny frail arms and sunken cheeks. "But you have to eat something to keep your energy going."

"I keep telling my mother to eat. But she keeps saying she doesn't have an appetite," wept

Ivey with a tear in her light brown eyes. "My mother is sick, Mrs. Brown," said Ivey as she rubbed a tear from her chestnut brown oval shaped face.

"Gloria hasn't been eating much lately. I've been fixing her small meals like potatoes and stuff," said Geneva, a neighbor who lived up the sidewalk from Mrs. Brown and Gloria.

"How you've been, Geneva?" asked Mrs. Brown, remembering that Geneva was known in Cloverdale for falling in love with a white man who got her pregnant and ran off to another state. Folks in Cloverdale were certain that Geneva was still waiting for that man to return even though it had been nearly thirty years since she last saw him.

"I've been hanging in there," sighed Geneva.

"How's Hilton?" asked Mrs. Brown as she looked at Geneva's café brown face.

"My son has been doing really good," uttered Geneva. "He's a psychiatrist now in Baltimore. I wish he would've married Tiffany."

Mrs. Brown smiled. "Well, Tiffany's married now. I remember he wanted to court Tiffany." A small chuckle escaped her lips.

"I remember," smiled Geneva.

"It seems like all of our children turned out to be good," said Mrs. Brown as her gaze bounced between Geneva and Gloria.

"I heard your son, Tony, is a dentist and Tiffany is a gynecologist," said Ivey.

"They are," said Mrs. Brown in a pleasant tone.

"My son wants me to move out of Cloverdale. But I told him that this is home for me," mumbled Geneva as she glanced out of the window.

"I've told my children the same thing, Geneva. Cloverdale is all I know." Mrs. Brown paused. "I guess our prayers helped our children be something in life."

She leaned back in the burgundy chair as she mumbled a prayer.

"Time for your medicines, mama," said Ivey as she handed Gloria a small medication cup filled with pills.

Silence flowed through the living room.

"You two have been my friends for over two decades," coughed Gloria as she looked at Mrs. Brown and Geneva. "I don't know how much longer I'll be on this earth. I've been sick for a long time."

"Mama had a doctor's appointment two weeks ago," said Ivey as her gaze dropped. "She will have to go into the hospice center in a few weeks."

"I am sorry to hear that, Gloria," said Mrs. Brown in a sympathetic tone.

A cool breeze swept through the living room mixing with the scent of Gloria's medicines weakening the lemon mist scent.

"The doctor told me that I only have a few more months on this earth if I can't get a donor," mumbled Gloria as she rubbed her small caramel brown hands together.

"What type of donor do you need?" asked Mrs. Brown in a curious manner.

"I need a bone marrow transplant. Some people call it a stem cell transplant," said Gloria as the words struggled to come out of her mouth. "The doctors said I have some type of cells inside of me that shows that Hope may be able to help me."

A streak of confusion rushed through Mrs. Brown. "What do you mean? I don't understand."

"The doctors said there is a process called fetal micro . . . microchimeric," coughed Gloria as she rubbed her nose with some tissue. "Ivey, explain it to Mrs. Brown."

Ivey exhaled slowly. "Mrs. Brown, I'm a nurse. So, I can explain it to you," said Ivey before pausing while gently patting her mother's hand. "Another word for fetal microchimeric is called mother-child cell sharing. Some people also call it fetal stem cell sharing."

"I don't really know much about science," interrupted Geneva.

"Me, neither," said Mrs. Brown.

A sharp sound pierced the air as Gloria coughed. Ivey handed Gloria a glass of water.

"Can you get your daughters' medical records to see if they can help you?" asked Geneva.

"I don't think I can do that because of HIPAA," muffled Gloria.

"*HIPAA?*" said Mrs. Brown in a curious manner.

"It's a law that says nurses, doctors and other professional people can't talk about my business without me signing a consent form," said Ivey.

Silence flowed through the living room as if life was being sucked out of Gloria.

"But what is that fetal *micro* thing?" asked Mrs. Brown.

Ivey tapped on Mrs. Brown's dark brown hand before speaking. "I'll explain the whole process in an easy way. I'm sure mama doesn't mind me telling you."

"I don't, Ivey," chattered Gloria as she coughed.

"A pregnant woman passes cells to her fetus . . . well, her baby," said Ivey at a slow pace. "At the same time, the baby passes stem cells to its mother."

"Okay," said Mrs. Brown and Geneva in unison as if they were starting to understand.

"The stem cells can stay in a mother for decades. Doctors can even test the stem cells to see which baby left stem cells in a mother," said Ivey. "Mama needs more of the stem cells to help slow down . . . or cure her leukemia."

"Really . . . I didn't know," said Mrs. Brown as if she was in a classroom.

"Apparently, mama still has some of my fetal stem cells inside her," said Ivey before dropping her head. "But I can't be a donor. I can't give her any of my stem cells 'because I have fibromyalgia." A single tear rolled down her face and dangled along the ridge of her chin.

Mrs. Brown inhaled slowly as she started feeling uneasy. She pondered whether Gloria had called her over to ask if she could be a donor.

Silence tumbled through the living room.

"Well, my health isn't good. I've got arthritis. So, I'm sorry. I can't be a donor," uttered Mrs. Brown as her gaze darted between Gloria and Ivey.

"Mrs. Brown, I know you probably can't be a donor," muffled Gloria painfully as she held her stomach.

"Oh, okay," said Mrs. Brown in a relieved manner. She paused for a split second, recalling that Gloria had mentioned earlier that Hope may be able to help her.

A loud sound echoed inside the house as a dumpster truck drove by. "I recall you said Hope may be able to help you," uttered Mrs. Brown.

"Yes, the doctor said the fetal cells inside me had to come from Hope and Ivey," said Gloria before closing her eyes. "There's a chance that Hope's cells can help me since Ivey can't. But the doctors will have to run some tests on her to make sure."

Ivey's gaze plunged toward the floor.

Mrs. Brown sat, recalling that Gloria hadn't seen Hope in over seven years.

"I called Hope several times but she ain't returning any of my calls," mumbled Gloria.

Ivey handed Gloria another glass of water.

"I've called her, too," said Ivey in a pitiful tone. "She finally answered my call."

"Did you tell her what was going on with Gloria?" inquired Mrs. Brown.

"Yes, ma'am," sobbed Ivey as she wiped tears from her eyes.

A pinch of empathy streamed through Mrs. Brown as she watched Ivey cry.

"What did Hope say?" asked Geneva.

Tears flowed down Gloria's caramel brown face. "She refuses to help me, Mrs. Brown," wept Gloria as her voice trembled. "I know I wasn't the best mother to her. I know I took her through a lot when I was out there on that crack. I know I didn't treat her right. I treated her bad 'cause those drug dealers had raped me . . . and I got pregnant with her. I took my anger out on her." Gloria tilted her head toward the ceiling. "I used to call her a *Bad Seed.* I was wrong . . . oh, *God,* . . . I was so wrong. But I can't erase the memories from her mind. I can't . . . I can't," screeched Gloria, causing her body to shake.

"You have to get some rest, mama," interjected Ivey.

"I know. But I have to find peace about this situation," said Gloria as she rubbed her slender face. "I couldn't cope with the fact that those drug dealers had raped me. I got so depressed after I had Hope I started smoking crack. I was

127

a good girl . . . before I got raped. I thought about taking my life. I needed help. My mother couldn't help me," wept Gloria as she buried her face in her small hands. "My mother's drug dealing friends had raped me while she was busy getting high on heroin."

Mrs. Brown collapsed her hands together in a praying position.

"Did you ever tell Hope what had happened to you and what led you to do drugs?" asked Mrs. Brown in a supportive tone.

Gloria's slender fingers combed through her stringy hair as if she was trying to hold on to the little dignity that she had. She had undergone several sessions of chemotherapy, resulting in a ripple effect of massive hair loss.

"No. But I've tried to reach out to Hope over the years . . . even before I got sick. I wanted to apologize to her. I wanted to tell her," uttered Gloria. "I wanted to seek her forgiveness. I wanted to show her that I could try to learn to love her the way she needed to be loved. But she left home seven years ago . . . and I've never seen or heard from her since then."

Ivey wiped a bead of sweat from Gloria's face. "I told Hope that mama was sick. She acted as if she didn't care. I spoke with Hope two weeks ago. I told her that mama had a doctor's appointment. I even told her that the doctors can't find a donor for mama. I told Hope that the doctors wanted to run some test on her. But Hope never showed up to the appointment. She doesn't care."

Mrs. Brown rubbed her dark brown hands together, contemplating whether she should reveal to Gloria that Hope had been calling her over the years. But she didn't want to jeopardize the relationship she had developed with Hope.

"Mrs. Brown, I know Hope had a close relationship with you when she was a teenager. I remember she used to love going to your apartment to watch you bake and cook. I think you were the only real mother figure she knew when I was on crack. So, if you speak with her, please talk to her for me. I really need Hope to allow the doctors to test her to see if her stem cells can help me," said Gloria as if she had a gut feeling that Hope had stayed in contact with Mrs. Brown.

"Ivey, did you tell Hope that y'all mother was sick?" asked Mrs. Brown in a low tone as if she was confused about Ivey's previous statements.

"Yes," said Ivey in between speaking and allowing a tear to roll down her face. "She's not going to do it. She told me that I better start planning funeral arrangements for our mother."

Words evaporated in the air.

"I have found peace with God," mumbled Gloria. "So, even if Hope refuses to allow the doctors to test her to see if she can help me . . . I still want to talk to Hope to seek her forgiveness. I know I wasn't a good mother to her.

But I need to hear Hope's voice one more time before I leave this earth."

Chapter 28

The morning sun beamed inside Hope's white Range Rover. Clusters of trees stretched along the streets as Hope drove through nearby cities, looking at different buildings. Her catering service was expanding and she wanted to step out on faith to transition her company from the back of her house into an official business location. She had formed a rapport with local hotels that permitted her to reserve small conference spaces when she wanted to meet a customer to provide food samples.

Hope had just dropped off the twins at camp. She enjoyed having a slight break from Sloan as well. He had a business meeting with Mr. Gavino at the new pizza pub in Charlotte which gave Hope a few hours to explore more buildings.

Soft melodies drifted from the speakers in the Range Rover.

Hope exhaled, reflecting upon Sloan's bizarre demeanor at Creative Marbles Museum. She tapped her slender fingers on the steering wheel, pondering why Sloan always had a hefty sexual appetite every time he returned from his business trips.

Hope pressed her head firmly into the headrest, remembering that she was scheduled to meet with Tiffany tomorrow to provide a small display of her catering meals. She had complicated feelings about seeing Tiffany after nearly seven years. On one hand, she was excited at the possibility of meeting an old friend; on the other, she dreaded that Tiffany would try to convince her to see Gloria. Hope was uncertain whether Tiffany had recognized her voice.

A touch of bitterness leaked through Hope's veins as memories of her dreadful childhood stormed through her mind . . .

A musty smell drifted through the abandoned building mixing with a cool breeze. She had forced herself to fall asleep, hoping to control the hunger pains that overtook her five-year-old body. Hope's eyelids slowly separated as she lifted her small head. She glanced around the building, hoping that Gloria had not left her. She slowly sat up, noticing that something was rattling inside her jacket as she moved. She slowly opened it. Her gaze landed on a bag of chips and an apple, snuggled inside—all of which she was certain Gloria had stolen.

A shaft of sunlight peaked through the cracked glass windows in the abandoned building.

Hope's gaze landed on an alabaster white man wearing a black police uniform. No one ran. No one stopped talking. The drug dealers kept selling dope. The drug addicts continued smoking and shooting up drugs. The officer's presence didn't stop the show. He positioned himself a few feet away from Hope permitting her to hear every word he said.

"What's up, Sergeant Smith?" said a tall white man with a golden brown tan.

"Don't what's up me, Supreme. Where's my money?" Smith said glancing around the abandoned building. "It seems like business has been growing," he chuckled as two guys stood in a corner counting money and shooting dice while a short chubby man wearing a gray business suit inched through the side door.

Supreme's well-structured body showcased the muscles protruding through his Polo sweater. His attractive features showcased the finest of his high cheekbones. "I've got you man . . . chill," he said while signaling for a tall guy to come to him.

"I see this is the *spot* to get cocaine, fentanyl, meth and whatever else that rocks their boat," chuckled Smith as he looked around. "I guess marijuana is no longer in the running game." He paused before speaking. "I used to smoke pot in college. But I've never thought about using anything stronger."

"Is that so?" smirked Supreme. "That's hard to believe."

"Are you calling me a liar?"

"Yes," Supreme said with confidence. "The way you act, I'm sure you sniff coke."

Smith leaned forward. "I see you've got a *tan*," he chuckled as he quickly diverted the conversation. "It almost matches that black chick I keep seeing you with in town. I must admit, she's a gorgeous black baby doll."

A frown flashed across Supreme's well-defined face. "Look, man . . . don't make any jokes about my Kimi," he snapped. "I don't have time for your racist comments." He sneered.

"Do you have time for your father's racist comments?" grimaced Smith. "What did your millionaire father say about Kimi? I heard he doesn't care much about *other types* of people. He was sued for housing discrimination a decade or so ago, right? I heard he tried to get a few folks deported," he chuckled.

Supreme ignored him.

"Man, your father must learn that money is green. I don't care what color a person is as long as I get my *green* money. But I'm surprised your father accepts Kimi."

Supreme bit his bottom lip before speaking. "Why not? Oh, because she is black! Listen, like I told my father . . . . my mother. . . my entire family, and now I will tell you the same thing. Kimi is a good girl. . . and I don't care if she is black. I don't care if she was green, I love her. And for the record, my father does not make racist comments about Kimi. He knows I would *never* allow it. Besides, he sees that she is a good woman. So, he has changed."

"Really? I guess the old saying it correct that all it takes is one good black woman to change *us*. I guess that's why slavery ended," laughed Smith "I wonder what type of *goodies* Kimi has that got you so sprung man," said Smith as he licked his lips.

Supreme leaned toward Smith. "You better not touch Kimi or her family." Supreme tapped the black gun dangling from his hip.

"Settle down, cowboy." Smith glanced around. "Does Kimi know what you do?" A ripple of laughter rolled off his tongue.

Hope's body flinched as Smith's laughter echoed through the building.

"No . . . and she better not find out," insisted Supreme while glaring at Smith.

Smith rubbed his forehead. "Oh, yeah . . . I bet she thinks you make dough solely from your chain of barbershops and beauty salons that you have up and down the west coast. Oh yeah, maybe she thinks most of your *dough* comes from your gaming centers where people pay big bucks to play video games and eat chicken wings and pizza," laughed Smith.

Supreme's eyebrows connected. "Yes, she does . . . but how do you know my business?"

Smith ignored him as a short olive-brown man inched toward them.

"You need something, Supreme?" asked the man in a Spanish accent with a silver gun peeking from his cream sweater.

"Yes, Papi Chulo. Go get the money from the hiding spot and come back," said Supreme. "Smith wants his cut."

"Okay. The usual amount?" he asked.

"Yes," confirmed Supreme.

"You can throw in a bonus in there if you like," laughed Smith.

"Whatever, man," snapped Supreme causing Smith's body to slightly flinch.

Hope glanced around noticing that the two pale white little girls who typically shared a spot on the cold concrete floor with her were asleep with a brown dingy blanket tossed over them. The little almond brown boy who typically slept near them was gone. But Hope noticed three new children were huddled in a corner, terrified, as they watched a man *wrestling* on top of their mother in a nearby corner.

Hope peered around looking for her mother. Gloria was still in the same corner smoking crack. She had been working overtime on the pipe and performing tricks all night. Hope's eyes widened as two men stood in front of her mother unfastening their pants.

Hope turned her head eating the unhealthy meal that her mother had managed to scrape together for her. A truckload of fear stormed through Hope as a tall skinny man wearing a black business suit walked toward the sleeping little girls.

"Wake up and come with me," whispered the man to one of the little girls sleeping on the floor.

The girl's eyelids slowly separated as she pulled her body to an upright position. "Why?" asked the little girl. "Where's my mommy?" she asked while looking around as fear built in her blue eyes. Her mother was nowhere in sight.

"Get up," said the man jerking on the girl's narrow arm as he looked around.

"I can't go with you. My mommy told me to stay right here," said the girl as her voice trembled.

"Get up, now!" he uttered while licking his lips.

"My mama is going to be mad if I get up."

"We're going over there to play a little game," said the man as he pointed to a corner while pulling the girl to her feet.

The girl stood and trailed behind the man as he led her to a dark corner. His black business suit shifted as he walked rapidly to a corner that was clustered with cardboard boxes. The stacked cardboard boxes resembled a skyscraper permitting a shield for the businessman to hide his unforbidden act.

"Has he paid for his services?" chuckled Smith as he pointed in the direction of the man.

"Yes. He's a regular," blurted Supreme. "I heard he's a lawyer."

"Really . . . that's interesting," smiled Smith while rubbing his chin. "How do you know?"

"I've got my connections. I can get the scoop on anyone. But, of course, he denied it."

"I've got to get to know him a little better." Smith grinned. "He's got to pull a few strings for me."

Supreme frowned. "A favor for a favor . . . is always your mission."

"You're right," blurted Smith. "I could've arrested you when I busted you trafficking dope to Cloverdale. But instead, I allowed you to run these abandoned buildings." He frowned. "Not to mention, I let you and your little runners transport dope hassle-free in and out of Cloverdale." Smith shrugged Supreme's shoulder. "Hell, I even let you know where there is heat along I-85 highway when you enter North Carolina from South Carolina."

"True . . . and we appreciate it," uttered Supreme.

"I even showed you how to cover up the windows so no one . . . not even police officers can see any light or action in here," Smith snapped.

"Yeah, it does camouflage the windows," said Supreme while looking at the windows.

"Even I couldn't see the flames from the fire burning in that container over there from outside," chuckled Smith while pointing to a large trash can in the corner.

"A few users brought it in here so the kids can stay warm," said Supreme.

"How nice," smirked Smith as laughter peeled off his tongue.

"I get tired of telling them to stop bringing their kids in here," said Supreme. "It's like a broken record. So, I stopped telling them."

"Who cares about all of that," snapped Smith. "Their children will grow up being like them . . . and my money will keep flowing from generations to come," he giggled.

"You're sick, Smith," said Supreme.

"Whatever! Where's my money?" Smith paused while glancing around. "What's taking your little runner . . . Papi Chulo so long?"

"Calm down. He's coming now." Supreme frowned.

"Here," said Papi Chulo handing a black envelope to Supreme.

Supreme opened the envelope and peered inside for a few seconds as his fingers combed through what was inside of it.

"Here's your cut," spouted Supreme. "It's all in there," he said as he watched Papi Chulo walk away.

A smile stretched across Smith's face as he reached for the envelope. "Okay. You can return to doing business as usual," chuckled Smith.

"Whatever, man," said Supreme as he drew closer to Smith. "I don't know how much longer I'm going to be doing this."

"What are you talking about . . . there's no getting out of it," Smith grappled.

"We had a deal man. You told me I only had to do this for a few months," shrieked Supreme.

"Deals are made to be broken," laughed Smith.

Supreme glared at him. "I'm marrying Kimi next year. She'll graduate from law school this year, and I want to do things right by her. I want to do right by these kids in here. I don't want this stuff to be on my conscience. This is not right." He coughed. "How can you sleep at night, man, knowing all of this is going on," he asked as glanced around.

Smith paused before saying, "Since when do a *big time* drug dealer like you sympathize with someone, especially with these low lives?"

A frown flashed across Supreme's oval shaped face. "Whatever . . .

mark my words, Smith," blurted Supreme as he drew even closer to him. "I'm done with this mess in a month . . . and don't try any funny stuff."

"Is that a threat?" smirked Smith.

"It's a threat and a promise," said Supreme. "You may be a Sergeant with a gun. . . a crooked one at that . . . but you know I will shed you no mercy if you step in my way."

Smith stood silent as if Supreme's words scared him. "I guess you will get your little runners to mess me up and leave me for wild dogs to eat . . . or set me on fire alive . . . or bury me in a landfill with cement poured on?" laughed Smith. "I heard that's what you have commanded your runners to do with the other people. I wonder if your father taught you how to do those things. He's a smart man that I need in my corner. I heard he has a few *wrinkles* that he hides behind his entrepreneurship but he funnels his money into real estate and other businesses. So, I can only imagine what you would *try* to do to me," he chuckled.

Supreme exhaled. "You can decide your own fate if you come after me or any of Kimi's family," said Supreme as he walked away and marched up the steps to another area of the building. That was the last time Hope had seen Supreme in the building.

"Well, I guess you better appoint one of your little runners to take your place . . . before you resign," laughed Smith as he pivoted his feet to walk away but not before he glanced in Hope's direction.

"My . . . oh my," Smith grinned as he walked toward Hope with a wide smile on his face. "Aren't you a pretty little cookie?" He licked his lips. "You're new here," he said. "What's your name?"

Hope looked around for her mother before saying, "Hope."

"Come with me," whispered Smith as he stretched out his hand toward her.

A loud sound from a car horn pierced inside Hope's white Range Rover as she veered into another lane. The sudden loud sound snapped Hope out of her journey down memory lane saving her temporarily from her dreadful past with Smith.

Hope drove down the street, passing a seafood restaurant that was hosting a grand opening. She watched as customers lined up along the narrow sidewalk to enter the restaurant. Hope yearned for the day that she could find a location for her catering company.

She glanced in her rearview mirror, noticing that a car had been traveling in the same direction for a while. She continued to drive by several buildings, glancing inside them to see their layouts. She wanted a business located in the heart of downtown but the rental fees exceeded her projected start-up budget. So, Hope settled with trying to locate a space on the outskirts of downtown Raleigh.

Loud screeching sounds pierced the air as cars pressed on their breaks to avoid running a red light.

Hope turned up the music in her Range Rover to allow soft jazz to flow inside as she waited for the light to turn green. Her gaze locked in on a billboard that displayed a telephone number for reporting human trafficking. Hope swallowed, thanking God that she was never a victim of that.

Hope glanced in her rearview mirror. A black Lexus continued to follow her. Her heart pounded as she wondered if someone was stalking her. She pressed on the gas hoping to create some distance between her Range Rover and the black Lexus.

She veered onto Highway I-85 North and noticed the black Lexus trailed after her, shortening their distance.

A nervous feeling gripped Hope, causing her hands to become sweaty as she held the steering wheel. Her heart beat faster and faster as the driver of the black Lexus pulled up beside her. It was Sloan. He was driving a rental car behind her.

Sloan apparently had a tracking device installed on her Range Rover. He was an engineer. He was capable of designing anything.

Hope was starting to feel like a prisoner within Sloan's exclusive world. Living with Sloan reminded her of Sergeant Smith's treacherous acts. She was Sergeant Smith's prisoner as a child and now she felt like Sloan's prisoner as an adult.

Chapter 29

Soft gospel music permeated Mrs. Brown's cozy apartment. The Saturday morning's bright sun glistened through the kitchen brushing against the cabinets.

"Oh, goodness, this is a delicious breakfast," uttered a medium-sized woman as her copper brown hand shoved cheesy grits into her round shaped lips.

"Thank you, first lady," said Mrs. Brown in a customary form whereby she called the pastor's wife, first lady.

"You sure do have a chef's hand," said a sandal brown man in a baritone voice as he launched a buttery soft biscuit between his lips while shifting his gaze between Mrs. Brown and his wife.

"Thank you so kindly, Pastor McCoy," said Mrs. Brown in a soft tone while wiping her mouth to make sure no grits were on her lips.

"I've been trying to get Doya to make biscuits like yours," chuckled Pastor McCoy while glancing at his wife.

"Well, you can keep praying 'cause my biscuits will never be as good as Mrs. Brown's biscuits," grinned Doya.

A ripple of laughter filled the kitchen nearly overshadowing the gospel music.

"How are your children?" asked Doya.

"They're fine," said Mrs. Brown. "What about your children?"

"They're good," replied Doya.

Pastor McCoy gulped down a glass of milk before parting his lips to say, "I'm glad you invited us over for this special breakfast," he uttered. "And . . . to do the special prayer for your friend," he said as his right eyebrow elevated toward the ceiling.

Mrs. Brown paused before speaking. "Yes, indeed, my friend and her daughters need a lot of prayers," said Mrs. Brown while closing her eyes as she reflected upon Gloria's declining health.

Though she felt comfortable talking to Pastor McCoy and Doya, she was uncertain whether Gloria wanted her to disclose her health condition and her situation with Hope to others.

Doya stretched her long arm across the table and gently tapped Mrs. Brown's hand.

"From what you have shared . . . it seems like they need a restoration of their family bond," uttered Doya.

"They need a favor from God," interjected Pastor McCoy as he closed his eyes while rocking side by side as if the wooden chair caused a degree of discomfort.

"Yes, sir, they do," sighed Mrs. Brown knowing Pastor McCoy would never complain about the chair.

Mrs. Brown always felt good when Pastor McCoy and his wife came to see her. They had no problem visiting her in Cloverdale. They treated her with respect and never declined any meal she offered them.

Pastor McCoy whipped out a white handkerchief and rubbed his forehead where sweat beads had congregated.

"Does your friend attend our church?" asked Doya as a wrinkle flashed across her forehead. "I want to make sure I didn't forget to add her to our sick and shut-in list."

"No, she doesn't. She went to a church on the other side of town before she got sick." Mrs. Brown exhaled recalling how people knew that church's pastor was adamant about never stepping foot in Cloverdale.

"Well, you know I'm always willing to pray for someone . . . even if they don't attend my church . . . and even if they don't believe in the God I serve," said Pastor McCoy in a firm tone. "So, it's no problem at all for me to pray for your friend."

"Thank you," Mrs. Brown said as she took a slow sip of pulp free orange juice. "My friend has had a very . . . very rough life."

"Well, I'm a firm believer that God can help your friend," said Doya.

"I know he can," Mrs. Brown paused. "I just pray that God touches her daughter's heart to help her mother if she can help."

"What do you mean?" asked Doya in a puzzling tone.

"I don't know much about medical stuff," Mrs. Brown inhaled. "But my friend needs her oldest daughter to get tested to see if she has some type of cells to treat her." She paused. "My friend's youngest daughter can't help her. She got some type of condition and can't help her mother."

"So, is her oldest daughter going to get tested?" inquired Doya as her eyebrows connected.

Mrs. Brown remained silent for a few seconds. "My friend doesn't think so. She feels that her daughter would rather let her die than help her."

"That's really sad to treat a mother like that," muffled Doya. "But God is in control."

Loud music penetrated through the apartment walls drowning out the soft gospel music as a jeep drove up the street.

Mrs. Brown glanced out of her window before speaking. "Her oldest daughter hasn't called or visited her in years."

"Then how does she know that her oldest daughter will not help her?"

asked Doya.

"Somehow, her younger daughter, Ivey, got in contact with her elder one, Hope," uttered Mrs. Brown. "Gloria feels like Hope wants her to die," said Mrs. Brown in a remorseful tone as she suddenly realized that she had said their names. But she was certain Pastor McCoy and Doya would never repeat their conversation.

"Interesting . . . interesting," mumbled Pastor McCoy as if he knew something that Mrs. Brown and Doya didn't. He clenched his fist together and bowed his head as he mumbled a prayer.

The conversation between Mrs. Brown and Doya ceased for a few seconds.

"I'm going to keep you uplifted in prayer, Mrs. Brown," said Doya. "I see this is bothering you."

"It does . . . but my faith is strong," said Mrs. Brown.

A ray of sunshine beamed inside the kitchen as if the clouds had parted to allow light to flow directly inside.

"God knows best," said Doya. "He knows the plans he has for all of us."

"I know," confirmed Mrs. Brown. "But I need God to work in favor of Gloria, Ivey and Hope."

Pastor McCoy slowly lifted his head. A wide smile flashed across his round face as he leaned forward before saying, "God works in mysterious ways. But you must remember that forgiveness must come freely."

A sense of peace flowed through Mrs. Brown.

Chapter 30

Hope sat at her small office desk inside her house. She strolled through her company's website to review the upcoming scheduled catering services. She leaned back, wondering why Sloan had followed her earlier today. She exhaled slowly as she reflected upon Sloan telling her that he didn't trust women. Yet, Hope had tried countless times to assure Sloan that she was a faithful wife.

A beeping sound echoed inside the house. Hope glanced at the caller ID.

"Hello, Sloan," said Hope in a pleasant tone.

"I am calling you to see if you need anything from the grocery store?" asked Sloan in an inquisitive tone.

"No. I have everything to prepare dinner," responded Hope.

"Where are the twins?"

"They are playing in the playroom. I already gave them a snack."

"Okay. I will be home shortly," said Sloan.

Hope slowly hung up the telephone. Her mind started racing, trying to rationale why Sloan had actually called the house. Hope paused as she realized that Sloan apparently knew that she had been reviewing her upcoming catering orders on her website for him to call and ask her if she needed anything from the grocery store. Hope was convinced that Sloan had designed a system to monitor what she reviewed on the computer.

But how? she thought.

A beeping sound echoed again. Hope looked at the high-tech caller ID. Her heart stopped beating. It was her mother. Hope listened as the telephone rang several times before coming to a halt. Her body flinched as the ringing sound pierced the air again a few minutes later. This time it was Ivey.

Hope tapped her slender fingers on her laptop. She was more focused on reviewing her upcoming catering orders than speaking with Gloria and Ivey on the telephone. Hope leaned back in her chair as her mind slowly traveled down memory lane . . .

A cold breeze wafted through the abandoned building. Hope's slender body held firmly to the flimsy blanket that her mother had given her before venturing off to perform endless tricks in a corner.

"Come with me," said Smith as his black police uniform blended with the darkness that was growing inside the building from the sun slowly drifting behind the moon.

Hope's head shifted from side to side. "No . . . I can't go with you," she said hoping her mother would hear her talking to the man. Unfortunately, her soft voice wasn't loud enough.

Hope glanced around noticing no one looked in her direction . . . not even her mother. Two little girls, one pale white and the other cinnamon brown sat nearby playing with rocks on the floor.

"I have to stay here with them," said Hope as she looked at the two little girls.

The two little girls' bodies flinched as they looked up at the man as if they knew something that Hope didn't know. Hope looked around, noticing that the girls' mother was busy *serving* a man while Gloria was entertaining two men.

"Get up now!" ordered Smith in a low tone as he jerked on Hope's skinny arm.

Hope looked in Gloria's direction. Her heart sunk when she noticed that Gloria was squatting in front of two men who had their pants pulled down.

"Can they come with me?" asked Hope in a nervous tone as she looked at Smith while pointing at the two little girls.

"No, I've already played a little game with them before," chuckled Smith as he tugged on Hope's arm. "We're only going to my patrol car. I want to show you something inside it."

Hope glanced at the two little girls while noticing the fear that unfolded on their faces.

"I can't go," repeated Hope as nervousness gripped her.

A river of tears formed in Hope's eyes as she glanced at her mother. Hope was too scared to scream because Gloria demanded that Hope remained quiet at all times when they were inside the abandoned building.

Smith applied a tight grip to Hope's wrist nearly dragging her as he strolled out of the building toward his patrol car.

Darkness consumed Hope's eyes as she looked around. The sun was no longer in sight preventing any light from shining in the dark alley.

"We're just going to drive to a secret cut in the woods," said Smith as he tossed Hope in the backseat. "Don't get any funny ideas of jumping out because this door automatically locks," said Smith as he slammed the door.

"I want to go back to my mommy," repeated Hope several times as she glanced out the window bypassing rolls of abandoned buildings before arriving at a cluster of tall trees in the woods.

"It's too late for all of that," barked Smith as he drove further inside the woods. He hopped out of the front of the car, opened the back door and flopped beside Hope's nervous body.

"Come here . . . and stop crying," Smith said firmly as he licked his lips while strolling his finger along the ridges of Hope's face. "We're going to play a little game."

Those were the last words that Hope heard Sergeant Smith say before she passed out from the unbearable pain that stormed through her body.

An hour later, a tearful Hope walked slowly through the abandoned building. Every step Hope took toward the corner where the two little girls were sitting reaped pain from her thighs up to the inner core of her stomach. The little girls' gazes lowered toward the floor as if they were familiar with the torture that Hope had endured.

A truckload of pain tumbled through Hope's little body as she fastened her pants, noticing that she no longer had on panties. She clenched her stomach trying to control the pain that stormed through her. She tried to sit down but the pain forced her to stand.

"Where's my crack?" hollered Gloria as the two men walked away from her.

"Here," said one of the men as he tossed something toward Gloria.

Hope's heart beat faster than a drummer as she walked toward her mother.

"Mama . . . my stomach hurts," said Hope in a nervous tone as she held her stomach.

"Go and sit down, Hope!" shrieked Gloria causing Hope to nearly faint.

A busload of fear rattled Hope's body. But she was in a lot of pain.

"Mama . . . somebody hurt my stomach," muffled Hope as she watched Gloria clamp her lip on a glass crack pipe smoking the crack that the man had tossed to her.

"Hope! Do you see me doing something?" blurted Gloria. "Go and sit down."

"But my stomach is hurting, mama," mumbled Hope in a painful tone. "A policeman hurt my stomach. He pulled down my panties and hurt me," cried Hope.

Gloria closed her eyes and her frail body shifted to the side while she allowed the crack to overpower her.

Tears streamed down Hope's five-year-old face as she watched Gloria close her eyes as if she was trying to enjoy every second of her high. Hope waited patiently for Gloria to respond. Time seemed to have come to a standstill as Hope watched her mother.

Rumbling noise echoed from a corner.

"Hey, where are you going?" yelled a skinny lady as a man ran out of the abandoned building pulling up his pants. "Give me my crack!"

Hope glanced at Gloria noticing that she was still in a daze from smoking crack. Hope slid to the floor as if she were a centipede. Pain ricocheted through her body like a cannon. She placed her small golden brown hand over her stomach trying to control the pain. Her body trembled like a leaf on a windy day. Her mind couldn't process what had actually happened to her. She didn't know the word for it. But she knew that a constant throbbing pain traveled from between her thighs up to the core of her stomach.

A tear rolled down Hope's face as the smell of Sergeant Smith's poignant cologne seemed to have glued to her shirt. She forced herself to go back to sleep wishing that she could disappear.

"Mama," winced Hope as the pain continued to travel through her body. "Mama, please help me. I'm scared," said Hope as she fell asleep praying that someone . . . anybody . . . a *Guardian Angel* would rescue her.

Unfortunately, Hope endured many more painful days at the wrath of Smith . . . and other men in the abandoned building without an ounce of help from her mother . . . or anyone.

These were the moments when five-year-old Hope's love for her mother slowly faded and hatred started to build.

Chapter 31

A bright sun beamed rays inside Hope's kitchen.

Hope closed her eyes as she reflected on the last conversation she had with Ivey. Peace spread through Hope as she realized that Ivey was right. Ivey's father was nice to Hope. He was the one who had rescued Hope from the routine ventures with Gloria to different abandoned buildings as if they were camping trips and vacation resorts. He was the one who removed her from the *painful acts* that routinely caused her stomach to hurt.

Hope slowly rubbed her hands as she recalled the day that Ivey's father became her *Guardian Angel* . . .

Five-year-old Hope pressed her eyes firmly together trying to allow sleep to overpower her hunger pains. The bright morning sun beamed inside the abandoned building. Hope rubbed her eyes as she noticed that a tall café brown man tugged on her mother's arm.

"Have you thought about what I asked you, Gloria?" asked the man as he pulled off a condom, tossing it in a corner.

Gloria used a condom with every trick she performed as if it was a cardinal rule. She'd gotten into countless arguments with men who begged her to let them go bareback. But Gloria was adamant about following her cardinal rule.

"I'm serious about what I said to you," uttered the tall man as he zipped up his pants.

Hope recognized him. He had been a frequent customer of Gloria for over two months.

The man glanced around the building. The sun's rays pressed against his navy blue business suit. It was obvious that he was on his way to work. But he made a pit stop to order a morning blowjob from Gloria.

Clusters of acne overtook his face, revealing every blemish. Without a doubt, his selection of women was slim to none—other than Gloria and perhaps other prostitutes. For some reason, it appeared that he had fallen in love with a bona fide crackhead.

"I'd like to take you home with me," he said glancing around. "This isn't a place for you," said the man as he straightened his jacket.

A prowling sound flowed through the abandoned building as a gray cat strolled through.

"Look, Eugene, you know what I do. You know that I'm a crackhead," shrieked Gloria as she slowly elevated from being on her knees to standing in front of him. "You don't need a woman like me," she said in a harsh tone.

"I know what you are, but I can help you change. I'll pay for you to get some help," he said as he reached for Gloria's caramel brown hand.

"It's not that easy," muffled Gloria as she looked in Hope's direction. "Let's go, Hope!" she bawled as she brushed off her red mini skirt while wiping her wet, crusty lips.

Hope peeped her head above a stack of small cardboard boxes that Gloria had placed around her, trying to prevent Hope from seeing the daily tricks that were conducted in the abandoned building. Yet, little did Gloria know, Hope had already seen countless sexual acts performed by the men and women prostitutes.

A loud sound pierced the air as car horns blew, causing Hope to flinch.

"Who is that?" asked Eugene as he looked at Gloria while pointing at Hope.

"*Why?*" asked Gloria in a hateful tone.

Hope's eyes widened as the tall man walked toward her. Her body trembled as if she were sitting on top of a washing machine that was spinning. Her mind raced, wondering if the man would take her to a dark corner and make her stomach hurt.

"What is your name, little girl?" asked Eugene in a calm tone.

Hope's lips felt as if they were cemented together as she walked toward Gloria.

"I didn't know you were over there, in that corner," said Eugene as his bushy untamed eyebrows connected. "In fact, I have never seen you in here."

Hope gawked at Gloria, hoping that her mother would not allow the man to take her to a dark corner.

"Gloria, is this your daughter?" inquisitively blurted Eugene. "Please don't tell me you've been bringing your daughter in here."

Gloria stood speechless as if she was a mannequin.

"Answer me, Gloria," shrieked Eugene as a shaft of sunlight flashed on his unattractive face.

Gloria sneered as if the man had no right to question her.

Eugene pulled out his cell phone, dialing a telephone number.

Gloria's eyes widened bigger than a walnut.

"I hope you aren't calling the police or child welfare," whispered Gloria.

Eugene walked toward Hope, grabbing her hand as he pressed the telephone to his perky ear.

For some unknown reason, a sense of peace enveloped Hope as her mind convinced her that Eugene would never harm her. His unattractive face made him appear scary. But he was not. Hope's small hand slowly gripped

Eugene's hand, hoping that he would persuade Gloria to permanently leave the abandoned building.

"Good morning, Mrs. Poole. This is Dr. Eugene Rankin. I will not be in the office today and possibly tomorrow," he said as his gaze shifted between Hope and Gloria. "Please reschedule all of my meetings for today and tomorrow."

Gloria squinted. "Are you a doctor?" she smirked.

"We can talk about all after we get out of here," said Eugene as he scratched his blemished forehead, revealing a burn mark on one side of his face.

"Who said my daughter and I were leaving with you?" blurted Gloria, causing Hope to flinch.

Eugene paused before speaking. "Listen, Gloria, if you don't leave this place right now, with or without me, I will call and report you."

Gloria glared at Eugene. "And I'll tell the police how you have been buying . . . *cookie* from me twice a day," shrieked Gloria as she looked at Eugene while snatching Hope's hand from him.

Clearly, Hope knew Eugene did not buy any cookies from her mother.

"You can't prove that I've bought anything from you. But I can prove that you have your daughter in this lowlife building," blurted Eugene as he pointed at Hope.

Gloria tilted her head toward the broken ceiling.

Eugene walked slowly toward Gloria, reaching for her hand. "Gloria, I don't want to argue with you. I want to help you and your daughter. I'm not a medical doctor. But I'm a researcher."

Rattling noises echoed in the air as birds flew around inside the broken ceiling.

"Gloria, let me take you home with me. I can help you get clean," he said.

Surely, he wanted to ensure he had access to her *cookies* on demand.

"No, I'm not going with you. I'm going to my own apartment," smirked Gloria.

"I didn't know you had an apartment," frowned Eugene.

"There's a lot you don't know," said Gloria as she walked away from Eugene while dragging Hope behind her.

"I'll give you and your daughter a ride. Please let me help you, Gloria."

Gloria's steps came to a sudden halt. The hot summer heat brushed against Hope's face as she walked toward the broken door.

"Let me help you and your daughter," whispered Eugene as he walked outside the abandoned building with them. "I can help you get clean."

Hope watched as a skinny man strolled inside the building with a needle in his hand as if he was a zombie. She glanced up at Eugene. The rays of the sunlight revealed layers of acne that bordered a large burn mark on his face. Yet, he had a peaceful demeanor about himself.

Eugene reached for Gloria's hand again. "Please let me help you and your daughter," he said in a sincere tone. "I will pay for you to get treatment."

Somehow, Eugene had eventually convinced Gloria to cease her interest to venture into abandoned buildings. He upheld his promise to take care of Hope and send Gloria to treatment. Of course, Gloria relapsed a few times before she finally mastered the ability to shake off her craving for crack.

Gloria and Hope eventually moved in with Eugene. Within a year, Gloria and Eugene got married and they had Hope's sister, Ivey. Gloria made sure Eugene underwent plastic surgery. As for Hope, she felt as though God had sent her a guardian angel—Dr. Eugene Rankin.

A soft, warm touch pressed against Hope's small hand, causing her to snap out of her dreadful memory lane. A warm smile stretched across Hope's face as she looked at her twins. She wrapped her long, slender arms around them, trying to embrace the moment.

The thought of someone ever harming her twins sent chills down Hope's spine.

Chapter 32

An elegant crystal chandelier dangled in the middle of the antique white painted ceiling. Hunter-green and gold lounge chairs assembled throughout the lobby creating an upscale appearance in Latham Springs Hotel. Crown molding decorated the oatmeal painted walls. Italian marble floors paraded around the lobby, highlighting the finest qualities of the luxury hotel.

Hope felt a little nervous as she assorted several food samples on gold trays. The delicious smells of lemon pound cake and red velvet cake wafted through the hotel's small conference room. The savory scent of lemon-peppered salmon mingled through the room, mixing with the barbeque chicken breasts.

Hope glanced at her white chef attire, making sure she did not spill any food on her shirt. Her clean pressed attire created a professional image. She walked outside the conference room glancing around the extravagant lobby as she waited for her customers.

A cluster of conversations from hotel guests could be heard throughout the lobby.

Hope's heart pounded rapidly as a slender caramel brown woman slowly approached her holding hands with a chestnut brown man. Hope's gaze scanned the man's muscular physique, perfectly trimmed mustache, and tamed beard that outlined his unblemished skin. His dimples defined his well-attractive face. Hope's gaze shifted toward a tall man whose light brown eyes locked in with hers as he walked beside the woman and the chestnut brown man.

"Hope," shouted the tall man as he nearly galloped toward her as she entered the small conference room. "I can't believe this is you," said the man as his well-groomed eyebrows connected creating a puzzling look on his face. "It's been such a long time since I last saw you," he said as he wrapped his long muscular arms around Hope.

"Hello, Tony. How are you doing?" Hope asked in a slightly uneasy tone, knowing that she had vanished without a trace seven years ago from Charlotte, North Carolina.

"I'm doing great," smiled Tony. "I see you're doing well for yourself," he said as he looked around glancing at the colorful arranged food samples on a table.

"So, I guess you're going to act like Tony is the only person in this room, Hope?" laughed the slender woman whose jet black hair showcased her high cheekbones and flawlessly beautiful skin.

"Hello, Tiffany," said Hope in a soft tone as she reached forward to hug Tiffany.

"I was uncertain whether it was you or not when I called the catering company a few weeks ago," winced Tiffany.

A cool breeze swept through the small conference room.

"I um . . . recognized your voice."

"You did?" muffled Tiffany before pausing. "Oh, Hope, this is my husband, Vance. He wanted to tag along with Tony and me to try some of the samples," chuckled Tiffany.

"Well, I'm glad that you called Serenity Catering Services," said Hope. "I am delighted that you drove here to meet me."

"It was no problem to drive here from Charlotte," smiled Tiffany as she gripped Hope's hand, brushing against her wedding ring. "Are you married?" smiled Tiffany.

"Yes," grinned Hope. "I've been married almost six years."

"Really?" said Tony as he glanced at Hope.

"We were childhood friends," said Tiffany as she looked at Vance while glancing at Hope. "I haven't seen Hope in over seven years."

Vance winced as his gaze shifted to Hope and Tiffany. "Is this the Hope that you told me about before?" inquired Vance.

"Yes," responded Tiffany as she smiled at Hope. "She vanished seven years ago," said Tiffany as a frown flashed across her caramel brown face.

"Seven years," said Vance.

Tony pressed his back against the ocean blue painted wall in the conference room.

Hope exhaled slowly, trying to maintain her professionalism. "I prepared a few items that I remember were your mother's favorites," smiled Hope as she walked toward the food samples, trying to change the topic of conversation.

Tiffany slowly strolled beside Hope toward the food.

"I hope that these samples taste as good as they look," laughed Tony.

"Trust me, they do, Tony," blurted Hope in a confident tone.

"I guess we will find out," grinned Tiffany as she nudged Hope.

Conversations ceased for a few minutes as Tiffany, Tony and Vance ate.

"It seems like my mother did teach you something," chuckled Tiffany as she planted a small piece of salmon into her mouth. "This is delicious, Hope. I know my mother will love this."

A peal of laughter leaped out of Hope's mouth. "I am sure she will. I added some of her favorite spices to the food."

"Tiffany, it seems like you have some competition," said Vance as he nibbled on a slice of lemon pound cake.

"Whatever," smirked Tiffany as she poked Vance in his arm.

"Don't hate, Tiffany," laughed Tony.

Hope and Tiffany joined Tony in a contagious laugh.

"So how long have you been working at Serenity Catering Services?" asked Tony as his teeth clamped down on a small piece of barbeque chicken.

"I'm the owner," said Hope in a proud tone as she noticed Tony looking at her hips.

"You are?" said Tiffany in an exciting tone. "I am proud of you. How long have you been operating this business?"

"I just started a few months ago. I worked at a few taverns to learn some tricks of the trade. I even went to a culinary school."

"Look at you, *Ms. Big Time*," blurted Tony. "I guess my mother contributed to your plans to open your own business," smiled Tony as he scratched his smooth forehead.

"Yes, she did," grinned Hope. "She definitely taught me how to cook and bake."

Footsteps strolled past the small conference room as hotel guests walked by.

"My mother will be surprised to have her seventieth birthday event catered."

"Don't try to take all of the credit," blurted Tony.

Laughter filled the air.

"You two are speaking as if you've decided to let me cater the event."

"Oh yes! You're hired," blurted Tony as he looked at Hope. "We will send all the details about what we want to your website."

"Don't tell mama we are trying to host this event, Hope," squinted Tiffany as if she already knew Hope had stayed in contact with her mother.

"Don't worry about that," smiled Hope.

"The food was good," said Tiffany as she wiped her mouth with a napkin. "Mama's birthday is November 2nd."

"I know," grinned Hope, recalling that November 2nd was also her twins' birthday.

"So, you've got three months from today to plan this event, " grinned Tiffany.

"Your mother told me that you're a dentist now, Tony," said Hope.

"Yes, that's correct," said Tony in a modest tone. "At the rate you're baking these delicious sweet cakes, I'm sure someone will get a cavity from them."

"*Whatever*, Tony. I know you wished your wife could cook like this," smirked Tiffany. "Maybe she should use her greenish-brown cat eyes to help her to read recipes to cook for you and your children."

A sense of calm overtook Hope as she laughed with Tiffany and Tony. She quickly reflected upon her teenage years of playing with them in Cloverdale. She did not have to worry about using the King's English around them.

"I saw your mother the other day, Hope. She didn't look well," said Tiffany.

Hope got quiet as if her lips were stapled together.

"Your mom said you're a doctor," said Hope, ignoring Tiffany's statement.

Tiffany's bow shaped lips slowly separated as she gazed at Hope.

"Yes, I am. I deliver babies and provide other services to women."

"That's good. I know your mother is proud of you," said Hope.

"Some days, it's not good," frowned Tiffany.

"What do you mean?" asked Hope puzzled.

"I've been getting a few young girls and women who have been through awful experiences," sighed Tiffany. "Some of them have been through human trafficking."

"*Human Trafficking?*" mumbled Hope barely above a whisper.

Overhead soft melodies flowed through the speakers in the conference room.

"It is becoming a growing issue in different states," uttered Vance in a low tone. "Now, it is becoming an issue here in North Carolina."

"He's the chief attorney with the FBI," said Tony as he looked at Hope while pointing at Vance with a prideful smile on his face. Without a doubt, Tony was elated that Vance was his brother-in-law.

Vance looked at Tony as if he didn't want Hope to know his occupation.

A beeping sound pierced the air as a text message appeared on Hope's cell phone. It was Sloan. Hope cleared her throat. "I'm glad you were able to meet me to taste a few items," she said in a hasty tone as if she had to finish her meeting.

"We are, too," said Tiffany in a puzzled manner. "Can I call you sometime?"

"Yes, you can call me," chuckled Hope. "I'm a big girl."

"Where do you live?" asked Tiffany in an upbeat tone.

Hope paused for a few seconds, capturing Tiffany, Vance and Tony's attention.

"I live here . . . in Raleigh," said Hope as she noticed Vance peering at her as if he detected something was not right.

"Where?" asked Tiffany as she brushed a crumb off her pastel pink shirt.

Hope glanced out of the window. She knew Sloan would never approve of anyone visiting their home. Her heart was torn between reuniting with her childhood best friend and upholding Sloan's orders. But she missed sharing secrets with Tiffany.

"I live on the other side of town," said Hope as she glanced at her watch.

A puzzled look formed on Vance's face as if he was using his FBI techniques to analyze Hope.

"I have to leave in a few minutes," smiled Hope while reading Sloan's second text message. "I have to pick up my twins," uttered Hope.

"Twins," shrieked Tiffany with excitement. "I have twins too. A boy and girl."

"Me too." Hope paused before speaking. "What a coincidence for you and me to have twins." She cleared her throat. "What about you, Tony?"

"I have a son and a daughter," said Tony as if he wanted to provide Hope with a quick update. "But they are not twins. How old are your twins?"

"Five."

"My twins are one," interjected Tiffany before saying, "What are your twins' names?"

"Jayden and Jayla," Hope blurted. "What are your twins' names?"

"Vance, Jr. and Via."

"What does your husband do?"

Hope hesitated before responding. "He's an engineer."

"Did he grow up in Cloverdale?" inquired Tony as if he was desperate to know.

Hope chuckled softly. "No, Tony," blushed Hope, remembering that Tony had asked her for a kiss in high school. But she had declined his offer.

"What is his name?" asked Tony as he opened a bottle of water.

"Are you interrogating me, Tony?" chuckled Hope as she packed up the trays, noticing that they had eaten most of the food samples.

"No, Hope," said Tony in a caring tone. "I'm just trying to figure out why you're acting so top secret."

Silence floated in the air like pollen.

"Is everything okay, Hope?" asked Tiffany in a familiar supporting tone that Hope remembered Tiffany used to comfort her when they were teenagers.

Hope closed her eyes as she tilted her head toward the cream painted ceiling. She felt torn because as a teenager, she felt comfortable telling Tiffany everything. They shared secrets. But now, things were different. Sloan made Hope feel trapped as if she lived a life of secrecy. She did not feel comfortable telling Tiffany that she felt like she was married to a stranger.

Chapter 33

The sizzling, evening sun beamed inside Mrs. Brown's apartment. A shallow breeze drifted through the front door, barely drowning out the heat waves on the first day of August.

"Mrs. Brown, you've got to turn on that air conditioner," blurted Mrs. Ruth as she entered Mrs. Brown's apartment.

"It feels okay in here to me," chuckled Mrs. Brown as she fanned herself.

"I understand, but you've got to reduce the heat in here just a little bit," said Mrs. Ruth as she turned on the air conditioner.

"Ruth, don't be coming in here running up my electric bill."

"I'm not. I'll cut it off in a few minutes," said Mrs. Ruth as she fingered through her wavy black wig while signaling for Jasmine and Taylor to have seat at the table.

The delicious aroma of the baked chicken breasts, macaroni and cheese and collard greens wafted through the small kitchen.

"I'm glad you let me cook for you and your grandchildren, Ruth."

"I'm not turning down any of your home-cooked meals, Mrs. Brown," said Ruth.

"It's going to be a sad day in Cloverdale when you stop cooking for your customers."

"Go and wash up, kids," smiled Mrs. Brown while ignoring Ruth.

"Yes, ma'am," said Jasmine as Taylor trailed behind her to the bathroom.

"Ruth, are you going to close my front door?" said Mrs. Brown as she squinted. "I can't cool down the entire Cloverdale."

Ruth strolled toward the door as her hot pink pants plastered around her hips.

"That don't make no sense, Ruth," blurted Mrs. Brown. "You ain't got no business wearing these *hot mama pants*."

"Mrs. Brown, I've been going through detox. It's a slow process," smiled Ruth.

"What detox?" squinted Mrs. Brown.

"Mrs. Brown, my grandchildren have really changed me."

"If you say so," said Mrs. Brown as she glanced at Ruth's tight cream shirt that revealed the creases of her cantaloupe shaped breasts.

"Give me some credit, Mrs. Brown," frowned Ruth. "I've stopped wearing my stilettos. Plus, I don't wear my colorful wigs or my halter tops anymore."

Pounding noise seeped through the walls in the small apartment, escaping from a deep blue metallic Tesla.

Mrs. Ruth quickly glanced out the window. "Oh, that's Chandy. I had some fond memories with him," she vaguely said while smiling.

Mrs. Brown closed her eyes as if she was saying a silent prayer for Ruth. "Nobody said you had to stop wearing your wigs. It wasn't the wigs, Ruth. It was your character and personality you had when you wore the wigs. Go and wash your hands," said Mrs. Brown as if Ruth had plucked a nerve.

"I'm going. I'm waiting on Jasmine and Taylor to come out of the bathroom."

"How are they doing?" whispered Mrs. Brown.

"I guess . . . they're doing a little better. They've been going to therapy," sighed Ruth. "But you know us folks don't do therapy. I've been told therapy is for people who don't have all of their screws tight in their head."

"I used to think the same way. But I've learned that therapy can be good," said Mrs. Brown. "Some days, I feel like I should've gotten therapy after my husband died. I took it really hard." She sighed.

"I remember," said Ruth. "But you know how we think about therapy."

"I know. So, will the girls be ready to go to school?" asked Mrs. Brown trying to slightly change the topic.

"I guess time will tell. This will be their first time ever going to a real school."

"I will keep them in my prayers," muffled Mrs. Brown.

Footsteps trailed back in the kitchen as Jasmine and Taylor returned and sat at the maple wood table.

"Mrs. Brown, have you seen Gloria lately?" asked Ruth in an unsettling tone as she stood, heading to the bathroom to wash her hands. "She looks bad off."

"I know," sighed Mrs. Brown. "I visited her a few weeks ago."

"Gloria told me that she needs something from her daughter, Hope, to help her condition," said Ruth as she slowly walked toward the bathroom. "After what Gloria put that girl through, I doubt Hope will ever help her."

"Go and wash your hands, Ruth," ordered Mrs. Brown.

"Well, it's the truth, Mrs. Brown. Everybody in Cloverdale knows how Gloria treated Hope. It was terrible."

"Go and wash your hands, Ruth," repeated Mrs. Brown firmly.

Mrs. Brown sat at the small maple wood table as she smiled at Jasmine and Taylor.

"How have you been, Jasmine?"

"I'm okay," muffled Jasmine as she adjusted a button on her purple shirt.

"What about you, Taylor?"

"I'm okay," mumbled Taylor as a small smile flashed on her face. "I'm glad me and my sister are with our grandmother. She helps us a lot."

"She really does help us," uttered Jasmine in a low tone. "She's funny too."

A peaceful feeling flowed through Mrs. Brown as she poured Jasmine and Taylor some homemade lemonade.

"I'm glad to hear that," said Mrs. Brown as she looked at Taylor's hair, noticing that hair had finally covered all of the previous patches on her small head.

Footsteps swarmed into the kitchen. "I'm back," said Ruth. "Now, let's eat."

Mrs. Brown peered at Ruth. "I thought you went to a bathroom in Vegas."

"I had to tend to some business in the bathroom," smirked Ruth.

Soft chuckles flowed from Jasmine and Taylor's mouths.

"Let's say grace," said Mrs. Brown as she bowed her head.

A few seconds later, Mrs. Brown lifted her small head. "Now, we can eat, Ruth."

"This food tastes delicious," mumbled Ruth while eating some collard greens.

"Jasmine and Taylor told me that they've been doing good," said Mrs. Brown.

"That's right," smiled Ruth.

Jasmine wiped her mouth. "Taylor has gotten better," whispered Jasmine as she smiled at Taylor. "She no longer pees in the bed," uttered Jasmine in a supportive tone. "She used to pee on herself every time she saw one of the leaders coming near her," muffled Jasmine as she slightly lowered her head.

"I was scared, Jasmine," mumbled Taylor. "I tried to control the pee, but the pee just kept running down my leg when I saw one of them."

Jasmine slid closer to Taylor. "I am happy that you got better," said Jasmine as she lovingly rubbed Taylor's hand. "She doesn't pee in the bed . . . or pee on herself anymore," sighed Jasmine. Perhaps, she was delighted that she no longer had to wake up smelling the astringent scent of pee roaming from Taylor's twin bed in their bedroom.

Taylor bashfully cut her eyes at Jasmine.

"That is good, Taylor. I am proud of you," said Mrs. Brown.

"Taylor had nightmares and peed in the bed for several weeks until her therapist and psychiatrist were able to help her cope with her PTSD and fear," Mrs. Ruth said.

Mrs. Brown cleared her throat. "PTSD? Are you talking about post-traumatic stress disorder?" asked Mrs. Brown as she slowly closed her eyes. She knew exactly what PTSD was because her brother Lamont had been diagnosed with it after he was discharged from the military.

"Yes," winced Taylor.

"I don't cut myself no more," said Jasmine in a slow manner.

"Cut?" inquired Mrs. Brown as her gaze pivoted between Jasmine and Ruth while pushing a spoonful of potatoes into her mouth.

"Yes, ma'am. I used to cut my legs and stomach with a paperclip or ink pen when I was . . . going through that stuff. I'm glad the leaders kept the knives and stuff locked up," chattered Jasmine in a low tone.

"Her therapist and psychiatrist said Jasmine did those self-injurious behaviors to cope with all of the trauma she was going through. But she has stopped doing them now," said Ruth in an upbeat tone as if she was trying to reassure Jasmine to refrain from harming herself.

A smile stretched across Taylor's golden-brown face as she smiled at Jasmine.

"Are you two ready for school?" asked Mrs. Brown. "It starts at the end of this month."

"I guess," muttered Jasmine. "We've never been to a regular school."

"I'm sure you will probably like it," said Mrs. Brown in a charming way.

"I have a school meeting next week," said Ruth. "It is something like a treatment team meeting. Their therapist and social worker will be there too. We are supposed to talk about a plan for Jasmine and Taylor."

"That would be nice," smiled Mrs. Brown as she watched Jasmine and Taylor nibble on their collard greens. "You'll be able to meet your teachers before school starts."

Taylor's head slowly lowered toward her olive green shirt, causing her chin to land on her chest. "I hope none of my teachers are part of that stuff."

"What stuff?" asked Mrs. Brown.

"Human Trafficking," said Jasmine. "The leaders had people working for them."

"Your teachers better not harm you or Taylor," shrieked Ruth in a stern tone, causing Taylor to flinch. "Let me know if you ever see somebody who used to work with the leaders. I'll make sure the real police get them."

Mrs. Brown cleared her throat, trying to cut through the sudden tense atmosphere. "Have you made any new friends?" asked Mrs. Brown in a slow tone.

"They've made a few friends here in Cloverdale," said Ruth.

"Now, that could be a good and bad thing," grinned Mrs. Brown.

A peal of laughter flowed off Taylor's tongue.

"We go to the community center," muffled Taylor.

"Okay, the kids there are good," said Mrs. Brown. "Tiffany and Tony went there when they were kids. They are volunteer tutors there now."

"Jasmine and Taylor met a few friends there," said Ruth as she poured herself a glass of lemonade. "They used to sit by themselves for the first couple of weeks. Now, they interact with the kids," said Ruth. "Plus, they get to see Tiffany sometimes."

"Yes, we do," smiled Jasmine. "We like Tiffany. Plus, we have one or two friends. But me and Taylor don't want them to know what we've been through," mumbled Jasmine as her gaze dropped.

Silence tumbled through the kitchen like a softball.

"They don't have to know," said Ruth in a supportive tone as she pressed her mahogany brown hand against Jasmine's pecan brown face to comfort her.

"I'm glad you're making friends," said Mrs. Brown. "They'll be the same kids you'll go to school with."

"I didn't know that," smiled Taylor. "I was scared about going to school. I thought we had to go to school with people we didn't know."

"At least, we will know somebody," muffled Jasmine.

"That's good," smiled Mrs. Brown while feeling delighted that Jasmine and Taylor were starting to feel relaxed and safe around others.

A cool breeze flowed from the air conditioner in the living room into the kitchen.

"Ruth! If you don't go and turn off that air conditioner," blurted Mrs. Brown, making Jasmine and Taylor laugh. "I'm going to tell you a thing or two that won't be nice."

"Goodness. Mrs. Brown, at least let us finish eating our food in coolness," chuckled Ruth as she slowly stood and headed toward the living room.

"I've already told you that the air conditioner is causing my bones to rattle."

"Okay . . . Okay, Mrs. Brown. I've turned it off. Jasmine and Taylor, please hurry up and eat before the heat waves return," chuckled Ruth.

"Trust me, Ruth, you have felt plenty of heatwaves," snapped Mrs. Brown.

"You are funny," smiled Jasmine. "I can tell you've been friends a long time."

"I know," laughed Taylor in a relaxed tone.

"This food was delicious, Mrs. Brown," smiled Ruth as she gathered the plates off the table and placed them in the sink, preparing to wash them.

Like clockwork Jasmine stood, pushing her chair under the table as she walked toward a corner to retrieve the broom and sweep the floor. She helped clean up every time she ate at Mrs. Brown's house. Taylor grabbed the dish towel and wiped off the table.

A sharp sound pierced the air as the telephone rang.

"Excuse me," said Mrs. Brown as she slowly stood and walked toward the telephone. Pain slithered through her ankles, signaling that arthritis had dominated her bones.

"Hello," said Mrs. Brown in a soft tone as she pressed the telephone to her ear.

"Mrs. Brown, I need to talk to you."

"Hold on," whispered Mrs. Brown. "I've got to take this call."

"Okay, we're leaving now," said Ruth as a frown stretched across her face as if she wanted to know who was on the telephone while closing the front door behind her.

"Hello. I'm back, Hope," uttered Mrs. Brown in a concerned tone.

"I need to talk to somebody," sobbed Hope in an alarming tone, causing uneasy feelings to storm through Mrs. Brown.

Mrs. Brown planted her small hand firmly against her chest as she listened to Hope sob endlessly on the telephone.

Chapter 34

Hope paced the tile floors of Charlotte Medical Hospital on the bright Monday morning. Her heart pivoted between worrying about the medical outcome of Jayla and Jayden's cochlear surgery and the excitement of her twins potentially being able to hear and speak.

Moisture built up between Hope's slender fingers as nervousness overpowered her.

"Hope, sit down," ordered Sloan while glancing at his watch.

"I can't, Sloan, I am so nervous. I pray everything goes well for the twins . . . especially Jayla," said Hope in an uneasy tone. "You know what Dr. Ericsson said about Jayla being anemic."

"I know. But Jayla's levels have improved, Hope."

Hope slowly closed her eyes. "But you know Dr. Ericsson said there was a chance that Jayla's levels could drop during the surgery," said Hope she continued to pace.

Chairs were neatly arranged in the waiting area, permitting several people to have ample space to sit. Some people sat with tearful eyes while others sat with a partial smile on their faces in the waiting area.

Sloan stood as he said, "Hope, sit down. I don't want you ending up as a patient too."

"I can't, Sloan," whispered Hope as she noticed Sloan glancing at his watch. "I hope you understand. I'm going for a walk in the hallway," said Hope as she strolled out of the waiting area.

Colorful pictures plastered against the alabaster white walls in the corridors as Hope walked, trying to ease her mind. Sunlight entered through the windows, balancing the cool breeze that flowed through the air conditioner vents in the corridors.

A tall well-groomed white man joined Hope in galloping up the tile floor.

"Hey, I'm Dean," said the man as he walked beside Hope.

"I'm Hope."

"I take it you have a loved one here in the hospital," said the man as a puzzled look flashed across his round shaped face.

"Yes, my husband and I are here with our twins," responded Hope as she glanced around, wondering why the man was talking to her.

A streak of curiosity flowed through Hope for a few seconds.

"Do you have a loved one here, too?" asked Hope.

"No, I'm here doing some work," responded the man.

Hope paused for a few seconds. "Oh, what type of work?" asked Hope.

"It's a long story," smiled the man as he glanced at his cell phone. "It was nice talking with you, Hope," said the man while heading toward another corridor.

Hope headed back to the waiting area. Sloan was no longer in there. Hope glanced around.

"Hello, if you're looking for the man who was sitting over there, he went that way," said a full-figured lady with a Spanish accent.

"Thank you," said Hope as she strolled out of the waiting area, looking for Sloan. Hope wondered why the strange lady kept staring at her. Something was not right.

Hope passed by a large window that overlooked a beautiful floral garden. Her gaze locked in on Sloan. She stood, watching Sloan's lips as he spoke with someone on the telephone while the sun beamed onto his navy blue shirt.

She felt puzzled as she read his lips, hoping that Sloan wouldn't see her. She continued to peer at his lips, focusing closely on every word that came out of his mouth. Sloan didn't notice Hope staring at him through the large glass window. She figured the glare from the morning sunlight prevented Sloan from seeing her standing there.

Hope continued to observe Sloan's lips as he said, "Things are getting a little questionable. You've got to slow down. Somebody has been trying to look at a few things on your system." He scratched his head. "I don't know. But whoever it is, they are using a high-tech system more advanced than mine. I will upgrade a few things on your system when I get there. I will fly out this evening." Sloan glanced at his watch.

Sloan hadn't told her that he had to attend a business trip with Mr. Gavino this evening. She paused, noticing that she didn't feel tired which was strange. Typically, the day before Sloan had to go on a business trip to meet Mr. Gavino, Hope always felt an intense level of fatigue. She figured stress had overtaken her body.

The bright rays of the sun beamed against the glass window, preventing Hope from fully seeing Sloan's lips for a few seconds. She moved to the opposite end of the large glass window, trying to capture a better view of Sloan's lips. She focused intensely on Sloan's lips as he said, "For now, you should only focus on selling the pizzas," paused Sloan. "Mr. Gavino! You don't need any more customers right now . . . or new staff. The pizza sales are doing great. Just focus on that for now. I'm telling you what is best," said Sloan as he slightly turned his head, which prevented Hope from seeing his lips.

A sharp pain pierced through Hope's heart. She wondered what type of business Sloan was really doing with Mr. Gavino. *Why did Sloan have to convince Mr. Gavino to only focus on selling pizzas?* thought Hope. *Something isn't right.*

Hope slowly walked back to the waiting area as if she was moving through quicksand. She glanced up the corridor, noticing that Dean was talking with a chubby chocolate brown man. Hope passed by them as if they were invisible as she continued to walk to the waiting area. Hope could feel them staring at her. *But why?* she wondered.

She flopped into a chair in the waiting room. Her heart pounded away as she tried to capture her breath from nearly jogging up the corridor.

A vibrating feeling pressed against her hip as her cell phone rang. She retrieved her cell phone from her hip as she walked out of the waiting area.

"Hello," whispered Hope.

"Hope, your mother has been rushed to Charlotte Medical Hospital," said Mrs. Brown in a startling tone. "Her sickness is taking over her body."

Hope's heart slammed against her chest. The thought of her mother being admitted to the same hospital where her twins were undergoing surgery sent chills down her spine.

Hope swallowed hard before speaking. "Mrs. Brown, I am here with my twins. I told you that they were getting their procedure done today."

"I understand that, Hope. But you should take the time to go and see your mother when she arrives there," begged Mrs. Brown.

Silence peaked on the phone. "I can't promise that, Mrs. Brown."

"Hope, please do it for me," begged Mrs. Brown. "Please have the respect to see your mother when she arrives. The ambulance is en route to the hospital."

An ounce of bitterness traveled through Hope's heart.

"I don't mean to be disrespectful, Mrs. Brown, but do you expect me to leave my children and go see Gloria?" spatted Hope.

"No, Hope. I'm am asking you to go see her when you get a chance."

Hope's gaze landed on Sloan as he walked toward her.

"I . . . I can't do that. I want to focus only on my twins right now."

"What is going on, Hope?" asked Sloan in a concerning tone.

Hope paused as if she wanted to ask Sloan the same question. She walked closer to him. "Mrs. Brown just told me that Gloria is en route to this hospital. Apparently, something has happened to her," Hope said in a nonchalant tone. "Mrs. Brown, I'll call you back later."

"Hope, please do it for me," begged Mrs. Brown. "God doesn't like this, Hope."

"I'm sure God didn't like how Gloria treated me either." Hope's head tilted toward the white ceiling. "So, please don't paint Gloria out to be a victim, Mrs. Brown. I'm the victim in this story." Hope paused. "I'm sorry, Mrs. Brown. I didn't mean to speak to you like that. But everybody got to stop making it seem like I've done something wrong."

"You've got to find it in your heart to forgive your mother."

Hope stared at the cell phone for a few seconds contemplating whether to hang up on Mrs. Brown before saying, "Well, today is not that day," mumbled Hope in a heartless tone. "I'm sorry . . . but I feel like you are trying to pressure me to forgive her. I've learned that forgiveness must be something someone volunteers to do. It shouldn't be forced."

Silence rippled through the cellphone.

"Hope, God has a way of touching our hearts," said Mrs. Brown in a soft tone.

"I know . . . but I . . . but I just can't do it for her," muffled Hope.

"Please think about it. I'll talk to you later," said Mrs. Brown.

A short white lady wearing a nurse's uniform dashed toward Hope and Sloan.

"Mr. and Mrs. Glover, please come with me. Dr. Ericsson needs to you right now."

"I've got to go, Mrs. Brown," said Hope as she shifted her gaze back to the nurse. "Is something wrong with my twins?" asked Hope in a panicked tone.

"Jayden is fine," said the nurse as she continued to rapidly walk up the corridor.

"And Jayla . . . ," inquired Hope as her eyes started to fill with tears.

The nurse hesitated to respond initially.

"Is Jayla, okay?" asked Sloan in a firm tone. "Did something . . . happen?"

"Dr. Ericsson will let you know," said the nurse in a flat tone as she opened the door.

A cold hand of fear gripped Hope's heart as her gaze landed on Jayla's limp body.

Chapter 35

Mrs. Brown wobbled up the corridors of Charlotte Medical Hospital toward Gloria's hospital room. Tiffany trailed beside Mrs. Brown, using her arm as a brace to assist Mrs. Brown to walk.

"Mama, you could've used a wheelchair to move around in this hospital," said Tiffany.

"I'm fine, Tiffany," said Mrs. Brown. "I'd rather let someone else use it."

"Are you sure, mama?" asked Tiffany as she continued to walk up the long hallway.

"Tiffany, I've told you already . . . I'm fine for now. I will need a wheelchair one day . . . but not today," smiled Mrs. Brown.

A clean scent of disinfecting supplies swirled through the hospital as the Monday mid-day sun glistened inside the hospital.

Mrs. Brown slowly opened Gloria's hospital room door. Loud beeping sounds flowed through the room from the monitors. The afternoon sun shined through the window, landing on the tile floor.

"Hello, Gloria," whispered Mrs. Brown as she wobbled inside the room.

Gloria slowly peeled her eyes apart. Her frail body rested within the white hospital bedsheets that snuggled her as if she was a mummy.

"I'm . . . I'm surprised you came here," said Gloria as she struggled to get the words out of her mouth.

"You're my friend, Gloria. Why wouldn't I have come?"

"I didn't know if your arthritis would stop you from visiting me," said Gloria.

Mrs. Brown sighed as she glanced down. Her lilac dress draped near her ankles.

"Hello, Mrs. Gloria," said Tiffany in a soft pleasant tone.

Tiffany pulled up a chair for Mrs. Brown close to Gloria's bed.

"Here, mama. Sit down," said Tiffany.

"Thank you, baby," smiled Mrs. Brown.

Gloria fingered through her thin hair as if she was trying to look presentable. Her hair was disheveled over her head as if she didn't know combs were discovered decades ago.

Tiffany walked over to Gloria, gently pulling her hair behind her ears.

"Thank you, Tiffany. You're so sweet," grinned Gloria. "My daughter just left."

"Which daughter?" inquired Mrs. Brown knowing that Hope was somewhere in the hospital with her twins. Mrs. Brown wasn't sure if she needed to tell Gloria.

"*Ivey*," said Gloria as her eyebrows connected as if she could tell that Mrs. Brown wasn't telling her something.

"What happened, Gloria?" inquired Mrs. Brown in a sincere tone.

A loud ruffled sound came out of Gloria's mouth as she coughed. "My leukemia started acting up a lot. I think I passed out or something. So, now I'm in here getting some treatment," said Gloria as she pointed to an IV needle inserted in her right hand.

"When will you get to go back home?" asked Mrs. Brown.

"I don't think I'll be going back home."

"Why not?" asked Mrs. Brown.

"I think they want to send me to the hospice center," coughed Gloria. "But I told my doctors that if I'm going to die . . . I want to die at home."

"Is there something that the hospital can do to help you while you're here?"

"They've done all they can do," sighed Gloria. "The only things that can help me now are prayers and a donor," coughed Gloria. "Hopefully, I can get a transplant soon."

"Can the hospital help you with that?" asked Mrs. Brown in a sincere tone.

"No. They can't find a donor for me. They've tried."

"Have you gotten in touch with Hope?" inquired Mrs. Brown, hoping that Hope had called Gloria.

Gloria tilted her head toward the cream painted ceiling. "Hope refuses to talk to me. I've called her and left several messages at her house," sobbed Gloria. "Ivey has even called and talked with Hope," she paused. "She told Ivey that she wasn't helping me."

A tear rolled down Gloria's caramel brown face.

"Mama, when you talked to Hope, did you tell Hope what was going on with her mother?" asked Tiffany in a respectful tone.

Mrs. Brown looked at Tiffany as if she had leaked classified information.

Gloria's eyes filled with tears. She slowly pulled her body to an upright position.

"Mrs. Brown, you've talked to *my* Hope?" asked Gloria in a nervous tone.

Mrs. Brown was a God-fearing woman. She did not want to lie to Gloria. But she didn't want to destroy her relationship with Hope either. She planted her small hand over her mouth as she closed her eyes.

"Yes," sighed Mrs. Brown.

Gloria slithered her frail body back under the sheets. She turned her head toward the window as she glanced out of it for several minutes. Her hand trembled.

"Mrs. Brown, you mean to tell me that Hope calls you but she doesn't have the decency to call me? Especially, if she knows I am *sick,*" said Gloria as she continued to look out the window.

Mrs. Brown sat silently as if she was a mannequin.

"Well, if truth be told . . . Hope really doesn't owe you anything," said Mrs. Brown as if reality was forcing her to see things the way Hope did.

"I know I've done wrong by Hope. I know I wasn't a good mother to her like you are to Tiffany," sobbed Gloria as she continued to peer out the window. "I hate myself for what I've done to her and for what I let happen to her. She didn't deserve it."

Mrs. Brown looked at Gloria without speaking.

"I was on drugs. I didn't care about anybody but my next high," coughed Gloria as her gaze fixed outside the window. "Eugene was the best thing ever in Hope's life. If it wasn't for him, I would've had Hope and Ivey in those slums with me. I was on drugs bad," cried Gloria. "But I've changed . . . I just want to see Hope one last time."

Mrs. Brown sighed as she reached for Gloria's hand.

A loud beeping sound echoed through the spacious living room from the monitoring devices. Gloria didn't even turn her head to look at the monitor.

The room door opened. A walnut-brown nurse strolled inside. "Hello, I'm Nurse Ashlyn. I received an alert at the nursing station," said the nurse as she looked at the monitors. "Your blood pressure is rising," said the nurse as she looked at Gloria. "I've got to let the doctor know."

"Okay," said Gloria as she stared out the window without looking at the nurse.

Nurse Ashlyn walked toward the door and closed it behind her.

Gloria slowly looked at Mrs. Brown.

"Please tell Hope that I don't care if she doesn't want the doctors to test her to see if she is a donor," cried Gloria. "But I want to see her one last time so I can make peace with her before I leave this earth. Though I doubt that she'll come."

Mrs. Brown glanced at Tiffany, noticing a single tear trickle down her face.

"My days are drawing near," said Gloria. "I might be dead and gone before Hope will ever think about helping me. So, if you know anything about her, please let me know so I can try to find peace."

Tiffany's hand snuggled Mrs. Brown's hand as if she was forewarning her mother that she was about to provide Gloria with an update.

"Mrs. Gloria . . . " said Tiffany in a calm tone. "I saw Hope last week for the first time in over seven years. My brother, husband and I met with Hope."

Mrs. Brown looked at Tiffany. She was unaware that Tiffany had met with Hope.

"Where?" inquired Gloria.

"In Raleigh," responded Tiffany.

"What were you all doing in Raleigh?" asked Mrs. Brown in a puzzled tone.

"We were taking care of something," smiled Tiffany.

Tiffany inched closer toward Gloria's hospital bed. "Hope has a catering company in Raleigh. She is married to an engineer," muffled Tiffany. "They have a set of twins."

A faint smile stretched across Gloria's face as tears flowed down her face.

"My Hope is a business owner of a catering company," grinned Gloria. "I am proud of her," she said as the words struggled to seep out of her mouth. "I guess you did a great job teaching Hope how to cook when she was a teenager, Mrs. Brown."

Mrs. Brown remained silent. She felt as if this was Gloria's time to express herself.

"I'm glad she's married to a *professional* man. Is he?" sighed Gloria.

"I've never met him," said Mrs. Brown.

"Me neither," said Tiffany. "But I think . . . well, I don't know for sure."

"What is it, Tiffany?" asked Mrs. Brown in a concerned tone.

"Nothing, mother. I really don't know all of the details."

Tears streamed down Gloria's face. "So, my grandchildren are twins."

"Yes, Hope and her husband have fraternal twins . . . a boy and a girl."

"I can't believe that I've never seen them and I don't think I'll ever get to see them," sobbed Gloria.

Gloria's words settled at the core of Mrs. Brown's heart. Mrs. Brown slowly exhaled while saying a silent prayer. She knew that the twins were somewhere in the same hospital. Plus, Mrs. Brown knew Hope and her husband were also at the hospital. But Tiffany didn't know that.

Mrs. Brown slowly stood. "I *might* be able to arrange for you to see your grandchildren . . . Hope . . . and her husband. But I can't make any promises."

Chapter 36

Words seemed to have evaporated in the air as Hope sat in the powder blue chair staring at Jayla. The rapid beat of her heart forced blood to her head faster than a rocket, causing Hope to feel dizzy. Her heart shredded into a million pieces when she had to leave Jayla's limp body in another room.

"So, explain to me what happened," sobbed Hope as her lips trembled.

"As I explained to your husband and you previously, there was a high chance that Jayla would encounter some complications," said Dr. Ericsson in a calm tone. "I explained that every procedure, not just the cochlear procedure, could potentially result in complications."

"We know all of that," shrieked Sloan. "But explain to us *what* happened to Jayla."

A short white nurse handed Dr. Ericsson a clipboard.

"Thank you, Nurse Ashlyn."

Dr. Ericsson paused for a few seconds. "As you know, Jayla was diagnosed with pediatric anemia."

"We know all of that," interjected Sloan. "But you told us that she was *okay* to get the procedure done!"

"Mr. Glover, I recommended that Jayla wait a few more weeks. You and your wife insisted that Jayla should have the procedure done simultaneously as her twin brother, Jayden."

Hope shook her head faster than a pendulum, signaling her level of disbelief as tears rolled down her face.

"You told us that Jayla was okay to get the procedure done," sobbed Hope.

Dr. Ericsson glanced at the clipboard, apparently reviewing Jayla's medical notes.

"I told you and your husband that Jayla's red blood cell count had improved some. I did say, at that time, Jayla should be okay for the procedure," paused Dr. Ericsson. "Days before the procedure, we tested her levels and they were fine."

"So, what happened?" sobbed Hope.

Dr. Ericsson folded her bow shaped lips together. "Jayla lost a significant amount of blood during the procedure."

A nervous feeling overtook Hope, causing her legs to shake like Jell-O.

"Are you okay, Mrs. Glover?" asked Dr. Ericsson in a pleasant tone.

"No," said Hope in a harsh tone. "I don't understand what happened to my child."

"My child looks like she was dead!" shrieked Sloan. "Is she dead?"

Silence rippled through the room like a tidal wave.

"I still don't know why you wouldn't allow us to go near Jayla in that other room," sobbed Hope.

"You and your husband were upset. I didn't think it was in the best interest of you two to remain in that room."

"Are you out of your mind! How did you expect us to react?" blurted Sloan through his pearly white teeth.

"If you calm down, Mr. Glover, I will explain to you what happened. Jayla lost a lot of blood. Her red blood cell count dropped significantly," said Dr. Ericsson.

"Please bypass all of the medical jargon and get to the point," said Sloan.

Dr. Ericsson gently tapped her slender finger on the clipboard.

"Red blood cells carry oxygen to the brain," uttered Dr. Ericsson, totally ignoring Sloan's directive about medical jargon. "Jayla's red blood cell count was low before the procedure."

A vibrating sound flowed through the room as Sloan's cell phone rang. He glanced at it for a few seconds as if he contemplated answering it. Hope watched as he turned it off.

Dr. Ericsson cleared her throat before continuing her medical explanation. "Jayla's red blood cell count decreased during the procedure when she lost a lot of blood," she uttered.

Hope glanced at Sloan, recalling his concerns about a blood transfusion.

"But why does she look like she is dead?"

"She's not," said the doctor.

A loud rumbling sound ricocheted through the room as thunder towered over the hospital, removing the bright sun that once resided in the sky.

"I'm trying to explain step by step to you and your husband," said Dr. Ericsson as she handed Nurse Ashlyn the clipboard. "Jayla has slipped into a slight coma."

"A coma," wept Hope as she stood. Hope paced the floor as if she was using her shoes to clean the floor.

"Jayla's red blood cell count is low. As I explained before, red blood cells are responsible for carrying oxygen to the brain," the doctor said as her gaze connected with Hope.

"I hope Jayla doesn't need a blood transfusion," said Sloan as a sneer formed on his face.

Layers of wrinkles formed across Dr. Ericsson's face. "Do you have a religious or personal preference for blood transfusions?" asked Dr. Ericsson.

Sloan paused before responding, capturing Hope's attention. "Is there another option for Jayla?" responded Sloan, avoiding the doctor's question.

A puzzling feeling gripped Hope, wondering whether Sloan actually had a religious or personal concept regarding blood transfusions. If he did, this was something Sloan had never shared with her.

"I recommend that Jayla remains in an induced . . . sedated coma for a period of time to allow her red blood cell count to increase."

"How long?" asked Sloan in a pitiful tone.

"It can take several weeks for red blood cell count to restore."

"Weeks," sobbed Hope.

Nurse Sarah handed Hope a Kleenex.

"Thank you," said Hope as she glanced at Nurse Sarah.

Raindrops splattered against the window, casting a gloomy foam against the glass.

"I don't anticipate that Jayla will need that much time."

"What about school?" asked Hope as she tilted her head toward the ceiling. "School starts in three weeks. Dr. Ericsson, we need to know what type of school to put my children in," said Hope in a frantic tone. "We had hopes of sending our children to a regular school," sobbed Hope.

"This is a process, Mrs. Glover."

"I just want my twins to be *normal*," wept Hope without considering how insensitive she sounded.

"They are normal, Mrs. Glover," uttered Dr. Ericsson in a pleasant tone. "This is what your twins probably define as being normal . . . since this is the only normalcy that they have known since birth."

Quietness settled into the room, mingling with the crisp scent of Lysol.

Hope closed her eyes reflecting on Mrs. Brown's words. She recalled Mrs. Brown had told her that God had a way of touching hearts. The condition that Jayla was currently subdued to definitely had Hope's complete attention. Every core of Hope's heart was slowly peeling away. Her mother-daughter relationship with Jayla was unbreakable. Yet, her mother-daughter relationship with her own mother was shattered. Hope slowly exhaled wondering if this was God's way of persuading her to forgive . . . and help her mother.

"Do you want an update on Jayden?" asked Dr. Ericsson in a calm tone.

"Yes," mumbled Hope in a heartfelt tone.

"The procedure went well for Jayden. He should be waking up in a few minutes," said Dr. Ericsson as her gaze shifted between Hope and Sloan.

"Do you think . . . um . . . Jayden will be able to hear?" asked Hope.

"Jayden will have to undergo habilitation treatment first."

"When can he start?" asked Sloan in a sincere tone.

"In a few days, after he recuperates."

A loud sound echoed in the room. Dr. Ericsson glanced at a pager on her hip. A frown slowly inched across her heart shaped face.

"What about Jayla?" asked Hope in a low tone. "When will she recuperate?"

Dr. Ericsson slowly allowed her pink lips to separate. "I will be better able to answer that question after Jayla wakes up in a couple of days."

"In a couple of days," sobbed Hope as she slowly closed her eyes.

The muscles in Hope's heart tightened.

The thought of Jayla never recuperating rattled Hope's soul.

The thought of only one of her twins being able to hear and speak pierced her heart. Hope loved them equally and wanted them to have the same opportunities in life.

Chapter 37

The Tuesday morning sun shined through the large glass windows as Hope strolled through the corridors of Charlotte Medical Hospital. Her heart slowly fluctuated as she walked toward Jayla's room. Her vineyard green summer dress shifted as she walked. She had just visited Jayden, who was progressing well without any complications. He had fallen back to sleep which granted Hope the opportunity to go to Jayla's room while Sloan remained with Jayden.

Hope's body was operating off of three hours of sleep. She hadn't eaten much. She hadn't drunk much. She was on the verge of being diagnosed with chronic fatigue.

Hope glanced inside several hospital rooms as she continued to walk toward Jayla's room. A prickled feeling pinched her heart as she noticed a young lady embracing an older woman while holding a vase filled with colorful flowers. Hope's heart skipped a beat as she wished she had that amount of love for her own mother.

Hope's mind raced as she recalled that her mother was hospitalized in the same hospital as her twins. Hope exhaled as if she was blowing a dandelion flower. She slowly opened Jayla's room door, hoping to see Jayla sitting up on the edge of her bed. Jayla rested on the hospital bed with tubes running through her limp body.

She was surprised as her gaze landed on Mrs. Brown sitting in a chair near Jayla's bed with her hands clamped together as if she was praying. "Good morning, Mrs. Brown," said Hope as she tiptoed toward her, hoping to avoid interrupting her prayer.

"Good morning, Hope," said Mrs. Brown as she slowly opened her eyes and relaxed her hands.

"How . . . how did you get here?" asked Hope in a puzzled tone.

"Tiffany brought me here this morning. She had to go to work. She'll be back around lunchtime."

"Did . . . did she see Jayla?" asked Hope.

"No. I haven't told her that your twins are here," responded Mrs. Brown. "But she knows your mother is here."

"How?"

"I told her. Tiffany brought me yesterday to see your mother."

"Did . . . Tiffany see Gloria too?"

"Yes, she did."

The room remained silent for a few seconds.

"Jayla is in . . . a coma," said Hope in a flat tone. "She was previously diagnosed with pediatric anemia. She already had a low red blood cell count," sighed Hope. "So, the doctor said her cell level dropped which prevented oxygen from getting to her brain. The doctor said she will put some medicine in Jayla's IV to wake up her soon."

Mrs. Brown grabbed Jayla's little hand and reached for Hope's hand. She bowed her head and mumbled a silent prayer. She slowly opened her eyes and asked Hope to sit.

A tear rolled down Hope's golden-brown face as she sat.

"This child means a lot to you," said Mrs. Brown as she caressed Jayla's face.

"Yes, she does, Mrs. Brown," sobbed Hope.

"She is depending on you to make the right decisions for her. She is depending on you to hold it together," muffled Mrs. Brown.

A river of tears flowed down Hope's face.

"Hope, I know you might not want to hear this. But God makes no mistakes," said Mrs. Brown as she pressed her lips firmly together. "It is no coincidence that Jayla is in this state of mind right now. It is no coincidence that your mother is in the *same* hospital as Jayla and Jayden . . . and at the *same* time."

Hope pressed her palms against her face, wiping away her tears.

"So, you are saying that God allowed this to happen to Jayla," sobbed Hope in an embittered tone.

Mrs. Brown adjusted her wired glasses on her nose. "I'm saying that God works in mysterious ways."

A clean scent of Lysol flowed through the room, mingling with the gentle breeze of the overhead air conditioner.

"Just like you are praying that God grants a way to heal Jayla . . . your mother is praying that God grants a way to heal her."

Hope stood. She walked over to the glass window and glanced out of it.

"Sometimes, we don't understand why God allows things to happen," uttered Mrs. Brown. "But in the end, it always works out for our good."

"How?" wept Hope as her heart felt as if it was crumbling. "My child is in a coma. I had hopes of her procedure going well. I had hopes of her being able to hear and speak without any complications," cried Hope. "I had hopes of holding her . . . playing with her by now."

"I understand. But God has a plan, Hope."

Hope walked over to Jayla. "I never thought this would happen to my child. I never thought I would be faced with possibly having one twin who could hear and speak and the other one . . . ," cried Hope. "This is not what I wanted. It's not fair to Jayla."

"Hope, you don't know if Jayla will never be able to hear and speak."

"I know. But I'm scared, Mrs. Brown. I don't want this to happen to my twins."

"I know. You told me when you called me that day crying on the telephone."

"But why is this happening to Jayla?"

A cluster of sun rays splattered on the tile floor.

"Hope, sometimes, we don't get to choose what happens to us," uttered Mrs. Brown. "We all face trials and tribulations," she said in a spiritual manner. "But what helps define us is our ability to have faith . . . and to *forgive*."

"So, are you saying that Jayla's condition right now might be a test of my faith . . . and my ability to forgive?"

"It might be, Hope. Only you and God know," responded Mrs. Brown. "Just think for a minute, Hope. Your child . . . who you love dearly . . . is in the hospital fighting for her dear life. And . . . at the same time, your mother . . . who you disown . . . is in the same hospital fighting for her dear life."

A loud weeping sound erupted from Hope's mouth.

"Mrs. Brown, nobody knows how Gloria treated me," sobbed Hope.

"God does, Hope."

"But my mother never loved me like I love Jayla."

"God doesn't use a measuring stick to determine his love for us, Hope."

"Gloria never loved me," shrieked Hope in a low tone.

"How do you know, Hope?" said Mrs. Brown as she squinted. "Maybe your mother loved you the *best* way she knew how to love a child."

"By being on drugs and hauling me to different abandoned buildings?" snapped Hope. "By allowing me to get molested in that nasty abandoned building while she got high," said Hope as her lips trembled.

Mrs. Brown stared at Hope for a few seconds.

"I apologize, Mrs. Brown. I didn't mean to sound disrespectful," said Hope as she walked toward Mrs. Brown, wrapping her slender arms around Mrs. Brown.

Mrs. Brown patted Hope's back.

"Your mother had a rough life as a child."

Hope leaned back, gawking at Mrs. Brown.

"Not like mine," muffled Hope.

"Now, Hope . . . you listen to me 'cause this has been going on too long," chattered Mrs.

Brown. "Gloria didn't choose the life of drugs, Hope. It was forced on her."

"Forced," sneered Hope.

"Gloria's mother used to do the same thing to her," sighed Mrs. Brown. "Gloria's mother used to haul her to Godless places, too. Gloria saw her mother, father, aunts and uncles do drugs. After Gloria was raped by her mother's drug dealing friends and they got her pregnant with you, she lost all hope. She didn't have anyone to talk to. She didn't have anyone to help her. She felt helpless. So, Gloria followed the same drug pathway as her family after she had you. It was the only life that she knew," said Mrs. Brown as she closed her eyes as if she had unleashed too much information into the atmosphere. "So, you should thank God that Gloria didn't pass down the drug-gene to you."

Hope walked over to Jayla, caressing her small hand.

"Gloria never told me," sobbed Hope. "But she never showed me any love."

"Maybe she didn't know how to do that, Hope. Please go and visit your mother," begged Mrs. Brown. "She is in room 516."

Hope's gaze shifted from Jayla to Mrs. Brown.

"I . . . I can't do that. I'm not ready yet."

"Hope, your mother is terribly ill right now," snapped Mrs. Brown in a tone that Hope had never heard. "You're in the same hospital where she is nearly dying . . . and you're still telling me you don't want to see her."

"I need time to think."

"Your mother doesn't have time, Hope," shrieked Mrs. Brown. "What if it was Jayla or Jayden in the same condition as your mother? You would want someone to help them, right?"

"Yes, ma'am," responded Hope in a low tone.

"So, you need to do what is right in the eyesight of God. You need to visit your mother. You need to stop calling your mother by her first name!" ordered Mrs. Brown without pausing, causing Hope to flinch.

"I hear you, Mrs. Brown," mumbled Hope.

"You need to allow the doctors to test you to see if you are a match for your mother," shrieked Mrs. Brown.

Hope stared at Mrs. Brown. "I need to think about it"

"Would you have to think about it if the doctors needed to test your cells to help Jayla right now?" blurted Mrs. Brown.

"No," responded Hope without any hesitation.

"So, you should be willing to allow the doctors to test your cells to see if you can help Gloria."

"Now, wait a minute, Mrs. Brown," said Hope. "This makes no sense to me. Jayla is an innocent child who harmed no one. Gloria abused and mistreated me for years." Hope inhaled as if she wanted to vanish. "Jayla and Gloria are not the same. Plus, Gloria definitely does not deserve my devotion like Jayla."

Mrs. Brown stood and propped her hands on her hips.

"If you can't find it in your heart to do it for yourself . . . please do it for *me* . . . do it for the sake of Jayla," demanded Mrs. Brown as she walked to the door.

Hope slowly closed her eyes as tears trickled down her face.

"Please stop trying to pressure me to do something I don't want to do," spatted Hope. "Gloria is not the victim."

"You're right, Hope. I'm sorry," sighed Mrs. Brown recalling that Reverend McCoy had told her that forgiveness must flow freely. "But your mother has changed. She's not like she used to be."

"Interesting," muffled Hope. "It seems like she's too sick to be cruel anymore."

"For real, Hope, your mother changed before she got sick." Mrs. Brown remained silent for a few seconds. "She told me that she had done a lot of bad things to you. She knows she didn't protect you . . . when you needed her." Mrs. Brown paused. "She used to cry and tell me how she missed you and how she wanted to apologize to you."

"Really, she used to ask about me?" asked Hope in a soft tone as if the layers of hatred were slowly peeling.

"Yes, but I never told her that you were calling me all of those years. I didn't tell her because I kept my promise to you that I wouldn't."

Hope exhaled. "I'm not ready to see her. I don't know if I ever will."

Mrs. Brown closed her eyes before saying, "I'm heading to your mother's room now. Your twins should meet their grandmother before she dies." Then she exited Jayla's hospital room without even saying goodbye to Hope.

Hope felt as though her heart had stopped beating.

Chapter 38

The next day, beige colored walls surrounded Hope and Sloan as they sat in the Charlotte Medical Hospital's habilitation room. Wednesday morning had come too soon and Hope had been uncertain whether Sloan would make it to the scheduled appointment. He had just returned from a one-day business trip with Mr. Gavino.

Hope's heart raced as she waited for Jayden to be transported from his hospital room to the habilitation room. Medical devices assembled around the room. Headphones positioned neatly on the large medical table. A computer rested on a desk in the corner. A projector screen dangled from the middle of the ceiling.

"Will Jayden be able to hear and speak?" asked Hope immediately as Dr. Ericsson and a tall ebony brown man walked into the room.

"We will find out soon," smiled Dr. Ericsson.

"Hello, Mr. and Mrs. Glover, I am Dr. Shaw. I am a speech pathologist. I specialize in performing cochlear implant speech therapy. I will conduct a series of tests on Jayden to test the device."

"What about testing whether he can hear and speak," interrupted Sloan.

"That is part of the series of tests," responded Dr. Shaw as he walked toward the computer.

"Before Jayden comes into the room, I want to show you a picture of how Jayden's cochlear implant looks from an internal and external view," said Dr. Ericsson as she pushed a button to turn on the screen projector.

Hope's eyes scanned the images on the screen projector. Her heart sunk as her gaze focused on how Dr. Ericsson had to shave Jayden's hair behind his left and right ears as part of the cochlear implant process. She cringed as she observed how Dr. Ericsson had to implant part of the device inside Jayden's ear. Hope gripped Sloan's hand as she noticed blood seeping from Jayden's head and ear where the device was implanted.

Several minutes later, Hope stood as the room's door opened. A warm feeling flowed through her as her gaze fixated on Jayden. A well-figured cocoa-brown nurse pushed Jayden inside the room as he sat in a wheelchair.

"He shouldn't need the wheelchair," smiled Dr. Ericsson as she looked at the nurse. "He has been progressing well."

"Hello, Jayden," sighed Hope hoping that Jayden would respond.

"Hello, son," said Sloan as a smile flashed across his butterscotch-brown face. His navy blue business suit cast an upscale appearance over his well-built physique.

Jayden squinted as he looked at Hope and Sloan's mouth as if he was reading their lips. He raised his small slender chestnut-brown hands toward his ears, touching the devices as he looked at Hope.

An ounce of sympathy rolled through Hope as she stared at Jayden.

"Jayden, can you hear us?" asked Hope in a calm tone as she squatted.

Jayden squinted again as he looked at Hope's lips.

"Mrs. Glover, please allow me to run a series of tests," demanded Dr. Shaw in a respectful tone.

Hope glanced up at Dr. Shaw as his fix-foot-six body towered over her. His hazel-brown eyes definitely highlighted his attractive unblemished facial skin, revealing the smoothness of his well-groomed mustache and eyebrows. Hope gawked at his hands for a few seconds, noticing that Dr. Shaw wasn't wearing a wedding ring. Hope stood, locking her gaze with Dr. Shaw's hazel brown eyes. She noticed how he quickly scanned her face as if he was admiring her beauty.

"Hope, have a seat so Dr. Shaw can perform the tests on Jayden," blurted Sloan as if he had noticed that Hope was admiring Dr. Shaw's facial features.

Hope strolled over to a chair behind Sloan as she smiled at Jayden. She sat in a black padded chair that provided sufficient support. A firm grip nestled on her upper thigh as Sloan placed his hand on her leg, squeezing it as he stared directly into her eyes.

Hope sat motionlessly. She was surprised that Sloan had done this to her. Sloan had never put his hands on her in this manner before. She wondered what had happened during the recent one-day business trip that he had with Mr. Gavino.

Hope exhaled, remembering that Sloan was typically aggressive every time he returned from his business trips. She wondered if Sloan's business affairs with Mr. Gavino were becoming stressful or if Sloan's aggressiveness aroused from something else.

Hope leaned back in the chair as if she was a child sitting in the principal's office.

"Hello, Jayden, I am Dr. Shaw. I am going to run a series of tests on you," said Dr. Shaw, instantly capturing Hope's attention. "I see that you have a twin sister, Jayla, here with you as well," said Dr. Shaw as he glanced at the computer screen.

Dr. Ericsson walked toward the nurse. "Nurse Petrina, please assist Jayden to the chair over there," she said while pointing to a small chair. "You can take the wheelchair with you. He will not need it."

Dr. Shaw cleared his throat. "Mr. and Mrs. Glover, I'm going to start the tests in a few minutes. I will not be able to respond to you because I have to focus on Jayden."

"Okay," said Sloan in a nonchalant tone as he glanced at his watch.

"I'm going to run a few tests on Jayden to send sound signals to his brain," said Dr. Shaw as Nurse Petrina exited the room, pushing the wheelchair out. "I will not be able to hear you once I place these headphones on my ears," said Dr. Shaw as he dangled the headphones in the air to show Hope and Sloan.

Dr. Ericsson typed a few notes onto the computer before looking up at Dr. Shaw. "I will leave now, Dr. Shaw. I will review your medical notes in the system," said Dr. Ericsson as she walked toward the door.

"Okay," said Dr. Shaw as he placed a set of soundproof headphones on his and Jayden's ears.

Dr. Ericsson walked toward Hope and Sloan. "I will follow up with you after Dr. Shaw finishes the tests. Jayden is scheduled to be discharged today."

"Today," said Hope.

"Yes. I kept Jayden an extra day just to provide additional observation. As I explained before, the cochlear implant procedure doesn't require an extensive hospital stay," smiled Dr. Ericsson. "But Jayden will still have to return for his cochlear implant auditory and speech therapy with Dr. Shaw for a while."

Sloan cleared his throat as if he wanted to get a point across. "Make sure the appointments are scheduled when my wife and I both can attend them," uttered Sloan as his gaze shifted from Dr. Ericsson to Hope immediately.

Loud beeping sounds flowed through the room as Dr. Shaw adjusted the volume on the auditory machine.

"What about Jayla?" asked Hope in a low tone as she stood.

"I will meet with you and your husband after Jayden is finished with his tests to discuss Jayla's prognosis," said Dr. Ericsson. "I'm headed to check on her now."

Hope slowly exhaled. "Dr. Ericsson, will Jayla be able to go home soon?"

"Not today," said the doctor in a low tone. "But a nurse is with her at all times."

Hope slowly sat wondering if Jayla's nurse was taking good care of her. Hope's heart pounded away as she reflected upon Mrs. Brown's words. She felt as though she was at the crossroad between helping her mother or forsaking her mother on her deathbed.

Hope closed her eyes. She yearned for the moment that she could hear Jayla and Jayden's voices. She yearned for the moment that the doctor would confirm that they could hear and speak. An excitement charged through Hope as she tried to imagine what their first words would be until Sloan's voice interrupted her peaceful thoughts.

"I saw you staring at Dr. Shaw," whispered Sloan in a stern voice as he gripped Hope's wrist. "How *dare* you disrespect me like that!"

"Let *go* of my wrist," said Hope as she jerked her wrist from Sloan's tight grip. "I wasn't staring at him. I only looked at him to show respect as he was talking to me."

"Go ahead and get all of your thrills from looking at him," muffled Sloan. "Make sure you think of him tonight because I might need three rounds after this."

"Are you serious, Sloan?" uttered Hope in a low tone as she glared at him. "We are here in this hospital with our twins. We should be focusing on their health, not on Dr. Shaw," said Hope as she noticed that Jayden was looking at their lips.

Hope placed her hand over her mouth to prevent Jayden from reading her lips. "Stop it, Sloan. Jayden is reading our lips."

Dr. Shaw stood and walked Jayden to another side of the room to conduct a different test. Hope was unable to see Jayden from the angle where she was sitting.

Hope and Sloan sat quietly in the room for nearly an hour.

"Hope, how much longer will this be?" asked Sloan as he looked at his watch.

"Do you have to be somewhere?" asked Hope in a low snappy tone.

"If I did, you would be the first to know, honey," whispered Sloan in a sarcastic tone. "I'm just checking my watch to see how much longer I have until I can get you in the bed. I want you to remember his name when I give you long deep strokes."

"Whose name?" whispered Hope as if she was in a whispering contest with Sloan.

"*Dr. Shaw*'s name," whispered Sloan.

"Whatever, Sloan," muffled Hope. "And why are you talking to me like that," uttered Hope barely above a whisper. "I'm not a whore or a prostitute."

A soft chuckle flowed out of Sloan's mouth.

"I don't see anything funny. I'm not that type of woman and you know it."

"Do I?" sneered Sloan. "The only thing I do know is what I want to order from the menu tonight."

"Do you hear yourself, Sloan?" mumbled Hope, hoping that Dr. Shaw wasn't listening. "You can't order me from any menu," blurted Hope in a low tone, as an image of the brochure she found inside Sloan's car suddenly flashed before her. "But I'm sure you probably can order other women from a menu."

"What did you just say?" whispered Sloan through his pearly white teeth while staring at Hope with a bewildered look on his face as if Hope had just unraveled an underground secret. "Who have you been talking to?" he asked as his eyebrows twitched. "Answer me, Hope Glover!" he gritted barely above a whisper. "Who have you been talking to?"

Hope swallowed hard before responding. "Nobody, Sloan," muffled Hope as she suddenly recalled Sloan had told her that the brochure that she found underneath the passenger's seat in his car reflected the pizza sales at one of the pubs.

A sense of uneasiness settled in her stomach as she felt that Sloan was slowly becoming an abusive husband. Then again, she wondered if Sloan already had a dominating alter-ego but controlled it when he was around her and the twins. She felt as though she really didn't know the real Sloan.

Footsteps trailed toward Hope and Sloan.

"Excuse me, Mr. and Mrs. Glover," said Dr. Shaw. "I need about another thirty minutes to an hour with Jayden. You may stay if you like or you may leave."

"We will come back," said Sloan in a hasty tone. "We will go and visit his twin."

"Okay, I will follow up with Dr. Ericsson to provide her with the results or you may schedule a time to meet with me to discuss the results," said Dr. Shaw.

"We will follow up with Dr. Ericsson," said Hope in a low tone, hoping to ease Sloan's tension and insecurity.

The excitement she had felt when she arrived at Jayden's habilitation appointment suddenly faded away.

Chapter 39

The next morning, Hope strolled through the corridors of Charlotte Medical Center. The Thursday morning sunlight pressed against her plum, long sundress. The inner crescent of her thighs and the soft tissues of her jewel box still throbbed from the intense pressure that Sloan had applied inside her last night. Her heart sunk, reflecting how Sloan had thrusted against the canvasses of her walls as if she was a stranger. The three scoops of sex definitely left her sore which prevented her from wearing jeans today. Sadly, the soreness made her reminisce about the pain inflicted by Sergeant Smith that she had experienced as a child. Though Hope was a grown woman now, there was no doubt in her mind that Sloan's level of sexual aggressiveness had become more intense than before as if he was a stranger attacking her. *But why*, she pondered.

Hope's gaze landed on Dean. She figured he worked at the hospital since he was always there when she and Sloan arrived every morning. She walked inside Jayla's hospital room while Sloan visited Jayden. Beige painted walls encased the room. A square shaped window granted a sufficient amount of sunlight to flow inside. A sky blue hospital sofa positioned underneath the window.

Hope's heart pulsated rapidly as she walked closer to Jayla. Her gaze landed on the back of a five-foot-seven woman, wearing a nurse's outfit.

"Good morning," said the nurse in a low tone, barely above a whisper, without turning around. "I will be with you in a minute. I'm changing the hospital gauge on Jayla's head," said the nurse as if she rather give Jayla her undivided attention instead of acknowledging who had walked inside the room.

"Okay," smiled Hope, noticing how gently and carefully the nurse was tending to Jayla.

Hope sat in a chair, admiring the craftiness of the nurse as she cared for Jayla. She observed the nurse clean Jayla's face after changing the gauge that had dried up blood on it. The nurse slowly pulled Jayla's hair to the side, gently brushing it. A warm feeling flowed through Hope as she continued to watch how the nurse took pride in tending to her daughter.

"Okay, all done," whispered the nurse. "Jayla, I will be back to check on you," said the nurse in a pleasant tone as if she had formed a rapport with Jayla.

The sunlight shined into the room, casting a glare on the side of the nurse's face. She walked toward the trash can, throwing away items in it. Hope could only see the nurse's back as she stood near the trash can.

"Good morning," said the nurse as she turned around.

A truckload of shock burst through Hope like a cyclone.

"What are you doing here?" blurted Hope in an alarming tone as she stood.

"Hope, is that you?" asked the nurse as she walked closer to Hope.

"Ivey!" gritted Hope, through her teeth. "What are you doing in here?"

A puzzled look spread across Ivey's face. "Hope, I work here as a nurse."

"No, no, no," repeated Hope as she shook her head. "Out of all places in the world . . . you work at this hospital!"

"Hope, please lower your voice," ordered Ivey as she glanced at Jayla. "She is resting now."

Ivey walked back toward Jayla. She readjusted the white hospital sheets over Jayla's body.

Then she inched back closer to Hope. "Is . . . is Jayla your daughter?" asked Ivey in a pleasant tone with a tiny smile on her bronze brown face.

She walked closer to Hope, extending her long arms to hug her. Hope slowly inched back as if she didn't want Ivey to touch her.

"You act like you didn't know," said Hope as she tilted her head.

"I didn't," responded Ivey. "You've never told me anything about yourself. You've been gone for almost seven years. You vanished like a thief in the night. You never called, visited, or e-mailed me . . . or mama after you disappeared. So, no, Hope, I didn't."

"I did tell you that I had twins, Ivey," uttered Hope as frustration coursed through her like the Nile River.

"I know. But I didn't think . . . Jayla was one of your twins," said Ivey as a puzzled look spread across her oval shaped face. "How was I to know that Jayla Glover was your child, Hope? I didn't even know your last name was Glover. You didn't tell me," said Ivey as she squinted. "I didn't even know that your twins were . . . deaf," mumbled Ivey in a heartfelt tone. "So, tell me, how did you expect me to know that Jayla was your child?"

"How did you know both of my twins were deaf?" asked Hope.

"I am the head nurse here. I oversee the other nurses. So, I review their materials. Plus, I am assigned to some patients."

"Whatever, Ivey. So, I guess you volunteered yourself to take care of Jayla and Jayden. What a real-live coincidence," chuckled Hope as if she was trapped in the middle of a nightmare.

"You have some nerve, Hope!" said Ivey in a low tone glancing at Jayla as if she wanted to make sure they didn't disturb her. "As I said, I didn't even know that Jayla . . . and Jayden were your twins."

"If you say so," blurted Hope in a sarcastic tone. Ivey closed her eyes before responding.

"Look, Hope, I was in here taking good care of a child who turns out to be my niece," said Ivey as a tear rolled down her face. "I've been struggling to come to work every day knowing that our mother is in the same hospital resting on her dying bed. But I still managed to take care of your twins and all of my other patients as if nothing was going on in my personal life."

"Your personal life, Ivey. What about my personal life?" blurted Hope in a low tone as she glanced at Jayla. "I'm the one who went through hell, living with Gloria . . . not you. I'm the one who got molested in those nasty abandoned buildings that our so-called mother used to haul me to so she could get high. I felt as if Gloria had exchanged my body to pay for her high," cried Hope as she paused between sniffles.

"Hope," said Ivey before being rudely interrupted.

"No . . . you listen to me," snapped Hope while wagging her slender finger in the air in front of Ivey. "I'm the one who lost sleep fearing the next time I would get molested again. I was even molested by Sergeant Smith in the woods more times than I could count." Hope covered her face.

"Oh, Hope. I heard he had done terrible things to people in Cloverdale but I didn't know he had hurt you too."

"Oh, it gets worse, Ivey," snapped Hope. "You can't even imagine what mama let him do to me while she was high," shrieked Hope. "I saw other little girls and boys get molested."

"Oh, no," sighed Ivey as a tear rolled down her face.

"Nothing ever happened to you, Ivey. I'm the one who went without food while Gloria got high" wept Hope as she turned away from Ivey.

Ivey grabbed Hope's hand. "Hope, you don't have to share all of that with me," said Ivey in a supportive tone as if what she had not even heard was an overload of information.

Hope slowly pulled her hand from Ivey. "No, I want you to know. So, you can stop trying to get me to feel pity for Gloria," smirked Hope before proceeding with her venting routine. "I'm the one who Gloria called a *'Bad Seed'* because drug dealers raped her and impregnated her with me. I'm the one who had to run off just to get peace of mind. I'm the one who slept in a shelter until I was able to find a job. I'm the one who married the first decent man that approached me without even really knowing him. There are some days I feel like I still really don't know him. I'm the one who birthed precious twins who turned out to be deaf. So, you tell me, Ivey, whose personal life is worse," sobbed Hope.

Silence filtered through the room like pollen.

"I didn't know you went through all of that," said Ivey as a tear rolled down her face. "I'm your sister. I want to be here for you, Hope, if you'll allow me."

"Thanks for taking care of them," mumbled Hope. "So, yes, Jayla is your niece and Jayden is your nephew. I don't mind you tending to them while they're in this hospital. But I don't want Gloria near them or I'll make sure you're fired."

"You can't threaten me, Hope!" shrieked Ivey. "I know how to resolve this issue. I am going to request that I'm removed from overseeing Jayla and Jayden because it is a conflict of interest," said Ivey as she walked toward the door. "It was nice seeing you after seven years. I pray that you have a nice life," said Ivey as she opened the door. "But I can't imagine you having a nice life when you're forsaking your dying mother and . . . you're struggling to adjust to what's going on with Jayla right now," said Ivey as her shoulder length dark brown hair bounced with radiance.

A sudden reality check kicked inside Hope's head. She paused, reflecting upon the high quality of care that Ivey provided Jayla. She was uncertain whether another nurse would render the same level of care. But she was certain she wanted to leave the hospital with her twins being able to hear and speak . . . without worrying about Gloria.

"Ivey, please don't leave," said Hope.

She flopped in the chair, crying as if the tear ducts in her eyes had erupted.

Chapter 40

A shaft of the Thursday mid-day sunlight sprinkled inside Mrs. Brown's apartment. She leaned back in the navy blue sectional chair, trying to entertain her guest.

"So, how is Gloria?" asked Ruth with curiosity dancing in her eyes.

"Ruth, why do you have on that little sundress?" asked Mrs. Brown without answering Ruth's question.

Muffled chuckles flowed out of Jasmine and Taylor's mouths as a small grin spread across Geneva's café brown face.

"Mrs. Brown, I knew your apartment would be about 200 degrees. So, I wanted to wear something to keep my body temperature down."

"There are other ways to keep your body temperature down," smirked Mrs. Brown as she paused before speaking again. "I guess I can't chastise you since the sundress does come to your knees instead of your thighs like in the past."

Ruth brushed her hands along her burnt orange sundress, trying to smooth out the wrinkles.

"How is Gloria doing?" repeated Ruth.

"Ruth and Geneva, let's go in the kitchen and talk," ordered Mrs. Brown as she stood. "We can let Jasmine and Taylor stay in here to watch television while we talk about grown folks' stuff."

"Turn the television on the cartoons," smiled Ruth as she looked at Jasmine and Taylor.

"Here, kids, I made some fresh ginger cookies," smiled Mrs. Brown before wobbling into the kitchen.

She sat at the maple wood table as Geneva and Ruth stared at her.

"Gloria isn't doing good," said Mrs. Brown in a remorseful tone. "She needs some type of transplant."

"Can the doctors find a donor for her?"

"They've been looking," uttered Mrs. Brown.

"I bet if Gloria had the good type of insurance, the doctors would find a donor."

"Ruth, it is not determined by the type of insurance you have," said Mrs. Brown.

"If you say so, Mrs. Brown," said Ruth as she draped her long auburn brown wig behind her perky ears.

"Has Gloria gotten in touch with Hope?" asked Geneva as she sipped on some homemade lemonade that Mrs. Brown had prepared.

"I don't think so," said Mrs. Brown as she pressed her lips firmly together. "I talked to Hope."

"You did," blurted Ruth. "What did she say?"

Chirping noises flowed through the kitchen window as a bird perched on the windowpane.

"I think Hope is still consumed with hatred from how Gloria used to treat her," sighed Mrs. Brown.

"Well, you know Gloria used to treat that girl really bad," muffled Ruth in a concerned tone.

"Folks in Cloverdale used to talk about it, Ruth," said Geneva in a low tone.

Mrs. Brown exhaled before speaking. "That's the past . . . and we have to leave the past in the past."

"I know Mrs. Brown but the truth must be said," interrupted Geneva. "From what I know, Gloria changed years ago . . . even before Hope had left home. But Gloria apparently had done so much damage to that Hope felt like she had to leave home in order to find peace of mind."

"Really?" inquired Ruth with a puzzled look on her face. "I hope she hasn't been living a harsh life. What if something terrible had happened to her?"

Mrs. Brown tilted her head toward the ceiling before lowering it and saying, "She's okay." Mrs. Brown paused before speaking. She didn't want to say too much but she didn't want them to speculate that something terrible had happened to Hope.

Quietness swept through the room. Whenever Mrs. Brown spoke everyone always listened as if it was breaking news.

"Hope has been living in Raleigh, North Carolina for the past seven years." Mrs. Brown pressed her lips together. "She made a good life for herself. She is the owner of a catering company. She wants to open a culinary school one day. She is married to an engineer and they have a set of twins."

"Twins," blurted Ruth. "Hope has a set of twins."

"How do you know all of that, Mrs. Brown?" asked Geneva with a bewildered look on her face.

Silence engulfed Mrs. Brown for a few seconds.

"Don't tell me Hope stayed in contact with you all these years?" whispered Ruth in a surprised tone.

"Not the entire seven years," muffled Mrs. Brown. "She waited about two or three months before she called me. I guess she wanted to be certain that I wouldn't tell Gloria before she started calling me almost every day." She paused. "It hurts my heart that I couldn't tell Gloria for years. I was scared Hope would stop calling me. I didn't even tell my own children."

"Really," gasped Ruth. "Well, folks in Cloverdale always said you can keep a secret."

Geneva nodded as if she was confirming Ruth's comment.

"I never told Gloria until the other day . . ." said Mrs. Brown as she sipped on some lemonade. "I didn't want to mess up my relationship with Hope. But I felt bad not telling Gloria."

"You shouldn't feel bad, Mrs. Brown. You did develop a good relationship with Hope," mumbled Ruth. "You would've thought Hope was your own child as much as she stayed with you."

"I remember how she used to try to cook like you back then," laughed Geneva. "But her cookies tasted like hot rubber bands."

"How you know what rubber bands taste like, Geneva?" laughed Ruth. "Don't you have food in your house? I hope you're not eating rubber bands."

"I'm just saying," chuckled Geneva. "Hope's cookies didn't taste like Mrs. Brown's."

"Well, Hope has come a long way with her cooking and baking skills since she was a teenager," affirmed Mrs. Brown. "She has her own catering company and several customers."

"Really," said Ruth. "I'm sure Hope did. She learned from the best."

A prideful feeling flowed through Mrs. Brown as she reflected upon how she taught Hope how to cook and bake.

"I pray that Hope will consider what I asked her to do," sighed Mrs. Brown.

"What did you ask her to do?" asked Geneva in a low tone.

Quietness surrounded them for a few seconds.

"It seems as if God has Hope at a crossroad right now," responded Mrs. Brown without directly answering Geneva's questions.

"Why do you say that?"

Mrs. Brown's gaze landed on the table for a few seconds. "Gloria is at Charlotte Medical Hospital resting on her dying bed. Hope's twins," paused Mrs. Brown. "Hope's twins are also at Charlotte Medical Hospital."

"For what?" inquired Ruth.

Mrs. Brown sipped on a glass of lemonade.

"Hope's twins had to get an operation."

"For what?" asked Ruth with a puzzled look on her face.

"They are deaf."

Geneva and Ruth's eyes widened larger than walnuts.

"But they got some type of operation the other day that's supposed to help them be able to hear and speak."

Ruth's pink glossed lips slowly parted. "Why did Hope have to bring the twins all the way from Raleigh to Charlotte for that operation?" asked Ruth.

"Hope said something like the doctor here specialized in that type of operation that the twins needed."

A gentle breeze flowed through the kitchen window.

"Oh, that's no coincidence, Mrs. Brown," said Ruth as she shook her head. "God planned all of this," blurted Ruth as she nodded. "God fixed it so Gloria was in the same hospital at the same time that Hope's twins were getting their operations."

"Yeah, you're right Ruth," said Geneva as she looked around. "Only God could arrange for Hope and Gloria to be at the same location and at the same time."

"I know," said Mrs. Brown. "I told Hope the same thing. That's why I am saying that Hope is at a crossroad."

"What crossroad you keep talking about, Mrs. Brown?"

"Gloria is in the hospital struggling to hold on to the threads of her life," paused Mrs. Brown. "And one of Hope's twins is struggling to recover properly from the operation," sighed Mrs. Brown. "The doctor kept her in a mini coma to help her 'cause she is anemic really bad and something is going on with the oxygen to her brain."

"Oh, no, Mrs. Brown," mumbled Ruth. "Please say it isn't so."

"God must be testing Hope," uttered Geneva.

"I know. I told Hope," sighed Mrs. Brown. "Those twins mean the world to her . . . especially her daughter," paused Mrs. Brown. "Hope wants to make sure she has a better relationship with her daughter than what Gloria had with her."

"Please don't tell me that it's Hope's daughter who's having complications."

Mrs. Brown closed her eyes as she responded, "Yes, Ruth. It's Hope's daughter."

Silence roamed through the kitchen.

"Mrs. Brown, you have to convince Hope to do what is right in the eyesight of God," said Geneva as she bowed her head as if she was praying.

Ruth bowed her head as well.

Mrs. Brown closed her eyes, mumbling a prayer. She opened her eyes and noticed that Geneva and Ruth were staring at her as if she had been praying for a long time.

Geneva exhaled slowly, "It will be sad if God takes Gloria and Hope's daughter to Heaven with him just because Hope can't find it in her heart to forgive Gloria."

Mrs. Brown slowly exhaled. "I don't think God would punish Hope by killing her daughter just because she doesn't forgive her mother." She paused. "Forgiveness cannot be forced. Plus, there are some really bad things that Gloria allowed to happen to Hope as a child. So, on one hand, I must respect how Hope feels but on the other, I understand how Gloria must feel."

"It seems like Gloria's situation is a matter of life and death, but what happened to Hope in the past was a crime," frowned Geneva. "Well, Mrs. Brown, you once said something about God's wrath."

"I know. I remember," said Mrs. Brown as her hands connected while she mumbled a quick silent prayer. "Surely, there has to be a more tactful way for me to encourage Hope to forgive her mother."

Mrs. Brown's cheeks got wet as tears streamed down her face.

Chapter 41

Hope exhaled slowly as she watched Ivey slowly close Jayla's hospital room door. The Thursday mid-day continued to unveil more tears than Hope could withstand.

"Go ahead, Hope. I'm listening," said Ivey walking toward Hope as if she was the older sister. "You've been gone almost seven years. But you're still holding on to the past. You must find a way to move forward."

"I've tried so many times to put the past behind me," sobbed Hope. "My mind will not allow me to forget the things that Gloria did to me."

"Stop, Hope. Just stop!" gritted Ivey between her teeth. "Stop calling *mama* by her first name. That is so disrespectful and you know it."

"My heart will not allow me to call her mama, Ivey," said Hope as she dropped her head. Her heart sunk, tugging away at the emotional scars her mother had inflicted upon her life. "I've cried many nights. I've lost a lot of sleep, trying to find a way to love her. But in the end, I find myself hating her."

A soft beeping sound could be heard through the hospital room from the monitor that was connected to Jayla.

"You have to learn how to forgive mama, Hope," whispered Ivey as if she didn't want to disturb Jayla. "It makes no sense for you to be in the same hospital where mama is . . . and still not find it within yourself to go and see her," said Ivey as she stared at Hope.

"Do you know how hard this is for me, Ivey? It isn't easy for me. I'm supposed to love her . . . I was supposed to help her . . . I was supposed to trust her," wept Hope. "But I can't, Ivey . . . I just can't."

"Hope, at least allow mama to meet Jayla and Jayden. They deserve to meet their grandmother."

Hope shook her head from side to side. "No, Ivey . . . I can't do that," muffled Hope. "My mind tells me to forsake her. My heart tells me to hate her."

"But what does your soul tell you, Hope?" asked Ivey as her right eyebrow elevated toward the ceiling.

Hope planted her hands on her face as she cried.

"Mama is going to die soon if she can't find a donor," sighed Ivey as she grabbed Hope's hand. "You should allow the doctors to run the test on you to see if you are a match for mama."

A gentle breeze swept through the room, brushing against Hope's wet face as tears flowed down her face.

"Do you remember what I told you about mother-child cell sharing?" asked Ivey in a supportive tone. "Some people call it fetal stem cell sharing. But doctors typically call it by the medical term of fetal microchimeric," paused Ivey. "The doctors said some of your cells are still in mama after all of these decades. Those cells are the ones that might be able to help mama, Hope."

Hope stood as she closed her eyes. She walked over to Jayla, rubbing her small hand.

"Who would've known that mama would need something so delicate from the child that she . . . ," muffled Ivey.

"The child that she what?" demanded Hope as her head swirled around toward Ivey. "Go ahead and say it," cringed Hope. "The child that she what!"

Ivey's head tilted toward the ceiling before responding. "The child that she mistreated," said Ivey in a low tone as she closed her eyes. "God has a funny way of doing things," babbled Ivey as she walked toward Hope, wrapping her arms around Hope.

Hope exhaled, trying to embrace Ivey's warm hug.

"Ivey, can you provide me with an update on Jayla."

Ivey glanced at Jayla. "She is getting better. She actually started pulling through a little last night. But she is resting now."

"She did?" said Hope as a peaceful feeling engulfed her.

"Yes," responded Ivey. "But she may recover slower than Jayden. But Dr. Ericsson will check Jayla again to make sure."

Hope's heart skipped a beat as the words flowed out of Ivey's month.

"Do you think . . . Jayla will be able to hear and speak?" mumbled Hope as she leaned over to rub Jayla's hand.

"Dr. Ericsson is the best person to answer that question for you, Hope."

Hope walked over to a window, staring out of it as tears streamed down her face.

"It will hurt my heart if I have one twin who can hear and speak . . . and the other who can't," cried Hope. "I came to this hospital with the hopes of leaving with both of my twins being able to hear and speak. It will just destroy me if they both can't."

Ivey joined Hope at the window.

"I read Jayden's test results, Hope."

Hope turned to look at Ivey with curiosity.

"What did they say?" asked Hope in a nervous tone.

"The test results show that Jayden will be able to hear and speak," smiled Ivey. "Dr. Shaw is really good. He will be providing Jayden's habilitation therapy."

Hope stood motionless. Hope's body pumped an array of mixed feelings through her. She didn't know whether she should be happy for Jayden or sad at the fact that Jayla may not be able to hear and speak.

"I will go and see Jayden in a few minutes. My husband is with him now."

Ivey looked at Hope for a few minutes. "What is my brother-in-law's name?" inquired Ivey.

"Sloan," sighed Hope as if she finally felt comfortable sharing information with Ivey. "He's an engineer."

"What about you, Hope?" asked Ivey.

Hope firmly pressed her lips together before slowly speaking. "I own my own catering company. I want to open my own culinary school one day."

"I guess Mrs. Brown taught you something in the kitchen," laughed Ivey. "I remember how you used to try to bake and cook like her."

The bright sun shined into the room, permitting rays to bounce against the beige colored walls.

"What about you, Ivey?" asked Hope in an inquisitive tone.

"I'm married, too," smiled Ivey.

"What does he do?" asked Hope hoping that Ivey's husband wasn't a drug dealer like the young guys who she used to date when they were growing up in Cloverdale.

"My husband, Orlando, is a minister," grinned Ivey. "We've been married a year now. We are planning on having children soon."

"A minister?" smiled Hope as a sense of relief flowed through her.

"Yes," responded Ivey as if she knew why Hope had inquired.

Soft chuckles flowed from Hope and Ivey's mouth.

"Hope, please help mama," said Ivey in a serious tone as if this was the perfect moment for her to plead her case to Hope.

Hope turned away from Ivey, looking out the window. She glanced at Jayla for a few seconds.

"Ivey, why do you want to spoil the mood right now?" asked Hope. "We were having such a nice conversation before you wanted to venture back to talking about Gloria."

"But, Hope, mama really needs your help," muffled Ivey.

Hope walked closer to Jayla's bed. Ivey joined her.

"I can't, Ivey. I'm sorry."

"Hope, if Jayla needed something from you to help her to hear and speak would you give it to her?"

"Yes," responded Hope without hesitating.

"So, how can you find it in your heart to help Jayla but not your own mother?"

"Because I love Jayla . . . and I don't love Gloria."

"How can you say that, Hope?" said Ivey. "God doesn't like this. Plus, it's not fair for Jayla. It's not fair for Jayden. They at least need to meet their grandmother before she *dies.* "

"I don't want them to meet her," said Hope as she sat in a chair near Jayla.

"Hope, please don't do this to your children. Just because you're mad at mama, it's not fair for you to deprive them of meeting their grandmother."

"Ivey, please don't try to tell me how to raise my children. They are better off not knowing Gloria."

"Hope, please don't say that," sighed Ivey. "You can't do this."

"Yes, I can and I will."

"Please listen to yourself. You're not being fair to Jayla and Jayden," muffled Ivey. "You have so much hatred in your heart for mama that you can't even see how it is affecting you! It is literally tearing you apart," shrieked Ivey.

"How dare you say that, Ivey!"

"Hope, it's the *truth*," cried Ivey. "You hate mama so much that maybe this is why God has allowed Jayla to have a slow recovery," sniffled Ivey. "God may be using Jayla to reach you. I'm sure you don't want her growing up hating you."

"Get out right now," blurted Hope as the thought of punching Ivey in the mouth crossed her mind. "Get out!"

"I'm not leaving, Hope! You are my sister and I want you to understand how your hatred is probably the reason why Jayla is healing slower than Jayden."

"Get out!" yelled Hope as she walked toward the hospital room door. "You have a twisted way of trying to manipulate me to think that my reaction toward Gloria is why Jayla is healing slowly."

"God is probably using this mother-daughter scenario to capture your attention."

"What are you talking about?" said Hope as she slowly walked toward Ivey with rage in her heart.

"Mama is your mother and she is here in this hospital with a medical condition," sighed Ivey in a calm tone. "You are Jayla's mother and she is here in this same hospital with a medical condition."

"It is purely a coincidence!" shrieked Hope.

"No . . . it is not a coincidence," said Ivey. "Did you ever wonder whether all this was God's plan?" She paused. "Maybe God is prolonging Jayla's recovery process to give you some time to do what is right?"

Hope closed her eyes. "Why is God doing this to me?" she mumbled.

"Hope, mama will die if you don't help her," said Ivey as she wiped a tear from her eye. "Please help mama. Do it for me. Do it for Jayden. Do it for

Jayla. Do it for God," sobbed Ivey.

A tear trickled down Hope's face.

"I can get the doctors to test you today if you'll allow them to do it," cried Ivey.

"It just doesn't seem right, Ivey," winced Hope. "Why should I help her?"

Ivey rubbed her hands together. "Well then at least allow your children to meet their grandmother before she dies," wept Ivey as she walked toward Jayla.

Hope scratched her temples as if she was trying to control her stress level. She started tugging on her hair knowing a bald spot was en route if she didn't stop. Her trichotillomania had caused some damage to her scalp but she had managed to the best of her ability. Certainly, her post-traumatic stress disorder was causing an intense level of panicked feelings to flow through her at this moment. She had planned to get some therapy but never convinced herself that it would help now since she was no longer being traumatized like when she was a child. But if she ever needed therapy, this was definitely the time to start considering it.

"I don't know," muffled Hope.

"If you will not do it for mama, do it for daddy," said Ivey knowing that Hope had always accepted Eugene as a father figure.

Hope slowly exhaled recalling when Eugene told her about the trauma he had experienced with his mother. He had learned to forgive and help his mother which tugged at Hope's heart. She remembered that Eugene had contemplated allowing his mother to burn up in the house because of the many bruises she inflicted on him as a child because his father had left her. Hope winced as she reflected upon him telling her that he risked his life saving her and his face got burnt. Hope loved Eugene and she figured if he could learn to forgive his mother, it was worth her considering.

"Look, Hope," said Ivey with an excited tone as she pointed at Jayla.

Hope swallowed hard as her gaze landed on Jayla. Jayla's eyes were open.

"Jayla, can you hear me?" asked Hope in a low tone. "You are going to be alight."

Jayla's gaze fixated on Hope and Ivey's lips.

"Jayla, please shake your head if you can hear me," pleaded Hope.

A tear trickled down Hope's face as she observed Jayla turn her head to look out the window as if she didn't want to look at Hope. A puzzled feeling flowed through Hope as she walked around the hospital bed to look at Jayla's face.

An ounce of uneasiness pumped through Hope as she noticed that Jayla refused to look at her.

"I think she's been reading our lips," muffled Hope. "She knows what we said."

Ivey put her hand over her round shaped mouth.

Tears streamed down Hope's face as she watched Jayla's slender fingers glide in the air to communicate in ASL without looking at Hope.

"What did she say?" asked Ivey in a curious manner.

Hope gasped for air as if she was taking her last breath. "Jayla . . . wants me to help my mother," cried Hope as if Heaven had opened the floodgates.

This was the first time, in several years, that Hope had acknowledged Gloria as being her mother.

Chapter 42

Thursday afternoon, Hope inched opened the hospital room door. Cream colored blinds dangled in the window. Two sky blue chairs pressed against the snowflake white colored wall. A small television mounted in the corner of the wall.

Hope slowly inched toward the hospital bed as if her feet were stuck in cement. Her heart pulsated with every step she took as if she was on death row.

"I don't want any food," said a woman with a faint raspy voice as she rested on the hospital bed with her back toward the door.

Hope sat, staring at the frail woman's white hospital gown. The woman made no effort to turn around to look at Hope.

"I'm not hungry. Just let me be. I'm better off this way," coughed the woman without lifting her head.

Hope's shallowed nervous breaths made her feel as though she should just leave the room. She didn't want to disturb the woman. She didn't even want to speak to her. In fact, she didn't want to be in the same room as her. Yet, her mind wouldn't allow her to rest anymore. Her heart wouldn't allow her to maintain hate anymore. Her soul wouldn't allow her to have peace anymore. And, it all surfed when Jayla's gentle request touched Hope's heart.

Hope cleared her throat, hoping that the woman would turn around to initiate the conversation.

"I've already told you I don't want anything to eat. So, please leave."

Hope pressed her back firmly against the chair. Every nerve within her body told her to leave. But every cell in her body told her to stay.

A harsh sound reaped through the air as the woman coughed. The woman placed her caramel brown hand over her mouth, trying to hold the coughs. Her thin, patchy, sandy brown hair bounced as she coughed. Hope figured the chemotherapy had taken a toll on the woman's hair.

"Gloria," mouthed Hope as if the woman could hear her. Hope's heart clenched as she forced her lips to open to call Gloria, her mother.

A tear rolled down Hope's face as she noticed that her mother was slowly fading away. Life seemed to have been seeping out of every pour of Gloria's body. Hope had never seen her in this poor state. Even when she was on drugs, Hope recalled that her body was full of life—and other stuff too.

Hope's muscles around her mouth contracted as she forced her lips apart.

"Mama," said Hope in a soft tone noticing that her mother didn't even turn around. "Mama," repeated Hope in a louder tone. "It's Hope."

The woman cleared her throat. "Get out of here," shrieked the woman causing Hope to flinch. "*My* Hope would never come and see me. So, if you think you can fool me . . . you're wrong," said Gloria without turning around. "Hope hates me to the core of her heart and soul." She paused. "So, stop trying to talk like her."

A dim glimpse of sunlight flowed inside Gloria's hospital room.

"Mama . . . it is me," mumbled Hope as a tear rolled down her face.

"Get on out of here! You're not *my* Hope," said Gloria as she pulled the covers over her head as if she didn't recognize Hope's voice. It had been nearly seven years since she last spoke with Hope. Yet, a mother should never forget her child's voice. But Gloria's health had taken a beating which caused her to slowly forget things.

"It's me," whispered Hope.

"I already told you . . . that my Hope wouldn't come and see me," said Gloria. "But I appreciate you for trying to make me happy by pretending to be her." She paused. "So, you can tell Ivey I said I don't need no fake person coming in here pretending to be my daughter."

Beeping sounds flowed out of the monitoring machine near Gloria.

Hope sat quietly for several minutes.

"All I want from my Hope is to see her one last time before I *die*," muffled Gloria through the white sheets as she continued to bury her head as if she was a mummy. "Hope doesn't have to help me. She doesn't have to let the doctors test her. She doesn't even have to give me the cells or the transplant. I just want to make peace with her," sighed Gloria.

Hope cleared her throat.

"Who would've thought I would one day need some cells to save my life . . . from the daughter that I treated so badly," exhaled Gloria before becoming silent for a few seconds. "I guess God has a funny way of doing things."

Hope glanced at the IV as medicine dripped down in Gloria's veins.

"I've done some really mean things to Hope. I didn't protect her. I didn't love her as I should have. I just didn't," cried Gloria. "I used to get high on crack in abandoned buildings. Can you believe I used to drag Hope in those nasty places with me?" wept Gloria. "She was just a child and I was a low-life drug addict. I let her down. I didn't even help her when she told me some men had hurt her stomach. I didn't know what she meant by that when she told me . . . 'cause I was too busy getting high instead of protecting her," sniffled Gloria. "I finally realized what she meant but it was too late . . . our mother-daughter relationship was already destroyed," mumbled Gloria as if she was preparing the words for her own eulogy. "I didn't protect her. I didn't help her."

Hope reached over and touched Gloria's right shoulder, caressing it. Hope's heart trembled as she felt Gloria gently pull her shoulder away from her hand, causing tears to tumble down Hope's face.

"I don't need no sympathy. You don't have to try to comfort me," mumbled Gloria as she pulled the sheets tighter over her head. "So, you can leave if you like."

Hope stood still as if she was a mannequin.

"I guess you're staying," sniffled Gloria as if she could sense someone was still standing near her. "I did my Hope wrong," said Gloria as though she wasn't finished unleashing her wrongdoings. "I didn't feed her sometimes. I didn't bathe her sometimes. I didn't even hug her sometimes," coughed Gloria. "I used to call her a *Bad Seed*. She didn't deserve it. But I took my anger and hatred out on her 'cause my mother's drug dealing friends had raped me . . . and got me pregnant with her."

Hope tilted her head toward the ceiling.

"I was a good girl. I wasn't on drugs when I got pregnant with her," she paused. "My mother was too high to even know that those men had raped me. I had no one to talk to. There was no one to help me. After I had Hope, I felt so depressed. I didn't know what to do so I turned to drugs. That was the only life I knew," wept Gloria. "I saw my mother do it. I saw my father do it and everybody else. So, I thought getting on drugs was the right thing to do."

Every seed of hatred in Hope's heart slowly peeled away as she listened to her mother try to make peace with herself.

"I heard that Hope has her own catering company. I am proud of her," paused Gloria. "I heard she is married to an engineer and they have a set of twins. I doubt it if I'll ever get to meet her husband or my grandchildren," wept Gloria. "I . . . at least . . . want to see my grandchildren before I die even if Hope doesn't want to see me. I don't blame Hope for being this way toward me."

Hope shifted in the chair as a tear rolled down her face.

"I blame myself 'cause God knows I didn't treat her like a mother should've treated her. But I can't take it back. I can't," sobbed Gloria. "All I can do now is try to make peace with her 'cause God knows I treated her wrong," said Gloria as if she was confessing her sins. "I pray that Hope can one day forgive me."

A river of tears flowed down Hope's face like a tsunami.

"Mama, it's me," said Hope as she slowly pulled the covers off Gloria's head.

Gloria firmly held the covers over her head.

"No, it is not!" shrieked Gloria.

"Mama, please, let me pull the covers off your head," cried Hope.

"Get away from me. You're not my Hope," blurted Gloria in a deranged tone.

Hope slowly slid her hands underneath the white sheets as tears rolled down her face. She gently placed her hands on top of Gloria's head massaging it to help Gloria realize that it was indeed Hope in the room with her. Hope recalled that her mother liked it when Hope massaged her head. Gloria used to say Hope had magic hands because Hope's massages helped ease her troubled mind and often time helped her to fall asleep.

Gloria slowly released the white sheets from over her head. She slowly turned her head toward Hope. Her body trembled as she forced herself to an upright position on the hospital bed.

The rays of the sun shined into the room creating a glow on the walls.

Gloria stretched her frail caramel brown arms toward Hope's face. She planted her hands underneath Hope's chin as if she was cupping the smoothness of Hope's skin. Tears flowed down Gloria's round shaped face like an avalanche as she pulled Hope's face closer to her as if she needed a better view.

"Mama, it's me, Hope," she sniffled while splinters of her heart slowly unraveled.

Gloria closed her eyes as her dry lips slowly opened to say, "Thank you, God."

Chapter 43

Thursday evening, Hope sat in the familiar beige painted habilitation room. A river of excitement flowed through her veins as she watched Dr. Shaw place the soundproof headphones on Jayla's ears and his ears. Dr. Ericsson didn't want to delay Jayla's auditory and speech habilitation therapy any further.

Hope sat quietly as she kept her eyes on Jayla. She could feel Sloan sporadically looking at her as he sat beside him. Hope made *sure* her gaze never connected with Dr. Shaw. Her jewel box couldn't withstand the harsh pounding from Sloan again.

A warm feeling flowed through Hope as she reflected upon the joy that her mother had felt at the sight of her face. Hope was delighted that God had answered her mother's prayers. Now, Hope was praying that God would answer her prayers. But she did not want it to seem as though she was bargaining their fates. Jayden's prognosis was hopeful. He was putting forth efforts to hear and speak. Jayla's prognosis wasn't hopeful causing Hope's heart to splinter nearly beyond repair.

"Jayden is making a lot of progress," smiled Sloan as he pinched Jayden's cheek. "Dr. Shaw has been working with him every day."

Hope leaned back in her chair, recalling Sloan preferred to meet with Dr. Shaw alone as he provided habilitation therapy to Jayden. She didn't mind because she didn't want any unnecessary tension from Sloan. In fact, Sloan's plan worked out because Hope was able to spend time with Jayla.

Hope looked at her son. "I am proud of you, Jayden," said Hope in a heartfelt tone as she reached across Sloan to hug Jayden.

Jayden slowly opened his mouth as words struggled to flow between his lips. Hope expected this to happen. Dr. Ericsson had forewarned her that Jayden needed to complete several auditory and speech therapy sessions before the words would smoothly flow out of his mouth.

Jayden slid out of his chair beside Sloan. He walked over to Hope, wrapping his chestnut brown arms around her. Hope inhaled, embracing Jayden's tight hug.

"Th . . . thanks," said Jayden in a flat tone that touched Hope's heart.

A pleasant feeling tumbled through Hope's heart. She was grateful that Jayden could hear her voice. She was grateful that Jayden would speak.

"Dr. Shaw said Jayden was making great strides," grinned Sloan in an exciting tone. "He turned out to be right," smiled Sloan as he looked at Hope.

"I am grateful that Jayden is able to hear and speak," said Hope, making sure her response focused on Jayden instead of Dr. Shaw.

"Jayden and I have been hanging out this morning," smiled Sloan as he looked at Jayden.

Jayden was discharged yesterday. Sloan had been spending more time with him than he ever did in the past.

"What did you guys do?" smiled Hope as her gaze shifted between Jayden and Sloan.

"We've been catching up on a few father-to-son stuff," said Sloan as he gently elbowed Jayden.

A delightful feeling rolled through Hope as she noticed the sparkles in Sloan's eyes as he spoke about the activities that he and Jayden had done earlier today.

"Did you have fun, Jayden?" smiled Hope.

"Ye...Yes," responded Jayden, causing a joyful feeling to flow through Hope as Jayden forced the words out of his mouth.

"When are you going to introduce me to your mother?" whispered Sloan.

Hope paused for a brief second. "Some time today if you like. She is resting now."

"And your sister?" inquired Sloan.

"If she is at work today, you can meet her too," responded Hope in a low tone.

"You sound like you don't want me to meet them."

"Sloan, please don't start anything in here," begged Hope. "I want to focus on Jayla right now."

"Do you plan on allowing the twins to meet their grandmother sometime today too?" asked

Sloan in a sarcastic tone as he glanced at his watch.

"I guess so," said Hope as she quickly gawked at him.

"This is like one big family reunion," chuckled Sloan. "Are you going to allow the doctors to test you to see if you can help your mother?" asked Sloan in a serious tone as he glanced at his watch again.

Hope ignored Sloan's questions as she glanced at Dr. Shaw, hoping that he couldn't hear them through the soundproof headphones.

"Maybe *Dr. Shaw* can give you the checkup," whispered Sloan as if insecurity was creeping inside of him.

A vibrating sound entered the air as Sloan looked at his cell phone. He cleared his throat.

"I have to fly out later on to meet Mr. Gavino."

Hope bit her bottom lip, trying to contain her composure in the habilitation room.

"I will return before noon tomorrow," said Sloan as he glanced at his phone again. "I am sure you can take care of things while I am away for a few hours."

"Can I go with you?" asked Hope in a low tone. "I can ask Mrs. Brown to watch Jayden since you and I would only be gone less than a day," said Hope, hoping that she had used the proper King's English. "I am sure Mrs. Brown wouldn't mind watching him since we are already in Charlotte," smiled Hope. She wanted to spend some quality time with Sloan to try to rekindle things.

"*No*," blurted Sloan without pausing. "I mean . . . I think it is best if you stay here with Jayla," he said as if he was seriously hiding something. "Plus, this is a business trip, Hope . . . not a vacation for you and me," he said as he turned away from Hope to face Jayden.

Hope watched as Sloan played with Jayden while they sat beside each other. She took this opportunity to quickly glance at Jayla. She noticed Dr. Shaw was communicating in ASL with Jayla. Suddenly, her gaze connected with Dr. Shaw's for a split second. Like before, Hope noticed Dr. Shaw had scanned her face. But this time it seemed as if his gaze shifted from her eyes to her breasts and quickly back to looking at Jayla.

Hope quickly shifted her gaze from Jayla toward the floor as she felt Sloan gently nudge her.

"Did you find what you were looking for over there?" mumbled Sloan as if he was trying to use his words carefully since Jayden was able to hear now.

"I was trying to see how Jayla was doing, Sloan," responded Hope while smiling at Jayden.

"Okay, I'm just making sure," smirked Sloan while placing his butterscotch brown hand near his crotch as if he was resting his hand. "I see I might have to do my *inventory* when I return from my quick business trip," smirked Sloan as he glanced at Hope's jewel box.

Hope exhaled, feeling as though Sloan was trying to conspicuously threaten her. She knew exactly what Sloan was implying when he placed his hand near his crotch.

She got nervous as she noticed that Dr. Shaw had continued to communicate with Jayla. This was longer than what Dr. Shaw had done with Jayden.

"What is Dr. Shaw saying to Jayla?" whispered Sloan.

Hope glanced at Dr. Shaw's fingers as he communicated to Jayla. She winced, recalling that Sloan still struggled to understand ASL.

"He is asking Jayla if she can hear him," responded Hope while carefully avoiding saying Dr. Shaw's name in any manner that would rattle a nerve within Sloan.

"What did Jayla say?" asked Sloan in an anxious tone.

"She didn't respond to him," cringed Hope.

Dr. Shaw stood. He removed the soundproof headphones from his head. He slowly walked over to Hope and Sloan. His luscious lips slowly parted.

"I need more time to work with Jayla," said Dr. Shaw as he cleared his throat.

Sloan stood. "Do you need an additional thirty minutes to an hour as you did during Jayden's first session?" inquired Sloan.

Dr. Shaw paused before responding. "No, Mr. Glover," replied Dr. Shaw as Hope noticed his gaze landed on her face as if he was trying to monitor his words carefully. "Jayla needs more time than that."

Hope swallowed hard. She didn't want to ruffle Sloan's feathers. But she needed to ask Dr. Shaw a few questions.

Hope slowly stood as her plum colored long sundress snuggled nicely into her flawless body.

"Is something wrong, doctor?" asked Hope in a flat tone, as she gripped Sloan's hand to reassure him of her respect for him.

Dr. Shaw glanced at Jayla before responding. "Jayla is not progressing like Jayden did," whispered Dr. Shaw.

"What do you mean?" sobbed Hope. "Jayla had the same operation as Jayden. She is receiving the same habilitation treatment as Jayden. So, what do you mean Jayla is not progressing like him?"

Silence flowed through the room as if it had been sucked inside a vacuum.

"I understand that this may be an emotional time for you, Mrs. Glover," said Dr. Shaw in a compassionate tone.

"That is an understatement, Dr. Shaw," snapped Sloan.

Hope looked at Jayden as he slid off the chair. A tear rolled down his chestnut brown face as he walked toward Jayla. Hope's heart plummeted as she watched Jayden wrap his small arms around Jayla.

"Do you think Jayla will ever be able to hear and speak?" asked Hope as her cheeks suddenly became wet from the trail of tears that flowed from her eyes.

Dr. Shaw's hazel brown eyes connected with Hope's gaze.

"Only time will tell," he responded.

Hope walked toward her twins. Her heart skipped a beat as tears streamed down Jayden's face while he removed the soundproof headphones from Jayla's ears.

Hope gawked at Jayla's fingers as she communicated in ASL with Jayden. She inhaled sharply as Jayla's light brown eyes locked into her gaze.

Hope's bottom lip trembled as she read Jayla's fingers.

"What did she say, Hope?" asked Sloan in a disturbing tone.

"Jayla said . . . ," sobbed Hope as if the words were painful for her to say.

"What did she say?" repeated Sloan as he walked closer to Hope.

"Jayla said it's okay if she never hears like Jayden," cried Hope.

Every core of sanity within Hope crumbled as she watched Jayla plant her head against

Jayden's small chest. Though Hope wanted Jayla to be able to hear, she still loved and accepted her.

Her hopes of Jayla and Jayden being able to hear and speak seemed to have shattered before her very eyes.

Chapter 44

Friday morning, Hope sat in the small medical room holding Mrs. Brown and Tiffany's hand as they prayed. A sharp pain pierced through her heart at the thought of Jayla never being able to hear or speak. The spotless tan colored walls surrounded her. Sky blue padded chairs assembled in the corner of the room.

"I'm glad you came, Mrs. Brown," said Hope. "And you too, Tiffany."

"No problem," uttered Mrs. Brown in a soft tone. "I'm glad you agreed to allow the doctors to test you to see if you're a match for your mother."

"All of this is so hard for me to accept," said Hope as a tear rolled down her face.

"I understand," sighed Mrs. Brown. "How long did the doctor say it would take for the results?" asked Mrs. Brown while brushing a lint ball off her burgundy dress.

"An hour or two," winced Hope. "That's why I wanted you to be here with me."

"I think you're doing what's right in the eyesight of God," blurted Mrs. Brown.

"I still don't know, Mrs. Brown," smirked Hope. "My mind has been so cloudy about what is going on with Jayla. I had plans for both of my twins to go to regular school in a few weeks," cried Hope. "But it seems as if Jayden will be able to hear and speak and Jayla will not."

Hope wrapped her slender arms around Jayden, pulling him closer to her.

"Maybe Jayla will make some progress soon," said Tiffany in a calm tone. "Don't give up on her yet," said Tiffany as she adjusted a button on her blue shirt.

"I'm not giving up on Jayla. I'm just preparing myself for the worse scenario. I just want both of my twins to be normal," said Hope as she watched Jayden walk into a corner to play with his toys. "Jayla is in habilitation therapy right now with Dr. Shaw. He has been working with her every day. I just want her to be normal."

"Jayla is normal. Jayla and Jayden were born normal," sighed Mrs. Brown as she looked in Jayden's direction. "You are the one who thought it was abnormal 'cause they couldn't hear or speak."

"It's not normal, Mrs. Brown. It's not right."

"It is, Hope. So, please stop saying it's not normal. You're acting like you are unable to accept the twins for how they were born."

"I can," cried Hope as she looked down.

"Well, act like it then and stop being so insensitive," scolded Mrs. Brown.

A tear trickled down Hope's face. "You're right," she said as she walked closer to Mrs. Brown to hug her before returning to her seat to sit.

Mrs. Brown slightly winced noticing that Hope's perfume was a familiar scent. *But from where?* she thought. She did not have time to inquire about the perfume scent because she was focused on talking to Hope about refraining from being insensitive.

Mrs. Brown firmly pressed her lips together before speaking. "It's hard enough how the world treats people who have some trouble hearing. Your twins don't need their own mother treating them bad and not accepting them."

Silence filtered through the air as if Mrs. Brown's voice had caused sound to disappear.

"God made a way for Jayden to be healed," said Mrs. Brown as she gently gripped Hope's chin to lift her head.

"What about Jayla?" asked Hope as her head tilted toward the ceiling.

"Maybe God isn't done with Jayla," sighed Mrs. Brown. "Maybe there is something else that God needs to do with her."

"Like what," cried Hope.

Mrs. Brown leaned back in the sky blue, padded chair as Ivey entered the room. "I don't know, Hope. But I do know that God works in mysterious ways."

"You are right, Mrs. Brown," confirmed Ivey. "Dr. Shaw said Jayden is making good progress," she smiled.

"I know. But even if he does go to regular school," paused Hope. "Dr. Shaw and Dr. Ericsson said Jayden would still need to continue auditory and speech therapy. So, I might just send him to the other school where Jayla will have to go," said Hope as her head drooped.

"Lift your head, Hope," ordered Mrs. Brown. "You don't have nothing to be ashamed about."

"I know. But it hurts my heart to know that Jayla may never hear or speak like Jayden," sighed Hope. She was obsessed with the idea of having perfect children because Gloria had called her a *Bad Seed.*

"God is in control, Hope," sighed Mrs. Brown. "I've been praying for them. But I know God makes no mistakes." Mrs. Brown paused before speaking. "So, please stop saying you want them to be normal. This may be normal to them."

Hope slowly exhaled. "I know. I just . . . I just want them to be okay."

Hope wept before speaking, "I want my children to have every advantage I can possibly give them. But if this is who they are, then there's nothing wrong with that."

A scraping sound echoed through the room as Jayden rolled his car toys across the tile floor.

"Where is your husband, Hope?" asked Tiffany.

"He is on a business trip. He will be here at noon today."

"What is his name?" smiled Tiffany.

"I told you before, Sloan," sighed Hope.

"He travels a lot," said Mrs. Brown as her eyebrows connected. "Do you ever go with him?"

"No," muffled Hope.

"Has he ever invited you to go with him?" asked Tiffany.

"No," responded Hope.

"Why not?" asked Tiffany as a puzzled look spread across her face.

"He doesn't like to mix business with personal life."

Tiffany pressed her lips together before proceeding with more questions.

"Speaking of family, does he have any sisters or brothers?"

"I don't know."

"What do you mean you don't know, Hope?" asked Mrs. Brown in a concerning tone.

"I've never met his family."

"Why not?" inquired Tiffany as she scratched her caramel brown face.

"He was raised in different foster homes ever since he was a little kid," sighed Hope. "His parents were on drugs. They didn't take care of him." So, Hope saw herself in him because Gloria was like that too.

"I'm sorry to hear that," mumbled Tiffany.

"Have you ever visited his hometown?" asked Mrs. Brown. "I'm sure he has aunts and uncles . . . or cousins."

"No," said Hope in a low tone as if Mrs. Brown and Tiffany were helping her to realize that she actually didn't really know Sloan.

"Where is he from?" asked Tiffany.

"New York."

"How long have you been with him?" asked Tiffany.

"Seven years," muffled Hope in a low tone.

"Have you met any of his friends . . . since you've never met any of his family members," asked Mrs. Brown in an inquisitive tone.

Hope was too embarrassed to respond. "No," answered Hope as she slowly felt as if she had married a stranger.

"What about his co-workers or business associates, Hope?" asked

Tiffany as her eyes widened like chestnuts as if she was in shock.

Hope paused for a few seconds. "Tiffany, why are you asking me so many questions about my husband?"

"No reason, Hope. I'm just trying to hold a conversation with you. Would you like to ask me questions about my husband? If so, I don't mind answering them," said Tiffany in a supportive tone as if she was trying to get Hope to realize that something wasn't adding up about Sloan.

Hope stood. She pressed her back against the tan colored wall.

Tiffany walked toward Hope. She wrapped her slender arms around Hope. "We have been friends for a long time, Hope," sighed Tiffany. "Even though it has been almost seven years since I last saw you . . . I still know when something is bothering you."

Silence sprinkled through the room.

"I've been under a lot of stress, lately," muffled Hope. "This issue with Jayla . . . and with . . . my mother," mumbled Hope, "It is getting the best of me."

"I see," said Mrs. Brown in a caring tone.

Hope glanced at Jayden for a few seconds. "I met Sloan when I arrived in Raleigh. I didn't know anyone. I didn't even really have friends other than two girls who I worked with," muffled Hope. "One day, it was raining while I was walking to work. Sloan pulled over and gave me a ride to work."

"You got in the car with a stranger!" shrieked Tiffany.

"Yes," mumbled Hope. "He gave me a ride to my job."

"How did he know where you worked?" asked Tiffany.

A puzzling feeling flowed through Hope as she recalled that she had never told Sloan where she worked. She remembered pondering that rainy day as to how he knew that she worked at Class Touch Tavern.

"Sloan said he figured out that I worked at the upscale restaurant on that same street."

"*Something* doesn't seem right, Hope," babbled Mrs. Brown in a low tone. "If you never told him where you worked . . . then how did he know?"

"Do you think he had been following you for a few days or weeks?" asked Tiffany in a bewildered tone.

"No," smiled Hope. "He isn't that type of guy."

A frown flashed across Tiffany's face. "I'm just saying, Hope," grimaced Tiffany. "Think about it. You were a young girl in a new city. You didn't have any family there. You didn't have any friends there. You didn't even know anyone," uttered Tiffany.

Hope swallowed hard knowing that Tiffany's words were true. "I know."

"Then out of nowhere comes this man who gives you a ride to your job even though you never told him where you worked," said Tiffany as if she was lecturing Hope. "It's like he was cruising the streets looking for a young girl. Then he married you really quickly. You've never met any of his family. You've never met any of his friends. And I assume, you've never met his co-workers or business associates."

A tear rolled down Hope's face.

"You don't know what you're talking about, Tiffany," muffled Hope.

"Yes, I do, Hope," said Tiffany as she slowly held Hope's hands. "You told me that day that Tony and Vance met you in Raleigh that your husband didn't like you having anyone at your house. We thought that was so strange for a grown man to tell a *grown woman* that she couldn't have any friends at her house. My husband is an attorney with the FBI. He thinks Sloan is controlling you as if you're his prisoner. You even shared with me that Sloan was older than you," paused Tiffany. "Something isn't right, Hope."

Hope buried her face in her hands.

Mrs. Brown walked over to Hope, caressing her hands. "Do you even know what type of life he had before he met you?"

"No," said Hope as she paused for a few seconds, realizing that Tiffany and Mrs. Brown had valid points. Hope allowed the floodgates to open as she said, "I was so naïve. I don't know much about him. I trusted him too easily," she winced. "I've always felt like I wasn't good enough for anyone because Sergeant Smith raped me. He stole my virginity from me." A tear rolled down her face. "Gloria made me feel like I was nothing and I've hated her all these years. But Sloan made me feel special. So, I married him out of fear that no one would want me. But I now see that everything he said and done were lies. I feel like I married a stranger."

The unbreakable bond that Hope once had with Sloan chipped away. Every speculation that she had been harboring about him was released into the atmosphere.

Chapter 45

An hour later, Hope continued to sit in the medical room. The threads of her sanity had slowly unraveled as she analyzed her marriage to Sloan. Her mind wouldn't allow her to ignore the warning signs. But her heart wouldn't allow her to overlook the fact that Sloan was the father of her twins. Even though Hope wished that Tiffany and Mrs. Brown had never helped her to see things clearly, she knew the truth would come out at some point.

Hope figured whatever Sloan was doing, she was determined to unveil it soon.

"Tiffany, please don't tell Vance what I told you," muffled Hope in a low tone as her heart raced away. "I don't want any problems."

Tiffany sat stiffer than a statue.

"Hope, you've been my friend since we were teenagers."

"I know, Tiffany. But you still haven't answered my questions," said Hope as her bottom lip started to tremble. "I don't want anything to happen to Sloan. We shouldn't make assumptions."

"What if the assumptions turn out to be something serious," whispered Mrs. Brown as she gawked at Hope.

Hope wrapped her arms around Jayden, covering up his perky ears. "I don't want to ruin my marriage. I don't want to ruin my children's relationship with their father. I don't want to cause any problems for Sloan just because of assumptions." Hope had forced herself to ignore Sloan's wrongdoings to keep her family.

A gentle breeze swept through the room, mingling with the fine hairs on the back of Hope's neck.

"How is your catering business doing?" asked Tiffany in a low tone as if she wanted to change the subject.

"It's doing fine," smiled Hope.

Mrs. Brown looked at her withered hands. "I don't know how much longer I'm going to keep baking and cooking. Maybe you can take my customers, Hope," sighed Mrs. Brown.

"I don't know, Mrs. Brown. Your customers have been with you for years."

"Well, they're going have to go to someone else anyway when I stop," exhaled Mrs. Brown as she rubbed her hands together as if her arthritis was acting up. "So, you should take them," winked Mrs. Brown.

A soft scraping sound could be heard as the medical room door opened.

"I have been looking for you, Hope," said Sloan as he strolled into the room. His cream linen business suit highlighted his well-groomed appearance.

Jayden dashed over to Sloan, hugging him as if he hadn't seen him in years.

"I am glad you made it back from your business trip," smiled Hope.

"I told you that I would return before noon today," uttered Sloan as he planted a kiss on Hope's cheek. "I checked on Jayla before I came here. She is still with Dr. Shaw and Dr. Ericsson. She will be discharged tomorrow."

"I have been in here with Tiffany and Mrs. Brown," said Hope as she wondered how Sloan knew her exact location in the hospital. She wondered if he had installed a tracking device on her cell phone. "I figured it was best for me to allow the doctors to work with Jayla without Jayden and me being in the room with her."

Hope stood as she straightened out a wrinkle on her canary yellow shirt. "Sloan, this is Mrs. Brown, my Godmother," smiled Hope.

"I have heard a lot about you, Mrs. Brown," smiled Sloan. "And I take it that this is Tiffany?" grinned Sloan.

"Yes, it is. She was my childhood best friend," said Hope.

"Hello, Sloan," said Tiffany in a flat tone as she squinted.

Quietness surfed inside the room.

"Has the doctor been in yet?" asked Sloan as he looked at Hope.

"No," said Hope. "We are still waiting," responded Hope as she noticed a bewildered look dance across Mrs. Brown's face.

"Has the doctor run the test on you yet?" inquired Sloan.

Hope glanced at Tiffany, noticing that she was staring at Sloan as if she was disgusted. Hope wished she hadn't shared with Tiffany anything negative about Sloan.

"Yes. The doctor took blood from me. He also did a cheek swab."

"Who is he, Hope?" inquired Sloan as he grinned while looking at his watch.

Tiffany sneered as she squinted.

"My mother's doctor. His name is Dr. Sterling."

"Okay," smiled Sloan as if he was delighted that it wasn't Dr. Shaw who had stuck a swab in

Hope's mouth.

"Why did Dr. Sterling have to put the swab in your mouth? What will the swab show?" asked

Sloan as he squatted in front of Jayden to play with him.

Hope looked at Tiffany. A puzzled look crept across Tiffany's face as she slowly shook her head from side to side, trying to avoid Sloan from seeing her do it.

"He said the swab would show whether I am a match for my mother."

"What do you mean?" asked Sloan.

A touch of uneasiness erupted within Hope as she looked at Mrs. Brown and Tiffany. Hope felt like a child responding to Sloan as if he was a warden. She disliked when Sloan returned from his business trips. He always had an overabundance of aggressiveness stored inside of him.

"Dr. Sterling used a swab to collect DNA from Hope's cheek," responded Tiffany as if she wanted to help Hope explain the procedure.

Sloan didn't even look up at Tiffany as if he was consumed with arrogance and being in control.

"The swab will detect a minimum of six or more HCL markers," sneered Tiffany as she looked at Hope. "HCL markers stands for Human Leukocyte Antigen. If the HCL markers in Hope match her mother's HCL markers, then Hope can donate cells . . . bone marrow to her mother."

Sloan stood. He clapped his hands as if he was applauding Tiffany.

"Thank you for that great explanation, *Dr. Tiffany*," said Sloan in a sarcastic tone. "You are a doctor, right?" asked Sloan. "I think Hope told me that you were."

"Yes, I am," blurted Tiffany as she stared at Sloan without breaking her gaze.

A touch of bitterness knocked on Hope's heart as she looked at Sloan.

"Mrs. Brown, I know you are proud of her," grinned Sloan.

"I am," said Mrs. Brown as she pressed her hands together in a praying position.

"*Dr. Tiffany*," said Sloan as he gawked at her. "I was expecting my *wife*, Hope, to explain to me what Dr. Sterling did to her. Hope needs to understand every step of the process if she agrees to do it," he smiled nonchalantly.

Mrs. Brown closed her eyes. Hope was certain that Mrs. Brown was praying this time.

The door slowly opened. A short white man walked into the medical room.

"Hello, I am Dr. Sterling," said a man as the wrinkles on his alabaster white face overtook his forehead. "I need to talk with Hope Glover in privacy."

Mrs. Brown slowly stood.

"I don't mind if they stay in here," said Hope.

"I would rather share the results only with you at this time," said Dr. Sterling.

"I am her husband, so I should be able to remain in here, right?" grinned Sloan.

Dr. Sterling paused for a few seconds.

"Due to hospital policies, sir, I need to talk with Hope Glover by herself."

Sloan stared at Dr. Sterling before grabbing Jayden's hand. He opened the door for Tiffany and Mrs. Brown. They exited the room as if they were on an assembly line.

Dr. Sterling turned on the small electronic device.

Hope sat patiently as Dr. Sterling reviewed something on the device. Hope leaned forward as Dr. Sterling spoke with her. She listened tentatively as he provided an overview of all the tests that he had conducted on her.

"Are you on any sleeping medicine?" asked Dr. Sterling.

Even though Hope's body was inside the room with Dr. Sterling, her mind was a million miles away. Her heart throbbed as she tried to rationalize why Sloan was always aggressive, dominating and disrespectful every time he returned from a business trip with Mr. Gavino. Somehow, after a day or two, Sloan always managed to transform into a loving, supporting and kind husband.

"Mrs. Glover, did you hear me?" asked Dr. Sterling.

"Yes," said Hope as she finally realized that Dr. Sterling was trying to get her attention.

"Did you eat or drink anything before you took the test?"

"I had a cup of lemon tea," responded Hope.

"Are you taking any sleeping medicine?"

"No," said Hope. "Why?"

Dr. Sterling stared at Hope as if her response puzzled him. "Well, the test detected sleeping medicine in your blood."

"That can't be correct," said Hope.

Dr. Sterling paused before speaking again. "Do you have any questions?" he asked as he scratched his forehead.

Hope paused, trying to recall the words that came out of Dr. Sterling's mouth.

"No," responded Hope in a low tone as she glanced at the door.

Dr. Sterling stared at Hope.

"Are you okay?" asked Dr. Sterling in a bizarre tone.

"Yes," mumbled Hope in an uncertain tone.

Dr. Sterling leaned back.

"You appear to be uninterested in the results," said Dr. Sterling.

"I . . . I am," muffled Hope.

Dr. Sterling tapped his long white fingers on the electronic device.

"But you didn't react when I announced the results to you," uttered Dr. Sterling.

"I don't recall you telling me the results, Dr. Sterling," said Hope while recalling that she had ventured off for a few minutes thinking about Sloan as Dr. Sterling was talking to her. "What did you say?" asked Hope as a touch of curiosity flowed through her.

Dr. Sterling's gray bushy eyebrows connected before his pink lips opened. "Are you okay?" he asked while looking at Hope.

"Yes, I was daydreaming for a few seconds. I've got a lot on my mind." She paused. "But what did you say about the results regarding Gloria?

"According to the test results, you are definitely a match to Gloria Rankin."

Chapter 46

The Friday morning gloomy clouds stretched against the massive sky. The sun struggled to find a corner to peek through the cloud.

A prickly feeling marched down Hope's spine. She sat in a padded chair inside the hospital.

Her mind raced faster than a leopard chasing its prey. But the slow beats of her heart made her feel as though she was daydreaming. Hope couldn't believe that she was physically in the same room with her mother, husband and children.

"Mama, I brought my husband and twins to meet you," said Hope in a flat tone.

Snoring sounds danced through the hospital room.

"Mama," repeated Hope as she gently tapped Gloria on her shoulder.

"Maybe we should come back later, Hope," said Sloan.

"Mama," said Hope as she slowly fingered through her mother's hair while gently massaging her scalp.

Gloria gradually opened her eyes. She sluggishly pulled herself to an upright position on the hospital bed. She pressed her small hands on her head, trying to press down the wild strings of her sandy brown hair.

"Who are all of these people, Hope?" said Gloria in a raspy voice.

"This is my husband, Sloan and our twins Jayla and Jayden," uttered Hope in a low tone.

"Excuse my appearance. I haven't seen a comb or a brush in a few days," she gently chuckled.

"That is okay," said Sloan as he stood near the hospital bed. "I'm glad I finally had a chance to meet you."

"Likewise," sighed Gloria as she gripped her green hospital gown.

"I met Ivey a few minutes ago in the hallway," smiled Sloan.

"That is good," coughed Gloria as she pulled the white sheet toward her neck.

"Mama, this is Jayden Lamar Glover," said Hope in a soft tone as she ushered Jayden closer to her mother.

"Hello," smiled Gloria as she looked at Jayden. "I am your grandmother," she said in a prideful tone.

"*Hel* . . . Hello," said Jayden at a slow staggering pace as he tugged on the bottom of his navy blue shirt.

Hope inhaled as she observed her mother squint as Jayden struggled to allow the words to roll off his tongue. Hope exhaled slowly, remembering that she had informed her mother that Jayden and Jayla were born deaf. She took pride in sharing with Gloria that the twins had their cochlear implant surgery completed this week.

"This is Jayla Michele Glover," said Hope as she ushered Jayla closer to Gloria.

Jayla stood, silent as she looked at Gloria. Her long ponytail brushed against her narrow shoulders. Her candy red shirt highlighted her youthful skin and white teeth.

"You are so pretty," uttered Gloria as she looked at Jayla. "You look just like your mother," sighed Gloria as if she was blowing out a match.

Gloria remained silent as if she was waiting for Jayla to speak.

"The doctor is still working with her," said Hope as if she wanted to explain to Gloria as why Jayla was not speaking.

Hope gracefully moved her fingers in front of Jayla to encourage her to try to speak. Jayla pressed her tiny bow shaped lips together. She glanced at Jayden before communicating with Hope in ASL. Hope's heart felt as though it was slowly withering like a pink rose on a chilly night.

"How did you learn sign language?" asked Gloria.

"I took some classes." Hope paused. "It's called ASL . . . American Sign Language"

"Oh," sighed Gloria. "I always knew that you were smart."

"What about you, Sloan?" asked Gloria. "Do you know how to do . . . ASL?"

Silence flowed through the room as if Sloan was contemplating whether to tell Gloria the truth or a lie.

"Not like Hope. I am still learning," said Sloan as he glanced at his watch.

Hope winced. Sloan had always relied on her to communicate with the twins.

"Jayla can understand you, mama. She can read lips," said Hope.

A small smile formed on Jayla's round face.

Gloria extended her lanky arms toward Jayla and Jayden. She stared at them for a second as if she was trying to capture a sparkle of love in their eyes.

Gloria rubbed Jayla's face for a few seconds as if she was reminiscing about when Hope was Jayla's age. "She will talk soon," said Gloria as if she knew something that Hope didn't.

Sloan pulled a chair closer to Gloria's hospital bed. "Have a seat, Hope."

Gloria reached for the remote. She turned on the small television in the hospital room. "They can watch cartoons," said Gloria as she handed Hope the remote control.

Hope motioned for Jayla and Jayden to sit near the television. Hope could see the back of their heads as they watched television.

"Jayla has hearing and speech therapy again today," uttered Hope.

"That's good," sighed Gloria.

A clean crisp scent floated in the air from Sloan's cologne.

"So where are you from, Sloan?"

"New Jersey," said Sloan while gawking at his watch.

A puzzled feeling flowed through Hope.

"I thought you told me you were from New York," smirked Hope.

"I am," said Sloan. "I meant to say, New York."

Hope started feeling very confused.

Gloria looked at Sloan for a few minutes with a slightly bewildered facial expression.

"What about your parents?"

"What about them?" inquired Sloan with a partial smile on his face.

"Where do they live?" coughed Gloria.

"They live in Florida," responded Sloan as he glanced at Jayla and Jayden.

A ripple effect of disbelief stormed through Hope. Sloan had always told her that his parents were deceased.

"Do you have any sisters or brothers?" muffled Gloria.

"Yes," said Sloan as he glanced at his watch. "I mean . . . no," uttered Sloan as he looked at Hope.

Hope blinked as if her eyelashes were heavy as she wondered why Sloan was uncertain as to whether he had siblings. Her mind forced her to see that Sloan was quickly unraveling. For some reason, Sloan struggled to keep his story consistent with what he had told Hope years ago when they met. Plus, he was looking at his watch a lot.

A raspy sound erupted in the air as Gloria coughed.

Jayla suddenly stopped watching television. Her head swirled toward Gloria. She stood and walked toward her grandmother. Jayla leaned toward Gloria, planting her small hand on Gloria's frail arm and Jayla rubbed Gloria's arm as if she could remove the crumbled coughs that came out of Gloria's mouth.

Hope winced, wondering how Jayla knew Gloria was coughing. Hope walked over to Jayla. She rotated her fingers in front of Jayla as she communicated in ASL. Hope was anxious to know whether Jayla had heard Gloria coughing.

A sharp noise echoed through the small room as Jayden dropped the remote control.

Jayla turned toward Gloria. She never responded to Hope.

Hope scanned Jayla's face. She noticed a twinkle in Jayla's eyes as Jayla looked at Gloria. Hope's heart skipped a beat as she reflected upon the days when she had pure love for Gloria. She was about the same age as Jayla. But Hope cringed as she remembered that her pure love for Gloria had turned into a bitter love.

"Have you told your mother, Hope?" asked Sloan in a low tone while peeking at his watch.

"No, because I wanted time to think about it," whispered Hope as if Gloria couldn't hear her. Her heat pounded, wondering if she had used the correct King's English. She didn't want Sloan to correct her in front of her mother.

"Hope, you don't have to do it," said Gloria in a soft tone. "I am at peace now. All I wanted was to see you before I left this earth," smiled Gloria. "My heart overly rejoices that I got to see my grandchildren . . . and your husband," muffled Gloria as if her throat wouldn't allow the words to flow out properly.

Hope paused as a river of uneasiness trickled through her veins.

"I didn't mean it like that mama," mumbled Hope. "I wanted time to think about it because there are risk factors for me too."

"But the doctor said you and your mother can do the surgery on Monday," said Sloan as if he was in a rush for Hope to undergo surgery.

Hope gawked at Sloan. A cloud of confusion floated through her mind as she wondered why Sloan was rushing her to make a decision.

Gloria planted her head further on her pillow. "Do not worry, Hope," smiled Gloria. "I am at peace."

Every core of Hope's heart fluttered when Jayla started signing something to her. She couldn't bear seeing her daughter cry.

"What did she say?" asked Sloan as he sat in the padded chair beside Jayden.

Hope glanced at Jayden. He was focused on the cartoon as if he was hypnotized.

"We can talk about it later," said Hope in a low tone.

"I think we should talk about it now," uttered Sloan.

Hope exhaled slowly as she continued to watch Jayla's fingers shift in the air.

"Hope, what is she saying?" asked Sloan.

Gloria chuckled softly. "Sloan, you have to learn ASL."

Sloan slightly sneered. "Hope usually takes care of that."

"I remember you told me that. But it would be good if you learned too."

"I will work on it," said Sloan as he gawked at his watch.

A rumbling sound echoed across the sky.

"That watch must keep you busy," sighed Gloria. "You keep looking at it."

Sloan stood silently as if his tongue was cut out of his mouth.

"Not really," chuckled Sloan. "But I do have to leave shortly. I have a business meeting," stated Sloan as he quickly peeked at his watch.

A vineyard of anger slowly harvested inside Hope. "Are you serious, Sloan? Do you have another business meeting? And why are you being disrespectful by constantly looking at your watch?"

Jayla's fingers glided in the air, communicating the same sentence to Hope.

"Hope, what is she saying?" asked Gloria as she touched Jayla's ponytails.

Jayla planted her small hand on Gloria's face in a loving manner. A single tear rolled down her face.

Hope wiped the tears from Jayla's face. Hope observed as Jayla motioned her small fingers in the air again, signing the same sentence.

The words slowly peeled off Hope's tongue. "Jayla told me to please help you."

Tears sprinkled down Gloria's face.

Chapter 47

The following Wednesday, beige walls positioned around the habilitation room. Large medical devices rested on a long white table, leaving no space for anything else.

"Please have a seat. Dr. Shaw will be with you in a few minutes," said a nurse.

"Where do you want me to put this?" asked Hope as water dripped from her black umbrella.

"You can place it in a bag near that small table," said the nurse as she pointed to the corner.

"Jayden has been doing good," said Sloan as a smile overtook his butterscotch brown face.

"I know," said Hope as she gently pinched Jayden's face.

A slither of wishful hope flowed through Hope as she looked at Jayla.

"Jayla is doing well, too," said Hope as she noticed Jayla was reading her lips. "I am still praying that she will hear and speak one day."

A soft smile crawled across Jayla's face.

"Thank you for bringing Jayla and Jayden to their appointments," said Dr. Shaw.

"We wouldn't miss it for anything," said Sloan as he stood.

"I will work with Jayden, first," uttered Dr. Shaw while ignoring Sloan's comment.

"Can you start with Jayla first?" asked Hope as if she was eager to know if Jayla would finally hear and speak. "I would like you to do that for me," said Hope in a heartfelt tone while hoping that Dr. Shaw would understand her request.

Sloan hastily cleared his throat while staring at Hope as if she had violated an unspoken rule.

Dr. Shaw stole a quick peek at Hope before shifting his gaze to Sloan.

"Mr. Glover, is that okay with you?" asked Dr. Shaw.

Sloan paused before responding as if he wanted to demonstrate to Hope that he was in total control.

An avalanche of hatred settled into the pit of Hope's stomach as she looked at Sloan.

"Yes," said Sloan as he looked at Jayla.

Hope sat in the soft padded chair as she watched Jayla trail behind Dr. Shaw.

Sloan sat behind Hope, gawking at the side of her head as if his eyes could electrocute her.

"Sloan, please don't start it," whispered Hope as she tried to rationale why Sloan was so jealous and insecure.

"It seems like you already started it," muffled Sloan.

Hope opened her large black purse. She had stored a few items inside to keep the twins occupied between their appointments. She reached in and pulled out a small ziplock bag of green grapes.

"Go and wash your hands over there, Jayden," she said trying to ignore Sloan. "Make sure you dry your hands so I can give you your snack."

"I wonder what else you have stashed away in that purse," mumbled Sloan as he leaned over Hope, trying to peek inside.

Hope glanced at Jayla, noticing that a different type of headphones snuggled against her ears. She noticed that Dr. Shaw had the same type of headphones.

"Jayden, did you have to put those headphones on your ears before?" asked a puzzled Hope.

Jayden peered in Jayla's direction as he tossed a grape inside his round shaped mouth.

"No," said Jayden, the word easily rolling off his tongue.

"I wonder why Jayla has to use those headphones," uttered Hope in a low tone.

"I don't know. I will ask Dr. Shaw when he is finished with Jayla," muffled Sloan as if he wanted to emphasize that he preferred to ask Dr. Shaw instead of Hope.

Thirty minutes later, Hope opened her purse again. She pulled out a coloring book and a pack of crayons for Jayden.

"Here, Jayden. Come and sit at this table with me," she said as she ushered Jayden over. "Go ahead and color," she said as she sat.

Hope glanced over at Sloan. He appeared to be more focused on something on his watch than observing Jayla.

"What are you looking at on your watch, Sloan?" whispered Hope, trying to capture his attention. "Why do you look at it so much?" muffled Hope as she stood and walked toward him.

Sloan did not budge. He kept his gaze locked on his watch without looking up.

Hope walked closer toward him as her black sundress cradled her body. She tried to glance at his watch. But she only captured a glimpse before he noticed her presence. He quickly covered it up.

"What are you doing?" muffled Sloan through gritted teeth as if Hope had entered unchartered territories.

"Nothing. I was talking to you. But you never responded. So, I got up and walked over here to you," whispered Hope in a bizarre tone.

"What do you want, Hope?" asked Sloan as he pressed a button on his watch, causing a black screen to appear. "Obviously, it was so important that you had to interrupt me from taking care of some business," whispered Sloan as if he didn't want Jayden to hear him. Certainly, Sloan didn't want Dr. Shaw to hear him.

"I didn't know you could take care of business through your watch," mumbled Hope as she walked back to the small table in the corner. "I guess I learned something new today," whispered Hope in a sarcastic tone.

Sloan bit his bottom lip as he glared at Hope.

Even though she could barely see the images clearly on Sloan's watch, Hope was certain he was watching some people walking around inside a house or a building.

Dr. Shaw slowly pulled the headphones off his ears. He walked toward them.

"Mr. and Mrs. Glover, is it okay if one of my colleagues reviews something?" asked Dr. Shaw in an unsettling tone.

"Why?" asked Sloan in an inquisitive manner.

"I want Dr. Milner to give me a second opinion about Jayla's results today."

"Okay," said Sloan.

"Nurse Maria, can you ask Dr. Milner to come in here for a few minutes."

Ten minutes later, a tall chocolate brown man opened the room door. His muscular physique protruded through his white lab coat. His clean shaved face displayed the fine hairs on his mustache. His light brown eyes highlighted his tamed eyebrows. His bald head showcased his breathtaking appearance.

Hope sat quietly as if she was mesmerized.

"Dr. Shaw, I was told you needed me to look at something."

"Yes, Dr. Milner. I want you to give me your opinion about something. These are the patient's parents," said Dr. Shaw as he pointed at Hope and Sloan.

Dr. Milner turned and looked at them.

"Hello, I'm Dr. Milner. I am an ear, nose and throat doctor," he said before his words came to a halt. "*Hope* . . . Hope Rankin," said Dr. Milner in an excited tone as his pearly white teeth leaped out of his mouth. "I haven't seen you since high school."

"Her name is Hope *Glover* now," blurted Sloan as he stood. "*Rankin* was her maiden name."

The oxygen in the room suddenly depleted as if jealousy had taken over

Sloan.

"Sloan, this is Blake. We used to live in Cloverdale together. We went to the same high school," uttered Hope as if she had to provide Sloan with a mini-biography of Blake. She glanced at Dr. Milner's hand, noticing that he wasn't wearing a wedding ring.

Sloan stared at Hope as if he could set her on fire with his glares.

"Mrs. Glover, it was nice seeing you again," said Dr. Milner as he turned toward Dr. Shaw. "What do you need me to do?" he asked while clearing his throat.

Dr. Shaw and Dr. Milner formed a beeline toward Jayla.

Hope watched as Dr. Milner's fingers glided in front of Jayla as he communicated in ASL with her. Hope was impressed. She recalled playing kickball with him in Cloverdale. They had attended the same high school. She remembered he ate ginger cookies nearly every day. They were his favorite cookies. She recalled that day in high school when Blake had told her that she would be his wife one day. She even quickly recalled that he had begged her for a kiss on his birthday. But she had refused to allow his *ginger cookie* lips to touch her lips. Now, part of Hope wished she had given him that kiss.

Hope strolled over toward the table where Jayden was still coloring. She didn't want to undergo interrogation from Sloan. Her heart pounded away as if a construction worker was drilling a hole through her chest.

Fifteen minutes later, Dr. Milner strolled to Hope and Sloan. "Thank you for allowing me to work with your daughter. Dr. Shaw and Dr. Ericsson will discuss the results with you," he said as he walked out of the room.

Dr. Shaw walked toward Hope and Sloan with a bewildered look on his face. "I will be ready for Jayden in a few minutes," said Dr. Shaw.

"Dr. Shaw, why did you use a new set of headphones with Jayla today?" asked Sloan.

"Because I wanted to do an advanced test on her."

"Okay. So, why did you have to bring Dr. Milner in here?" asked Sloan.

"I wanted to get a second opinion on something."

"Why?" asked Hope, in a muffled tone as her heart fluttered.

An ounce of disappointment flowed through Hope. Her ears were not prepared to hear Dr. Shaw tell her that Jayla would never be able to hear or speak.

"Will Jayla ever be able to hear or speak?" asked Sloan in a rattling tone.

Jayden walked over toward Hope as if he wanted to hear Dr. Shaw's response.

"Has Jayla *tried* to speak at home?" asked Dr. Shaw, ignoring Sloan.

Hope looked around. "No," she mumbled as if some pain had pierced her heart.

"Does she look at you when you call her name?" inquired Dr. Shaw.

"No," said Hope as she felt wetness starting to form inside the sockets of her eyes.

Jayden reached for Hope's hand as if he was trying to comfort her. Hope looked at Jayden. Her heart sunk, causing her to try to accept that Jayla would never hear or speak. Hope felt as though she had fallen short of God's grace.

"Why are you asking us these questions?" asked Sloan.

Dr. Shaw pressed his lips together before the words flowed out of his mouth. "The results show that Jayla *can* hear and speak."

A river of confusion flooded Hope's mind. "Then why doesn't she talk with us?" asked Hope as her heart slowly crumbled while looking at Jayla as she continued to sit at a table with headphones on her ears. "All this time, I thought . . . she couldn't hear or speak." Hope didn't know whether she should be happy or sad. More shocking, she didn't understand why Jayla had declined to reveal to her that she could hear and speak.

Hope glanced at Jayden as curiosity consumed her. She wondered if Jayden and Jayla had been harboring a secret. They were twins and certainly had an undivided bond since birth. "Jayden, can Jayla hear and speak?" asked Hope.

Jayden looked at Jayla before responding. A single tear rolled down his face.

"Yes . . . but . . . only with me," muffled Jayden as he slowly dropped his head as if he had broken Jayla's trust.

Moisture gathered in Hope's mouth. She was too heartbroken to speak while splinters of her heart slowly embedded into her soul. The reality of knowing that Jayla did not want to talk with her shattered her.

Chapter 48

A week later, the sun shifted across the blue sky forming a massive shadow over Cloverdale. Eggshell painted walls stretched around the small living room. The Friday afternoon provided a great opportunity for friends and family to be together.

"That chicken casserole was *delicious*, mama," said Tony as he walked toward the door, wiping a few lingering crumbs from his linen shirt. "I have to leave. I have a meeting," he said, rubbing his stomach as if he was trying to savor memories of the food.

"Whatever, Tony. You just want to eat and run," laughed Tiffany. "Plus, I'm sure your wife has ordered you to come home."

"I see you have jokes," chuckled Tony as he planted a kiss on Mrs. Brown's head. "Maybe

Vance didn't come to get a plate from mama because he needed a slight break from you," laughed Tony as he left.

"I have to go, too," said Hilton as he looked at his mother, Geneva. "Plus, I'm sure all of the women in here want to catch up on some gossip," chuckled Hilton.

The sun beamed onto Hilton's six-foot-nine chestnut brown chiseled body as he walked toward the door. His biceps protruded through his linen cream shirt. His stallion shaped, sexy physique overshadowed every male professional exotic dancer.

"Where are you rushing off to, Hilton?" asked Geneva in a soft tone.

"I have to take care of something, mama," said Hilton.

"I remember when you were a tiny fellow standing in my kitchen," smiled Mrs. Brown as she looked at Hilton. "I was surprised you wanted to learn how to cook."

"Or maybe he was trying to court Tiffany?" chuckled Ruth, as Hilton walked out the door, leaving a trail of his cologne. "Do you know he's a psychiatrist now, Tiffany?"

"And he is married, just like I am," smirked Tiffany as she looked at Ruth.

A cloud of laughter filled Mrs. Brown's apartment.

"Hilton has a priceless shaped body," mumbled Ruth as she peeked out of the window as Hilton walked down the sidewalk. "He has a stride in his walk as if he was a professional exotic dancer," she said while perching her lips firmly.

Mrs. Brown squinted. "Ruth, control your words."

Horns honked from a distance echoing into the apartment.

"I bet somebody was honking at Hilton," chuckled Ruth.

"The tossed salad was delicious, Mrs. Brown," said Hope, totally ignoring Ruth's comments as she wiped her mouth. She was relieved to be around familiar people and glad that she didn't have to use the King's English around them.

"Yes, it was," said Tiffany as she sipped on some iced tea.

"Thank you for preparing this meal for my grandchildren and me," said Ruth.

"It really was good, Mrs. Brown," chattered Ivey in a soft tone.

"Thank you," uttered Mrs. Brown. "I wanted to do something special for all of you. I'm glad that God blessed all of us to be together again," she sighed.

"Amen to that," smiled Ruth. "It's like we're having a Cloverdale reunion."

A cluster of laughter burst into the air, rekindling their fond memories.

"Hope, I'm glad you came to visit your roots," said Ruth as she sipped some tea.

"I know," chuckled Tiffany as she interjected into Ruth and Hope's conversation.

"I never forgot about Cloverdale," exhaled Hope as she slowly looked at Gloria.

"I'm glad you reunited with your mother," said Mrs. Brown in a soft tone.

"Me, too," muffled Gloria in a low tone as she looked at Hope.

Jayla and Jayden sat quietly as their eyes remained glued to the television. Hope noticed that Taylor sporadically kept looking at her. *But why? she wondered.*

"God definitely works in mysterious ways," said Ruth as she fingered through her long curly sandy brown wig. "By the way, these are my granddaughters Jasmine and Taylor. They live with me. I forgot to introduce them before we ate."

"Hello," said Hope. "These are my twins Jayla and Jayden," smiled Hope as she tried to figure out why Jasmine and Taylor were living with Ruth.

"Hello," said Jasmine as she gently smiled.

"Hello," mumbled Taylor as Hope noticed that Taylor had difficulty maintaining eye contact while she messed with a button on her peach shirt.

"So, are they Julia's children?" asked Hope as she smiled as she walked closer to Jasmine and Taylor.

"Yes," said Ruth as the word crumbled off her lips.

Taylor stared at Hope before muttered a few words. "Your perfume smells nice. You are wearing the same perfume that my mama used to wear."

"That is a coincidence because my perfume is imported," said Hope in a prideful way, but that level of pride was soon to evaporate.

"I know," said Taylor in a humbling voice. "It is *E'Zanti* perfume."

Silence tripped through the air, causing an eerie feeling inside of Mrs. Brown. She wondered how Hope and Julia wore the same type of imported perfume. "Were did you buy your perfume, Hope?"

"I didn't. Sloan always gets it as a gift for me," said Hope in a puzzled way as if she had started to realize that it may be more than just a coincidence that she and Julia wore the same perfume.

"Well, it is a lovely fragrance," interjected Geneva as if she had suddenly taken notice of the scent.

"Where is Julia?" inquired Hope as she noticed Ruth was acting strangely.

A screeching sound erupted through the living room as a blue jeep slammed on breaks, preventing from hitting a kid who dashed in the street after a ball.

"I know you have a lot of fond memories of Cloverdale, Hope," uttered Mrs. Brown as if she wanted to change the topic of the conversation. She rubbed her hands together as if she could remove arthritis from her hands.

"I do," said Hope as she caressed her mother's hand.

"We sure do," snickered Tiffany.

"I remember we used to play kickball with milk cartons," laughed Ivey.

Laughter slithered out of Hope's mouth as her mind back peddled to those days.

Mrs. Brown stretched her dark brown arms toward a plate of homemade lemon cookies. "Here, take a few cookies," she said as she passed the plate of cookies.

A pleasant feeling flowed through Hope as she glanced around Mrs. Brown's apartment. She was very familiar with this place.

"Hope, I heard you are married now," smiled Mrs. Ruth.

"Yes, I am," sighed Hope as she glanced at two girls sitting behind Ruth.

"Why didn't your husband come with you?" asked Tiffany.

Hope hesitated. "He had to travel out of town on a business trip."

"Before anybody asks me," blurted Ivey. "My husband had to take care of something at the church," she said while looking around as she laughed.

"What type of work does your husband do, Hope?" inquired Geneva.

"He is an engineer. He designs a lot of high-tech devices," she replied in a prideful tone.

"What type of devices?" asked Ivey as she sipped on a glass of iced tea.

"Websites, caller Ids, alarm systems, cameras and other stuff."

Gloria slowly opened her mouth. "What about his watch?" she asked. "Did he design it, too? I noticed he looked at his watch a lot that day."

"You're right," said Tiffany. "When I met him, he kept looking at his watch."

"Me too. I also noticed that," babbled Mrs. Brown as she adjusted her glasses. "When I met him, he acted like he was watching something on his watch."

"If he is an engineer, there is no telling what his watch really does," uttered Ivey.

Silence sprinkled throughout the living room.

Hope's lips were cemented together. She realized that they were right. She was convinced

Sloan must have designed devices to track her when she left the house. Hope exhaled, remembering that Sloan had installed cameras in the house.

"What does his watch look like?" asked Jasmine in a bewildered tone.

A cloud of confusion overpowered Hope's mind.

"Why?" asked Ruth as she leaned forward.

"I just wanted to know," said Jasmine as her sentence quickly ended.

"Jasmine, my husband has different types of watches," responded Hope.

A lingering smell of the homemade lemon cookies drifted through the living room, mingling with the overabundance of silence.

"Well, I'm really enjoying this moment," muffled Gloria, breaking the silence. "I'm happy to be in the same room with my daughters and grandchildren."

"How do you feel, Gloria?" asked Ruth in an inquisitive tone.

Gloria slowly cleared her throat as Jayla stared at her. "I'm doing okay," mumbled Gloria. "I'm glad God touched my heart . . . and Hope's," uttered Gloria as she smiled at Hope. "I don't eat much 'cause I don't have an appetite."

Jayla stood. She walked over to Gloria as her ponytails trailed behind. She handed Gloria one of her cookies. "Please . . . eat . . . grandma," said Jayla as the words slowly peeled off her tongue.

"Oh, that is so sweet," sighed Mrs. Brown as she looked at Jayla. "Hope, I'm glad Jayla finally revealed to you that she could hear and speak," sighed Mrs. Brown as she looked at Hope and Gloria. "It is as if Jayla waited until after you helped your mother before she wanted to tell you," uttered Mrs. Brown in a pleasant voice. "I strongly believe that God used Jayla as a vessel between you two."

A river of compassion for Gloria brushed against Hope's heart as she detected a sparkle in Jayla's eyes as she looked at Gloria. Hope sighed, noticing that Jayla had an abundance of love for Gloria. She wondered if she had never donated the bone marrow to her mother whether Jayla would have never disclosed to her that she could hear and speak.

"How was the procedure, Gloria?" asked Ruth in a low tone.

"The doctor said I am getting better," muffled Gloria. "I was a little sore when I woke up. But I can't complain. I am just grateful that Hope helped me," she said as her gaze floated toward her rosemary pink sheet. "I still have to see my doctor periodically."

"What about you, Hope?" inquired Tiffany.

"I'm okay," mumbled Hope. "I was a little sore. But I'm fine now."

A sense of peace tumbled through the living room.

"I'm glad to hear that," smiled Mrs. Brown.

"Are you ready for school to start?" asked Hope as she looked at Jasmine and Taylor, trying to divert the conversation. "It starts next week right after Labor Day."

"Yes, they're getting ready," exhaled Ruth.

"They might go to the same school I graduated from," uttered Hope.

"What school did you go to, Mrs. Hope?" asked Jasmine in a soft tone.

"I went to South Charlotte Middle School."

"I think that's where we are going too but I'm not really sure," uttered Jasmine. "My sister and I might have to go to a different type of school."

Hope got a feeling that something wasn't right.

Ruth brushed a crumb off her green blouse as she nibbled on a cookie. "They've been through something. So, I have to make sure that their school is right for them."

"Do you want another cookie?" asked Gloria as she looked at her grandchildren.

Jayden slid off the burgundy chair. He grabbed a few cookies for himself and Jayla. His black pants shifted as he walked.

"Well, whatever school you go to, I hope you like it," said Hope.

"Me too," muffled Jasmine as her gaze landed on her orange shirt.

"I just hope I don't see any of the leaders at the school," mumbled Taylor.

Hope glanced around the room, trying to figure out what Taylor was talking about.

"What leader?" inquired Hope in a bewildered tone.

Ruth batted her eyelashes as if they were wrestling. "They were involved in human trafficking," babbled Ruth as if Jasmine and Taylor had given her permission to disclose their painstaking experiences.

"Human trafficking," uttered Hope as confusion stormed her mind.

Ruth perched her lips together before slowly speaking. "Julia went missing years ago . . . on my birthday. It wasn't long after you left Cloverdale," muffled Ruth while looking at Hope. "Julia was forced into a terrible life of human trafficking. A guy named Rock stole Julia from me. He kidnapped Julia and forced her into human trafficking. It seems like Rock got Julia pregnant with Jasmine and Taylor," exhaled Ruth.

Hope's lips slowly parted. "So, where is Julia?" asked Hope while breathing slowly.

Ruth closed her eyes. "Jasmine and Taylor told me that the main leader killed Julia. He was

Rock's brother."

"Why?" asked Hope as a river of sympathy flowed through her veins.

"Jasmine told me that Rock's brother killed Julia because she kept trying to escape from that life," said Mrs. Brown.

"Do you know his brother's name?" asked Mrs. Brown.

"No," responded Mrs. Hall.

Hope cleared her throat. "How do you that the main leader who killed Julia was Rock's brother?" asked Mrs. Brown as she scratched her elbow.

"I heard my daddy tell mama a long time ago. Mama cried a lot. She used to ask daddy why he allowed his brother to control him," Jasmine slowly uttered. "Daddy smacked her for saying that to him."

A cloud of empathy hovered along the popcorn white ceiling.

Ruth tilted her head toward the ceiling. "Thank God, Jasmine and Taylor were able to escape all of that. Social services placed them with me. Now, they're in therapy and stuff," exhaled Ruth as if she had to provide Hope with a mini-memoir of Jasmine and Taylor.

Quietness tumbled through the living room like a rollercoaster.

"I am so sorry to hear that," sighed Gloria in an uneasy tone.

Hope sat as if she was in a state of shock. She slowly exhaled as she observed Taylor rubbing her hands together as if she was trying to set a campfire. Hope sensed that Taylor was nervous. Hope had a million questions that she wanted to ask about her experience being trapped in human trafficking, but she didn't want to create an uncomfortable atmosphere for Taylor.

"We've gotten a little better," whispered Jasmine.

Hope listened tentatively without moving. She couldn't believe the words that were pressing against her eardrums.

"I don't have nightmares much about the leaders," Taylor said as her lip trembled.

Tiffany's lips slowly peeled apart. "Do you remember what the leaders look like?" asked Tiffany as if she didn't just hear what Taylor said.

"Yes. But I hope I don't see them ever again."

A truckload of trepidation reaped through Hope.

"Taylor has gotten better," mumbled Jasmine as she gripped Taylor's hand. "She used to get scared and pee on herself whenever a leader came around us," said Jasmine in a low tone as if she suddenly realized that she was sharing too much information.

Hope pressed her back into the chair as she listened to Jasmine and Taylor speak.

She felt as though she was trapped inside a horror movie.

Chapter 49

Two weeks later, loud ringing sounds echoed through the building. Brown chairs assembled in a square shaped room in multiple parallel lines. Almond painted walls encased the books, computers and desks. The mid-September weather permitted a ray of sunshine to flow into the room, mingling with the gentle breeze that surfed the air conditioner.

"Welcome, grandmothers, to Ericston Vance Academy," said a short ivory lady with platinum blonde hair who communicated in ASL as she spoke.

Hope overheard a lady say, "I'm not a grandmother. I'm a nana."

"I am Mrs. Reid. I am your grandchildren's school teacher," said the teacher as she totally ignored the lady's comment. "We are delighted that you are participating in the Grandmothers' Day event at our school today. We hope you enjoy your lunches with your grandchildren. We will be eating in this classroom today. Every teacher has to do the same."

A peaceful feeling overtook Hope as she looked around the classroom. She was delighted that the twins were able to remain in the same classroom— even though the school had recommended otherwise. Hope didn't want to separate them. She was excited that the school was designed to encourage students to speak as well as to use ASL.

"Grand . . . grandma," said Jayla as the words slowly rolled from her pink tongue. "I'm glad . . . you came," muffled Jayla as a massive smile stretched across her face, nearly touching her ears. Her navy blue uniform accented her light brown eyes.

"Me, too, Jayla," said Gloria as she hugged Jayla.

"Make sure you eat, grandma," smiled Jayden as he slid closer to her.

A ray of love seeped through the veins in Hope's heart. She was at a loss for words. She couldn't believe the level of love that Jayla and Jayden had for her mother as if they had known her for years.

The savory smell of baked chicken, green beans, macaroni and cherry cobbler soared through the classroom.

"Hope, I'm sure you can cater a meal like this," said Gloria.

A soft chuckle rolled out of Hope's mouth. "I bet mine would be better," teased Hope. "But this food is good, too."

"I'm sure," snickered Gloria as she planted a piece of baked chicken on her tongue. She tucked the fine hairs of her sandy brown wig behind her perky ears. Her previous chemotherapy had taken a toll on her hair.

Hope watched as Jayla stood. She walked toward a little girl who was sitting at a table by herself. Hope planted her hand on her chest as she observed

Jayla reach for the little girl's hand and guide her to their table.

"This . . . is Sunny. She . . . she's my friend," said Jayla as she held the little girl's alabaster white hand. "She doesn't have a grand . . . grandma here today," stumbled Jayla as if she still had some slight difficulty speaking at times. This didn't bother Hope. She was delighted that Jayla could talk. More importantly, Hope was overly rejoiced that Jayla finally started speaking.

"You can sit with us," said Gloria in a soft tone.

"Yes, Sunny, sit here," uttered Hope.

Hope noticed Sunny's fingers moving in a familiar pattern. She looked at Jayla and Jayden.

"She can talk, mama. But Sunny still uses ASL. She thinks her words aren't clear when she says them," uttered Jayden without stumbling over his words for the first time since he had the procedure done.

A warm feeling of happiness coursed through Hope.

Hope's fingers moved elegantly in front of Sunny to communicate with her. She reassured Sunny that it was okay for her to speak to them.

"Tha . . . Thank you," said Sunny in a soft muffled tone.

Hope stood. She walked over to retrieve Sunny's meal from the table.

Hope glanced around the classroom. Her heart rejoiced as she watched Jayla and Jayden's classmates speaking and using ASL. She noticed that several of their classmates had the cochlear procedure conducted as well. She could see the small devices attached near their ears. Hope was certain that this made Jayla and Jayden comfortable being around them.

"Here you are, Sunny," said Hope, handing her a tray of food.

"Thanks," muffled Sunny.

"Hope, you are really good with sign language," said Gloria.

"Thank you," responded Hope in a pleasant tone. "It's called ASL," whispered Hope.

"Since you're thinking about hiring staff one day, have you thought about hiring people who know ASL?"

Hope paused for a few seconds. "Yes," said Hope. "I also want to create a culinary school one day designed for people who are deaf and have a hard time hearing. I want to organize it where I can still take catering orders and be able to teach people how to cook."

"That would be fantastic," said Gloria as a smile plastered on her face. "Who would you teach?"

"I want to teach children and adults."

"Children?"

"Yes, I want to have summer camps too. But the only thing is, I have to make sure that some of my employees understand ASL."

"That is great, Hope. I've never heard of that before. But I'm sure you will find employees who know ASL."

Hope inhaled as she watched Gloria interact with her twins. A sense of serendipity marched through Hope as she reached over to hug her mother. She couldn't believe that her mind, body and soul had intertwined to permit her to love her mother again after all of these years. Her soul finally felt at peace. She recalled the art of forgiveness that Eugene had helped her to understand. She had forced herself to focus on healing from her trauma with her mother and Sergeant Smith.

"Where is your husband, Hope?" asked Gloria as she nibbled on a green bean.

"He had to go out of town on a business trip," sighed Hope.

"He goes out of town a lot. Do you ever get to go with him?" asked Gloria.

Hope glanced around at the nearby desks and tables, hoping no one could hear their conversation.

"No. He never allows me to go with him," said Hope as if she needed to vent a little.

"I don't want to get in your marriage. God knows, I don't want to do anything to mess up our relationship," said Gloria as she gently tapped on Hope's hand. "But something isn't right, Hope."

A river of trepidation pierced through Hope's heart.

"I know, mama. I'm starting to realize it," mumbled Hope as she glanced at Jayla and Jayden, hoping that they were not listening to her conversation. They were busy talking and playing at the table. "It took me a long time to even recognize certain things about my husband. It was naïve."

Gloria continued to gently tap on Hope's hand.

"But I feel trapped, mama. I feel like I have to stay with him 'cause we have the twins together," whispered Hope as if her mother had suddenly been hired as her therapist. Hope felt relieved that she didn't have to use the King's English around her mother.

"I don't want to tell you what to do, Hope. But there are plenty of women who have survived in life after they left their husbands," whispered Gloria. "But try to figure out what is going on with him before you make any decisions."

A loud noise ricocheted inside the classroom as a student dropped his lunch tray.

"I know. But he is starting to change and it makes me feel uncomfortable," whispered Hope in a barely audible manner.

"Hope, maybe he was always like this and you're just starting to notice it," said Gloria as she caressed Hope's hand. "But you have to do what is best for you and your twins," paused Gloria. "So, I'm not going to tell you what to do with your marriage. All I will do is support your decision the best way I know how."

"I know," muffled Hope as she hugged Gloria.

Jayla plucked through the cobbler on her plate searching for the cherries.

"You are just like your mother," laughed Gloria. "You used to do the same thing, Hope."

Clusters of conversations flowed through the classroom.

"This was really fun, today. I—I never did this before," uttered Gloria in an uneasy tone. "It seems like I missed out on things like this when you were in school," said Gloria as her gaze shifted toward the floor.

Hope exhaled slowly. "It's okay, mama. You have time to make up for it with Jayla and Jayden," said Hope as she gently nudged Gloria with her elbow.

"Make sure you eat your green beans," said Gloria as she looked at Jayden.

"We will be here for a *hundred years* before he eats green beans," chuckled Hope.

Laughter plunged out of Jayla and Sunny's mouths as they ate.

"I don't like green beans," babbled Jayden.

"You have to eat your vegetables so you can grow up to big and strong," smiled Gloria as she pinched Jayden's cheek.

Two minutes later, Mrs. Reid walked toward the front of the classroom.

"On behalf of Ericston Vance Academy, I want to thank all of the grandmothers who came to this awesome event today. We have only five more minutes to enjoy this lunch. I hope everyone will come out again when we host this event again," she smiled.

Hope looked at her mother.

"This meant a lot to Jayla and Jayden," whispered Hope as she looked at her mother. "Especially, Jayla," mumbled Hope as she recalled how Jayla had cried at her summer camp because her friend's grandmothers had attended the grandmother-grandchildren event and her grandmother was not present. Hope winced, recalling that Jayla had refused to look at her that entire day which caused Hope's heart to slowly chip away.

"I can tell. But I feel bad that I didn't do things like this with you," sighed Gloria while her words slowly ceased as if she finally realized that she had significantly deprived Hope of her childhood.

"It's okay. I will invite you to other school events," said Hope in a reassuring tone.

Even though this event had ended, Hope was convinced that it had helped rekindle her relationship with her mother.

Chapter 50

Red, yellow, and brown leaves masked the dried out grass, overshadowing the lush green leaves that once predominated the trees. October had settled in, bringing a cool breeze that blanketed the air.

"Thank you for meeting with me," said Hope as she looked at Tiffany. "We have to finalize the plans for your mother's event."

"You are welcome. I want to make sure this is a special event for my mother's seventieth birthday party," smiled Tiffany.

"This works out for me since the twins are in school. I have to return before they get out."

"How was the drive from Raleigh to Charlotte?" asked Tiffany.

"I had some problems with my brakes. I had to stop by the mechanic. He said the brake line had been cut. But I got it fixed. So, hopefully, I will not run into any traffic on my way back."

"The brake line?" asked Tiffany.

"Yes. But it got fixed."

"I'm glad you made it safely."

"Me too, because I needed to see the layout of this ballroom to determine where to set up the food for your mother's event in two weeks," sighed Hope.

"My mother is going to be surprised," grinned Tiffany.

"I know," laughed Hope. "My twins and your mother share the same birthday."

"For real?" smiled Tiffany. "Is November 2nd their birthday as well?"

"Yes," responded Hope. "So, I have to make plans for my twins' birthday party and your mother's birthday event."

"I guess you better get started with the plans," laughed Tiffany. "Because I know my mother . . . and your twins would prefer that you cater their events."

"Of course," smiled Hope as she looked around the room.

Cathedral ceilings reigned throughout Chandler Convention Center creating an elegant appearance. Greek style columns positioned in every corner. Light gold painted walls boarded the hunter green trimmed paint. Marble tile blanketed the spotless floor. Chairs and tables were arranged in an orderly fashion.

"This is a beautiful small ballroom," said Hope as her eyes became mesmerized by the astounding elegance throughout the room. "The size will be just right for Mrs. Brown."

"I agree. She doesn't like large rooms. So, Tony and I reserved this small ballroom for her."

"She is going to love it."

"I know. We wanted it to be special for her."

"Okay, so let's get to business," said Hope as she opened her laptop. "These are pictures of the meals that I will prepare."

"I already *tasted* them so I know they're delicious," laughed Tiffany.

"Thank you," smiled Hope. "But I want you to see how they will look on the different colored plates."

"I didn't know that catering involved so much"

"Yes, it is a delicate art," uttered Hope. "You have to tell me what color plates, napkins, chair covers, forks, spoons, and knives you want. Also, I need to know what type of glasses you want."

"Chair covers?" asked Tiffany.

"Yes, I decorate it for some of my customers," grinned Hope.

"Are you serious?" laughed Tiffany.

"Yes," paused Hope as she stared at Tiffany.

"Seriously, I didn't know it involved all of this," said Tiffany. "I'm impressed."

Soft instrumental music flowed inside the small ballroom.

"These are some examples," said Hope as she strolled through the myriad of pictures on her laptop. "I even bought a few so you can feel the texture of the napkins and chair covers."

"This feels really nice," said Tiffany as her fingers fumbled through an apple green colored tablecloth. "And this salmon pink napkin is nice," she uttered.

"Tiffany, this event is for your mother, not you," smiled Hope as she noticed Tiffany touching the pink and green samples.

"Well, you know I'm proud to be an Alpha Kappa Alpha." A rollercoaster of laughter leaped off Tiffany's tongue.

"I know," smiled Hope.

"Do you have any burgundy and yellow?" asked Tiffany. "They are my mother's favorite colors. So, why did you bring the pink and green items?" smirked Tiffany.

"Just in case you liked the texture of the materials, not the colors," smiled Hope. "I can get the items in any color and texture. I just want to know which one you prefer," laughed Hope.

"I hear you, Mrs. Caterer of the year," snickered Tiffany.

"Girl, you haven't changed at all after all of these years. You can't get your way all the time," chuckled Hope.

"I know and you can't be in control of everything all the time," snapped back Tiffany. "I remember how you used to set all of the rules for the kickball games."

Laughter filled the room.

"I hope you don't put any polyester chair covers on the seats," chuckled Tiffany. "You know my mother loves that mess."

"I know," grinned Hope. "But once again, this is your mother's event, Tiffany."

"I know, but Tony and I are paying for it," smirked Tiffany.

"In that case, you can decide the texture," laughed Hope. "But make sure it's something you think your mother would like. I want Mrs. Brown to be happy on her birthday."

Hope closed her laptop. She placed all of the samples of her catering items into a large sophisticated rolling container.

"Look at Mrs. Big Time," chuckled Tiffany. "You look so professional."

"Of course," said Hope. "I take my catering business seriously."

"I see," smiled Tiffany.

"Oh, by the way, do you want me to wear a white or black catering chef uniform?"

"Are you kidding me, Hope?"

"No, I need to know. I typically allow my customers to pick the color."

"Whichever one you think is best, is fine with me," smiled Tiffany. "I am really proud of you," said Tiffany as she cleared her throat. "Have you found a business location yet?"

"No, I'm still looking."

"You should get one in Charlotte so you can take over my mother's customers."

"I don't know if I want to do that," said Hope.

"I think it would be good for you. My mother has already established a large network."

"I know," sighed Hope. "Your mother asked me already. I told her that I would think about it."

"To be honest, the toughest part will be her customers. I'm not sure how you can convince them that your cooking is as delicious as my mother's," laughed Tiffany.

"I know," laughed Hope. "You know how folks in Cloverdale are about food. They have been used to your mother preparing meals and cakes for special arrangements for years."

"You're right," said Tiffany. "But I have invited a lot of her friends to the event."

"I thought you invited the entire Cloverdale projects when I looked at the number of people that I need to prepare food for," chuckled Hope.

"I'm sure you can handle it," grinned Tiffany.

"I will get a few contracted employees to help me."

"Okay," said Tiffany. "But I still think this may be a way for you to convince folks in

Cloverdale that you have magical cooking hands too. Besides, I'm sure my mother will let them know that she taught you how to cook."

"I still have to think it about it. So, I don't want to make any promises," said Hope, in a shallow tone. Though this was a golden opportunity to establish herself to expand her customers, Hope realized that she still struggled with self-confidence. Her past and current traumas nearly destroyed her self-esteem, an area that often caused self-doubt.

Tiffany pressed her lips together before slowly allowing them to part. "Why are you hesitating about potentially accepting my mother's customers?"

"No reason," mumbled Hope.

Tiffany paused. "We were friends as kids, Hope. So, I know when something is bothering you."

"It's okay. I'll be fine."

Tiffany slanted her head to the side as she looked at Hope. "Well, I can't make you talk to me if you don't want to do so."

The elegant white doors to the small conference room slowly opened.

"Excuse, me," said a short man with an Italian accent. "Do you know how much time you need in this ballroom because we have to set up for an event?"

"We will be finished in a few minutes," responded Tiffany.

The man slowly closed the doors.

"I still don't know why you are so reluctant to possibly accepting my mother's customers," said Tiffany as if she wanted to quickly resume their conversation. "I know it's not anything related to your mother because you two have restored your relationship."

"No, it's not that."

"Then what is it? I am your friend and I know something isn't right."

"I'm okay," said Hope, trying to prevent from speaking negatively about Sloan.

"Is it your husband, Hope?" asked Tiffany as if she hadn't forgotten their previous conversation. "I'm not trying to get in your marriage, but something isn't right," paused Tiffany. "My marriage isn't picture-perfect. But it's nothing like yours."

A cloud of silence filtered through the room barely below the instrumental jazz that flowed out of the speakers in the room.

Hope flopped down in a black padded chair as she rubbed her forehead.

Endless heartfelt words streamed out of Hope's mouth as if someone had unlocked the floodgates causing Tiffany to wrap her slender arms around her.

Chapter 51

Two weeks later, pink and blue balloons dangled from white padded chairs. Colorful artwork decorated the walls of the rectangular shaped room. Canvas boards positioned in the middle of the room near small square shaped tables.

Paint brushes glided up and down on white sketch paper as children laughed and peeked at one another's artwork.

"I want to take this time to thank everyone for coming to Imaginary Art Gallery," said a short, penny brown woman as her right hand gripped a turquoise paintbrush. "This is an awesome place for Jayla and Jayden to celebrate their birthday party," she uttered while brushing a layer of green paint on a canvas. "Please continue to enjoy this event."

A warm feeling flowed through Hope as she watched Jayla and Jayden paint.

"Happy Birthday, Jayla and Jayden," smiled Hope as she took their pictures.

"This is really nice, Hope," said Gloria as she patted Hope on her back. "I can see that my grandchildren are having a lot of fun."

Clusters of laughter tumbled through the room. Hope's gaze landed on several children who congregated near Jayla and Jayden to observe the amateur pictures that they had painted.

"I am glad that some of their friends from school could come to this event," said Hope.

"Where is Sloan?" asked Gloria as a frown unfolded on her face.

"His flight was delayed," sighed Hope. "But I think he will still make it to the twins' birthday party."

Gloria stared at Hope, causing an awkward feeling to run through Hope.

"I will be back, mama," said Hope, trying to reduce the sudden tension in the air.

Hope walked toward her kids. She stretched her arm wide so she could hug both of them.

"What are you drawing?" asked Hope as she looked at Jayla.

"I am making butterflies for you and grandma," responded Jayla.

"I'm making a bike," blurted Jayden.

Lovely feelings pumped through Hope as she watched smiles unfold on her twins' faces. They were enjoying themselves as they painted with their friends.

"Where . . . where is daddy?" asked Jayla in a soft tone.

"I talked to him early this morning. He is trying to make it here," said Hope as she forced a smile on her face.

Hope walked toward an empty canvas. She applied a few coats of paint onto a pink piece of paper, trying to ease her mind. *Where are you, Sloan?* wondered Hope.

Familiar voices approached Hope.

"I'm glad you invited my twins," said Tiffany as she smiled at Hope.

"I am glad that you came," said Hope.

"I might have my twins' next birthday party here," chuckled Tiffany while handing her twins a paintbrush.

"I think that will be a great idea," said Vance as he walked Vance, Jr. toward an empty canvas.

"Where is Sloan?" asked Tiffany.

A touch of disappointment coursed through Hope as she looked around the art gallery room.

"He had to go out of town for a business meeting yesterday. He was scheduled to return this morning. But his flight was delayed."

"His flight," sneered Tiffany. "This is the most important day for the twins."

"I know," mumbled Hope as she glanced around the room.

A warm breeze flowed through the room.

"Hello, Hope. Thank you for inviting us," said Tony as he ushered Heather and his children inside the room.

"I am glad that you and your family could make it," grinned Hope as she handed Heather two aprons. "These are for Carmen and Anthony, Jr. so that they don't mess up their nice outfits," she smiled.

Hope watched as Heather walked Carmen and Anthony, Jr., toward a set of canvases.

"It is amazing that I can't even smell the paint in here," uttered Tony.

"Are you trying to sniff the paint?" whispered Tiffany as she poked Tony in the arm. "There are other ways to get high," she laughed.

"Whatever, Tiffany," responded Tony in a hasty tone. "I've never done any drugs."

"You two better be good," chuckled Hope.

"I'm just kidding with you, Tony," laughed Tiffany.

"The paint is odorless. It is safer for the children," said Hope.

"Where is your husband, Hope?" asked Tony as his eyebrows connected.

"I just asked her the same thing," muffled Tiffany.

Hope slowly exhaled. "Sloan had a business meeting out of town and his return flight has been delayed."

Tony peered at Hope for a few seconds.

"Daddy, come and paint with me," said Carmen in a soft voice.

Hope was delighted that Carmen had interrupted Tony's conversation with her. She pulled out her cell phone, hoping that Sloan had sent her a text message to give an update on his whereabouts. She huffed, realizing that Sloan had not texted or called her.

A shaft of sunlight brightened the room, highlighting the colorful art paintings on the canvases.

"It's time to cut the cakes," announced Hope. "Jayla and Jayden, come over here."

"How did you find time to bake *two* cakes?" asked Tiffany.

"I am a professional," laughed Hope.

"Well, I hope you have applied those professional skills to my mother's cake and food," chuckled Tony. "Her event is this evening."

"I haven't forgotten, Tony," laughed Hope. "I will have everything prepared."

"I hope so," giggled Tiffany. "Make sure everything is perfect for our mother."

"It will be," smiled Hope.

An hour later, Hope glanced around the art gallery. Sloan still hadn't arrived.

"Let's draw a picture together," said Gloria as she caressed Hope's right hand.

Hope wondered if her mother could sense the overload of disappointment that she was feeling.

Chapter 52

The evening clouds created a path for the sun to cast a rainbow of rays inside the Chandler

Convention Center's ballroom. White square shaped chairs with stained gold bows draped on the back of them assembled throughout Chandler Convention Center's ballroom. Burgundy linen tablecloths blanketed round shaped tables. Small glowing candles floated above the water inside the heart shaped vases creating a shimmer throughout the room that paralleled the sparkling lights from the Victorian style chandelier that dangled from the ceiling. Greek style columns rested in the corners, permitting a graceful backdrop of the light gold and hunter green painted walls.

Men, women and children marched inside the small ballroom wearing clean nicely pressed clothes. Hope wasn't expecting the guests to wear tuxedos or evening gowns. But she was certain that Tiffany had advised everyone that blue jeans were not permitted. From the appearance of everyone in the ballroom, it seemed as if Tiffany got her point across to Mrs. Brown's friends in Cloverdale projects.

Hope placed several business cards and a brochure on the edge of a table in the front.

Soft instrumental music flowed throughout the room creating a peaceful atmosphere.

"This is absolutely beautiful," said Mrs. Brown as a tear rolled down her dark brown face. "This is truly a surprise," she sniffled as her gaze scanned the room. "I thought everybody forgot that my birthday was November 2nd since nobody said anything to me about it."

"I am glad you like it, mama," said Tiffany in a soft tone.

"We had to turn into detectives to organize this event for you," said Tony. "We just knew one of your friends would sneak and tell you."

"No, baby. Nobody peaked a word out," said Mrs. Brown as she wiped her face. "I'm just surprised that Hope was able to organize her twins' birthday party earlier today and still have the energy to host this event for me."

"You did a nice job for my sister," said Lamont as he smiled at Hope while hugging Mrs. Brown.

Hope glanced around, making sure her contracted employees were serving the meals and beverages as she had instructed. A sense of pride flowed through her as she watched the contracted employees parade around the ballroom, wearing her company's black uniforms. She was delighted to have a size suitable for the employees.

The delicious savory smell of lemon peppered salmon swirled throughout the ballroom, mingling with the crisp scent of barbeque chicken breasts. The sweet aroma of lemon pound cake and red velvet cake wafted inside the room.

"Ruth, I am glad you brought your granddaughters with you," smiled Mrs. Brown as Ruth walked up to the table.

"Me too," grinned Ruth as she looked at Mrs. Brown.

"They look beautiful," said Hope as she glanced at Jasmine and Taylor's dresses.

"This is the first time we've ever been to an event like this," uttered Jasmine as she looked down at her purple dress.

"We didn't get to go anywhere when we were at that place," winced Taylor.

Hope exhaled. She knew exactly what Taylor meant.

"Excuse me," said a tall contracted employee in a baritone voice. "Your seat is right here," uttered the man as he pointed to a table beside Mrs. Brown's table.

"Okay," grinned Ruth as she glided toward the table as her black evening gown trailed behind her.

"I didn't know Mrs. Ruth had any long dresses," laughed Tiffany.

"She had to buy a new wardrobe when her granddaughters came," mumbled Mrs. Brown in a humorous tone.

"Thanks for allowing my twins and my mother to sit at the table near you," said Hope.

"No problem, Hope," said Mrs. Brown as she looked at the table beside her.

"Mrs. Brown, you look so beautiful," said Gloria as her voice flowed from her table to Mrs. Brown's table. Her cinnamon brown dress highlighted her mahogany skin.

"She sure does," said Geneva as she fastened a button on her forest green dress while sitting beside her son, Hilton.

"It was nice to meet you today," said Heather as she looked at Hope. She sipped on some lemonade.

"Likewise," said Hope as her gaze locked into Heather's greenish brown eyes. A soft chuckled sparked inside Hope as she remembered Tiffany had said Heather had cat eyes and couldn't cook.

"It was nice to meet you, too," said Heather in a soft mellow voice. "And this is our daughter, Carmen and our son, Anthony Jr.," blurted Heather as if she wanted to make sure that Hope knew that Tony was the father of her children

"Heather, Tony and I went to school with Hope," said Tiffany as if she wanted to interrupt Heather's next sentence. "Did you forget that Hope already met the kids when we went to their birthday party at the art gallery?" smirked Tiffany, knowing that Heather was being passive-aggressive and a queen at being sarcastic.

Heather wiped her cupid shaped lips while she kept her gaze on Tony.

Tiffany glanced at Hope as a sneer flashed on her lips. Hope was familiar with that look. She figured Heather had plucked one of Tiffany's nerves.

"Hello," said Hope while glancing at Vance, Jr.'s dark brown eyes.

"Hope, this food is absolutely delicious," complimented Vance.

"Yes, it is," smiled Tiffany.

"Mama, you definitely taught Hope how to cook like you," said Tony in a supportive tone without noticing that Heather was staring at his left temple as if he had an argument forthcoming at home.

"Does anybody need anything else?" asked Hope as she glanced around the table. She was glad that the table was large enough for Mrs. Brown, her grandchildren, her children and their spouses.

"Maybe *a second* plate at some point," grinned Tony as if Heather had been depriving him of home cooked meals.

"I second that motion," said Vance.

"Vance, you're not in *court*. So, you don't have to motion anything," chuckled Tiffany.

"Settle down," chuckled Mrs. Brown. "Hope, I'm really proud of you."

"Thank you, Mrs. Brown," smiled Hope.

"Where is your husband?" asked Mrs. Brown.

"He had to go out of town for a business meeting. But he will be here soon."

Vance glanced up at Hope while taking a quick break from his salmon.

"I look forward to meeting him," said Vance in a conspicuous tone.

Hope paused for a second. "I will be back. I have to check on the other guests."

"Okay," smiled Mrs. Brown. "I'll walk with you."

"You don't have to do that, Mrs. Brown," smiled Hope.

"Oh, it's no problem. I have enough energy to walk around in here with you."

Hope looked at her mother. "I will be back, mama," smiled Hope.

"It's okay, Hope. I know Mrs. Brown is trying to steal you for a few minutes."

"I know," said Ruth as she laughed with Gloria.

"Jayden, make sure you eat your vegetables," said Hope as she looked at him. "Mama, please don't let Jayla eat too much cake."

A partial frown flashed on Jayla's face. She was definitely addicted to sweets.

Hope strolled through the ballroom with Mrs. Brown, making sure that the guests were pleased with the services.

"Hello Mrs. Arlene and Mrs. Dinah," said Hope while passing their table. Hope never forget how Mrs. Arlene taught her how to do her hair while living in Cloverdale. Though she had never been to cosmetology school, Mrs. Arlene could work wonders with a straightened comb and curlers and she showed Hope. A small chuckle escaped Hope's lips as she recalled how Mrs. Dinah tried hard to teach her how to sew. After a few pricks with the needles, Hope quickly abandoned her interest in sewing. Mrs. Brown helped Hope to find her true gift in cooking. It was a heartfelt experience that Hope never forget. "You two look beautiful."

"Thank you, Hope" said Mrs. Arlene as she sipped on a glass of tea.

"Hope, this food is delicious," said Dinah.

"Thank you," smiled Hope as she continued walking with Mrs. Brown.

"How was the food, JoAnn?" asked Mrs. Brown as she approached a table.

"It was delicious, Mrs. Brown," said JoAnn as her silver hair sparkled with the lights. JoAnn routinely ordered meals from Mrs. Brown every holiday and cakes for all of her grandchildren's birthdays. "If this is your event, then why did you have to cook?"

"I didn't cook this food," smiled Mrs. Brown.

"Well, it sure enough tastes like you did," said JoAnn as she looked at the people sitting at her table.

Mrs. Brown paused. "Why are you looking like that, Thelma?" asked Mrs. Brown as she looked at the woman who was sitting beside JoAnn.

"So, *who* cooked then?" asked Thelma who was known as Cloverdale's internal news anchor. People flocked to her apartment to get the latest scoop on news.

Mrs. Brown leaned against the table as if she was bracing herself. "Hope Rankin-Glover cooked this food. She is the owner of Serenity Catering Services," she said as she signaled for Hope to come to her.

Mrs. Brown ceased her conversation for a split second. "This is Gloria Rankin's daughter," smiled Mrs. Brown. "She cooked all of the food . . . not me."

Thelma gawked at Hope. "Child, you sure do cook like Mrs. Brown. You had us fooled," said Thelma as her salt and pepper colored hair brushed against her shoulders.

"We were sitting over here feeling sorry for Mrs. Brown. We thought her children made her cook all of this food for her own event," sneered JoAnn.

"Yes, I cooked all of the food," smiled Hope. "Mrs. Brown taught me."

"Did it take you several years to learn how to perfect meals like her?" inquired Thelma as if she was conducting a newspaper interview with Hope.

"Yes, it took a few years," smiled Hope. "She taught me when I was a teenager."

"What made you want to learn how to cook?" asked Thelma.

"I developed an interest when I was young," smiled Hope, quickly recalling the many nights and days she went to sleep hungry while trailing behind Gloria in abandoned buildings. Hope wished she had known how to cook those days. She would have cooked a feast for the children with whom she shared a small space in the corner of the abandoned buildings. From those dreadful hunger days, she promised herself to become a chef when she grew up—a dream that finally came true.

"Stop trying to be a news anchor," blurted JoAnn as she gawked at Thelma.

Thelma buckled her lips together.

"It was nice meeting you," smiled Hope as she looked at JoAnn and Thelma.

Hope continued to stroll by several tables. Of course, Mrs. Brown felt the need to stop and conduct a survey of the food with the guests and to introduce Hope. A sense of acceptance flowed through Hope as the guests finally realized that she had cooked all the food.

"I'm ready to sit down now," said Mrs. Brown.

"Okay," uttered Hope. "I know what you were doing, Mrs. Brown. You were trying to pass along your customers to me," giggled Hope.

Mrs. Brown rubbed her hands together as if her arthritis was cradling her bones. "I guess I couldn't fool you," grinned Mrs. Brown. "I wanted to introduce you to some of my customers who are here. In this case, they would have already tasted your food. Now they know you have roots from Cloverdale and that I taught you how to cook," she smiled. "Trust me the word will surely spread like a wildfire. Everybody will know that Gloria Rankin's daughter can cook like Mrs. Brown."

At the rate that Mrs. Brown was trying to recommend new customers, Hope was certain that her catering business would reach higher grounds quickly.

Hope walked toward her mother and twins.

"Where is your husband, Hope?" asked Gloria in a pleasant tone.

"I don't know, mama. But he told me he was coming."

Hope glanced at her cell phone. She didn't have any missed calls.

"Where are you, Sloan?" mumbled Hope.

A familiar streak of disappointment flowed inside Hope, causing her heart to wither like a rose.

Chapter 53

Two hours later, crumbs congregated on the catering trays. Residue lingered inside the iced tea and lemonade canisters. The number of guests in the ballroom was decreasing as the evening progressed with time. But there were still several guests mingling with one another at different tables.

Hope walked past the table where she had placed several business cards and a brochure. She noticed all of the business cards and brochures had vanished.

"Mrs. Brown, I hope you enjoyed your event," said Hope in a pleasant tone.

"I did, Hope," winked Mrs. Brown as she leaned back in her chair.

"This was really nice what you did for my mother," smiled Tiffany.

"And the food was absolutely delicious," said Heather, capturing everyone's attention.

"Thank you," uttered Hope as her mind still tried to speculate on Sloan's whereabouts.

Hope glanced at her cell phone again. There were no missed calls or text messages from him.

"Hope, I have to take Jayla to the restroom," said Gloria.

"Thank you, mama," said Hope as she tried to force a smile on her face. She was still wondering why Sloan had not arrived.

"I have to use the bathroom too," said Taylor as she slowly stood.

"I will go with you," said Ruth as she strolled behind Taylor. "Come on, Jasmine," ordered Ruth. "You know I don't let you two out of my sight unless you're at school."

"Mama, make sure Jayla washes her hands in the bathroom. Also, can you take Jayden with you too? I can't watch him while I work," smiled Hope.

"Sure, Hope," grinned Gloria.

"Thank you, mama. You have been a big help today."

"No problem, Hope. I'm glad I could help you," said Gloria. "This really means a lot to me."

Hope shifted from one table to the next. People were still holding conversations about the delicious food. A warm feeling flowed through Hope as she glanced at the contracted employees while they cleaned up several areas. They had done a great job.

"Hope," said Mrs. Geneva. "Your mother and Ruth said they are taking the kids for a brief walk through this convention center."

"This place is so beautiful," said Geneva. "So, I guess I'll go for a walk with them."

"Okay, but don't forget we have to leave shortly. We only reserved this place for four hours."

"Okay. I'm sure we'll be back in a few minutes. I will tell them to hurry up."

Hope continued to stroll past the tables. Some people were gathering their coats. But several of Mrs. Brown's closest friends were still lingering inside the ballroom.

A gentle tap landed on Hope's back. She slowly turned around. Her gaze landed on Sloan.

"I'm glad you were able to make it, Sloan," uttered Hope. "But the event is almost over."

"I guess it is better to be late than never, right?" he smiled.

His black suit cradled the finest creases in his muscular arms.

"You missed the twins' birthday party earlier today," huffed Hope.

"I tried to make it. But my flight was delayed," he grinned.

"You could have called or texted me to let me know," said Hope.

"I couldn't. The battery in my cell phone died."

Hope allowed her mind to convince her that Sloan was telling the truth. She handed Sloan a glass of water. "You look nice."

"Thank you," said Sloan as he planted a kiss on Hope's forehead.

"I see you have been working hard in here," Sloan said as he gently pinched Hope's cheek. "I'm proud of you, Hope," he said while stepping closer to Hope. "I want to spend the next couple of days with you and the twins. I canceled several business trips."

A warm feeling danced in Hope's heart. "Thank you, Sloan. I am glad to hear this. Now, the twins and I will be able to have more time with you."

Sloan wrapped his arms around Hope as he glanced around the ballroom.

"I am glad that you are proud of me," grinned Hope.

"I will show you how much I am really proud of you when we get home," whispered Sloan in Hope's ears as he perched a kiss on her ear.

A soft chuckle flowed out of Hope's mouth.

"Oh, by the way. I will book us a flight to travel to Europe for the Christmas holiday," grinned Sloan. "Make sure that your passport and the twins' passports have not expired."

A ripple effect of love tumbled through Hope's heart. "That is so nice, Sloan. Where are we going this time?" inquired Hope.

"France and Germany?"

"Wow."

Sloan paused before speaking, while glancing at his watch as if he was reading a message. "We will go to Dubai as well."

"Really," smiled Hope as excitement flowed inside.

Sloan cleared his throat as he looked at his watch again. A frown formed on his face. "I have to go to Dubai by myself. But I take you and the twins to France and Germany before I travel to Dubai. Where are the kids?" asked Sloan as a frown formed on his face.

Hope stood like a statue as a touch of disappointment sparked in her. "They went to the bathroom and to walk around with my mother."

"Okay. But I hope she keeps a close eye on them."

"She will. Let me introduce you to a few people," said Hope in a pleasant tone.

"I'm good," said Sloan. "Plus, I need to sit down."

"Please, Sloan," begged Hope.

Sloan paused for a few seconds. "Okay, I'll go to one or two tables."

Hope ushered Sloan to Mrs. Brown's table.

"Everybody, this is my husband, Sloan," said Hope in a proud tone.

Silence formed at the table as everyone looked up at Sloan.

"It is nice to put a face to a name. Hope always talks about you," said Tony as he stood.

"That's good," smiled Sloan.

"I'm Tony. Mrs. Brown is my mother and Tiffany is my sister," said Tony as he leaned toward Sloan to shake his hand. "And this is my wife, Heather, and our children."

"Nice to meet you all," said Sloan as his gaze slightly landed on Heather's breasts, sparking a ray of jealousy in Hope's heart.

"You already know, I'm Tiffany," said Tiffany as she looked at Sloan. "This is my husband, Vance."

Vance stood. He shook Sloan's hand without uttering a single word.

A fake smile unfolded on Sloan's face.

"And this is Mrs. Brown," smiled Hope as she pointed at Mrs. Brown.

"I see that you had a lovely event," said Sloan as he looked at Mrs. Brown.

"Yes, I did and your wife did a wonderful job," uttered Mrs. Brown in a pleasant tone.

"I hate that I missed it," smiled Sloan. "I had a business meeting and my flight was delayed coming back," said Sloan as he glanced at his watch.

"Where did you go?" asked Vance as if he was analyzing Sloan.

Sloan squinted as if Vance's questions had sparked a nerve. He didn't like to be questioned.

"I went out of town," responded Sloan in a hasty tone. "It was nice meeting everyone," he said as he walked to the next table.

"I'll be back, everybody," said Hope as she trailed behind Sloan.

"Hello, Mrs. Geneva, this is my husband, Sloan," said Hope in an uneasy tone while trying to figure out why Sloan was short tempered with Vance.

"Nice to meet you," said Mrs. Geneva. "Hope talks about you all the time."

"I hope she is saying good things about me," smiled Sloan as he placed his empty glass on Mrs. Geneva's table.

"Of course, Sloan," grinned Hope.

Chattering noises flowed inside the ballroom.

"Daddy," said Jayden as he ran toward Sloan.

"See, even the kids missed you," mumbled Hope. "You've got to stop going on all of those business trips."

"It's how we pay the bills," grinned Sloan through his teeth as if he didn't want anyone to hear his response. Sloan hugged Jayden for a few seconds before turning toward Jayla. He wrapped his arms around her slender body. "Come here, little princess," smiled Sloan as he hugged her. "Thank you, Mrs. Gloria, for helping Hope with the kids while I was away on a business trip."

"You are welcome," said Gloria as she sat.

Laughter rolled into the ballroom as Ruth and her granddaughter walked inside.

"Hope, is that your husband?" asked Ruth in a loud tone while walking toward Hope and Sloan. "It's about time I finally get to meet him."

"Yes, it is," responded Hope from a slight distance.

Ruth stopped in her tracks. Apparently, she realized that Jasmine and Taylor were no longer walking in the ballroom beside her.

"Come on Jasmine and Taylor," ordered Ruth as her gaze shifted from Hope to them. They were still standing at the front door, staring inside.

Tiffany stood. She walked toward Jasmine and Taylor.

"Sloan, I will be back," said Hope. "Something is going on."

Sloan froze at the mere sight of Jasmine and Taylor.

"I have to go, Hope. I will see you at the house," said Sloan in an uptight tone while looking around as if he was searching for an alternate exit door.

A puzzled feeling rattled Hope's heart. "Please don't leave, Sloan. I have to see what is going on over there."

"I will meet you at the house," demanded Sloan while rubbing his chin. "The twins should spend more time with your mother tonight," said Sloan as if he knew something that Hope did not.

Hope paused. "Sloan, that means the twins will have to wait until I finish cleaning up this room. Then, I'll have to drive from Charlotte back to Raleigh," she sighed. "They will be tired. So, please go ahead and take them with you," begged Hope.

Sloan shrugged. "Hope, listen to me. Let your mother watch the twins. It is best that she watches them. I'm sure she wants to spend more time with them."

Hope exhaled. "Okay, Sloan. I love you."

Sloan embraced Hope as if it was his last time touching her. "I love you, too," he uttered while looking around as though he was a fugitive.

"Are you okay?" asked Hope as her heart fluttered.

Sloan ignored Hope's question. He dashed toward Jayla and Jayden, hugging them as if he would never see them again. Hope noticed that Sloan held Jayden for a longer time as he patted Jayden's back several times. She winced, trying to figure out what he was doing. Without glancing back at Hope, he nearly sprinted toward a side door as if he was late for a flight.

"That is the wrong door, Sloan," said Hope.

"I don't want to go that way," said Sloan in a hasty tone as he pointed in Ruth's direction. It seems like something is going on over there," he uttered as he vanished.

Hope walked toward Tiffany, Ruth, Jasmine and Taylor. "Is everything okay?"

"We don't know," responded Ruth. "I've never seen the girls react like this."

"They will not talk to us," said Tiffany as Vance slowly approach her.

"What is that?" asked Hope as she looked toward the floor. "I think somebody spilled something. I'll get one of the contractors to clean up the mess."

Ruth slowly walked closer to Jasmine and Taylor. She rapidly inhaled and exhaled as her gaze shifted between Taylor and the floor.

"What's wrong, Ruth?" asked Mrs. Brown as she wobbled toward Ruth.

"Oh, my God. It is pee," cried Ruth. "Taylor did you see one of the *leaders* in here?" asked Ruth in a serious tone, capturing nearly everyone's attention.

"What leader?" asked Vance.

"A human trafficking leader," responded Tiffany in a panicky tone.

Vance walked into a corner. He pulled out his cell phone and called someone.

Mrs. Brown walked toward them. She gently rubbed their faces.

Silence wrapped around their lips as if they were permanently glued together.

"Jasmine, please talk to me," begged Ruth.

Ruth turned her head toward Taylor. "Please talk to me."

Mrs. Brown grabbed Jasmine and Taylor's hands as she mumbled a quick prayer.

Jasmine planted her hand on Taylor's face as a tear rolled down her face. "Tell them, Taylor," mumbled Jasmine in a faint voice as she hugged Taylor.

Taylor slowly opened her mouth as pee continued to run down her legs like a faucet, splattering onto the marble tile floor in the ballroom.

The words that came out of Taylor's mouth nearly caused Hope to faint.

Chapter 54

The next morning, the large gloomy clouds stretched across the grayish black sky.

"Has anyone heard from Hope today?" asked Mrs. Brown as she looked at Ruth and Gloria.

"No," said Geneva. "I saw the FBI place her in the police car."

"That was so embarrassing," mumbled Gloria as she hugged Jayla and Jayden. "I can't believe this has happened."

"It's such a shame," said Mrs. Brown. "I would've never thought Hope was involved with something like this."

"Me neither," said Geneva. "How did she let all of this go on right under her nose?"

"Has she called you, Gloria?" asked Mrs. Brown.

"No," said Gloria as she hugged Jayla and Jayden. "I told her that I would watch the kids for her last night. I think she is still with the FBI. There was too much going on," exhaled Gloria.

"You can say that again," snapped Ruth as she rocked back and forth in a burgundy chair as if she was on a swing, staring at Gloria with rage in her eyes.

"Calm down, Ruth. It's not Gloria's fault. It's not Hope's fault," shrieked Mrs. Brown. "So, calm down, please," begged Mrs. Brown. "Hope's husband apparently had a lot of people fooled. I know something wasn't right about him. But I never thought it would be something this terrible."

"But why did Hope have to get involved?" blurted Ruth. "She had me fooled."

"Ruth, stop it," shrieked Gloria. "You don't know if Hope was involved in that mess."

"Well, the FBI didn't place her in handcuffs for nothing," blurted Ruth. "I pray they find her so-called husband."

Gloria wrapped her arms around Jayla and Jayden.

"I want my daddy," mumbled Jayden, instantly drawing everyone's gaze toward him as if they wanted to throw darts at him.

"Don't start it, Ruth," snapped Gloria. "He's just a kid."

"Ruth, you have to calm down," said Geneva in a soft tone as she tugged on her the blue scarf around her neck.

"I just can't believe it," sniffled Ruth. "This is a small world."

Loud rumbling sounds echoed across the sky, causing the glassware on Mrs. Brown's wooden stand to rattle.

"I still can't believe what happened last night either, Ruth," said Mrs. Brown as she closed her eyes. "But deep down in my heart I just can't accept that Hope could also be involved."

"Mrs. Brown, the FBI took her into custody," sobbed Ruth as she tucked her auburn brown wig behind her perky ears.

"That doesn't mean she has done anything," said Mrs. Brown.

"So, why did the FBI say that they had been watching her?" asked Ruth.

Quietness slithered through the room.

"Ruth is right, Mrs. Brown," mumbled Geneva. "I heard one of the FBI agents say they had been monitoring Hope for a few weeks."

"I didn't hear that," said Gloria as she continued to hug Jayla and Jayden.

"I did," snapped Ruth, causing her wig to vibrate. "His name was Agent Dean. He was one of the FBI Agents who talked to Taylor," said Ruth. "The other FBI agent's name was Garcia. She talked to Jasmine."

"I heard the FBI agents say that they saw Hope when she was at the hospital with the twins.

They had been trailing her."

Gloria cleared her throat. "Maybe they were trailing her just to get closer to her Sloan."

Ruth leaned back in the chair. "I need to talk to Hope. I can't believe this," mumbled Ruth. "Why did she allow him to change her? She was a good girl. I can't believe she was involved," said Ruth as she looked at Jasmine and Taylor.

"Ruth, please stop saying that," said Gloria.

"It's the truth. We all have to stop being in denial," blurted Ruth. "It's like Hope played this sweet innocent role around us. She acted like she was having so many problems with her husband just to distract us from focusing on the real issue."

"Ruth, you ought to be ashamed of yourself," uttered Geneva.

"Listen, everybody, face it. Hope fooled all of us," shrieked Ruth. "And I can't believe I'm sitting in here with Gloria. Hope is your daughter and she has been living with that lowlife husband," cried Ruth.

"Ruth, show some respect," said Mrs. Brown. "You shouldn't be talking like that around Jayla and Jayden."

"Ruth, you know you're wrong," mumbled Geneva. "Please show some respect."

"I'm trying," cried Ruth. "But they need to know what type of father they have."

Gloria stood. "Ruth, you're not going to keep disrespecting my grandchildren. We'll leave," said Gloria.

"Don't leave, Gloria. Please sit down," ordered Mrs. Brown. "We can't allow all this to mess up our friendship."

A river of tears streamed down Ruth's face.

"I know this is hard for you, Ruth," mumbled Gloria. "I would feel the same. But we have to do what is best for your grandchildren."

"My grandchildren went through a lot and everybody is expecting me to think that it is okay," sighed Ruth. "It's like my grandchildren were part of a horror movie," slurred Ruth in a heartfelt tone as she looked at Jasmine and Taylor. "I nearly passed out when I realized that Taylor had peed on herself. I didn't want to accept what was going on. I was in shock. But I knew I had to keep it together for Taylor."

A crisp scent of lemon lavender wafted through the living room.

Taylor slowly opened her mouth. "I was scared. I felt like running," said Taylor in a panicked tone. "But everything I told the FBI was the truth."

"We are proud of you, Taylor," sighed Mrs. Brown. "I'm glad you were able to pull yourself together to talk to the FBI."

"I was scared, too," muffled Jasmine. "I wanted to run. But my body froze up."

Mrs. Ruth looked at Jasmine and Taylor. "I love you."

Gloria tilted her head. "I'm sure this is painful for Hope," uttered Gloria. "I can't imagine how she feels," she paused. "I'm sure the FBI is going to tell her everything."

A loud rumbling sound ricocheted through the glass window.

"The FBI took the tape from the convention center last night," said Ruth. "They got Taylor and Jasmine to point out Sloan on the tape."

"They also got a glass that he left at my table," uttered Geneva. "The camera showed where he had placed it. I heard the FBI said they were going to run fingerprints."

Jasmine stared at Ruth as a single tear inched down her face. "Taylor, please tell them," sobbed Jasmine.

Taylor closed her eyes.

"What's wrong, Taylor?" asked Ruth.

Silence bolted Taylor's lips.

"If he was the leader that did that to mama, I hope you told the FBI," mumbled Jasmine.

"What are you talking about?" asked Ruth as her hands trembled.

Silence floated through the living room like a feather.

"Was he the leader who done that to mama?" asked Jasmine in a soft tone as she rubbed Taylor's hand.

Taylor's chin slowly lowered toward her chest. "Yes," sniffled Taylor. "He ordered a man to kill mama."

"How do you know that?" asked Mrs. Ruth.

"Mama was doing my hair in her cell," said Taylor.

"Cell?" blurted Mrs. Ruth.

"They kept mama in an underground cell because she was always trying to escape," mumbled Jasmine.

"Let her finish telling us, Ruth," said Mrs. Brown in a soft tone.

A puddle of tears forms underneath Taylor's chin before she spoke. "Jasmine was in her cell sleeping. Mama and I could hear them talking about killing her. I was scared. Mama told me not to cry and to hide. Mama hid me underneath a pile of clothes in a corner. She told me to be quiet regardless of what happened. I saw it all," she cried. "He beat up mama really bad. She passed out and he raped her before he killed her."

"I heard the FBI say that Rock and Sloan were brothers," mumbled Geneva.

"I think mama said the same thing one day, but daddy always denied it," said Jasmine. "I think he didn't want mama to know."

"Something isn't right," frowned Geneva. "Why would Sloan order Julia to be killed if she was the mother of his brother's children?" She glanced around. "Why would their uncle do that?"

Mrs. Ruth's eyelids collapsed as a loud muffled sound echoed out of her mouth. She spoke as if she had a delayed response to what she was hearing. "You mean to tell me that Sloan got somebody to kill my Julia," wept Mrs. Ruth as she stood and headed toward the front door. "I can't believe that Sloan is my grandchildren's uncle!"

"Ruth, please don't leave," begged Mrs. Brown as she slowly grabbed Ruth's hand.

Ruth jerked her hand from Mrs. Brown. She glared at Gloria as tears streamed down her face. "You mean to tell me that Hope was married to the monster who ordered my Julia to be killed!" screeched Ruth. "If Hope wasn't so naïve and dumb for Sloan, then maybe she could have saved my Julia!"

"Ruth, please calm down," pleaded Mrs. Brown.

"Let's go, Jasmine and Taylor," ordered Ruth before storming out the front door. "It seems like Sloan trained Hope too well. There's no telling what she might do for him!"

"I don't think she's trained. I think she's fearful of him," responded Gloria.

"Whatever!" snapped Ruth as she left.

A sharp sound pierced the air as the telephone rang.

"Excuse me," said Mrs. Brown. She wobbled over to the telephone.

"Hello," she said in a flat tone.

"Mrs. Brown, this is Hope. I know everybody is probably over at your house," sniffled Hope.

"So, please tell Mrs. Ruth that I am so sorry."

Mrs. Brown planted her dark brown hand over her heart.

"Please tell Jasmine and Taylor that I wish I could erase their past but I can't."

Mrs. Brown could feel an intense level of stares focused in her direction.

"Mrs. Brown, I am so sorry. All of this seems like a nightmare," sobbed Hope.

"Hope, where are you?" asked Mrs. Brown. "Your children and mother need you."

"I love my mother and my children, Mrs. Brown. But I also love my husband."

An unsettled feeling pierced Mrs. Brown's soul. She suddenly recalled that Hope had expressed this same level of emotions right before she vanished for seven years.

"There are things that you don't know about your husband," uttered Mrs. Brown.

"I don't care, Mrs. Brown," shrieked Hope. "I love my husband. I have to be with him. He is the only man I've ever loved. He's never done any of that stuff to me. He's never harmed my children. So, I just can't believe any of that stuff," cried Hope. "Please tell my mother to take care of my twins. I'm sorry, Mrs. Brown, but I have to be with my husband."

"Hope, don't do this," uttered Mrs. Brown, clenching her chest. "Sloan has a stronghold on your mind. Please don't be in denial. Please don't do this, Hope," pleaded Mrs. Brown.

Hope's voice faded away without even saying goodbye on the telephone.

Chapter 55

An hour later, rain burst through the clouds like a cyclone. An overwhelming sense of trepidation knifed through Hope's heart, body and soul. Her mind couldn't process the words that the FBI had said about Sloan. Her heart slowly deteriorated as she walked around her house, contemplating an escape plan to join Sloan. *But where would we go? Will he force me into human trafficking? Or will he protect me?* she thought. But reality kicked in.

"Hope, I know this is a lot for you to process. I've been trailing you ever since I saw you at the hospital with your twins," said FBI Agent Dean as he stared at Hope while showing her the search warrant again.

Hope exhaled slowly as she recalled the day that FBI Agent Dean spoke to her at the hospital.

"Chief agent Vance is good," said FBI Agent Garcia with a Spanish accent. "He told us that he profiled you after meeting you one time. He has never been wrong thus far."

"Profiled me?" asked Hope, recalling how Tiffany's husband, Vance, had stared at her that day as if he was analyzing her. She winced, recalling that she had met FBI Agent Garcia at the hospital as well.

"Yes, it is a technique that FBI agents learn to detect certain behaviors. But Chief Vance has mastered the technique," blurted an FBI Agent while strolling inside the living room. "By the way, I'm FBI Agent Wang," he said as his almond shaped eyes glanced at the papers in a box

Several FBI agents streamed into the living room like a broken dam as if they had been on a scavenger hunt throughout the house with electronic devices in their hands.

Hope closed her eyes, wishing that she had never met Vance. But deep down, she had always felt like something wasn't right about Sloan.

"It hurts my heart to know all of this has happened," sobbed Hope.

"I know that was painful for you to make that telephone call to Mrs. Brown," said FBI Agent Dean. "But I'm sure Sloan wired your cell phone to listen to all of your calls and we needed him to think that you wanted to run off with him."

A river of disbelief flowed through Hope. She couldn't believe what was going on.

"Sloan had more cameras in this house than the Pentagon," said FBI Agent Garcia. "But our engineers have manipulated the cameras to make Sloan think that you're the only person in here."

Hope glanced out of the window.

"Where are your cars?" sniffled Hope.

"We parked several yards away and walked through the woods behind your house. We had to make sure we located and infiltrated his high-tech cameras," said FBI Agent Dean. "I think he wired a few other things. I'm checking into it now," he said while looking at a device in his hand as he pressed it against the walls in the living room.

Hope glanced around, looking at the family portrait of her, Sloan and the twins. A busload of denial tried to seep through her pores. But her mind erased all traces of denial.

A loud banging sound echoed against the door. Hope's heart slammed against her chest as her gaze trailed the FBI agents' hands as they gripped their guns.

The door slowly opened. "It seems like he has already been here," said an FBI Agent as he walked inside the house as if he had a key.

"How do you know?" asked FBI Agent Morgan.

"I see the tire marks in the grass," uttered FBI Agent Dean.

Hope winced, realizing that the other FBI agents wouldn't know that because they entered through the back door.

"But Sloan's cars are still in the garage," said FBI Agent Garcia. "We searched the house. He isn't in here," she uttered. "We're waiting on FBI Agent Latham to send us the satellite report that will show us the activities in this area over the last few hours."

"Hope, how long have you been living here?" asked FBI Agent Dean.

"About five or six years. Why?"

"Did he have this house before you married him?"

"Yes," responded Hope as a sense of nervousness rolled through her.

"Did he tell you this was his house?"

"Yes," answered Hope. "And he put my name on the deed two years ago. Why?"

FBI Agent Morgan scratched his jet black hair.

"Hope, this house didn't belong to just him," paused FBI Agent Morgan.

"What do you mean?" asked Hope as she leaned back in the chair as if the oxygen in the room made it hard for her to breathe.

"This house belongs to him and his real wife, Amber."

"Wait! Wait!" cringed Hope. "What do you mean real wife?" asked Hope as tears rolled down her face.

The FBI agents looked at one another as if they had dropped a bombshell.

Chapter 56

Ten minutes later, darkness drifted across the sky, depriving the moon of finding a space to peek through the thick clouds.

Hope sat on the edge of the chair. Her heart raced faster than a leopard chasing its prey.

"What do you mean Sloan's real wife?" asked Hope in a pitiful tone.

FBI Agent Garcia inched toward Hope. "We ran the fingerprints on the glass that he left on a table last night at the event," she sighed. "His real name is Roland Lamar Gloverstone. But we've learned that his *alias* name is *Sloan*."

The blood in Hope's veins came to a slow chilling halt. "I don't believe you," sobbed Hope, recalling that Sloan had declined to allow her to name their son after him.

"We don't have any reason to lie to you, Hope. Your marriage to Sloan was not valid," said FBI Agent Garcia. "We pulled a court file on him as well. His wife, Amber, was in a strange car accident right around the time Sloan met you. He received a lot of money from her life insurance policy. And he kept the death certificate," said FBI Agent Garcia.

Hope shook her head. "His wife!" shrieked Hope as if her heart couldn't take any more. "I'm his wife," she cried as she planted her face in the crease of her hands. "If his wife is dead . . . like you are saying, then he is a widower which makes my marriage valid."

The FBI agents stared at one another as if there were more to the story.

"Trust me, your marriage is not valid. When did you meet Sloan?" asked FBI Agent Garcia as she looked at a death certificate.

"June 30th, on my mother's birthday," said Hope, recalling that when she had met Sloan, he had told her that he was coming from court due to his ex-girlfriend hitting him.

FBI Agent Garcia slowly walked toward Hope. "June 30th is the day that he had to go to the courthouse to get the death certificate and the money from the life insurance policy," she said as she showed Hope a document that Sloan had inside the box.

Hope's mind forced her to accept that Sloan had lied to her.

"Hold that thought, FBI Agent Garcia. I don't think Amber was his real wife, either," said FBI Agent Wang as he combed through the box, sorting things.

"Are you kidding me," sniffled Hope. "This can't be happening."

FBI Agent Wang fingered through his grayish-black hair as he looked at Hope. "I scanned the walls in this house. I found several hidden safes built in the walls," uttered FBI Agent Wang. "I had to use this device to open them," he said waving an electronic device in his hand.

"He used a fake name when he married Amber," uttered FBI Agent Wang. "Goodness, Sloan has several aliases," he shrieked, flipping through several fake driver's licenses and passports with different names.

"Fake name?" inquired Hope as her heart crumbled. "What else is in that box?"

Silence flowed through the living room for a few seconds.

"There are two fake marriage licenses in here," said FBI Agent Morgan. "And there is one with your name on it."

"You mean to tell me that he has been married three times," sobbed Hope.

"None of the marriages were valid," said FBI Agent Garcia in a soft tone.

"There are three life insurance policies in here," said FBI Agent Wang.

"Three?" inquired Hope as tears tumbled down her face.

"Yes, one for each of his fake wives, including one for you," said FBI Agent Wang. "There is a policy in here for someone named Amber and Crystal. It seems like he got married every *seven* years.

"Somehow, Amber and Crystal died mysteriously after Sloan was with them for seven years," said FBI Agent Garcia as she read the death certificates. "At the rate Sloan was going, it seemed like he would have killed you before the end of your seventh year with him," she sighed.

Hope closed her eyes as a gust of fear swept through her bones, causing sweat to seep through her pores. She recalled her brake line had been cut, nearly causing her to wreck. *Was he planning to kill me?* she wondered.

FBI Agent Garcia peered at a document. "Wow, he had a relationship with Julia from

Cloverdale? She was missing for years. It seems like he was engaged to her. I see that he filed for a marriage license, but I don't see the actual marriage license."

Hope's heart stopped beating for a few seconds. "Wait a minute . . . are you telling me that Sloan and Julia were married or they were about to get married."

A warm breeze swirled in the living room from the vent.

"It seems like Sloan wanted Julia for himself," said FBI Agent Wang as he looked at information on a device in his hand. "But it appears somehow Rock started having an interest in her."

Hope felt like she was trapped in a nightmare.

"From what we've learned, Sloan ordered Julia to be killed because of the rivalry he and Rock had over her," said FBI Agent Garcia.

Hope closed her eyes as shock consumed her. *Were Jasmine and Taylor her twins' sisters?* she thought.

Hope's lips slowly opened. "Who is the father of Jasmine and Taylor? Rock or Sloan?"

Silence filled the room.

"It seems like he had a thing for young women," said FBI Agent Dean as he ignored Hope's questions. "They were your age when he married them," he said while looking at a form in the box. "Sloan probably had planned to kidnap the women including you. But something made him keep all of you for a while."

Hope rocked nervously in the chair as her legs shook like Jell-O. Her heart couldn't withstand any more pain.

"I'm sure that was the reason," said FBI Agent Wang as he glanced at the life insurance policies and a device in his hand. "The death certificates are showing that Amber and Crystal died in strange car accidents."

Hope sunk into the chair, wondering if Sloan had planned to kill her. Fear sprung to her heart.

"We learned that he had some connections with Worldwide Express Pizza last night," said FBI Agent Garcia. "We've been trying to connect the dots."

Hope stared at FBI Agent Wang as he pulled one of Sloan's high-tech watches out of the box. She noticed there were about seven watches in the box. Her gaze trailed his white gloves as he placed the watch on the table. He appeared to be tech-savvy like Sloan as he hooked a device to the watch.

Several minutes passed by before FBI Agent Wang looked up. "Bingo, we have action," he said as the device in his hand turned on the mystery watch.

"We knew you would crack open the watch," uttered FBI Agent Morgan.

"Hold that thought," uttered FBI Agent Wang. "It seems like Sloan has a secondary security block on this watch," he said. "He is good. We should've hired Sloan long before he got into this human trafficking lifestyle."

Several minutes passed by before FBI Agent Wang looked around the room. "Can someone bring me the black briefcase?" he asked.

"Sure, Agent Wang. It seems like you've met your match," said Agent Morgan. "Apparently, Sloan configured the watch really good."

"Well, he is an engineer like me. So, he should know the tricks of the game. But I'm sure my FBI computer engineering skills will prevail," he snickered.

Hope sat in the chair, praying that she was dreaming. But she wasn't.

FBI Agent Morgan handed FBI Agent Wang a black briefcase with a keypad lock.

FBI Agent Wang opened the briefcase, retrieving a device. He opened the device, permitting a large screen to show. He hooked the device to the watch.

"Hope, where are your twins?" asked FBI Agent Dean in an alarming tone while glancing at a device in his hand.

"With my mother," responded Hope in a panicked tone as fear pumped through her veins. "Why are you asking me this all of a sudden?"

Several FBI agents hurdled around the monitoring devices like vultures.

Chapter 57

Two hours later, rain pounded against the window like a power drill. Mrs. Brown sat at the wooden table in the kitchen.

"Mrs. Brown, I can't believe Hope would do this," sighed Gloria. "I can't believe she is willing to put a man before her children. She should know how painful that will be for them," uttered Gloria. "I did that to her when I put drugs before her."

Mrs. Brown sat quietly as she stared at Gloria. Her gaze shifted to Ivey and her husband.

"All we can do is pray for Hope right now," sighed Ivey's husband, Orlando.

Mrs. Brown slowly exhaled as she looked at him. He was a minister and Mrs. Brown needed the extra spiritual guidance to get through this storm.

"I think we should say a word of prayer for Hope," recommended Orlando. "It seems like prayer is the only thing that will help her."

Heads bowed at the table in unison as words of prayer soared into the atmosphere.

"Amen," sighed Orlando.

"I pray that God heard our prayers," exhaled Mrs. Brown as she rubbed her hands together.

"We have to stay positive," sighed Ivey in a soft tone.

Gloria rubbed her face. "I agree. We have to stay strong for Hope's children," she said while standing. "I'm going to check on them."

Popping sounds echoed inside the apartment.

"I don't know why people like shooting guns in the air," shrieked Mrs. Brown.

"Well, you know that is a tradition here in Cloverdale."

"Well, that's not safe for kids," said Mrs. Brown.

"Those drug dealers been doing it for years," snapped Ivey.

"I don't know why the community police officer let them do it," sighed Gloria as she returned back in the kitchen.

"What are the twins doing?" asked Mrs. Brown as if she wanted to change the subject.

"They are asleep on your sofa. I'm sure they will want a snack when they wake up," said Gloria.

The popping sound echoed in the air again.

"I'm glad one of those stray bullets didn't come this way," blurted Ivey. "The police shouldn't let those guys do stuff like that."

Mrs. Brown squinted. "There's a lot that the community police officer let them do," she uttered. "There's a lot of crime that goes on over here."

"I know," said Ivey. "Sometimes the officers pay the boys to do it."

Mrs. Brown sighed. She recalled a few horror stories and rumors that she had heard about the community police officers. She even recalled Tiffany telling her that Sergeant Smith had raped her. So, his death was no surprise to Mrs. Brown or the people in Cloverdale.

"It used to be really terrible when Sergeant Smith roamed through here," said Gloria.

"I know. People were raped, robbed, shot and a lot of other stuff right under his watch and some of the other officers were corrupted too," mumbled Ivey.

"That is really sad," said Orlando.

Mrs. Brown closed her eyes as she recalled painful things that Sergeant Smith had done to people in Cloverdale. Quietness sprinkled through the room as conversations ceased.

"My heart hurts really bad," said Gloria. "I wish I could fall asleep and wake up to know that this all was a nightmare."

"I just can't believe Hope has done this. I think her husband pressured her to run off with him," said Ivey.

"There are a lot of people at my church that were victims of human trafficking," said Orlando.

"We have support groups for them. They like to be called *survivors* instead of victims."

Mrs. Brown looked at Orlando. "That's good."

"Does anyone know when Hope will come and get the twins?" asked Ivey.

"I had thought that by now Hope would've been here to get the twins. They still have on the same clothes from last night. I hope she didn't run off with Sloan," she muffled.

"I can buy them some clothes, mama," said Ivey in a low tone.

"Thank you, Ivey. But I don't know how to explain all of this to them," sobbed Gloria. "I don't want them to grow up without a mother. I wasn't there for Hope. Now, she's not here for her children," blurted Gloria. "I never expected this out of her."

Crackling sounds echoed through the kitchen's window as rain splattered against it.

"I called Tiffany to see if she could get any information out of Vance," muffled Mrs. Brown.

"What did she say?" asked Gloria in an anxious tone.

"Vance refused to give any information."

"But does he know that Hope has run off with that lowlife man? The twins will grow up without their mother," said Gloria as a tear rolled down her face.

Mrs. Brown leaned back against the chair. It pressed firmly against her bones in her buttock. "I need my pillow," said Mrs. Brown as she wobbled back into the living room.

Conversations fizzled out in the kitchen.

Mrs. Brown turned the corner, noticing that the twins had awakened. "You can have the rest of those cookies," said Mrs. Brown as she looked at Jayla and Jayden stretched across her burgundy sections, watching cartoons.

Mrs. Brown paused as she stared at them. An ounce of sympathy for the twins inched through her veins.

"Is my mommy coming to get us?" asked Jayla in a pitiful tone.

Words seemed to have glued to Mrs. Brown's tongue. "We're trying to figure it out," she sighed as she looked into Jayla's light brown eyes.

"Jayla, mama is going to come and get us," mumbled Jayden as if he knew something that

Mrs. Brown didn't, "Mama loves us, Jayla. She will come and get us," he repeated.

Jayla stared at Jayden with hopeful eyes.

Mrs. Brown slowly wobbled back into the kitchen as if she had bricks strapped around her ankles.

"The twins miss Hope," exhaled Mrs. Brown.

"I don't know what to do, Mrs. Brown," said Gloria.

"I've been calling Hope. But she isn't answering her cell phone," babbled Ivey.

"I think Sloan brainwashed her," said Gloria. "He was so controlling toward Hope when I met him at the hospital. He talked to her like she was a little child."

Mrs. Brown pressed her lips together.

"All we can do is pray for her," repeated Ivey.

"I know," muffled Gloria. "I hope Ruth can heal from all of this."

"I pray that she can," said Mrs. Brown as she glanced out of the kitchen window.

Loud banging sounds echoed through the apartment.

"Who is knocking that hard? Were you expecting any company, Mrs. Brown?" asked Gloria.

"Goodness."

Banging sounds traveled into the kitchen again.

"One minute," hollered Mrs. Brown as she slowly wobbled toward the front door.

Mrs. Brown glanced at the twins. They had fallen back asleep on the sofa. She figured they had cried themselves to sleep.

She slowly opened the wooden door.

Silence sealed her lips instantly. She gripped her chest as her gaze landed on two clean shaved men. The tallest man quickly pressed his index finger against his round shaped lips, signaling for Mrs. Brown to be silent. The shorter white man quietly opened the door as he pointed at the twins.

Mrs. Brown did not doubt that the men had come for them.

Fear stormed through Mrs. Brown's trembling body.

Chapter 58

The next day, a burst of nervousness flew through Hope as she watched FBI agents comb through her house. Lemon sized holes scattered on her walls as if someone had been playing baseball inside. The agents had drilled holes in areas where their devices detected various items. Hope's heart skipped a beat every time an FBI Agent showed her items that they had pulled out of the walls.

FBI cars clustered in front of her house as if she was hosting a car show.

Hope sat in the living room with her hand planted across her forehead. She had barely slept last night with all of the foot traffic. FBI agents rotated shifts searching through every inch of the house. Deep down, Hope's heart forced her to find a way to escape with Sloan. But her mind told her otherwise.

The acrid smell of coffee hovered in the air.

"Good morning," said FBI Agent Dean while sipping on a cup of coffee.

"Why did you ask me where my twins were?" inquired Hope in an anxious tone.

FBI Agent Dean paused. "I think Sloan put a tracking device on one of them."

Hope stood. "What do you mean?"

Hope paused, recalling that Sloan held Jayla and Jayden as if it was his last time seeing them. She remembered how Sloan had patted Jayden's back in a strange way.

"I think it is Jayden," mumbled Hope. "I remember he kept patting my son's back in a strange way."

"He probably implanted a tiny device on his clothing," said FBI Agent Morgan.

"Why?" asked Hope in a nervous tone.

"So, he can listen in on our conversations," uttered FBI Agent Wang. "The device is tiny. You wouldn't even notice it unless you were close up on it."

"That means wherever Jayden is, Sloan can locate him," said FBI Agent Dean.

"It also means wherever Jayden is Sloan can hear any conversations around him."

"But that would mean that Sloan had to be somewhere near Jayden to hear through the tiny device, right?" asked Hope as a scary feeling crept through her body.

"Not necessarily," said FBI Agent Wang. "The way he designed this watch and other devices, there is no telling the range he installed for the bugging devices."

A busload of fear burst through Hope. "Please don't let him kidnap my children," she begged.

"I doubt that he would risk going to your mother's house. He probably knows that agents will surveillance the area," said FBI Agent Wang.

FBI Agent Morgan walked into the living room. "Good morning," he said while looking at a report in his hand.

"Did you get an update on the twins?" asked FBI Agent Dean.

"What do you mean?" asked Hope as a thick cloud fogged her mind.

"We sent two officers to your mother's house to check on the twins," said FBI Agent Wang. "But they were not there."

"What do you mean," blurted Hope. "Where are my twins?"

"They are safe," said FBI Agent Wang. "The agents found them at Mrs. Brown's house with your mother."

A sense of peace flowed through Hope.

"But we found several wiretaps in this house yesterday. So, we were certain he had to plant a few wiretaps on you and the children," said FBI Agent Garcia.

"Are you serious?" said Hope as an ounce of curiosity roamed through her.

"Yes," responded FBI Agent Morgan as he handed Hope a tiny device. "We found a lot of those in the collar of your shirts and throughout this house."

Hope closed her eyes. She finally realized how Sloan was able to locate her in the hospital that day and when she was driving on the highway. Her blood came to a sudden halt. She realized that Sloan probably heard her conversations when she spoke with Tiffany.

The sun hid behind the massive cloud, preventing light to seep from any corner.

Hope slowly cleared her throat. "You never told me what you saw on Sloan's watch."

"I had to get another device to break the security code on the watch," babbled FBI Agent Wang. "We're scanning a few things right now," he said in a short tone as he looked at a monitor.

FBI Agent Morgan glanced at a device in his hand as he stood in front of the window. "I have the Skymarker surveillance report."

Hope paused, hoping the Skymarker would reveal that Sloan was innocent. Her heart struggled to accept the truth. But her mind told her otherwise.

"A tall European man picked up Sloan last night," FBI Agent Wang.

"Why did it take you so long to get the report?" asked Hope.

"It didn't take a long time," blurted FBI Agent Wang. "We've had the report since last night," he paused. "The person who picked up Sloan was a European man that we have been looking for."

"How can you see that it was a European man if it was night?" muffled Hope.

"Our system can do a lot," responded FBI Agent Dean.

A chill overtook Hope's fatigued body as an ounce of confidence slithered away from her.

"We did a face recognition scan of the man's face with one of our devices," said FBI Agent Dean. "He is wanted for kidnapping and abduction in another country."

"What! This can't be real. Please, tell me this isn't real," cried Hope. "I can't believe Sloan *knows* someone who kidnaps people," uttered Hope, hoping that the FBI was talking about a different Sloan.

"It is reported that the European man trafficked girls from other countries," said FBI Agent Wang, ignoring Hope's comments. "We were told he visited parks, museums, amusement centers, skating rinks and other places to lure victims. His first name is Seven."

"Seven," flinched Hope. "If you know all of that, why haven't you caught him?" snapped Hope as a river of frustration flowed through her.

FBI Agent Garcia walked closer to Hope. "He moves around a lot. To be honest, there is a group of them doing it. But we have footage of Seven entering a skating rink with an attractive woman and a little boy."

The oxygen in the living room suddenly became thin.

"He portrays a scheme like he is at an event with his family. But in actuality, he is really there to kidnap or abduct a victim," said FBI Agent Garcia

"No, no, no. This is so wrong," she sobbed. "If you know all of that, then why haven't you caught him?"

FBI Agent Garcia paused. "Trust me, the FBI is aware of that sick game," she paused. "Plus, Jasmine and Taylor told me about this scheme when I interviewed them last night."

Hope closed her eyes as if she wanted to literally die. "How do they know?"

"Jasmine and Taylor recalled playing that sick game with human trafficking leaders," blurted FBI Agent Garcia.

FBI Agent Morgan drew closer to Hope. "The FBI did a face recognition of the woman that had accompanied the European man to the skating rink. Her first name is Myla. She has been missing from California for over ten years," said FBI Agent Morgan.

"Apparently, Seven forced her into the life of human trafficking when she was around 18," said FBI Agent Dean. "Now, he has her helping him lure other women. She is a *Madame*."

Hope winced. "What is a madame?"

"Women who become trapped into a negative lifestyle to the point they surrender to the negativities around them just to cope with it," mumbled FBI Agent Garcia in a bewildered tone.

"Why do the women do that?" sobbed Hope.

"Some women become madames so that they are not killed or tortured. Some of them have helped human trafficking leaders lure other victims, kill people, torture people, etc.," responded FBI Agent Garcia.

Hope pressed her eyelids firmly together, trying to capture her tears.

"We've been told that several human traffickers have been doing this same scheme in different states along I-95 North," said FBI Agent Wang.

Hope cringed, wondering if Sloan was part of the scheme. She knew Worldwide Pizza Express pubs were located along Highway I-85 and Highway I-95 from Richmond, Virginia to Miami, Florida.

"How does Sloan know . . . Seven?" asked Hope in a faint voice.

"We're still trying to figure that out," blurted FBI Agent Dean.

"We will know soon," interjected FBI Agent Wang as he glanced at a device.

A sharp sound pierced the air as the house telephone rang. Hope stood. She walked over to the high-tech caller ID.

"It's my mother," she said. "Can I please answer the telephone?"

"No," demanded FBI Agent Dean. "We can't take any risks."

FBI Agent Garcia cleared her throat. "It was nice of you to help your mother at the hospital."

Hope's muscles tighten up in her face. "How did you know my mother needed help?"

"I work for the FBI. I can find out anything," smirked FBI Agent Garcia.

Hope's heart slammed against her chest as if a crane had fallen on her. "I need to see my children, please."

Fear and desperation flowed through Hope. "I want to see my mother," wept Hope. For the first time in her life, she realized she needed her mother to comfort her.

Clouds congregated in the sky, blocking all hope of any moonlight from shining inside the house.

"Do you recognize this man?" asked FBI Agent Dean as he gawked at

Hope.

Hope slowly walked as if her feet were shackled as she closed her eyes.

"Hope, you can't see the screen if your eyes are closed," grappled FBI Agent Wang. "You have to let us know if you know this person."

Hope exhaled as if she was blowing out a million candles. She slowly opened her eyes. Her gaze locked on the image of a man on the screen.

"Oh my God!" blurted Hope.

Hope couldn't believe her eyes. She recognized the man. It was the same European man that she saw at the Creative Marbles Museum when Sloan took her and the twins there.

"This is a picture of Myla," said FBI Agent Dean as Hope looked at the screen.

Hope's heart nearly leaped out of her chest. It was the same attractive woman who had entered into Creative Marbles Museum with the European man.

"Apparently, they're working with Sloan," confirmed FBI Agent Dean.

Without a doubt, Hope was convinced that Sloan was a human trafficker.

Chapter 59

The morning clouds gathered together creating a blanket over the grayish black sky. Rain overpowered the sunlight that previously dominated the sky.

Hope nibbled on some crackers, trying to regain her energy. Her body was fatigued. She didn't get much sleep last night because of the massive conversations among the FBI agents, the loud beeping noises from the FBI's devices and the FBI's rapid footsteps inside her bedroom to routinely check on her whereabouts.

Hope peeled herself off the California King sized bed. Her gray slacks nestled around her body. She figured there was no need wearing lingerie to bed as she had routinely done before Sloan went missing. Plus, her house was clustered with FBI agents.

"Are you going somewhere?" asked FBI Agent Garcia as she dashed into Hope's bedroom.

"No. But I would like to get out of the bed if that is okay with you," sneered Hope.

"I'm just checking," stated FBI Agent Garcia.

"Can you please take me to get my twins?" asked Hope. "Or, arrange to bring them to me?"

"That's not going to happen anytime soon."

"Why not?"

"Because it is protocol. But I can tell you that your twins are safe."

Hope slowly exhaled. "Is it okay if I use my bathroom?" asked Hope in a sarcastic tone.

"Yes. But please don't sneak out of the bathroom window," snapped FBI Agent Garcia. "I don't want you making plans to meet up with Sloan," she said. "For the life of me, I still don't understand why you never knew that Sloan was a human trafficking ringleader."

Hope winced. "I didn't and I don't have any reason to lie to you."

"That's what they all say," blurted FBI Agent Garcia. "By the way, I saw those nice clothes in your closet. I wonder if Sloan was preparing to auction you into human trafficking."

Hope's heart fluttered and her mind surfed like tidal waves. She often wondered why Sloan insisted on taking pictures of her in different poses and uploading them to his computer. It was a routine he did after they had arguments. When she questioned him about it, he told her that he needed a visual of her to keep his mind occupied. But she wondered if FBI Agent Garcia was right. She couldn't believe that she had unintentionally helped a human trafficking ringleader portray a fake marriage and lifestyle.

Ten minutes later, Hope strolled into the living room as FBI Agent Garcia trailed closely behind her.

"Have you figured out what's on Sloan's watch?" asked Hope in a nervous tone, while rubbing her eyes.

"Why do you want to know?" asked FBI Agent Dean in a sarcastic tone. "We typically don't allow people to interact with our stings. We do things privately. But since you are a key piece to this whole puzzle, we figured we should allow you to observe a few things."

"A key piece?" asked Hope.

"Yeah," smirked FBI Agent Dean.

"Any updates on Sloan's watch?" asked FBI Agent Garcia while sneering at Hope.

"We are still waiting for activity to take place on his watches," said FBI Agent Dean. "Sloan has tried to shut down the watch from a remote location. But I manipulated the system to make him think the watch is deactivated."

"He will know," muffled Hope while glancing around her living room.

"I doubt it," smirked FBI Agent Wang.

Hope exhaled as her gaze darted around the living room. Electronic surveillance devices, computers, wiretaps and monitors clustered around the room as if Hope was in the middle of a military base.

"Trust me, he will not know," affirmed FBI Agent Dean in an arrogant tone.

"Hope claims she did not know about Sloan's scheme," blurted FBI Agent Garcia.

"Well, you know there have been women who never knew they were married to serial killers. Spouses hide things from each other all the time," said FBI Agent Wang.

"Yeah, you're right. Killers have been married with children while killing their victims right under their family's nose," said FBI Agent Dean.

FBI Agent Wang tapped his black ink pen on the edge of a clipboard as he looked at FBI Agent Garcia.

"It seems like you've married a monster, Hope," said FBI Agent Garcia.

"I need to get some water," said Hope in an uncomfortable tone as she walked toward her kitchen. She needed a break from the screening in her living room.

"I'll go with you," said FBI Agent Garcia as if Hope needed an escort.

Hope strolled back into the living room as if she was on death row.

"Hello, I'm FBI Agent Locklear," said a man.

"He's our high-tech FBI locksmith," chuckled FBI Agent Wang. "He can crack open any locks. We need him to open up something for us."

A stream of silence flowed through the room.

"We finally figured out how Sloan knew Seven," babbled FBI Agent Wang.

Hope slowly exhaled. "How?" she asked in a rattling tone.

"It appears that Sloan and Seven attended the same study abroad program in Spain while they were in college," smirked Agent Wang.

Hope pressed her slender fingers against her temples. She recalled Sloan telling her that he had attended a study abroad program in Spain. But he never disclosed that he had developed the grassroots of his future human trafficking scheme while he was there.

"It seems like Sloan knew more languages than what you think, Hope," said FBI Agent

Wang. "From the reports we received, Sloan was highly intelligent. He was fluent in English, Spanish, Italian, and Arabic. There may be other languages as well," he exhaled.

"What!" blurted Hope. "But he acted like he was struggling to learn ASL."

"That's not true," interjected FBI Wang. "We found out his mother had a hearing impairment. The same type as your twins. He learned ASL from his mother. We found out she had a procedure done and she gained some hearing abilities."

Tears streamed down Hope's face clouding her vision. "Are you kidding me? You mean to tell me that he knew what was going on with our twins and he said nothing! He knew ASL but acted like he didn't! He knew that the procedure would work for our twins! Why did he hide all of this from me? Why?"

"Maybe he didn't want you to know everything about him."

"We found out that his father made him learn several languages as a requirement in the human trafficking business so he could communicate with victims and business partners from different countries."

Tears streamed down Hope's face. "I was married to a stranger. Why was I so naïve?" she cried. "Sloan told me he grew up in foster care."

"He did," responded FBI Agent Wang.

FBI Agent Dean entered the living with a startling look in his eyes. "I heard FBI Agent

Locklear say Sloan had a hidden door behind the bookshelf in his office."

"Huh!" blurted Hope, feeling weakness overtake her body as if she was about to faint.

"We know," said FBI Agent Wang as he glanced at Hope as if he didn't want Hope to know.

"FBI Agent Locklear is down there cracking open that mystery door."

"He already did that," uttered FBI Agent Dean. "He was able to walk through this house, underground, like a ninja," he chuckled.

"What do you mean," asked Hope as confusion stormed through her, wondering how all of this took place in their house without her knowing.

"Sloan had a small pathway behind the bookshelf in his office. He could walk through most of this house without being seen if he wanted to," said FBI Agent Dean. "He has a mini-apartment underneath the basement. There are bedrooms, a bathroom, a kitchen and other stuff down there," he uttered.

"I would have never found the secret dungeon if I didn't use this device to scan the walls throughout this house," said FBI Agent Kimber who held up a device in front of Hope. "Sloan was crafty. He specially designed the walls in his office, especially behind the bookshelf. That is the true work of an engineer. I've never seen anything like it."

Hope flinched before saying, "So, he had a mini apartment underneath our house?

"Not an apartment, Hope. It was a dungeon because people were forced to live there," said FBI Agent Wang.

"The secret dungeon also had two exit doors that lead to different secluded spots in the woods behind your house," interjected FBI Agent Dean.

"But those two exit doors are not on the floor plan for this house," said FBI Agent Morgan as he looked at a form in his hand.

"Sloan could even access the garage from the hidden dungeon," blurted FBI Agent Dean.

"How?" asked Hope.

"Through the custom made bookshelves in the garage," responded FBI Agent Dean. "When the other FBI agents moved the bookshelves . . . they realized that a hidden door was behind them that led to some steps."

"How did you know there was something behind the bookshelves?" sighed Hope.

"Our device detected images behind them," said FBI Agent Dean.

A touch of disbelief pumped through Hope's veins. "If Sloan had all of these hidden places in this house, how do you know that he is not still in here?" mumbled Hope.

"Our heat sensor would have located him in this house by now," blurted FBI Agent Wang.

"I don't believe none of this!" blurted Hope as her lips trembled. "I want to see the bookshelves and the secret dungeon!"

"I don't think Hope needs to see anything right now," blurted FBI Agent Garcia as she entered the living room.

"Why *not*?" asked Hope in a pitiful tone.

"We don't think it's in your best interest," responded FBI Agent Garcia.

"Why not?" shrieked Hope.

Beeping noises trailed in the air from the devices assembled on a table.

"We found chains in the hidden dungeon," replied FBI Agent Locklear as he twirled a cluster of keys in his olive cream hands.

"Chains," interrupted Hope in a shocking tone as her head shook.

FBI Agent Garcia stared at Hope. "Yes, agents are down there taking pictures."

"We found chains hooked up to a bed that was bolted down to the floor."

Hope flopped down on the sofa as if she wanted to vanish.

"We found a few purses down there," said FBI Agent Wang.

"Purses," shrieked Hope. "This can't be true. I don't recall Sloan ever bringing anyone here."

A sudden panicky feeling gushed through Hope's body, causing her to feel dizzy.

"From the way things look, Sloan held women hostage in the secret dungeon. It seems like he has been doing this for a long time," uttered FBI Agent Garcia. "The dungeon had a bathroom, a few bedrooms, a studio room where he took pictures of the women and other things." She paused while glancing at Hope. "He built a closet with fashionable clothes for the women to wear. Some of their dresses were similar to the outfits that you have in your closet, Hope."She paused.

"We even found pictures that he took of you in the dungeon."

"What!" yelled, Hope. Now she knew why FBI Agent Garcia made the early comment about Sloan contemplating whether or not to auction her into human trafficking.

"But he didn't upload your pictures to the computer downstairs like he'd done with the other women's pictures," interjected FBI Agent Locklear.

"Maybe he had second thoughts," said FBI Agent Garcia. "Maybe he really loved Hope."

"Or, maybe he was waiting on the right price," commented FBI Agent Kimber.

The oxygen in the room seemed to have decreased, causing Hope to nearly faint.

Chapter 60

Hope gasped for oxygen as if her lungs were on the verge of collapsing.

"You mean to tell me that Sloan held women hostage downstairs in this house!" cried Hope as she pointed toward the floor. "Now, I understand why he used to spend so many hours in the basement," she shrieked as her hand trembled.

Ruffling sounds flowed throughout the house as the FBI agents moved items to search them.

"We found pictures and IDs downstairs. We are running the names through our system," said FBI Agent Wang. "It appears that Sloan liked to keep souvenirs of the women he abducted."

"I don't recall any women being in this house," sobbed Hope.

FBI Agent Garcia stared at Hope as if she could see her soul. "You wouldn't hear them, Hope."

"Why not?" sobbed Hope while her heart throbbed.

"The secret dungeon is soundproofed," uttered FBI Agent Wang before pausing.

"We had to get a locksmith to open the door to the dungeon," smirked FBI Agent Garcia. "The locksmith said Sloan apparently had the key specially made. It resembled the old medieval keys."

Suddenly, Hope recalled on several occasions that Sloan's office had a soft, lingering smell of different perfumes. She even recalled on several occasions that Sloan's body had a crisp aroma of different perfumes when she entered it. Yet, Hope had never bothered to interrogate Sloan because he had been in the house several days prior and after she had smelt the scent of the different perfumes. Now, Hope knew why Sloan used to remain in the basement for several hours. He had confined several women inside the secret dungeon. Even though Hope had never physically seen the women, she had definitely smelt their perfumes.

"Are you okay, Hope?" asked FBI Agent Garcia.

"No," responded Hope in a bitter tone realizing that every time she smelt a woman's perfume on Sloan, he had declined to be intimate with her. Even though he did not leave the house during those times, Hope figured Sloan was soaking his royal oats inside the women whom he had confined in the basement.

"I realized I needed to cut you some slack," said FBI Agent Garcia. "It is true that some women don't know the dangerous things that their husbands do. But some women are also dangerous."

Hope buried her hands in her face trying to hide from the shame. She wished she had questioned Sloan about the medieval key that she had found hidden in his toolbox.

"It seems like you didn't know a lot about Sloan." FBI Agency Garcia paused before allowing her lips to say, "We also found sleeping medicine."

"Are you serious?" asked Hope as she suddenly realized why her body felt tired the night before Sloan ventured on his business trips with Mr. Gavino. Now, she realized why Dr. Sterling had asked her if she was on any sleeping medicine.

"Yes, I am serious. It is the type of sleeping medicine that disappears out of your system within days unless you have advanced testing done," responded FBI Agent Garcia.

FBI Agent Dean strolled back into the room with a bizarre look on his face.

Hope closed her eyes, hoping that she was dreaming.

"We found a computer and a camera downstairs," sighed FBI Agent Garcia. "He was taking pictures of the girls and sending them to somebody."

"You mean to tell me . . . all of that was going on in this house and I didn't know it?" shrieked Hope in a shocking tone.

"Do you really expect us to believe that you didn't know any of this was going on?" blurted FBI Agent Dean. "You can't be that naive!"

"I didn't!" hollered Hope. "I didn't," she sobbed as she nearly balled up in the chair like a pretzel. "I would have never allowed this to happen."

A herd of FBI agents ushered into the living room.

FBI Agent Dean looked at a device in his hand before asking Hope, "Did you work with Harmony Brookstone?"

Hope wiped her eyes as she slowly lifted her head. "Yes, I used to work with her."

"I know," blurted FBI Agent Dean. "I wanted to see if you would tell the truth."

"Why?" asked Hope in a pitiful tone as her heart fluttered.

FBI Agent Dean handed Hope a naked picture of Harmony. "Sloan apparently held her hostage downstairs," sighed FBI Agent Dean. "That's the bed downstairs," he said pointing to the picture. "Harmony looks like she was drugged up on sleeping medicine or something else."

A river of tears flowed down Hope's face like an avalanche. She was convinced Sloan transported the women in and out of the house after drugging her with sleeping medicine. She recalled Sloan routinely prepared her some of his famous lemon tea every time before he left. Though the tea was delicious, she had no doubt now that Sloan had mixed sleeping medicine in the lemon tea.

She would sleep for hours. She used to wonder why she always felt sleepy before Sloan went out of town. But she had found it cute that he always prepared her a delicious cup of lemon tea before he left which became her favorite tea. *How could I be that naïve?* she thought.

"Yes," said FBI Agent Wang. "We found different fingerprints down there that match a few women."

Hope closed her eyes for a split second.

"Hope, we need you to look at these pictures and tell us if you know these young women," said FBI Agent Garcia.

"I can't look at those pictures," cried Hope as her lips trembled like Jell-O. "I don't want to look at them. This is so wrong. I can't believe Sloan did this to those girls. I can't believe he did this to our family. I can't believe he did this to *me!*" she shouted. Hope felt as if her sanity was slipping away from her. "I need to see my children," she wept. "I can't take it anymore."

"Hope, you have to cooperate with us," said FBI Agent Garcia while pulling her wavy black hair behind her ears.

"I'm trying," she cried, fearing that the FBI agents were on the verge of arresting her.

"Do you know Melody Smithfielder?"

"Yes," sobbed Hope. "Please, please don't tell me that Sloan did something to her," said Hope as she finally realized that Sloan had transported women in and out of their house while she was living there.

"Based on the pictures downstairs, Sloan abducted a lot of women just to force them into human trafficking," said FBI Agent Dean as his blue eyes peered at Hope.

Hope shook her head as if she had lost the muscles in her neck.

"I'm sure Sloan had plans to abduct you and force you into this lifestyle when he gave you a ride that day," said FBI Agent Garcia. "But he kept you for himself for some reason."

"It seems like Sloan replaced Julia with you," said FBI Agent Dean as his fingers combed through some papers. "Sloan and Julia were in a relationship," he mumbled. "Interesting . . . it seems like Sloan ordered Julia to be killed the same day he married you."

A sickening feeling pierced Hope's stomach.

"Can I go and take a shower?" asked Hope as if she was a child seeking permission. "I don't feel well."

"Sure, but I have to follow you," said FBI Agent Garcia in an authoritative tone. "But you also should eat something."

Hope flinched like a withered leaf.

"After all of this," said Hope, as she glanced around at the high-tech devices that had overtaken her living room. "I don't have an appetite," she said while standing.

"Hope, before you leave," said FBI Agent Dean. "Did, Sloan go on a lot of business trips?"

"Yes," responded Hope in a low tone.

"Do you know where he went?" asked FBI Agent Dean.

"He told me he had to meet Mr. Gavino for business stuff."

"Where?" asked FBI Agent Dean.

"Different cities where the pizza pubs were located," responded Hope.

"It appears he traveled to the different states," responded FBI Agent Dean as his lips snuggled together as if he knew something that Hope didn't. He cleared his throat. "Perhaps, he was checking on the abducted women."

"No, no, no," said Hope.

"Hope, based on the setup downstairs, it is a possibility that Sloan held the women hostage in different states wherever the Worldwide Express Pizza restaurants were located."

Hope pressed her hands firmly against her ears as if she wanted to block the FBI agents' conversations from entering her ears.

"The system is finally detecting activity on Sloan's watch," uttered FBI Agent Dean while pulling up a chair in front of the monitor that was hooked up to Sloan's watch. "It looks like we'll have enough evidence to lock him away for life," he said while staring at the monitor that was hooked to the high-tech watch.

Hope stopped in her tracks as her fatigued body trembled like a flag on a windy day.

Chapter 61

The afternoon clouds cascaded the sky, permitting only a single shaft of sunlight to beam onto the snow that blanketed Cloverdale projects.

Mrs. Brown pressed her back firmly against her burgundy sofa.

A buttery, sweet smell of homemade lemon cookies floated in the living room.

"I am glad that I have someone to talk with about this situation," said Gloria in a bewildered tone. "I feel so helpless. I can't get in touch with Hope. I don't know where she lives in Raleigh. I don't know where the FBI took her."

"Maybe Hope will call soon," said Mrs. Brown in a hopeful tone.

"I hope so," said Gloria as she looked at Jayla and Jayden.

"What if Sloan tries to come and get the twins?" asked Mrs. Brown.

"The FBI told me that they will be keeping a close eye on the twins," said Gloria.

"Do you want to watch cartoons?" asked Mrs. Brown as she walked toward Jayla and Jayden to hand them the tray of lemon cookies.

"Yes," said Jayden as he reached for two cookies. "Thank you."

A warm feeling clung to Mrs. Brown's heart as she observed Jayden hand Jayla a cookie.

Mrs. Brown wobbled toward the television. She flipped through a few channels.

"Do you like this cartoon?" asked Mrs. Brown.

"Yes," responded Jayden as if he was the spokesman for Jayla and himself.

Jayla sat quietly. Her peach sweater highlighted her light brown eyes.

"Gloria, let's go in the kitchen so we can talk," said Mrs. Brown.

"Don't open the door for anybody," said Gloria as she looked at Jayla and Jayden.

"Okay," said Jayden as he nibbled on his cookies.

"Is . . . is . . . my mommy . . . coming to get us?" asked Jayla as the words nearly struggled to come out of her mouth while her eyes filled with sorrow.

Mrs. Brown's heart slammed against her chest.

"I've been trying to get in touch with your mother," responded Gloria in a heartbreaking tone.

"Mama . . . will come for us, Jayla," mumbled Jayden as he grabbed Jayla's hand.

Silence tumbled through the living room.

Mrs. Brown stood. "I'm taking your grandmother to the kitchen so we can talk," said Mrs. Brown as her gaze fixated on Jayla and Jayden.

Mrs. Brown wobbled inside the kitchen. Arthritis rippled through her entire body.

"Sit down, Gloria," said Mrs. Brown as she observed Gloria pace the kitchen floor.

"I can't, Mrs. Brown. My nerves are shot," responded Gloria. "Jayla keeps asking me where is her mommy. Jayden keeps asking me where is his daddy."

"They don't know better, Gloria," sighed Mrs. Brown. "They are probably confused about what is going on."

Gloria slowly sat on the wooden maple chair. "My stomach churns every time Jayden asks me about his daddy," sneered Gloria.

"Calm down, Gloria," said Mrs. Brown. "He is too young to know what is going on."

"I pray that Jayden doesn't turn out to be like his father," said Gloria.

"Please don't wish any bad luck on that precious child," ordered Mrs. Brown as she squinted.

"I'm not," said Gloria as she rubbed her small hands together.

Loud screeching sounds echoed inside the apartment from cars.

"Those drivers better be careful out there on these icy roads," blurted Mrs. Brown.

"There is no way I would be driving out there in all of that snow," said Gloria.

"Me neither," said Mrs. Brown as she leaned forward to rub her ankles.

Silence wrapped around Gloria's lips for a few seconds.

"Please tell Tony and Tiffany that I said thank you for buying the twins some clothes," mumbled Gloria.

"No problem," said Mrs. Brown. "Tony and Tiffany figured the twins needed clothes since they only had on what they wore to the event the other day."

"Thank you," said Gloria. "I was going to buy them some clothes."

"Don't worry about it. Tony and Tiffany know that you and I are on fixed incomes," muffled Mrs. Brown.

Gloria pressed her brown lips together.

"What are the twins doing about school?" asked Mrs. Brown as she looked at Gloria.

"Since it is snowing so bad, the schools have been closed," uttered Gloria. "I'm glad."

"Why?" asked Mrs. Brown.

"I don't know where their school is located in Raleigh," uttered Gloria. "Plus, I don't want to drive in this terrible snow."

"Well, the twins need to be getting as much education as they can," babbled Mrs. Brown.

"I understand. But I wouldn't feel comfortable driving from Charlotte to Raleigh every day during the school week. I might have to find a school here in Charlotte for the twins if the FBI locks up Hope," said Gloria as she tilted her head toward the popcorn ceiling.

"Don't jump to conclusions, Gloria," demanded Mrs. Brown.

"I'm not jumping to conclusions. I'm just trying to think ahead about the things that I might have to do with the twins."

"In that case, I'll ask Tiffany to start checking into a few things for you," said Mrs. Brown.

"Thank you so much, Mrs. Brown. You have really helped me to keep my nerves under control. I've got to keep my stress down so that I don't get sick," sighed Gloria. "So, thank you for helping me."

"I am supposed to help you, Gloria. You are my friend," uttered Mrs. Brown.

A warm breeze swept through the kitchen from the heater, overpowering the bone freezing temperature outside.

"What about the twins' speech and hearing therapy?" asked Mrs. Brown, recalling that Hope had previously told her that the twins had to attend therapy twice a week.

"Ivey took them to their appointment yesterday," said Gloria.

"Can you believe that Hope used to travel back and forth from Raleigh to Charlotte twice a week to bring the twins to their appointments?"

"Yes," responded Mrs. Brown. "I guess she was willing to make a sacrifice to make sure her twins received good care."

"I'm surprised the doctor's office is open. There is too much snow for anything to be open," said Mr. Brown while glancing out of the kitchen window.

Gloria paused for a few seconds. She leaned toward Mrs. Brown.

"I'm surprised that Sloan didn't try to sneak and see the twins when Ivey took them to their appointment. I'm sure Sloan knows when the twins have appointments with that doctor. I am sure he knows that the FBI agents are watching."

"You're right," huffed Mrs. Brown.

"I'm sure he was probably somewhere looking at the twins," muffled Gloria.

"I wouldn't doubt it," whispered Mrs. Brown.

"Me neither," affirmed Gloria.

Mrs. Brown rubbed her hands together. "This cold weather got my bones aching."

"You should get some cream from your doctor to help you with your arthritis."

"Nothing is going to help me. I've just got to deal with the wear and tear of old age," chuckled Mrs. Brown as she looked at her hands.

They looked up as they heard footsteps approaching the kitchen.

"Grand . . . Grandma . . . we . . . are hungry," said Jayden as he held Jayla's hand.

"Okay," smiled Gloria. "Grab your coats so we can go home."

"Don't leave, Gloria. I'll fix them something to eat," smiled Mrs. Brown. Her gaze landed on their cochlear devices near their ears. She thanked God that the devices helped them to hear and that they were able to speak.

"Are you sure?" inquired Gloria. "I thought your arthritis was bothering you."

"It is," smiled Mrs. Brown as she stood. She wobbled toward the refrigerator. "But I'm not going to allow my arthritis to stop me from feeding children."

Chapter 62

The full moon positioned in the sky, casting a glow across the midnight horizon.

Hope sat, watching the FBI agents gallop throughout her house as if they were in a parade.

Her gaze landed on the multiple computer monitors that had overtaken her living room as if she was inside a military command center.

FBI Agent Dean's blue eyes widened larger than walnuts. "I hope this is not what I think it is," he said while staring at a monitor that was hooked to Sloan's high-tech watch.

FBI agents quickly went toward the monitor.

"Is that a warehouse?" uttered FBI Agent Garcia as her arched ash brown eyebrows drew in.

"But where," she said while frowning.

Hope slowly stood, hoping to look at the monitor.

"Please sit down, Hope," commanded FBI Agent Dean. "I don't think you need to see this," he uttered in a firm tone.

A busload of frustration stormed through Hope as she sat. She slowly closed her eyes hoping that the FBI agents would leave soon.

"Yes, it is," said FBI Agent Morgan as he walked toward the monitor while holding a device in his hand.

Hope figured FBI Agent Morgan had been on another scavenger hunt in her house. Every time he returned to the living room, he brought more and more evidence as if he was the delivery man for the FBI.

"Where are these women being housed?" asked FBI Agent Garcia while scratching her hair as she glared at the monitor.

"There is no telling," said FBI Agent Dean. "But wherever they are, they are inside a large warehouse."

"How do you know?" asked Hope in a pitiful tone as a tear rolled down her face.

"Because I can tell by looking at the ceiling inside the building," responded FBI Agent Dean as he continued to peer at the monitor.

"Are those bedrooms inside the warehouse?" asked FBI Agent Garcia before her voice came to a sudden halt.

FBI Agent Wang leaned toward the monitor. "Yes."

Conversations soared through the living room for a few minutes.

"Is that the European man who picked up Sloan last night?" asked FBI Agent Garcia.

"Yes, it is," said FBI Agent Morgan before pausing. "That means if Seven is in that warehouse, then Sloan is with him too."

Hope swallowed hard.

"Sloan was good," said FBI Agent Wang. "He programmed his watch to see inside several human trafficking houses and warehouses," he said while looking at the monitor that was hooked up to Sloan's watch.

Hope leaned forward to peek at the monitor. Her gaze swept the different images on the monitor. Her heart sunk as she observed different women walking around inside a large house. Her gaze shifted toward another image that showed women sitting at a large table in another house.

An ounce of trepidation swept through Hope as her gaze landed on a group of women wearing lingerie. They were stationed inside a building that resembled a warehouse. Hope slowly inched closer toward the edge of her chair while maintaining her gaze on the monitor. The oxygen in her lungs reduced as her gaze landed on a group of businessmen parading through a building as if they were preparing to make a business transaction.

"We need images of their faces," blurted FBI Agent Morgan.

"I'm already on it," said FBI Agent Dean.

A gust of warm air surfed inside the living room from the heater.

"Hope, tell me what do you know about Worldwide Express Pizza," asked FBI Agent Wang as he glared at something on the screen while inserting another tiny cord into Sloan's watch.

"I don't know much about it," sighed Hope as her gaze landed on an image on the monitor that resembled the brochure that she had found under Sloan's passenger seat in his car.

"You know if you lie to us, it will create problems for you," shrieked FBI Agent Morgan. "You may end up in prison for life."

"I'm *not* lying," sobbed Hope. "I don't know anything about that pizza pub."

"Is that what Sloan told you it was?" asked FBI Agent Garcia as she squinted.

"Yes, and he also brought pizza home from that pizza pub several times."

"Have you ever been there?" asked FBI Agent Garcia.

"No," responded Hope. She closed her eyes as if her eyelids were heavy. "I've never been there. I've never met any of his co-workers. I've never met any of his friends. I've never met any of his family members," she shrieked as tears tumbled down her face like an erupted volcano.

"You've never met his family?" asked FBI Agent Dean.

"No!" snapped Hope "Sloan told me he didn't have any *real* family."

"Hope, he has three brothers," said FBI Agent Dean while looking at a device.

"Three?" inquired Hope.

"The FBI headquarters sent me Sloan's profile," said FBI Agent Dean while looking at a device in his hand. "Sloan has three brothers who are intertwined with human trafficking as well." He squinted, before parting his lips. "They were diagnosed with bipolar disorder and obsessive compulsive disorder."

A cyclone of fear rippled through Hope, riveting memories of Sloan's sudden mood swings, aggressive outbursts, grandiose, hypersexuality, and other tendencies she cared not to recall.

FBI Agent Garcia interjected. "Based on our conversation with Jasmine and Taylor, they believe that one of Sloan's brothers, Rock, was their father." She paused. "There is a strong possibility that either Sloan or Rock may be their father. But it seems like Sloan didn't want Julia to interfere with his relationship with his brother so he had her killed."

Hope's heart slammed against her chest as if a freight train had crashed into her. She recalled Jasmine and Taylor telling her that their father's name was Rock. Hope's lips trembled as she struggled to speak. *But was Sloan really their father,* she thought.

"Jasmine and Taylor told us that they didn't know their father's real name," said FBI Agent Dean. "But we were able to track down a life insurance policy Rock apparently took out on Julia . . . with Rock's *alleged* real name."

Silence swept across Hope for a few seconds. "If you know all of that . . ., why haven't you arrested any of them?" shrieked Hope as pieces of her sanity slipped away.

"It's not that easy, Hope. Rock used a fake name on the life insurance policy. But he was able to cash in the policy somehow," uttered FBI Agent Garcia. "We just found out about this entire human trafficking ring."

"There is no telling how many other men and women are out there like Sloan and his brothers," said FBI Agent Morgan.

Sirens roared from a distance as fire spread through Hope's veins like wildflowers.

"Based on the report," repeated FBI Agent Dean, "It seems like Sloan and his brothers are familiar with this lifestyle. His father was a human trafficker too," he huffed "Sloan's mother was a victim of human trafficking."

"If you know that, why didn't you catch him!" cried Hope.

"By the time we found out everything, Sloan's father had vanished and his mother died in a *mysterious* car accident. Sloan and his brothers were placed in foster care."

Hope dazed out the window as painful words seeped through her ears.

"It appears that Sloan was the mastermind behind Worldwide Express Pizza," said FBI Agent Morgan.

"Well, from what we have figured out, Worldwide Express Pizza did more than just sell pizzas," said FBI Agent Garcia.

"FBI Agent Garcia, we may have just received the evidence," said FBI Agent Wang as he stared at the monitor.

"What do you mean?" asked Hope in a nervous tone.

"Somebody just ordered a medium sized Mexican pizza. I can see the purchaser's names, address and picture," smiled FBI Agent Wang. "So, it appears that the customer is Mr. Franklin Masterstoner. He lives in Atlanta, Georgia."

"Wow, Sloan was good. This system even gives us Franklin's address."

Hope closed her eyes, knowing that Sloan had designed the system to detect a lot of information on every person who called their house and Worldwide Express Pizza. Once again, Hope wished she had questioned Sloan more about why the pizza pubs needed a high-tech caller ID system and what the numbers really represented underneath the women. Now, the pieces were finally coming together.

"Sloan definitely designed a powerful high-tech system that has backfired on him," blurted

FBI Agent Dean as if he was watching his favorite movie on the monitor.

Silence filled the room as the FBI agents continued to stare at the monitor.

"Okay, here we go," blurted FBI Agent Dean. "A picture of five medium-sized women who look Mexican appear on the screen."

"Is Franklin ordering the specific type of women he wants?" asked FBI Agent Garcia as if she was disgusted.

"It seems like it," asserted FBI Agent Morgan as he hooked a device to the monitor. "Customers access a conspicuous web link to access unique pizza orders."

Hope's gaze landed on a woman who appeared to be Mexican.

"Okay, Franklin has ordered the woman he wants," blurted FBI Agent Dean.

"Who did he order?" asked FBI Agent Garcia.

"Franklin ordered a medium sized Mexican pizza with 18 slices," responded FBI Agent Dean.

"But it is really a medium-sized, 18-year-old woman that he ordered," said FBI Agent Morgan.

Hope slowly lifted her head. "How do you know that the woman is 18?" sighed Hope.

"I've been tracking the pattern of the sales for hours. Now, I've figured it out. The number underneath the women represents their age."

Hope sunk into the chair wishing that she could wake up out of this nightmare.

"I see why the pizza pub is called Worldwide Express Pizza," said FBI agent Garcia while staring at the monitor. "The women on this monitor appear to come from different countries worldwide," she uttered. "And it appears you can order the women's services in an express process."

FBI Agent Wang pulled out his phone as he walked out of the living room.

"Please stop," cried Hope, wishing she had questioned Sloan more about the brochure she found in his car instead of accepting his lame excuse.

"I'm sorry if this is painful for you. But women are going through worse things than you right now!" snapped FBI Agent Garcia.

"FBI Agent Morgan, contact the FBI headquarters in Atlanta, Georgia. Give them this address," said FBI Agent Wang as she displayed the address.

FBI agents stared at Sloan's watch and the computer monitor.

"Okay, Franklin has keyed in his credit card information," said FBI Agent Dean.

"I wonder why Franklin would risk giving his credit card information?" inquired FBI Agent Garcia.

"It seems like that is the only way customers can purchase their top of the line pizzas," responded FBI Agent Dean as he continued to peer at the monitoring device.

A busload of anxiety reaped through Hope's heart, mind and soul.

"Franklin has finalized his order with Worldwide Pizza Express," uttered FBI agent Wang.

"I've never ordered a pizza that costs this much," he frowned. "This is more than my mortgage."

Hope slowly allowed her lips to peel apart. "Can I see the watch?" asked Hope.

"I can't allow you to touch it," said FBI Agent Wang as he adjusted his white gloves on his hand. "But you can stand here and look."

Hope's body felt as if she was walking through quicksand.

"As you can see, Sloan was heavily involved in human trafficking. It seems as if he designed his company, *High-Tech Digital Revolutions*, solely for that purpose."

FBI Agent Morgan returned to the living room, wearing white gloves. "The team in Atlanta is getting a search warrant right now. They are en route to Franklin's address," he paused. "It appears that Franklin is married with three children. His wife is a lawyer."

"Are you serious?" blurted FBI Agent Garcia.

"And get this, he is a doctor," said FBI Agent Morgan.

Curiosity stormed through Hope as if a vessel had burst inside her head.

"You mean to tell me that whoever this Franklin is," blurted Hope in an alarming tone. "He is a doctor! He has three children! And his wife is a lawyer!"

"Yes," affirmed FBI Agent Dean. "Human trafficking involves a lot of scumbags."

"Why is he ordering women on an undercover human trafficking site?" asked Hope.

"Maybe you should ask Sloan that question," snapped FBI Agent Morgan.

Hope twirled her fingers through her hair nearly pulling it out. Her mind shifted to her childhood years of having difficulty controlling her trichotillomania and post-traumatic stress disorder.

Chapter 63

The next morning, Hope's perky ears absorbed the FBI agents' words like a sponge. She exhaled, realizing that she actually did not know Sloan. He had lived, ate, breathed and portrayed a fake life around her and the twins. Hope's mind convinced her that Sloan had something more than obsessive compulsive disorder.

Hope's gaze shifted along the monitors stationed throughout her living room. She noticed that the FBI agents had been tracking customers' specialized orders that appeared on the monitors. The agents ignored the ordinary pizza sales. They focused on pizza orders that were associated with pictures of women.

A gust of warm air flowed through the room.

Hope wondered why the agents had designated her house as the headquarters for tracking Sloan. She figured that they preferred to remain at the house since they were discovering more and more evidence as they searched it.

"How did I overlook all of this?" mumbled Hope as guilt started to strip away her conscience.

"Did you say something, Hope?" asked FBI Agent Locklear.

"I was talking to myself," Hope huffed.

The FBI agents stared at Hope as if they were assessing her mental status.

"I'm alright," sighed Hope as she closed her eyes.

"You don't have to stay in here with us," blurted FBI Agent Dean. "You can go back to your bedroom if you like."

"I'd rather stay in here," mumbled Hope.

"Why?" smirked FBI Agent Dean.

"You took away my laptop. You took my cellphone," huffed Hope. "I have to ask for permission to *pee*. I have to ask for permission to eat. I have to ask for permission to walk throughout my house. I have to ask for permission to see my children," blurted Hope as the blood in her veins nearly boiled.

"Are you finished!" snapped FBI Agent Garcia.

Hope gritted her teeth. "Yes."

"So, sit down!" ordered FBI Agent Garcia. "And be quiet!" She paused. "And technically, it is not your house if you look at all of the facts."

Hope sat on the edge of the sofa, wishing that she could teleport into space. A river of frustration rushed through her body.

"From what I've gathered thus far, Sloan is the main ringleader of this scheme," asserted FBI Agent Dean.

"I don't believe that," said Hope in a painful tone, even after all of the saga she had already heard.

"Well, you had better believe it!" said FBI Agent Dean. "Because we are going to arrest your *fake* husband," snapped FBI Agent Dean.

"He can't be," said Hope as a tear rolled down her high cheekbone.

"If Sloan is not the main leader, then who is, Hope? It seems like you know something that we don't," shrieked FBI Agent Wang, holding a paper in his large hand.

"Maybe somebody by the name of Mr. Gavino," said Hope as a tear rolled down her face.

Silence dripped through the living room like a water faucet.

"Mr. Gavino is not the main leader!" shouted FBI Agent Wang. "I have connected the dots to this whole human trafficking ring" he blurted. "Mr. Gavino is Sloan's main recruiter along Highway I-85 and Highway I-95 . . . from Richmond, Virginia to Miami, Florida."

"The main recruiter?" inquired Hope as her throat tightened, recalling the locations of the pizza pub that Sloan had told her.

"Seven Gavino recruited wealthy customers for Sloan," said FBI Agent Wang.

"No, this can't be real," mumbled Hope as if she wanted to vanish. "You mean to tell me that

Seven and Mr. Gavino are the same person?"

"Yes, but Sloan created the Worldwide Pizza Express to sell pizzas," uttered FBI Agent

Wang. "But the pubs are also used to orchestrate his underground human trafficking ring," he said. "I've located the conspicuous web link that his customers use to order specialized pizzas."

"This is unreal," mumbled Hope.

"This thing is bigger than what you think, Hope," said FBI Agent Kimber. "Sloan and all of his brothers and father are heavy into the human trafficking ring."

A river of doubt flowed through Hope. Her heart wouldn't allow her to believe that Sloan was capable of doing all of this. Even though she questioned some of Sloan's bizarre actions at times, her mind wouldn't allow her to accept the truth.

"Based on the evidence from the credit card transactions we've reviewed, all of Sloan's customers were businessmen, doctors, religious figures, lawyers, dentists, school teachers, truck drivers, and so forth," announced FBI Agent Wang.

"Truck drivers," smirked Hope.

"Yes, we believe Sloan hired truck drivers to traffic the women."

Hope planted her hand on her forehead.

"We gathered information about the customers' careers," said FBI Agent Dean.

FBI Agent Morgan scratched his chestnut brown forehead. "This human trafficking scheme is larger than what we thought," he said while glaring at the monitor.

Beeping sounds echoed through the living room as the FBI's electronic devices extrapolated information from Sloan's watch.

She slowly walked toward FBI Agent Morgan as if she was moving through a time zone. She peered at the paper in his hand. A large web like image appeared on the paper that showcased several pictures of men and women. Hope noticed that all of the webs connected back to Sloan. Her sanity level slowly faded.

"No, no, no," cried Hope as she recalled reading Sloan's lips several times when he advised Mr. Gavino that they didn't need any more customers.

"There are more specialized orders," blurted FBI Agent Dean. "A school teacher just ordered an extra large white cheese pizza."

Hope glanced at the monitor as her gaze landed on an extra large white woman.

A few minutes later, Hope listened as she heard FBI Agent Garcia say, "A lawyer just ordered a small asiago cheese pizza."

Hope's gaze landed on a small figured woman who appeared to be Asian.

Shortly thereafter, Hope's ears captured FBI Agent Morgan saying, "A pastor just ordered a medium sized Swiss cheese pizza."

Hope closed her eyes, refusing to look at the monitor. But her mind told her otherwise. She glanced at the large monitor that nearly overtook one corner in her living room. Her heart sunk as her gaze landed on a woman who appeared to be from Switzerland.

"She looks like a model," said FBI Agent Dean while looking at the picture.

The specialized orders continued to pop up on the monitor. The FBI agents dispatched to FBI headquarters in different states to process search warrants.

"A bank's president just ordered a medium sized brunost cheese pizza," said FBI Agent Dean.

"What type of cheese is that?" asked FBI Agent Garcia.

"It is a brown colored cheese," responded FBI Agent Morgan. He peered at the monitor. "Wow, she is gorgeous," he said while staring at the mahogany brown medium sized woman. "Where are they finding these women?"

"It seems like most of these women have been trafficked from different countries. This is awful," shrieked FBI Agent Garcia. "All of these women look very young."

"You are absolutely correct," uttered FBI Agent Wang. "I've been doing face recognition with our equipment. Most of them have been missing for over 5 years. They are all between the ages of 18 to 30."

Silence tumbled upon everyone in the room for a few seconds.

"There is an order for two small Greek feta cheese pizzas," said FBI Agent Wang. "The customer is a judge."

"Are you kidding me?" snapped FBI Agent Garcia as she looked at the screen.

A few minutes later, Hope listened as her ears absorbed FBI Agent Dean saying, "Can you believe this? Someone just ordered 15 American cheese pizzas. The order consists of small and medium sizes. I will monitor this one."

Hope's heart pounded away. She felt as though her ears were deceiving her.

"This customer is a dean of a university. I wonder if this customer is ordering women for some athletes."

"Get out of here," blurted FBI Agent Morgan. "This is crazy."

"I guess we will see once the FBI Agents raid this event," said FBI Agent Dean.

"That type of service didn't come with my scholarship when I played sports in college," laughed FBI Agent Morgan.

"This isn't funny," sobbed Hope while listening to the agents' chatter.

"Nobody said it was funny! We are holding a conversation about the stuff your fake husband masterminded," snapped FBI Agent Morgan.

Hope's dignity slowly chiseled away. She was at a loss for words.

"That specialized order of 15 American cheese pizzas has been processed. The customer selected women that ranged from tan white to chocolate brown women," said FBI Agent Dean.

"That is a huge selection of women," uttered FBI Agent Wang.

Hope sunk into the sofa. She felt as though she was in the middle of a twilight zone. She watched, intensely, as the FBI agents clustered around the monitor.

A hush swept through the room. The FBI agents had stumbled on a classified secret.

Hope slowly slid to the edge of the sofa, trying to capture a glimpse of the activity on the monitor. Her gaze landed on pictures of a man that appeared on the monitor. Now, she understood why the FBI agents were silent.

"I can't believe this," shrieked FBI Agent Dean while pointing at a man who appeared on the monitor. "Is FBI Agent Poindexterleaf in on this scheme with Sloan?"

"I hope not," blurted FBI Agent Morgan. "He is an FBI Agent like us. He knows prostitution and human trafficking are illegal."

"Obviously, he doesn't value his career," snapped FBI Agent Garcia. "If he did, he wouldn't be ordering a woman from this website."

Hope felt as though her ears were deceiving her.

Chapter 64

Ten minutes later, the FBI Agents congregated in the living room.

"We have to figure out whether FBI Agent Poindexterleaf is a real customer or not," uttered
FBI Agent Morgan.

"No, FBI Agent Morgan, we have to process it accordingly. So, call chief FBI Agent Vance. He has to process this for us," sneered FBI Agent Dean as if he was disgusted that an FBI Agent may potentially be intertwined in the human trafficking scheme. "Chief FBI Agent Vance has to process the investigation and the search warrant since Poindexterleaf is an FBI agent."

A shocking feeling stormed through Hope.

"Make sure you report all of these details to chief FBI Agent Vance," ordered FBI Agent Dean as he looked at FBI Agent Morgan while handing him a document that he printed from the computer.

Hope closed her eyes, recalling that it was chief FBI Agent Vance who had initiated the investigation on Sloan. It was chief FBI Agent Vance who had analyzed her. It was chief FBI Agent Vance who had ruined her life. But then again, she ruined her own life by not following her gut suspicions about Sloan. More heartbreaking, Hope felt crushed knowing that chief FBI Agent Vance was Tiffany's husband.

"It appears that FBI Agent Poindexterleaf processed a specialized order for one small white cheddar cheese pizza and one medium Mexican cheese pizza," said FBI Agent Morgan in an alarming tone.

"Maybe he ordered the women as part of a sting," uttered FBI Agent Wang. "So, let's not jump to a conclusion."

"Regardless of the reason, we are going to proceed with this transaction accordingly just in case," snapped FBI Agent Dean without pausing. "FBI Agent Garcia, contact chief FBI Agent Vance right now and give him the details," demanded FBI Agent Dean in a sharp tone while looking at the monitor.

FBI Agent Garcia grabbed a document out of FBI Agent Morgan's hand. "I will provide the details to chief FBI Agent Vance," she said before dashing out of the living room.

FBI Agent Morgan cleared his throat. "If Sloan designed this system to detect the customers' careers, etc., then I am sure that Sloan knows that this customer is an FBI agent."

"You've got a point," said FBI Agent Dean.

"Do you think Sloan has been manipulating the system to lead us on a wild goose chase?" asked FBI Agent Wang.

FBI Agent Dean pecked on the keys on the computer for a few minutes. "I doubt it," he said in a confident tone. "I have blocked Sloan's access to the system. He can't even shut it down. He can't even stop any transactions that are coming in."

"How do you know for certain?" asked FBI Agent Morgan.

"Because Sloan has been trying," blurted FBI Agent Dean. "But I have been overriding his efforts," he chuckled. "So go and contact chief FBI Agent Vance."

Hope inhaled as if she wanted to take her last breath. She recalled, reading Sloan's lips one day when he told Mr. Gavino that someone had been trying to look at a few things on the system. She also recalled Sloan telling Mr. Gavino that someone was using a high-tech system more advanced than his. Now, it all made sense to Hope. She figured it was the FBI that had been trying to access Sloan's system.

"You think you've got skills," chuckled FBI Agent Morgan while looking at FBI Agent Dean pounding on the keys on the computer.

"I do," blurted FBI Agent Dean in a confident tone. "Sloan and I have been battling it out for the past few hours on this system," he chuckled. "Trust me, he is good. But his skills are no match for my FBI skills."

"Is the system detecting his location?" asked FBI Agent Morgan.

"Like I said, Sloan is good. He keeps manipulating the system to show that he is in a different country every minute."

"Get out of here," laughed FBI Agent Wang. "It seems like Sloan put a lot of time into developing this system to perfect his human trafficking scheme."

"Well, I am on trailing his steps," smirked FBI Agent Dean.

Despite FBI agents Dean's efforts, Hope had no doubt that Sloan was several steps ahead of the FBI.

A truckload of hatred flowed through Hope as she slowly removed her wedding ring from her hand. Reality kicked in as she analyzed the entire situation. "Why did Sloan do this to me?" she mumbled. "Why was I so naive? Maybe I could have helped those women if I had paid closer attention to what Sloan did in the house." She paused. "Maybe I could have saved Julia."

A disgusting feeling ricocheted through Hope's jewel box as she speculated upon the many women that Sloan tortured in the past.

Even though it was heartbreaking, Hope realized that her marriage to Sloan was fake. She did not doubt that she needed therapy regardless of the taboo comments that tumbled through Cloverdale . . . or what anyone said.

Hope's heart splintered, beyond repair, as she finally accepted that

Sloan was the ringleader of a human trafficking scheme.

Chapter 65

Two months later, the clouds clustered together across the gloomy sky. The ground was buried underneath a large white blanket that covered any evidence of life within the grass. The snow had dominated the grass on the ground. January had welcomed a heightened level of snowstorms.

Hope strolled through the house, wishing she could turn back the hands of time. But she couldn't. Her heart cringed. She couldn't believe she had been living with a human trafficking ringleader. She couldn't believe that her marriage was fake. She couldn't believe that Sloan had lived a double life.

A streak of frustration knifed through her heart. She couldn't believe that her twins' father was the mastermind behind Worldwide Pizza Express. She couldn't believe she didn't see the warning signs sooner. She couldn't believe how Sloan had taken her innocent, pure demeanor for granted.

"Mama, thank you for helping me pack," said Hope as she glanced around at the boxes stacked up throughout the house.

"You are welcome," said Gloria. "I'm your mother. The least I can do is help you pack."

"Thank you for letting the twins and I stay with you over the past few weeks," said Hope. "I couldn't stay in this house after all of that." She paused. "It seems like the only good thing Sloan did years ago was to pay off the house and put my name on the Deed."

"I wonder why he did that," signed Ivey.

"Maybe he wanted to make sure that Hope and the twins had a place to stay if something happened," said Tiffany.

"Well, that was the only way I could get the house because I was not considered Sloan's real wife. But I don't want this house," sobbed Hope.

"I know it was tough on you to change the twins' school and everything," said Ivey in a soft tone while wrapping her arms around Hope. "I know this has to be tough on them too."

"I know this is hard. I'm sorry that it had to turn out this way," said Tiffany.

A slight streak of anger flowed through Hope as she looked at Tiffany. Her mind struggled to accept the fact that Tiffany's husband, Vance, was the chief FBI Agent who had initiated the investigation on Sloan. But deep down, Hope knew it was not Vance's fault.

Hope exhaled slowly, "It was for the best, Tiffany," sighed Hope. "Even though my heart still hurts, I'm glad that the FBI was able to get some information from Mr. Franklin Masterstoner about the identity and locations of some of the women."

"Who is he?" asked Mrs. Brown.

"The FBI said Mr. Masterstoner was a huge investor as well as a customer," said Hope.

"I guess he told the FBI where some of the women were located in exchange for a lesser sentence," said Tony as he placed some items in a box.

"Tony, move your weak self out the way," laughed Hilton as he carried a box.

Hope sighed. "But Sloan took the FBI on a wild goose chase for several hours," she paused. "He kept manipulating the system to mislead them."

"He probably did that to get the FBI off his trail," uttered Lamont.

"I was shocked to find out that one of the FBI agents had been ordering women," blurted Hope.

"That is terrible," said Mrs. Brown.

A stream of warm air flowed out of the vents.

"I thank God the FBI finally believed you," sighed Mrs. Brown.

"I'm glad that the court didn't lock you up in prison," muffled Gloria.

"Me too," exhaled Hope.

The sun glistened onto Hilton's muscular body, capturing Hope's attention. Hope paused, recalling Ruth's comment that Hilton had a priceless shaped body that resembled a professional exotic dancer's physique.

"Can you pick up that box, Tony?" chuckled Hilton as he pointed at a tiny box in the corner.

"Whatever, Hilton," chuckled Tony.

Quietness reigned in the house. Hope was delighted that her childhood friends, Tony, Tiffany and Hilton, had come to help her move. She was delighted to see that her mother and Mrs. Brown had come to give her emotional support.

"This is a beautiful home, Hope," said Mrs. Brown as she looked around.

"Yes, it is," muffled Lamont as he placed a box on the floor.

"Thank you, Lamont, for helping me pack," said Hope, recalling how he had successfully recovered from his drug addiction.

"My sister told me you needed some help," said Lamont while hugging Mrs. Brown.

"Please have a seat, Mrs. Brown. You've helped me enough," said Hope.

"Well, I'll watch the twins for you while you keep packing," said Mrs. Brown.

"Hope, where do you want me to put this box?" asked Lee

"Over there," said Hope as her heart crumpled. She didn't want to pack Sloan's clothes. She had allowed Orlando, Hilton, Lamont and Tony to do it for her.

"Do you want me to take the clothes to a clothing bank?" asked Tony.

"I don't care where you take them," said Hope in a heartfelt tone. Her heart still couldn't fathom what Sloan had done.

"These are some very expensive business shoes and suits," said Orlando.

Hope glanced at the myriad of custom made business suits and European designed shoes that assembled through the room neatly. "You can take all of those clothes and shoes if you can fit them or give them to someone at your church," sighed Hope.

"I'd rather take them to the clothing bank," muffled Orlando in a humbled manner.

Tiffany slowly walked over to Hope. "It's going to be okay, Hope."

Hope sighed slowly. She was delighted that no one had asked to see the secret dungeon in the basement. In fact, Hope had used some of the closing money from the sale of the house to pay contractors to create an expanded basement, leaving no evidence that a secret dungeon had ever been built in the house.

A tear rolled down Hope's face. "I'm just glad that everyone is helping me move," said Hope as she looked around the house. "I had to list it on the market to sell it."

"The house didn't stay on the market long," said Tiffany. "I'm surprised you were able to sell it so quickly," uttered Tiffany as she adjusted her brown skirt.

"I know," said Ivey. "Usually, people want all of the stuff moved out before they want to tour a house."

"I'm glad that wasn't the case," said Hope. "But I was surprised that the court allowed me to sell the house even though I wasn't legally married to Sloan."

"I'm sure the court allowed you to sell the house because Sloan had added your name to the house deed," said Tiffany.

"So, it seems like you were able to get something out of this entire situation," uttered Mrs. Brown in a supportive tone.

"Yeah, but it makes me wonder why these people are in a rush to buy the house," said Hope. "Especially after they know what took place in it."

"How did they know?" asked Mrs. Brown in a puzzling tone.

"Because it has been all over the news, mama," said Tiffany.

"But how did the court allow you to sell the house if Sloan's name was on the deed too?" asked Ivey in a bashful tone.

"Since Sloan had used a fake name to get the house, the court did not consider that name. The court only considered mine since it was my real name on the deed," uttered Hope. "I'm glad because I didn't want the house. There was no way I could keep staying in here," babbled Hope. "I'm glad the court allowed me to use my last name," she said in a low tone. "And change the twins' last name as well."

Silence disbursed through the house for a few seconds.

"I can't believe Sloan had a secret dungeon in this house," whispered Tiffany.

"Me neither, Tiffany. That's why all of this is still so painful for me to accept."

"I couldn't imagine going through this, Hope," uttered Ivey as she held Hope's hand. "You're a strong woman. So, I know you'll get through this. I'll always be here for you."

"I'm glad I was able to sell the house. Now, I'll have money to get a location for my culinary business and school," sighed Hope. "I already finished my business plan a few months ago."

"That is great, Hope," said Mrs. Brown. "God works in mysterious ways."

Jayla walked toward Hope as her khaki pants shifted as she moved. "Mama, I'm hungry," said Jayla as she tugged on Hope's hand.

Hope stared at Jayla's beautiful light brown eyes. "Okay, Jayla," uttered Hope in a lovely tone. "Come on Jayden."

Jayden continued to sit on a small yellow chair that he used to sit in when he used to color with Sloan.

"Come on, Jayden, so I can fix you something to eat."

Jayden's lips slowly opened. "Mama, where is daddy?" asked Jayden.

Hope looked at Jayden while struggling to hold back the tears that invaded her face. "Daddy isn't here, Jayden," sobbed Hope in a hopeless tone.

"It's going to be fine, Hope," said Gloria in a motherly tone. "But it's going to take some time before Jayden will ever understand."

"Hope, I'll get them something to eat," said Mrs. Brown as she grabbed Jayla and Jayden's hands while wobbling toward Hope's kitchen.

A sharp ringing sound pierced the air causing Hope's body to flinch. A river of nervousness flowed through her body as the noise pierced through the front door again.

"Maybe it is the moving company at the door," said Tiffany.

"But nobody has ever come to this house," said Hope in a nervous tone. "Even the mailman has always put the mail in the mailbox along the street."

Hope slowly walked toward the front door, carefully opening it.

A man in a brown uniform stood at the door, holding a postcard and white roses.

"Are you Hope Rankin?" asked the man as she glanced at the delivery truck.

"Yes," said Hope, noticing that the man identified her by her maiden last name instead of the fake marital name that Sloan had given her.

"I have a postcard and flowers for you," said the delivery man.

A river of fear flowed through Hope. "Who is it from?" asked Hope.

Hope could feel Tiffany and Ivey standing near her.

"I don't know, ma'am," responded the man in an innocent manner. "All I know is the person paid for our company to deliver this postcard and flowers to this house."

Hope's trembling hand reached for the postcard and white roses.

"Thank you, ma'am," said the man as he left.

Hope slowly closed the front door. She peered at the roses. There was no doubt that the roses were from Sloan. White roses were her favorite.

"Who are the flowers from, Hope?" asked Gloria.

"The delivery man said he didn't know who ordered them, mama," said Ivey.

Hope exhaled slowly as fear seeped through her veins. "I'm sure they are from Sloan," mumbled Hope. "He knows white roses are my favorite," she said as she placed the roses on the small table.

"I wonder how the FBI wasn't able to catch Sloan," uttered Tiffany. "They need to know about this postcard and the flowers, Hope."

Hope stared at Tiffany for a few seconds. Her mind had forced her to think that Tiffany had ruined her marriage. But Hope had to accept the reality about Sloan.

Hope's gaze shifted toward the postcard. She noticed words were typed on there instead of any handwritten information. Her eyes scanned the postcard. Her heart slammed against her chest as she read the card.

"What does the postcard say, Hope?" asked Gloria in a soft tone as she placed her hand on Hope's shoulder in a comforting manner.

"It's from Europe," muffled Hope as a tear rolled down her face. She figured Sloan had used a fake passport to travel to Europe to escape the wrath of the FBI.

Hope closed her eyes, recalling that Sloan had promised to take her and the twins to Europe during the Christmas holiday. She guessed he had decided to leave earlier than expected.

"What does it say?" asked Ivey in a curious manner as she walked closer to Hope.

Words struggled to seep out of Hope's mouth as her heart skipped a beat.

Chapter 66

A month later, love danced throughout the air in Charlotte, North Carolina. Valentine's Day had sparked an influx of catering orders for Hope.

Hope slowly exhaled as she leaned back in the chair. Her feet were sore from pacing the floor as she prepared several heart shaped cookies, cakes and cupcakes. Her customer list had quickly increased. She had inherited Mrs. Brown's customers. Hope was certain she had to find a business location soon.

Hope closed her eyes. Her heart cringed as loneliness overtook her. She had spent her twins' birthday party, Thanksgiving, Christmas, the New Year and *now* Valentine's Day without Sloan. Yet, a part of Hope yearned for a vase of white roses from Sloan. But her mind was at peace. She no longer had to suffer the wrath of Sloan's sporadic aggressive behaviors.

Hope looked around the spacious living room, admiring her ability to transition from Raleigh to Charlotte. Her gaze landed on the chocolate brown couches that adorned the living room. Coconut tan painted walls and gold curtains draped in front of the bay window created an astounding appearance. Marble end tables were in every corner of the living room, presenting an upscale image. Sandy brown plush carpet paraded across the floor. A large floral vase towered in a corner, showcasing the finest of art.

"Thank you, mama, for watching the twins while I prepared those orders today," huffed Hope as if she was out of breath.

"You are welcome."

"Where are the twins?"

"They are asleep."

"Thank you for getting them in the bed for me. I had a lot of orders to do."

"I'm glad you adjusted to living back in Charlotte," said Gloria.

"Me too," said Hope. "Now I don't have to travel from Raleigh to Charlotte twice a week to take Jayla and Jayden to their speech and hearing habilitation therapy session. Now I can just travel a few blocks to their sessions."

"Why did you bring them all the way here for their speech and hearing therapy? I'm sure there were speech specialists in Raleigh."

"I didn't want to change their doctor."

A crisp scent of lemon lavender candle wafted through the living room.

"You did a good job, Hope," smiled Gloria. "And I'm proud of you. I'm glad you were able to finish all of those orders within a short period."

"Me, too," signed Hope. "But I see now I need to find a location for my business and school," she said in a soft tone. "I used a lot of gas, delivering those orders."

"You will have to hire some employees one day, Hope."

"I know. I'm working on it."

Sunlight peaked between the curtains, casting rays onto the soft carpet.

"Hope," said Gloria in a heartfelt tone. "I'm so proud of you. I thank God that you turned out to be a good girl . . . especially after what I've put you through," she said before pausing. "But God found a way to reunite us."

"We don't have to talk about it, mama. It's in the past."

"But, Hope, it seems like God was putting all of the pieces together in your life," she said while rubbing her hands together. "Then your life crumbled when you found out about the *real* Sloan."

Hope closed her eyes as if her mother's words hurt her eardrums.

"I'm sure God had a reason for all of this happening," said Hope in a sorrowful tone. "I'm glad Sloan didn't try to convince me to be part of all of that stuff."

"You decorated your house really good," said Gloria as she looked around. "This is a nice three bedroom house. I didn't know houses came with three bathrooms," she smiled while looking at Hope.

"I didn't want the twins fussing over a bathroom," she chuckled.

"I see you bought new furniture, too," said Gloria.

"I didn't want anything from the house. So, I sold it all," she sighed. "I want to erase every memory of my past with Sloan from my mind."

Gloria stared at Hope for a few seconds.

"Hope, you can never erase all of the memories of Sloan. You have a set of twins with him," uttered Gloria as she patted Hope's hand.

Hope cleared her throat. "Mama, you can come and live with me," said Hope in a soft tone.

Gloria paused before responding. "I'm fine living in Cloverdale."

"Why, mama?"

"It's all I've known for the last couple of decades," she sighed. "I'm used to the ups and downs of Cloverdale. Plus, that's where all of my friends live."

"But I can find you an apartment close to Cloverdale if you don't want to live with me."

"Hope, it's not that I don't want to live with you, baby," she uttered. "I like living in Cloverdale. Even though a lot of bad things have happened in Cloverdale, it is where I prefer to live. I have gotten used to the nonsense."

"Okay," mumbled Hope. "But always know that the option is on the table."

Gloria stared at Hope. "I'm sure I'll never change my mind. I'm just glad that God has reunited you and me," she said softly. "I'm also very happy that God rescued you from Sloan."

Hope leaned back in the chair, reflecting upon the words that were on the postcard. She recalled that Sloan had typed the words instead of leaving any handwritten evidence. Her heart cringed as she recalled the last couple of sentences. Her mind surfed as the words invaded her mind.

Hope closed her eyes, recalling Sloan's last few sentences on the postcard.

"I will always love you, Hope. You have helped me to see that there are some good women in this world. But I want you and the twins to start a new life without me. I know you will learn 'hurtful' things about me. It is the only lifestyle I have known since I was a child. I am truly sorry but that is the real me and I will never change."

"Hope, at some point, you've got to move on with your life," said Gloria as she slightly adjusted her wig.

Hope glanced at her mother's wig, knowing that her mother's treatment in the past had stripped her of the finest of her natural hairstyles.

"I know mama. But my heart still hurts and my mind still thinks about Sloan."

"But you have to think about what is best for your children. I remember you said Sloan told you to start a new life. So, *do it,* Hope."

"I know, but it hurts," said Hope as a tear rolled down her face. "All I wanted was to be a good wife, a good mother . . . and a good child," said Hope as she recalled all of the things that had splintered her heart.

Gloria pressed her lips together. "I can't change anything that I've done to you. But I will make sure that I treat you the best way I can the rest of my days on this earth," she sighed as she leaned toward Hope to hug her.

A crisp smell of lemon lavender wafted in the air from a candle.

"I'm glad God pulled us back together," said Hope in a pleasant tone.

"You've done well for yourself in a short time," smiled Gloria. "You have a career, a beautiful home and beautiful twins."

"But mama, I have no husband," huffed Hope. "I don't want my twins growing up with no father. I didn't have them out of wedlock," she wept.

Gloria tapped Hope on her hand in a supportive manner. "Do you want to go and see a therapist like the FBI Agent had recommended?"

"I'll be fine, mama. If I feel like I need therapy . . . I promise I will go," sighed Hope.

"I'm sure you will find somebody else. You're a beautiful woman," said Gloria.

"But I don't want to find anyone right now," said Hope as she stared at her hands. They looked bare without her wedding ring. "I stopped wearing my wedding ring. It's been three months since I last saw Sloan."

A shaft of warm air floated through the living room from the heater.

"It is for the best," said Gloria as she glanced at Hope's hands. Gloria cleared her throat. "Ivey said a nice guy asked about you. She said he went to school with you."

Hope tilted her head toward the ceiling. "I'm not ready to get married again."

"Nobody is saying you have to get married. There is nothing wrong with a date."

"I'm not interested in any dates right now, mama," uttered Hope in a hasty tone. "I don't even know who Ivey is talking about."

"Hope, baby, please don't spend the rest of your life being alone," begged Gloria. "If you do, you'll *allow* Sloan to keep your mind in bondage."

Hope exhaled. "I felt trapped living with Sloan. I couldn't have friends. I couldn't hang out. I couldn't do anything unless he was with me."

"Now, you have an opportunity to be mentally and physically free again," sighed Gloria as if she wanted to ensure that Hope left no stone unturned.

"Sloan used to think that every woman was a whore," mumbled Hope as a rollercoaster of emotions surged through her body. "But I found out that his father planted that in his and his brother's heads when they were children. His father was a human trafficking ringleader, too. So, Sloan grew up seeing men dominate women, sell them, force them to have sex, and confine them."

Gloria's eyes widened like golf balls. "Hope, you can't feel sorry for Sloan."

"I'm not feeling sorry for him. I feel bad that he had to grow up like that."

"Hope, at some point, you've got to move on with your life. I don't think Sloan will ever risk coming around you or the twins again. He knows that the FBI is on his trail."

"What about my twins?" cried Hope. "They need their father!"

"Hope, you've got to move on! There are plenty of women who survive without their children's father!" snapped Gloria as she took control of the conversation. "I didn't raise you to be weak. If anything, I raised you to be a fighter . . . a survivor!" shrieked Gloria.

Hope exhaled, realizing that her mother was right. "You are right. I went through some tough times with you," said Hope. "But I was a child then. I am an adult now."

"It doesn't matter, Hope," babbled Gloria. "After all, I took you through as a child, you should have tough skin . . . thicker than an alligator," she uttered. "So, at this point in your life, nothing should bother you! Nothing should break you down! Nothing should weaken your hopes!" cried Gloria. "I've already done all of that you and I regret every second of it."

"Don't cry, mama," sobbed Hope. "I've got to find a way to erase Sloan from my heart."

Gloria closed her eyes. "You need to erase him from your heart and your mind," muffled

Gloria. "There is no telling whether he would've killed you or forced you into human trafficking. Look what Sloan's father did to his mother. You remember you told me what the FBI said about Sloan's fake wives," she sighed. "Plus, you found out that Sloan was the main leader who killed Julia."

A tear trickled down Hope's face. "You don't have to remind me, mama."

"I'm not trying to remind you, Hope. I'm trying to help you realize why you should move on with your life!" snapped Gloria in a firm motherly tone. "There is no telling what Sloan would've done to you. The man built a secret dungeon in that house!" blurted Gloria as she slid closer to Hope. "You told me that he had you dressing up every day and taking pictures of you all the time. What was he doing with all of those pictures, Hope? Why was he video recording you walking around the house in lingerie and stilettos? Do you even know? Do you!"

"No, mama."

"Where were the twins when you were prancing around the house half naked for him?"

"Sleep."

"What about those sex scenes he recorded? Who has he shown?"

"I do not know mama. But I only allowed him to record us one time. I did not feel comfortable doing that so I told him to turn it off."

"He probably kept recording without you knowing."

"I do not think so, mama. He wouldn't do that to me," said Hope as if she suffered from Stockholm Syndrome.

"Hope, please stop being in denial! He has done some terrible things to a lot of women. He had women trapped in a dungeon and now he has your mind trapped."

A tear rolled down Hope's face. "I know, mama. But I feel so bad. I used to smell the scent of women's perfume in his office," she sobbed. "I used to smell the scent on him sometimes, but I couldn't figure out why I was smelling it. Especially, since he hadn't left the house at all on those days. After the FBI told me about the secret dungeon, I finally realized why I was smelling the different types of perfumes." She grasped for air. "I should had inquired more when Taylor told me that Julia wore E'Zanti perfume too. The perfume is expensive and imported. I later found out that it was an exclusive perfume and only certain people could order it. So, I should had at least asked Sloan if he knew Julia. But, I did not."

Loud honking sounds echoed inside the house.

"I feel like I am trapped in a nightmare," mumbled Hope.

Needless to say, it was a nightmare that was destined to linger for an eternity.

Chapter 67

Two weeks later, Hope sat quietly in her living room glancing around hoping that she had been in a nightmare. Reality kicked in when her mother's voice interrupted her afternoon nap.

"Thank you, mama, for watching the twins while I took a nap."

"You're welcome, Hope. The twins are in the playroom playing."

"I feel so sad at times, mama," she muffled. "Deep down . . . one side of me hates Sloan and the other side of me . . . still loves him."

Gloria tilted her head toward the coconut cream painted ceiling. "You what!" shrieked Gloria. "Sloan used *to secretly drug* you with sleeping medicine. He was the ringleader of a human trafficking scheme! He even had an insurance scheme going."

Hope buried her face in her small hands. "Please . . . don't remind me."

"I think he was going to kill you and collect on a life insurance policy just like he had done with his other fake wives, " snapped Gloria. "Just like his brother, Rock, had collected life insurance money from Julia's death! It seems like Sloan and his brothers had an insurance scheme and human trafficking scheme going on."

"I feel so naïve," sobbed Hope.

"There was no way you knew Sloan had a secret life," said Gloria as she hugged Hope. "He was a heartless man because he abandoned a good woman like you and his own flesh and bone . . . the twins."

"I saw a therapist earlier today," muffled Hope.

Gloria leaned forward as her eyebrows connected. "You did?" asked Gloria.

"I'm in therapy, mama," said Hope in a sheepish tone.

"Oh, now you want to go to therapy," Gloria said sarcastically. "Why now? You were adamant about not going when I asked you in front of the FBI."

"I've been thinking about it."

"I bet you have," she squinted as if she was wondering if Hope still had a plan to reunite with

Sloan.

"No, mama. I need to work out a lot of things that happened . . . in my childhood . . . being molested," She paused as a tear rolled down her face. "I needed therapy for what I've been through with Sloan . . . and what you took me through."

Gloria leaned back in the chair as a puddle of tears filled her eyes. "So, this is about me."

"I . . . think you and I should go together too," said Hope.

"I don't care much about therapy," uttered Gloria. "People my age don't go to therapy."

"Why not?" asked Hope. "Please don't tell me it is taboo for black people because I've heard it all," snapped Hope. "Why is there so much stigma about therapy?"

Gloria closed her eyes. "I don't think I need therapy . . . right now . . . but you can go."

"Why are you so reluctant to go?" asked Hope. "It is funny how you volunteered me to go and now you have an issue with it."

"Old black folks like me don't go to therapy," shrieked Gloria. "People don't want to help us."

"Then why did you insist that I go to therapy?"

"You need it," muffled Gloria.

"You do too, mama."

"No . . . ," sneered Gloria. "I don't want nobody knowing my past . . . my wrongs . . . my guilt . . . my pain," she muffled. "I'm too embarrassed. I'm ashamed to spill my guts to a stranger."

"Mama, it would be confidential. Therapists and psychiatrists can't spread your business."

"I can't do it . . . I don't want anybody thinking I have a few loose screws."

"Mama, it's not about what others think. It's about you getting the help you need. You've been through a lot, too . . . and I've been through a lot."

A loud sound echoed from the playroom as twins apparently turned on cartoons.

"I've had help. I went to the rehabs . . . you remember," said Gloria as her gaze lowered to the floor. "That was an uncomfortable feeling. I was the only black person at the rehab center. I felt like a specimen but my Eugene kept paying for me to go back."

"Mama, it's not like that now."

"Oh yes, it is." Gloria spouted. "You young folks see things differently than older black folks like me."

"But it is time for people to start thinking differently, mama," insisted Hope. "I heard that

Mrs. Ruth was in therapy and enrolled in a GED program."

"Well, she has a lot to work on. There's no secret that she's addicted to sex. Plus, she never healed from Julia being forced in human trafficking and being killed. "

"You have a lot to work on too, mama," mumbled Hope. "Besides, I realized I want to be mentally healthy."

"*Mentally* healthy?"

"Yes, mama," said Hope. "I've been through a lot of trauma."

Gloria closed her eyes before speaking. "I think you need to focus on the mess that Sloan took you through first and how it may impact the twins."

"I am going to work on everything," sobbed Hope.

A river of tears streamed down Hope's face. "We all need therapy," said Hope as her head lowered toward her chest.

Reality finally settled into Hope's splintered heart.

Even though her mother's words were painful, they were true.

Chapter 68

Four months later, the bright sunlight radiated across the blue sky as puffy white clouds danced around on the horizon.

Hope stood outside of a 7,000 square foot building in the heart of downtown Charlotte, North Carolina. Her heart pounded faster than a drummer in a parade as she read the business' name on the building: *Serenity Tavern & Culinary School of the Arts.*

Colorful balloons assembled along the sidewalk in front of the one story building. Large clear double paned windows marched along the bricks on the building. Customers congregated in a beeline that extended from inside the building to particularly wrapping around the building.

"Master Chef Hope, this is a wonderful grand opening," said a familiar voice.

"Mrs. Brown, I am so glad you made it to my grand opening," said Hope in an excited tone, knowing that the first day of summer in June was perfect for her grand opening event.

"I wouldn't miss it for nothing in the world, Hope. I am so proud of you," said

Mrs. Brown while hugging Hope. "Plus, I knew today was your birthday."

"Hope, you know my mother kept reminding me of your grand opening," smiled Tiffany.

"Come on in, Mrs. Brown, and have a seat," smiled Hope.

Hope slowly exhaled, taking pride in the scenery around her. Sunflower yellow paint covered the top half of the walls. A strip of vineyard green paint paraded around the bottom half of the walls creating a professional upscale image throughout the building. A thick trim of crown molding bordered the ceiling, casting a dazzling image. Cream colored tables and chairs were throughout the building.

"It is so beautiful in here, Hope," said Mrs. Brown while wobbling.

"Thank you." Hope walked Mrs. Brown to a table where her mother was sitting.

"Hello, Mrs. Brown. I'm glad that you came to the grand opening," smiled Gloria.

"Me too," said Mrs. Brown while glancing around. "There's a lot of people in here. It seems like you've done great for your first day."

"Yes, that is definitely a good thing," said Ivey as she sat at the roundtable.

Hope leaned toward Jayla. She planted a kiss on her forehead. She stretched her hand toward Jayden, gently pinching his cheek. "I want a cookie, mama," said Jayden while tugging on Hope's hunter green uniform.

"Come with me, kids," she smiled as she reached for their hands.

Hope strolled over to a glassed shelf. "Which cookie do you want?" asked Hope.

"I want a lemon cookie, mommy," said Jayla as her eyes glistened.

"Here you are, Jayla," she said as she handed Jayla one cookie.

"I want two chocolate chip cookies and two lemon cookies," uttered Jayden.

A peal of laughter leaped off Hope's tongue. "Jayden you can't have chocolate chip cookies *and* lemon cookies."

A frown formed on Jayden's face. "*Daddy* used to let me eat different cookies."

Hope's lips smashed together. A slight touch of bitterness flowed through her.

"You can only have one cookie," repeated Hope, holding firm to her parental instincts. She stared at Jayden for a few seconds as images of Sloan's facial features plastered onto Jayden's face.

"I'll take the chocolate chip cookie," pouted Jayden.

Hope galloped back toward Mrs. Brown and her mother.

"I see you finally got your culinary business up and running," said Tony as he walked toward Hope with his arm stretched out, embracing her. "You remember my wife, Heather," said Tony as he pulled out a chair for Heather.

"Yes," said Hope. "Hello, Heather. I'm glad you could make it."

"I am glad that Tony told me about it," smiled Heather.

"It seems like the entire Cloverdale community is up in here," chuckled Tony.

"There are other customers in here from different places, Tony," said Tiffany as she ushered her twins into their chairs. "So, this isn't a Cloverdale family reunion."

"You two better be good," laughed Hope as she looked at Tony and Tiffany, wondering whether Vance was coming to the grand opening.

"Hello, Hope," said Vance as he walked up behind Hope. "Congratulations."

Silence buckled Hope's lips for a second. "Thank you, Vance," she smiled.

Hope glanced around, admiring her employees' work ethics as they tended to the customers. A sense of pride flowed through Hope as she watched her employees parade through the building with their hunter green uniforms that displayed the business' logo on the left hand side of the shirts in gold letters. Her heart fluttered as she read the letters on their shirts that displayed: *Serenity Tavern & Culinary School of the Arts.*

"This is neat how you have your culinary tavern on this side of the building and the culinary school on the other side," smiled Heather.

"Thank you," said Hope in a humbled tone as her gaze landed on a customer.

Conversation soared from every direction in the building.

Hope watched as the customer's hand move fluidly in the air to order from the menu. A prideful feeling flowed through Hope as she observed the waiter's fingers glided in the air to communicate in ASL to the customer.

"Hope, that is so nice that you have employees who know sign language," said Geneva as she slowly sat at a table near Mrs. Brown.

Hope paused before speaking, "Thank you, Mrs. Geneva. I'm glad you could make it," said Hope. "It's called ASL."

"Her culinary school is for people who use ASL," said Gloria in a prideful tone.

"ASL?" asked Geneva as a puzzled look flashed across her face.

"It's called ASL for American Sign Language . . . not sign language," said Gloria in a soft tone.

A charming feeling flowed through Hope.

"That is nice," said Hilton as he approached Hope.

"Thank you," said Hope as she glanced at Hilton's diesel chest that protruded through his linen white shirt.

Hilton cleared his throat. "This is my wife, London."

"Nice to meet you," said Hope as she looked at London.

"Likewise," smirked London as if she had noticed Hope glancing at Hilton's chest.

"It is nice how you have designed your business," she uttered in a soft tone.

"I wanted to dedicate my company to help individuals who are deaf or hard of hearing," smiled Hope. "I also have a culinary school on the other side of this building."

"That is really nice, Hope," said Mrs. Brown. "God has turned your experience with your twins into something beautiful."

"You are right, Mrs. Brown," said Mrs. Ruth as she walked up behind Hope and Mrs. Brown. Her peach shirt highlighted her chestnut brown wig.

A sense of peace flowed through Hope as Ruth hugged her.

"Hello, Mrs. Hope," said Jasmine with a soft voice as she sat beside

Mrs. Ruth.

"Hello, Jasmine and Taylor," smiled Hope. "I am so glad that you came."

The sweet savory smell of pastries wafted past Hope's nose.

"Make sure you get some cookies," smiled Hope, looking at Jasmine and Taylor.

"This is a lovely place, Hope," said Mrs. Ruth as she grabbed the menu from the table and allowed her eyes to stroll along with the words.

Hope watched as a smile unfolded on Mrs. Brown's face. She recalled Mrs. Brown telling her that Mrs. Ruth's granddaughter had taught her how to read and she had completed a GED program.

"Thank you. I'll be back," she said while glancing around at her employees. "By the way, I am so proud of you."

"Thank you," responded Mrs. Ruth as if she had no doubt that Hope was referring to her ability to read now.

"Hope, before you leave, I want to let you know I invited somebody to come to your grand opening," blurted Ivey in an upbeat tone.

"Who?" asked Hope, puzzled.

"You'll see," said Ivey as a smile stretched across her round face.

Hope strolled through the building, capturing a glimpse of the customers' conversation as she read pleasant words that formed on their lips. She winced, realizing that Sloan wasn't there. He had not contacted her in several months as if he had forsaken her and the twins. Hope was delighted because Sloan's absence helped her to move on with her life. She wondered if the FBI would *ever* catch him. Her heart cringed, wondering how many people in the world had human trafficking schemes like Sloan. She walked toward a large black door and swiped a business card at the door to gain access to her culinary school. As she entered, she paused, observing her first culinary class of students who mingled together in a large kitchen. She smiled as she watched their fingers move elegantly in the air to communicate with one another. The students' skin tones represented a diverse pool of learners.

A short caramel woman reviewed the culinary school's curriculum with students.

"Hello, Master Chef Hope," said the woman as she communicated in ASL to make sure that the students understood what she was saying to Hope.

"Hello, Mrs. Poole," said Hope while gazing at Mrs. Poole's long gray hair.

"The students are excited that you opened a culinary school," smiled Mrs. Poole while signing as well so the students could understand what she was saying to Hope.

"I am glad, too," said Hope as she glanced around at the students. "It is my hope that they will one day work in my culinary business as well," said Hope as she communicated in ASL. "Some of them may even want to open their own culinary school one day," smiled Hope, knowing that some of her future competitors were in her first class. This didn't bother Hope. Her skills were top-notch.

Hope walked closer to Mrs. Poole. "I'm delighted that you are one of my instructors," she said, knowing that Mrs. Poole was a certified culinary educator like her.

A tall white man approached Hope. His fingers shifted elegantly in the air.

"Hello, Mr. Randy," said Hope as she glanced at his wavy blonde hair.

Words struggled to flow out of Mr. Randy's mouth. "I'm . . . I'm glad you did this for the students and me," he said in a slow tone as he spoke and signed at the same time.

"You are welcome, Mr. Randy," said Hope as she signed the words as well. "I'm glad you are one of my instructors as well," said Hope, recalling that she had attended culinary school with Mr. Randy in Raleigh. "Thank you . . . for hiring me," said Mr. Randy as he smiled. "My wife is happy too," he said while walking away.

Hope watched as Mr. Randy and Mrs. Poole co-facilitated the culinary class. Her heart fluttered like butterflies, knowing that she had finally accomplished her dream to own a culinary school designed for individuals who were deaf and hard of hearing. She was glad to receive several grants to assist the students to attend it.

Hope's business was destined for greatness.

Chapter 69

Two hours later, clusters of sweet, savory pastries and freshly cooked meals whirled through Serenity Tavern & Culinary School of the Arts.

Hope strolled through the building as she glanced around at the customers who had formed beelines from the door to tables. Her gaze landed on employees who paraded to tables to take orders.

A stream of rays from the sun flowed inside the building.

Hope paused, picking up a high glossed butterscotch colored menu. An array of pictures neatly plastered on the menu, highlighting classic dishes that were offered for breakfast, brunch, lunch and dinner.

A warm feeling flowed through her. She exhaled, admiring her accomplishments. Her culinary school had reached its capacity of enrolled students. Within two hours of operation, the tavern had already exceeded the projected weekly profit.

"Hello, Hope. I thought you left the building," said Ivey in an exciting tone.

"I had to check on the students in the culinary school," said Hope as her gaze landed on several customers whose skin tones represented a spectrum of colors.

"I am so proud of you, Hope," smiled Ivey.

"Thank you, Ivey. It means a lot to me that you are here," uttered Hope in a lovely tone.

"Me too," grinned Ivey.

A cloud of conversations flowed through the buildings.

"Look at all of these customers," said Ivey as a smile stretched across her bronze brown face.

Customers streamed through the front door.

"I'm glad that I prepared enough food for my grand opening," sighed Hope.

"Here comes Cloverdale's news anchor," chuckled Ivey.

Hope looked toward the door. A soft giggle leaped out of her mouth.

A tall, pecan brown woman with salt and pepper colored hair wobbled toward Hope with a fancy walking stick.

"Hello, Hope. Do you remember me?" she asked while peering at Hope.

"Yes, ma'am. I remember you, Mrs. Thelma," said Hope recalling she had met Mrs. Thelma at Mrs. Brown's seventieth birthday party. She remembered that Mrs. Thelma had questioned her at the event as if she was conducting a newspaper interview. "This is my sister, Ivey," smiled Hope.

"I know who she is," muffled Thelma. "How are you, Ivey?" she asked.

"I am doing well, Mrs. Thelma."

"Good," said Mrs. Thelma. "How is your husband?"

"He is also doing well," responded Ivey.

"So, *when* are you going to give your husband a child?" squinted Thelma.

A silence flowed among them for a split second. Hope figured word had traveled throughout Cloverdale that Ivey and her husband didn't have children.

"Soon, Mrs. Thelma," responded Ivey.

"Make sure you give him a child real soon," demanded Mrs. Thelma as if she controlled Ivey's ovaries.

Thelma pivoted her gaze toward Hope. "I see that you finally opened your restaurant and school," smiled Thelma. "I came to check out a few things."

"I am glad that you came, Mrs. Thelma," grinned Hope, knowing that Thelma only came to the grand opening to observe the scenery.

A short, chubby, caramel brown woman quickly approached them.

"I had a hard time finding a parking space out there," said the woman as she gasped for oxygen.

"JoAnn, stop complaining," blurting Thelma. "You needed the exercise."

"I'm not complaining, Thelma," smirked JoAnn. "The next time I will make you walk with me instead of dropping you off at the front door," she snapped.

Thelma gawked at JoAnn.

Hope signaled for an employee to usher Thelma and JoAnn to a table.

"Mrs. Thelma and Mrs. JoAnn, this is Genesis. She will take you to the table."

"Who said I wanted to sit with Thelma?" smirked JoAnn.

"Come on, JoAnn," blurted Thelma as she trailed behind Genesis.

A sneer unfolded on JoAnn's round shaped face. "Thelma better be glad that we've been best friends for over fifty years," said JoAnn as she leaned toward Hope. "She is here to spy on you," she whispered. "You know she is a news anchor."

Laughter rolled off Hope's tongue.

"They are too funny," laughed Hope.

"I know. They are like that all the time. Mama said she is surprised that they have remained best friends all of these years," chuckled Ivey. "They fuss all the time."

"Maybe that is their way of communicating with one another," grinned Hope.

Hope glanced around, noticing that customers had filled every inch of the tavern.

"This is awesome, Hope," said Ivey while hugging Hope.

"I am so happy. I didn't expect this many people to come," smiled Hope.

"Well, you did a great job marketing the grand opening," smiled Ivey. "Your brochures and newspaper ads were nice. And the radio announcement sure helped."

"I am glad," smiled Hope.

"Oh, don't forget I want you to meet someone," said Ivey as if she wanted to remind Hope.

"Who?" inquired Hope.

Ivey glanced at her cellphone. A small smile slowly formed on her face as she read a text message. "You will find out in a few seconds."

"I don't like surprises, Ivey. I've had enough in my life," mumbled Hope as she started walking toward the table where her mother, Mrs. Brown and her twins were sitting.

"Oh, this will be a *good* surprise," affirmed Ivey.

Hope slowly exhaled.

"Mama, how are your oatmeal raisin cookies?" smiled Hope.

"They are delicious."

"What about your lemon cookies, Mrs. Brown?" inquired Hope.

"Of course, they are delicious too," grinned Mrs. Brown.

Hope glanced at her twins. Cookie crumbs had gathered around their mouths.

"Wipe your mouths," smiled Hope as she looked at Jayla and Jayden.

"I think it is best if they wait until after they finish their cookies before they wipe their mouths," laughed Gloria. "The crumbs will return again."

"I see," chuckled Hope as she watched Jayla and Jayden nibble on the cookies.

A whirlwind of laughter flowed from the table before quickly fizzling out. Hope felt a sense of relief knowing that Gloria had finally agreed to attend therapy.

Hope winced, wondering why her mother, Ivey and Mrs. Brown has suddenly stopped laughing.

"Hope . . . somebody's here for you," said Ivey while staring at someone who was standing directly behind Hope.

A hush nearly filled the room.

A river of stiffness overtook Hope's body. She was too nervous to turn around. Her heart couldn't take any more heartaches. Her mind couldn't take any more turmoil. Her soul couldn't take any more disappointment. She didn't know who was behind her and she prayed it was *not* Sloan.

Every fiber of Hope's heart slowly became entangled.

Chapter 70

Ivey remained silent for a few seconds before finally smiling.

Hope tried to read Ivey's facial expression to give her a sense of comfort. Stiffness had nearly settled at the core of her bones. The thought of Sloan standing behind her launched a river of fear through her soul. She was not prepared to see him . . . *ever* again. Her heart had been splintered too many times.

Hope silently pleaded with God for a few seconds praying that Sloan was not the person standing behind her.

"Hope, I want you to meet somebody," said Ivey, gently gripping Hope's hand as if she sensed an uneasiness in her.

A sense of serendipity slowly replaced the busload of fear that once occupied her body. God had delivered a truckload of reassurance and protection to her.

Suddenly, Hope erased all levels of fear. She was determined not to allow Sloan to keep her heart, mind, body, or soul in permanent bondage.

Stiffness evaporated from Hope's veins, permitting her to build the courage to pivot her body within the next few seconds.

"Excuse me, Master Chef Hope. I would like to order some *ginger* cookies," said a man who was standing behind her.

Hope recognized the voice. She knew of one person who *loved* ginger cookies.

She mumbled a quick silent prayer again.

"Excuse me, Master Chef Hope," repeated the man.

Hope stared at her mother, Ivey, Mrs. Brown and her twins. Smiles spread across their faces as if they were watching a fairytale movie.

She watched as her mother and Mrs. Brown shifted their hands in the air to signal for her to turn around.

She slowly turned around to face the man who had been standing behind her for a few seconds.

"Blake," sighed Hope as her heart pounded while she thanked God that it was not Sloan. "Or do you want me to call you, *Dr. Blake Milner*?"

"You can call me Blake," he grinned, displaying his pearly white teeth.

Footsteps marched around the building as customers and employees interacted.

"What are you doing here?" asked Hope in an upbeat, pleasant tone as her gaze landed on the ridges of his muscles that protruded through his white shirt.

"I told Ivey to let you know that I was coming," he said while hugging Hope as his crisp cologne wafted underneath her nose. "I didn't want to miss your grand opening."

"Hope, this is the surprise customer that I wanted you to meet today," smiled Ivey. "I thought it would be a great idea for Blake to come to the grand opening."

The slow beats of Hope's heart convinced her that Ivey's intentions were as pure as gold.

"Ivey and I have been talking about you," said Blake.

Blake's ebony brown skin glistened as the sunlight pressed against his clean shaved face.

Hope cleared her throat. "I hope Ivey said nice things about me," she smiled while glancing at Blake's hands, praying that he wasn't married.

"Maybe I can tell you all about it over dinner this weekend," grinned Blake.

Hope glanced at Blake's hands again.

A soft chuckled leaped from Blake's cupid shaped lips. "I'm not married, Hope."

"Me, neither," said Hope in a soft tone while thanking God that the court had considered her marriage to Sloan as a *void marriage* since he had used a fake name during the ceremony at the Justice of the Peace. Now, she was legally free to use her birth name—Hope Michele Rankin.

A smile stretched across Blake's smooth face causing Hope to reflect back to that day in high school when he had told her that she would be his wife one day.

"Your mother and Mrs. Brown have already given me the approval to take you on a date this weekend," grinned Blake.

"And me, too," interjected Ivey as a smile flashed across her face. "I think a nice dinner this weekend would be perfect," she said before she took a seat at the table with Mrs. Brown, their mother and Hope's twins.

A soft chuckle flowed out of Blake's mouth.

The sun beamed inside the tavern, casting a trail of bright rays in front of Blake. Hope wondered if God was telling her that Blake was indeed the man for her.

She paused, recalling that Blake had a crush on her since high school. She had never forgotten that he had told her and her high school friends that she would be his wife one day. It seemed as though his dream was finally coming to fruition.

A small chuckle sparked inside of Hope.

Blake cleared his throat as he slightly walked closer to Hope.

"I'm sure Jayla and Jayden wouldn't mind if a really nice man took their mother to dinner . . . this weekend," grinned Blake as he gently grabbed her hand.

Hope peered down at her hand. She slowly exhaled, realizing that she hadn't been touched by a man in several months.

The gentle, warm touch from Blake's hand recharged all of the veins and arteries in her body. A glimpse of moisture nearly built in a precious spot inside her body.

Her gaze slowly inched from Blake's hand to his eyes.

Butterflies fluttered inside her.

She glanced at the table where her mother, her twins, Ivey and Mrs. Brown were sitting. They were smiling as if they were confirming their approval of Blake.

A peaceful feeling overtook Hope as the splinters in her heart completely vanished.

She looked into Blake's hazel brown eyes. She felt a level of trust, knowing without a shadow of a doubt that he was different from Sloan. She quickly reflected upon their childhood days in Cloverdale and how Blake was always kind and respectful.

"Yes, dinner this weekend would be nice."

Author's Quotes

Wisdom is not achieved by learning fancy words. It is developed by simplicity.

Kimberly Morton Cuthrell

Willpower is not measured by strength. It is determined by the ability to push beyond endeavors.

Kimberly Morton Cuthrell

Every expression does not require a reaction.

Kimberly Morton Cuthrell

Sometimes, silence is more powerful than spoken words.

Kimberly Morton Cuthrell

Our journey in life is not determined by positive or negative experiences. It is determined by how we internalize experiences to achieve our truest and greatest potential.

Kimberly Morton Cuthrell

Life would be simpler if we learn to measure people by their efforts instead of their failures.

Kimberly Morton Cuthrell

When you lose sight of your purpose in life, you allow the virtue of your character to be undermined.

Kimberly Morton Cuthrell

About Dr. & Atty. Kimberly Morton Cuthrell

Greetings!

Dr. & Atty. Kimberly Morton Cuthrell is an attorney, doctoral-level clinical therapist, suspense author, researcher, mediator, and currently a medical school student. She has a quest to create new inroads in suspense novels with behavioral health twists to destigmatize perceptions.

Kimberly is a self-publishing consultant/mentor whereby she paved a landscape as a writing coach, ghostwriter, proofreader, professional editor, and beta reader. She is the founder/managing attorney of her law firm as well as the owner of a behavioral health agency where she ensures the highest quality of legal and clinical written content.

Kimberly's interest to write evolved from reading books, writing proposals for grants and contracts that were awarded, composing corporate compliance and policy/procedure manuals within provisions of state and federal laws, and developing behavioral health accreditation manuals whereby she secured a corporation's Three-Year Accreditation three consecutive times.

Kimberly's unique writing skills advanced as she crafted her dissertation in her doctoral program. Her dissertation was published in an international scholarly journal and was recognized as the 'Most Read' research article within the first month on ResearchGate. In law school, she received the CALI Award for earning the highest grade in her legal writing class. Her writing skills continued to elevate in law school while competing in the Susie M. Sharp Intra-School Moot Court Competition in which she and her law school team member presented legal oral arguments and demonstrated legal advocacy skills, advancing to the octo-finals. In medical school, her writing flourished when she served as the principal investigator/lead researcher of a research team and won third place in a medical school research competition. She is a research mentor assistant in medical school and has guided several medical school students to finalize research projects to compete in research competitions in which some mentees have ranked in the top three places. Kimber has authored and co-authored research articles that are published in international scholarly journals. Her research findings and content have been cited in other researchers' published articles.

In her fiction work, Kimberly draws from thought-provoking imaginary situations, the art of wisdom, and diverse viewpoints. Kimberly, a member of Alpha Kappa Alpha Sorority, Incorporated, writes to intrigue readers' minds about *potential* real-life situations and inspire them to advocate for positive change and make meaningful impacts in their communities.

When she is not writing, Kimberly can be found playing her favorite board game, mentoring individuals to pursue their greatest potential, and spending time with her family. She is from North Carolina but has lived in Maryland and on Saint Vincent Island. She also spent many years residing in Portugal, Greece, Turkey, and Spain where she became proficient in Spanish before returning to the United States of America. A lifelong learner, she enjoys promoting confidence and wisdom in others.

www.kimberlymortoncuthrell.com

www.ingramcontent.com/pod-product-compliance
Lightning Source LLC
Chambersburg PA
CBHW070642180626
46817CB00006B/2210